# ENVY

 This Large Print Book carries the
Seal of Approval of N.A.V.H.

# ENVY

## A SEVEN DEADLY SINS NOVEL

# VICTORIA CHRISTOPHER MURRAY

**THORNDIKE PRESS**
A part of Gale, a Cengage Company

A Cengage Company

Farmington Hills, Mich • San Francisco • New York • Waterville, Maine
Meriden, Conn • Mason, Ohio • Chicago

LIBRARY OF CONGRESS CIP DATA ON FILE.
CATALOGUING IN PUBLICATION FOR THIS BOOK
IS AVAILABLE FROM THE LIBRARY OF CONGRESS

ISBN-13: 978-1-4328-5412-6 (hardcover)

Published in 2018 by arrangement with Touchstone, an imprint of Simon & Schuster, Inc.

Printed in the United States of America
1 2 3 4 5 6 7 22 21 20 19 18

It is crazy that I would think something like this would never happen. Just wasn't reasonable to believe that my mom, who was eighty-four and in failing health, would live forever.

But that's what I thought.

And then, on September 24, 2017, reality paid me a visit.

I've lost so many, but losing you, Mommie, has been the hardest. I haven't yet figured out how to paste my heart back together, but because of who you were and who you raised me to be, I believe that I'll be able to do it.

I still cry and my heart still aches, but my soul sings because I know where you are. And at night when I close my eyes real tight, I can hear your whispers and feel your hugs.

So this, my thirtieth novel, is dedicated to you, Jacqueline Christopher. The best mom on earth, who is now resting at your home in heaven.

I will love you forever and I will continue to use the gifts that I was given and that you nurtured.

God bless you, Mommie.

# 1
## KEISHA JONES

*My mama was a whore.*

Those words played in my mind as I stared at my mama's photo, then pressed the picture frame against my chest.

*My mama was a whore and that was what killed her.*

I held no judgment about how my mama lived. From the time I was a little girl, I knew Daisy Jones was a hustler, doing whatever she had to do to put a roof over us and food inside of us. So I could never judge a woman who took care of more than her business, she took care of her child.

Daisy Jones was more than my mother, she was my mama, and there is a difference. It was my mama that I loved, not the woman who serviced men at the truck stop right off I-530.

And anyway, what else was she supposed to do, having been born in White Haven, Arkansas, all the way back before the millennium became new? Not that I had any issues with my hometown or with 1977, the year my mama was born. It was just a fact that if you were a black girl with only a middle school education, your choices were limited to cleaning somebody's house, frying somebody's fish, or going for that higher hourly position turning tricks.

My mama went for the dollars, and again, no judgment. Because if she hadn't worked hard for that money, I would never have been born.

Whatever she did, at least she worked until she couldn't. At least she kept a roof over my head until now.

Pulling the picture away from me, my fingers traced the outline of her jaw. If I closed my eyes again, I was sure I would be able to see her, feel her. Because she had just been here yesterday.

I swept my fingers over the glass frame as if I were combing her hair. Her beautiful hair, which was poofed into an Afro, silver, even though she was only forty.

I guess that was what a hard life did to you. Turned your outside old and your insides out before it was your time.

"Keisha?"

I faced the voice and the nurse standing in the doorway. She wore flowered scrubs again; today, they were blue. And she wore the same tight-lipped smile she'd been giving me all week. I gave that smile right back to her, even though I suspected hers was sincere. Mine was only proof that for everything Daisy had done wrong, she'd done her best to raise me right.

"You good?" Nurse Burns asked me.

Again, because I'd been raised right I didn't tell Nurse Burns she'd just asked the stupidest question in the history of stupid questions. How could I be good when my mom had died less than three hours ago? So instead of cussing her out, I turned back to my mama's bathrobe, which I'd just folded.

While the nurse stood not saying a word, I reached for Mama's comb and brush. Next, I went for the plastic case that held my mama's dentures, but the nurse said, "Don't take those."

I tilted my head. I wasn't sure what I was going to do with the teeth for the bottom left side of her mouth. I didn't know if I wanted to keep them as some kind of memento that my mama had half a mouth of fake teeth — yeah, at forty.

The nurse walked over to the table and handed me Mama's toothbrush.

Really? She didn't want me to keep her

teeth, but she was giving me her toothbrush?

She said, "The administrator has some papers for you."

I wondered what kind of papers were needed for death.

Nurse Burns must've seen the question on my face because she explained, "You have to sign where you want them to take your mother."

Take her? "What?" I frowned.

"Which funeral home?" Her tone sounded like she thought I was slow. "I was thinking you wanted her over at Brown's, but you have to sign the papers and tell them that."

I paused. "If I take her to Brown's, won't I have to give them some money?"

She nodded and then she stared as if she were trying to figure me out. Well, it was my turn to explain some things to her. "I don't have any money."

"You don't have to use your own money. The insurance will take care of this."

For a second, I waited for her to laugh, and when she didn't, I did. "My mama didn't have no insurance. She didn't even have medical insurance."

"What about relatives? Or your church? Surely there are people who will help bury your mother."

That only made me laugh harder. People

who would help me? I guess since she didn't live in White Haven, she didn't know my life. "Look, I don't have no money, I don't have no insurance, I don't have no friends. So the people here, they're gonna have to bury her."

Her eyes widened. "No, Keisha, you don't want to do that. You want to give your mother a proper burial. If you leave her here, and leave her to the state" — she lowered her eyes, shook her head — "you'll never know what happened to her."

"I know what happened to her." I paused. "She died." And then, I went right back to doing what I'd been doing before the nurse interrupted me with this foolishness. It wasn't that I didn't love my mama — I loved her lots. But with her death, we had parted.

Looking at my mama's robe, I gathered the comb and brush, her dentures and toothbrush into the center. With the exception of a few things she'd left at home, this was all my mama had in the world.

"Let me get you something to carry that out."

"Nah, I'll carry everything in this." I folded my mama's worldly possessions inside the robe, then pressed the bundle to my chest.

I nodded at the nurse, pursed my lips again into that tight smile, and walked past her.

She said nothing until I was at the door. "Keisha, wait."

Turning, I faced her and stared as she held up the book in her hand. "You forgot this."

I started to shake my head, but one of the things I'd learned about Nurse Burns over the weeks of my visits to this hospice was that she was one of those pushy broads who kept talking until someone shut her up. So instead of saying what I wanted to say, I decided I could show her better than I could tell her.

I tucked my mama's bathrobe bundle under my arm, then took quick steps to Nurse Burns. My eyes were on hers when I grabbed Mama's Bible and my eyes stayed locked with hers when I dumped the book into the trash next to where my mama had laid her head.

Nurse Burns gasped, and stumbled back and away, like she thought lightning might be about to strike.

I almost laughed, though I didn't because I pitied her more than I found her funny. So I said, "Bye," and turned.

But when Nurse Burns called my name again, I whipped around. "What? I'm not taking the Bible."

She shook her head, swallowed, and pointed to the other picture that Mama had brought to the hospice with her. The picture that I always kept away from my glance.

"What . . . what . . . about . . . this?" She sounded as if she were afraid of me now. As if my blasphemy might be contagious and it was an illness she didn't want to catch.

I was pissed, but I couldn't take that out on Nurse Burns. How would she know that photo wasn't really a photo, but a dagger that sliced my heart?

I shook my head, but then, Nurse Burns got her groove back. Because even though I'd threatened her life by tossing that Bible into the trash, she still lifted the picture and held it toward me. She was doing that pushy thing again, and now, because she hadn't left it alone, she was 'bout to get her feelings hurt — again.

That meant I had to walk across the room once more, though this time, I didn't look at Nurse Burns. My glance was somewhere over her shoulder, looking out the window — my insurance that my eyes wouldn't drop to the picture by accident.

I grabbed the frame, and with my gaze still somewhere on the horizon, I tossed the picture to the right.

My aim was great. The photo landed with a thump. Right on top of the Bible. Right in the trash, where they both belonged.

Again, Nurse Burns gasped, but this time there was more sadness than shock in her sound. And this time, when I walked to the door, I made my way all the way through because Nurse Burns didn't have another word to say to me.

# 2
## GABRIELLE WILSON FLORES

"Mommy, I finished my cereal and I'm ready to go."

I looked up from where I sat at the edge of my bed, trying to squeeze my foot into this gorgeous new black pump with a metallic heel that I'd been dying to wear since I'd made this fabulous purchase at an end-of-season sale last February.

But I forgot all about my shoes when I took in the sight of my daughter. I wasn't sure if I should cry out in horror or if I should bust out laughing. The way the snickers began to rise up, told me which emotion was winning.

It wasn't that Bella had done all that bad of a job. By themselves, the green tights would have worked . . . without her pink tutu, red-striped hat, and black patent leather Mary Janes. And on any day walking down a Los Angeles street, I was likely to see someone four times Bella's age wearing the same thing.

But while her clothes worked in LA, they wouldn't work at her Beverly Hills pre-school. "Bella, sweetheart . . . what happened to the clothes that I laid out on your bed?"

She bounced into the room. "I wanna wear this instead."

"Babe," Mauricio began as he burst into our bedroom from his closet in the master bath. "I need help with this tie. Can you . . ." He paused as he took in our daughter. "Oh, Bella. You look . . . lovely."

"Thank you, Daddy." She scooted onto our bed.

I gave my husband a hard side-eye. Now what was I going to do? As soon as I told Bella she had to change, she would call on the name of her father. She would cry and tell me her daddy said she looked . . . lovely. I took a deep breath. It would serve him right if I made him take her to school wearing that circus attire.

"You gonna help me, babe?" Mauricio said, turning his attention to me.

I stood and hobbled over to him since I was wearing only one four-inch shoe. I grabbed the end of the tie and resisted the urge to wrap it around his neck and pull — my revenge for the position he'd put me in with our five-year-old.

But it was standing in front of him that made my distress fade away. Because this Latin flame still set my heart (and other parts of me) on fire. He was so hot, blazing even more now than he'd been when I married him six years ago.

With just a few folds and bends, I had Mauricio set.

"Thanks, babe." He kissed my cheek. Turning to Bella, he said, "So, you're ready for school?"

Bella and I spoke at the same time.

"Yes," she said.

"No," I shouted. "Really, Mauricio?"

"What?"

"Stop playing," I said before I turned to the only female in the world who could go to war with me and sometimes win. "Bella, you can't wear that to school."

From the corner of my eye, I saw my husband tiptoeing from the room. Chicken!

Bella folded her arms. "I wanna wear this."

"You have to wear the clothes I laid out for you."

She pouted. "I don't want to wear those clothes."

"Today is picture day, so you can't wear your tutu."

She squinted. "Those clothes are too ugly

for pictures."

I raised my eyebrows. Was this little girl questioning my taste in fashion? And then, I wondered, why was I having this debate with a five-year-old? I was the mama, a black mama.

So I did the only thing that gave me the upper hand. I put that bass in my voice and then *I* folded *my* arms, *I* pouted, and *I* squinted. "Bella!" Then, I extended my arm, pointed toward the door, and even though her tears flowed right away, she scooted off the bed and rushed past me — in fear.

That part didn't make me feel good. I wanted to raise my daughter to think her own thoughts and speak her own mind and always feel free to do both. But when it was seven forty-three and I had to leave by seven fifty if I wanted to drop Bella by eight fifteen and then get over to my office by nine — I just didn't have time for a free-thinking, self-speaking, pink-tutu-wearing child.

As I hobbled back to the bed to slip on my other shoe, my husband peeked into the room.

"Imagine this is a white handkerchief," he said, waving his hand before he stepped inside.

I rolled my eyes, but he'd come prepared to fight. He reached into his arsenal and gave me one of those dimpled grins that disarmed me, and I melted. The way I always did.

He said, "The only reason I told her she looked so good was because it's important to build our little girl's self-esteem."

"How in the world will letting her go out dressed like a clown help?"

"I'm sure there was a time when you dressed just like that." Before I could call him all kinds of things that had nothing to do with his name, Mauricio pressed his lips against mine — another one of his weapons. But not even a full second passed when my cell phone vibrated on the nightstand. Mauricio reached for it, glanced at the screen, then answered the call, "What's up, Pops?"

I frowned. My father never called this early in the morning. Not that he wasn't awake. By six, he was at his desk at the trucking company I'd encouraged him to buy nine years ago when I was getting my MBA. His mornings were always chaotic, getting the schedules set and truckers on the road, which was why him wanting to chat at this time was so unusual.

"Yeah, she's right here," Mauricio said. "You good?"

My husband nodded as he listened to my father's words, though I saw a bit of concern in his eyes.

"Okay, here she is."

I grabbed the phone. "Hey, Daddy."

"Morning, sweetness. Listen . . . I know you're busy."

"No, I'm not," I said as I eyed Bella sulking back into our bedroom. She'd done what I'd asked. But then she'd put her tutu on top of the khaki pants. I sighed as I returned my attention to my father. "I'm good," I told him. "What's up?"

"Can you stop by and see me this morning? Just for a few minutes. I have something I have to . . ." The way he paused made the frown in my mind deepen. "I have something I need to talk to you about."

"Okay. I'll drop Bella off and then swing by your office . . ."

"I'm at home. Come here."

At home? After six in the morning? "Daddy, is everything all right?"

"I'll talk to you when you get here." Then he hung up without *I love you, have a great day,* without any kind of his normal goodbye. I stared at the phone as if my cell could give me more insight.

"What's up with Pops?" Mauricio's voice cut through my thoughts.

"I'm wondering the same thing." I shook my head. "Daddy wants me to stop by his house." Looking up at my husband, I added, "Something's wrong."

Mauricio gave me a slow nod. "Well . . . it doesn't make sense to speculate when all you have to do is get over there and find out what's going on. So this is what we'll do. You finish getting dressed and get over to your dad's, and I'll" — he turned to Bella, who had once again scooted onto our bed — "take Bella to school."

"Yay." Bella clapped, then jumped up and into her father's arms.

Mauricio planted her onto the floor, then, holding her hand, he twirled her around, and her giggles were a song that filled our bedroom. He said, "I'll take you to school, and you can even wear your tutu."

"Yay!" Bella sang again.

Thoughts of my father shot right out of my head. But before I could call my husband all kinds of crazy, he added, "Yup, you can wear it all the way to school and then you'll leave it in the car and put it right back on when I pick you up and take you to get some ice cream."

There were more cheers from our daughter as she looked at me, her brown eyes filled with triumph as if she'd won the war between us. I shook my head at both of them.

"Go get your backpack and meet me downstairs."

"Okay, Daddy."

Bella ran to the door, but then, made a quick U-turn and charged back into the room. She wrapped her arms around my neck. "Bye, Mommy. Have a good day." And then she smacked a kiss onto my cheek.

"Thank you, sweetheart. You have a great day, too."

She dashed out of our bedroom and I turned my attention back to my husband. "Really? She can wear the tutu *and* get ice cream?"

"Look, you just witnessed a high-powered negotiation," he said, nothing but seriousness in his voice. "Everybody won. Bella's going to school dressed exactly the way you want, but before and after, she gets to be the prima ballerina she's determined to be."

"And who's the winner with all of that sugar she'll have before dinner this evening?"

He shrugged. "In any good negotiation, you have to give a little to get what you want. And what I wanted most was for you to focus on your father."

Inside my mind, thoughts of Bella and her tutu and ice cream screeched to a halt.

"Thank you," I said. "I do need to get over there."

"So call me after you talk to him, okay?"

I nodded and he kissed my cheek.

"And do what Bella said. Have a good day. And don't worry."

"I won't."

He glanced back over his shoulder. "Liar. But you're such a beautiful one."

I watched Mauricio strut from the room, and like always, he left me with a smile. But then when I thought about my dad, the cheer that I'd felt dimmed.

Mauricio was right, though. There was no need to worry when I didn't even know what was going on. So I slipped on my other shoe, then rushed into my closet for the matching jacket to my skirt.

I needed to get to Venice as fast as I could and find out what the heck was going on.

# 3
## KEISHA

I didn't want to open my eyes. Because if I did, then I'd have to face the first morning, the first day, the beginning of the first week, month, and year without my mama. But if I kept my eyes closed, maybe I could stop time from ticking. And if I could stop time from ticking, maybe I'd be able to figure out a way to rewind it and take back all that God had taken away.

So I kept my eyes closed and snuggled under the most valuable of Mama's possessions — this afghan that one of her johns had given to her. She loved it so much she hadn't even taken it with her to the hospice.

"I don't want all that sickness getting up in this," she told me when I'd brought it to her. "Take it home so it'll be waiting for me when I get out of here."

I'd only done what she said because I wanted her to have the hope in her last days that I didn't have. And if taking this home

24

made her smile (and it did), then I was going to do it.

The fragrance of her perfume lingered in the yarn, and it made me remember the day when she told me that John — that's what she called all of the men, her regulars and her one-nighters — had given her this as a gift.

"John brought it back for me from Morocco," she told me with pride swelling her chest.

That day, all I did was smile, and I kept it to myself that I'd seen a whole bunch of these in the Walmart when I went up there one day to get money from my boyfriend, Buck. I just let her have her fantasy and now, I wanted to have mine. And if I didn't open my eyes . . .

But then, the rattling of the front door made my eyes spring open. When the banging started, I stiffened at the force of the knock that made the door vibrate.

"Keisha! If you're in there . . ." Mrs. Johnson's shouts echoed through the neighborhood, I was sure. "Keisha!"

Even though I was in the back room (there were only two rooms in this shack), I did my best not to blink or breathe. Not even when I heard the doorknob jiggle. Then the sound of the key in the lock almost made my heart stop, even though I knew Mrs. Johnson couldn't get in. Buck had changed the locks last week while Mrs. Johnson was at work because I'd been prepared for this moment.

"Keisha! If you're in there, this is your notice. I'm calling the sheriff."

After another moment or so, I heard her footsteps stomping along the driveway. It was only when I heard her back door slam shut that I exhaled. Still, I stayed in my mama's bed for a few seconds before I swung my legs over the side and, wearing nothing but my bra and panties, tiptoed across the chilly wooden floor to the window. I held my breath as I slipped open a single blind and peeked through just to make sure Mrs. Johnson didn't have a new trick to get her rent money. I saw nothing and so I bounced back onto the bed. I was glad I'd been in the back room instead of on the sofa in the front, which was my normal resting place. If I'd been up there, Mrs. Johnson may have seen my shadow, and if she'd thought that I was in here, she would have tried to break the door down.

This game of me hiding and Mrs. Johnson seeking was not going to play out much longer. Mama and I hadn't paid the rent in three months, not since she went into that hospice and Medicaid took everything from her — the few dollars she had in the bank and even her Social Security check. They didn't care nothin' 'bout me, saying that I was old enough to take care of myself. But I'd been taking care of my mama. And when I did have a chance to work, my tips at Beryl's House of Beauty weren't enough to pay attention, let alone this five-hundred-dollar rent.

Lying back, it was unbelievable that at twenty-two I wasn't any better off than when I'd been two. At least it felt that way. I mean, Mama did all she could to take care of me. But we'd always struggled, moving from shack to shack when we didn't have enough money to pay the rent.

But one thing we'd never had to do — we'd never had to live out of our car, which was the move it seemed I was going to have to make. I was going to have to add "a house to sleep in" as another thing that I didn't have because of what God had done to me.

It wasn't that big a deal, I guessed. I'd been used to "not having" my whole life. I never had any friends, never had any new clothes, never had a real Christmas. I was raised with "not having."

I got used to most of it. But no matter

what I did, no matter how hard I tried, I could never get used to not having a daddy.

That thought made me open my eyes, sit up, scoot to the top of the bed, and rest against the wall where a headboard was supposed to be. Pulling my knees up to my chest, I wrapped my arms around my legs and remembered . . .

I stomped up the stairs, then threw the hard plastic backpack that Mama had gotten from the Goodwill onto the porch. My school books were so heavy the bag hit the wooden planks with a thud, making the porch rattle. But I didn't even care that Mama didn't like me doing that; I just swung the screen door back, then pushed the front door open. "Mama!" I called out.

"Keisha! Hush with all that noise."

I paused. Her voice was coming from the bathroom, so I marched back there, making my steps hard so before I even got there, Mama would know I was mad. I stopped at the open door, only because there wasn't enough space for the two of us to fit inside that bathroom and Mama took up most of the room just by standing in front of the sink. She was brushing that red stuff on her cheeks, and that meant she was going out to work tonight. And if she was going to work, then I was going to be stuck having a peanut butter and jelly sandwich for dinner again. Which wouldn't be bad if I hadn't had it for lunch this whole week.

She said, "And what did I tell you about calling me Mama? My name is Daisy. Just like I call you Keisha, and I don't call you *child* or *daughter,* I call you by your name and I want you to call me by mine."

That was something that I hated. All the other kids had to call their mothers Mama. I didn't want to call her Daisy. But right now, that was not what I wanted to talk to my mama about.

Looking at her through the mirror, I said, "Mama . . . I mean, Daisy, Mrs. Burgess said in school today that everybody has a daddy."

"You don't," she said, and for a moment, I was stuck, kinda fascinated at how my mama could put mascara on without blinking.

But then I got right back on the subject. I crossed my arms. Now she was adjusting her blond wig, the one that had hair flowing all the way down her back, stopping at her butt. She only wore that wig for special johns — that was what she told me. But I couldn't let her go out and have a good time when today was the most miserable day of my whole life.

"All the kids in class laughed at me. Because when we were talking about reproduction, I told them that I didn't have a daddy."

"You don't," she repeated.

I stomped my foot. "I do! Mrs. Burgess said that I do. She told me everybody has a mama and everybody has a daddy. That's how we all got here. It's called biology."

"Well" — Mama smacked her lips and then patted her lipstick with a piece of toilet paper — "your teacher doesn't know anything. She certainly doesn't know what she's talking about."

"She knows a lot because she went to college," I said.

My mama's hands stopped moving and she glared at me through the mirror. My heart started beating fast — that look that she gave me sometimes came with a backhand right in my mouth. But even though I was scared that she might pop me, I didn't care if I got in trouble. I glared right back at her because I always asked my mama about my daddy and she always told me I didn't have one. But today, for the first time, I knew that wasn't true. I knew now that she had been lying to me my whole nine years on earth, and I wanted to know who was my daddy?

"Young lady, I don't care if she went to college." Mama turned around and faced me. With her face so smooth and her lips so red, she almost looked like a movie star. She said, "If your teacher said everybody has a daddy, then everybody does . . ."

I smiled. Finally, she was going to tell me the truth.

Then, Mama said, "Everybody but you."

Even now, that memory made me sigh. That was the way the story always went — at least the story that came from my mama. She never did tell me, but years later, when I was in the ninth grade, I found out the whole truth — though it didn't come from her. And finding out came at a really high price for a fourteen-year-old girl.

That was something I didn't want to remember, at least not right now. So I rolled over and thought about my mama. But right away, I was sorry because I began to wonder what did those people at the hospice do with her? Where did they put her? Was she in one of those graveyards behind one of the churches? Had they buried her yet?

Would they tell me where she was, and if they did, would I ever go to see her?

"No!" I said aloud. I didn't go to cemeteries.

I rolled over, and grabbed my cell phone. Looking at Instagram was way better than filling my mind with thoughts of my mama. I clicked on that app, then went straight to the page I always checked out first. Scrolling through, I was disappointed there weren't any new posts since I'd checked yesterday; actually, there had been nothing new since Friday, and I always hated when that happened. I lived a different life through all of those glamorous Instagram pictures, and with the way I was feeling today, I needed to imagine myself in the photos standing next to celebrities, wearing all of those designer clothes, having my hair and makeup done by people who knew what they were doing. But without anything new posted on her page, there wasn't anything new I could imagine.

Still, I checked out the hundreds of photos that I'd seen thousands of times. That kept me busy and my mind away from my troubles for about an hour. But now it was almost nine, and I had to get over to Beryl's to at least make enough money to eat.

It was going to be a bit of a challenge to

get out of here. I wouldn't be able to take a shower because I didn't want Mrs. Johnson to hear the water running. So I'd just wash up, then climb the back fence because I couldn't walk past the front house. I had parked my truck about six streets over so that Mrs. Johnson would never know when I was home. Just thinking about all of that sneaking around made me tired already, but I was my mama's child — I was going to do what I had to do.

Looking at the last photo one more time, I took a minute to imagine myself at that party. Then, I clicked off Instagram. But I didn't move for a moment. I pressed the cell phone to my chest and closed my eyes. *One day.* Although I didn't yet have a plan, I had a purpose. *One day soon.*

# 4
## GABRIELLE

My assistant Pamela's voice floated through my car's Bluetooth connection. "Nope, you're free this morning. I cannot remember another Monday like this."

"I guess it's because Justus is out of town," I said, referring to my agency's biggest client.

"Yeah. Probably." The way Pamela sighed, I could tell she was glad her only dealings with our star client would be over the phone for the next week.

Justus was a great guy, a friend — and a little more — from back in the day. His star had risen, and then he'd remembered mine. He'd helped me and my best friend, Regan, start and put our PR firm, Media Connections Consulting Group, on the map, and then he became our PR when he told everyone how I'd been central to his success.

While he was a blessing, there was the other side, too. His demands grew in direct

34

proportion to his success. While he may have been about 50 percent of my company's revenues, he was 99 percent of our time and effort.

"Okay, great. So I don't have to cancel any meetings," I said, grateful that Pamela knew my calendar because with all that was on my plate, I never knew where I was supposed to be. "This works. I'll be in the office around ten."

"Gotcha. We're good. I'll let Regan know."

"Okay," I said, knowing that my best friend and my assistant would hold it all down for me while I took care of . . . what? I started worrying all over again — what was going on with my father?

I was so glad I'd spoken to Pamela all the way on my short but rush-hour-traffic-filled drive from Santa Monica to Venice where my dad still lived in the house where I was raised. For a moment, I let my thoughts drift back on those memories of growing up just six blocks from the beach, on a street where I knew everyone who lived in every house, but never realizing then how special that was.

Venice had one heck of a bad reputation back in the eighties and nineties, but I was an insider with a different view. What outsiders never saw was a residential community filled with family and longtime friends.

Just driving down Lincoln Boulevard altered my thoughts. My dad's call was probably nothing more than him needing some advice for his trucking business. Yup, that was probably what it was. My dad had been a truck driver from the moment he graduated from high school. And for twenty-five of those years, he'd worked for one company — Moss Trucking. But then in 2008, under a special project that I was working on during my first year of business school, I convinced my dad to buy the company, which had been up for sale for two years.

Parents were supposed to be proud of their children, but I always loved that scripture in Proverbs that said parents were the pride of their children. Because Elijah Wilson had made me so proud when, after balking at first, he'd stepped out on major faith and without a college degree or any kind of training, had purchased the company. Then my father had not only turned a profit the first year, but was managing to slowly grow the company each year.

I only knew my father's company's financials because I was on his board — a board of one . . . then two, once Mauricio and I married. But there wasn't much Mauricio and I had to do. We reviewed his sales and banking records because even though Daddy had an accountant that Mauricio had interviewed and hired, my dad didn't trust anyone except for family.

*Maybe that's why Daddy wants to see me. Something to do with the board.*

That was my thought as I made a right turn onto Brooks Avenue, then slowed my roll as I steered down the residential street. Two blocks down, I swung into the driveway and pulled up behind my dad's Ford Explorer. When I glanced at the clock on my dashboard, the time brought all of my concerns back. Nine thirty-eight. By now, my dad would usually have put in almost half a day at work.

I raised a stop sign in my head. Why was I stressing when I was right here? Slipping from my car, I locked it, then walked onto the porch, which creaked with each of my steps. I pushed open the guard gate, then knocked once before I used my key to enter.

"Daddy," I called out.

"Gabrielle . . . is that you?"

I frowned. When my dad walked into the living from the hall that led to his bedroom, his gait was slow, his steps seemed heavy. But what was most telling — he was still in

37

his plaid pajamas, covered by his bathrobe. This was a man who rose before the sun. My first words to him were, "What's wrong, Daddy?"

"Why're you asking me that?"

Once again, I took in his bathrobe, then decided to answer his question in a different way. "Because you called me by my government name when I came in, so I know something is up."

"That's not just your government name," he protested the way he always did when I kidded him that way, though today, there was a lot more bitter than sweet in his tone. He hugged me, then stepped back. "That's the name your wonderful mother gave to you."

As I moved over to the sofa next to my dad's recliner, we shared a couple of moments of silence. This was something that always happened when my dad spoke of my mom, Mary. She'd been gone for seven years, and while that was supposed to be God's number of completion, there wasn't any kind of finality in my dad's tone when he spoke of the woman whom he said was the love of his forever. He spoke of her like she was the blessed mother, and the void her death left behind still made my heart ache. But what pained me more was that I knew that, seven years after my mother died from heart failure, my dad still cried for her.

"I'm sorry, sweetness," my dad said as he dropped onto the recliner. "I didn't mean to snap that way. It's just that . . ."

I scooted to the edge of the sofa. "What's wrong?" I didn't want to go through a whole lot of nothing before we got to the something part of this conversation. My dad already knew how I was, how Mauricio was, how Bella was. He already knew that I was busy at work, and I knew all of that about him, too.

My dad nodded like he agreed — he wanted to get to the point as well. He said, "I needed to talk to you . . . about this." He pulled a letter from the pocket of his bathrobe, but when I reached for it, he held it back. "I need to tell you something, and I'll make this as quick as I can."

Now my mind swirled with a single thought — my father was ill. That letter was from some doctor giving the prognosis of my father's demise. I had to fight to hold back the tears. I wasn't ready to lose my father. I had just started breathing after living seven years without my mother.

He said, "Years ago, when I was on the road . . . I had an affair."

My thoughts came to a screeching halt,

backed up, and I blinked to press replay on my father's words.

"What?"

He repeated what he'd said, then he tried to hand me the letter. But I didn't take it.

"What?" I said again.

"Read this." Again, he pushed the letter toward me, but it wasn't a simple handoff because of the way both of our hands shook. I held the letter and held it and held it, just staring at the proper cursive writing that had written my father's name and company address on the envelope. In the upper corner, there was an address — a post office box in Arkansas: White Haven.

"Read it, Gabby. It's easier . . . for me . . . if you read it."

Now I looked up at him.

He said, "Read it and I'll explain everything."

And so I did what my father told me because despite my shock, he was still the dad. I slid the single page from its hiding place, unfolded the paper, and began:

It's been so many years, my dearest Elijah. You were the only man whose name I cared to know. But there is something that you have to know now. I didn't have that abortion I told you I was going to have over twenty years ago. I went ahead and had the baby because I didn't want to kill something growing inside of me. I know you didn't think the baby was yours. I know that was why you never came back. But this little girl, she is your little baby, she is your little girl. And now, I'm not going to be here much longer, and I can't leave Keisha by herself. We don't have no family and we hardly have any friends. I'm dying, and my little girl, our little girl, will be all by herself. I never told her about you because I didn't want her to feel the rejection I felt and I still feel every time I look at her face. But I'm hoping that you'll do right by one of your own. Just look at her picture and do the right thing. This is my final request on earth.

The letter was signed formally . . . twice: *Sincerely, Yours Truly, Daisy Jones.* I read the letter again, mostly because I didn't want to look up at my father. But when I began reading it for the third time, he called my name.

Now I had no choice. I looked up, but what was I supposed to say?

I was glad when my father spoke. "It's all true," he said. "You can ask me anything you want about this, but it's true."

"But . . ."

Before I could get any more words out, my father pulled something from the other pocket of his bathrobe. He handed me a photo, and the moment I looked down at it, I gasped. No one would deny that my father was this girl's father. She had everything that belonged to him — his bushy eyebrows, the cleft in her chin . . . and then there was that mole, right above her lip, in the same spot as my father's. It was like someone had taken all of his DNA and glued it onto her face.

"Oh my God," I whispered, pressing my fingertips against my lips.

My eyes returned to my father, and he nodded. "I can't . . . I don't even have the words for all of this. But the picture tells the truth."

"So you had an affair?" I knew that was what my father said when we started, but I was thinking he didn't really mean an affair-affair. I was thinking more of some kind of social media thing, and I couldn't be mad at that. My mom was gone and my dad spent so much time working, it would have been good for him to have some kind of social life.

But that was just my denial, because he'd said *affair* — and *affair* meant a relationship one wasn't supposed to have because one was already involved, right? And this picture — this was a picture of a young woman . . . twenty, maybe. This picture told the story of an affair that happened long ago. When my mother was alive.

"I did have an affair. It's not something I'm proud of, and it's not something I ever admitted out loud until today."

I blew out a breath because it was so difficult to wrap my mind around this. My father, who adored my mother, who'd gotten on his knees and cried at her funeral because he couldn't imagine his life without her. That man . . . had cheated on his wife? And then I had a thought. "Did Mom know?"

He shook his head. "No, I told you, I never spoke of it, and Mary never suspected because it was a thing I carried on for about a year when I was doing that route cross-country delivering to Walmart. It was just . . ." He looked down and away. "It was lonely on the road. On those long-distance trips, I hated being by myself night after night." But then, my dad's head shot up. As if he wanted me to see his eyes for his next words. "It had nothing to do with your mother. I loved her with everything in me, and if she had been able to be with me when

43

I traveled . . ." He sighed. "You believe me, don't you?"

His plea was inside his tone, and I nodded, even though that was not the most important part of this conversation. I wanted to talk about the letter — and what this Daisy Jones said . . . and the young woman . . . who looked just like my father.

"So, the baby . . . you knew you had a baby?"

"No." The way he shook his head, he'd have a headache by morning for sure. "I never knew about her."

"But the letter . . ."

"She told me she was pregnant, but I didn't believe it was mine. Daisy was . . ." He paused as if he was trying to find kind words. "She was a woman who made her living by keeping men company."

If this weren't my father, weren't so personal, weren't so serious, as a PR professional, I would have paused, just to relish in the brilliance of that spin.

He said, "I was only with her five, maybe six times through that year. I didn't stop by every time I was in Arkansas 'cause I just couldn't do it. I felt guilty every single time. So when she said she was pregnant, I asked her why was she telling me."

I flinched.

He held up his hands. "I wasn't trying to be disrespectful; it was just like I said, she kept company with many men. I wasn't fool enough to believe that she was only doing . . . that with me."

"You told her to get an abortion?"

Again, he shook his head. "No. Because I knew the baby wasn't mine. How could it be? Five, six times? When she was with so many other men? And we'd used protection." He paused. "Most of the time."

Just a minute ago, I appreciated my father's words, but right now, he made me sad. His denials sounded like so many of the men who sat in my office, pleading for my help to spin them out of paternity claims.

My father said, "After she told me about the baby, after I asked her how could it be mine, she told me she was gonna get an abortion 'cause she didn't have a lifestyle conducive to a baby. I didn't give her an opinion one way or the other. I just walked out of that diner and never saw her again."

"So . . . you weren't ever curious enough to follow up with her?"

He looked down at his hands again. "Please don't judge me, sweetness. You have to see this the way I did, for what it was. Being with Daisy was nothing but a temporary solution to being lonely on the road. She was convenient . . ."

"And she got pregnant," I interrupted him, holding up the picture. "Clearly with your child."

He gave me a slow nod.

"Wow."

"I know, it was a wow for me when I got this letter last week."

Those words made my eyebrows rise almost to the top of my forehead. "You've been holding on to this all that time?"

"I just didn't know what to do." He shrugged. "I wanted to digest it a bit and then . . . figure it out. Though, from the moment I read that letter, I knew what I had to do, what I wanted to do."

I nodded, knowing what he meant and agreeing with him. "So did you call" — I glanced at the letter again — "Daisy? Keisha?"

"Daisy didn't give me any phone number, no address, just a post office box. I have no idea why she would write and tell me this, then not give me any information."

Frowning, I looked at the letter again. "It sounds like — Is she dying?"

"What's on that paper is all that I know. But I'm hoping you can help me. Is there a way you can trace this letter back to White

Haven? I mean, I could go down there and see if she's still . . . working in the same places."

"No," I said, "I mean, yes. No, you don't have to do it. I'll do it. I'll find Daisy and Keisha."

"And you'll bring them here?"

I paused for a moment. Bring them here? To Los Angeles? "Is that what you want?"

He nodded.

I gave him a smile. "Then that's what I'll do."

His relief was palpable as he exhaled, his burden lifted. Together, we sat in silence, each with our own reflections. I wasn't sure what my father was thinking, but I had one thought.

After a minute or so, I voiced it. "Wow, I may have . . . a sister."

He nodded. "How do you feel about that?"

I shifted through all that was in my head and my heart. "It's . . . shocking. But . . ." I paused. Even though I felt his relief, I still felt so much of his distress. Leaning forward, I placed my hand over my father's. "If she's your daughter, then I can't wait to meet my sister."

His eyes became glassy. "So we're still in this life together, huh?" my father said, repeating the words that he'd uttered often right after my mom passed away.

"All the time and all the way." I spoke the same words I always said back to him.

We stood and then my father held me. Now he stood tall and strong, the way I was used to seeing my fifty-seven-year-old father. He was still a good man. That was a truth that would never go away. So, I would help him find Keisha and greet her and accept her with everything in me.

As I thought about it, I began to smile. Wow. In just these few moments, my life had totally changed. But I was ready. I couldn't wait to take the ride — for my daddy.

# 5
## GABRIELLE

I knew what it was like to be a zombie. Because from the moment I left my dad's place, I was on autopilot — or maybe auto-zombie. That was the only way to explain why I didn't remember getting on the 10 Freeway or exiting onto LaCienega and rolling up that boulevard all the way to my Beverly Hills office on Wilshire. I made that trip without having a single thought. Really, my mind was blank, even though I kept pressing, trying to think of something.

I guess the Lord didn't allow me to think because He knew I needed all of my mental capabilities to focus on performing my basic life functions: breathing, blinking, staring straight ahead so that I could maneuver my car without incident.

But now that I was here, all I could do was stumble into the office suite, past Pamela's empty desk — thank God she had stepped away — and then make it into my office. Every morning when I entered this space, I pushed open the door and paused for a moment to thank God for what He had given to me. The Media Connections Consulting Group may have only been in business for five years, but Regan and I were experiencing the success of an agency that had been around for so much longer. It wasn't just our client list of more than one hundred celebrities and companies that was impressive — this space with its top-to-bottom windows that covered two walls of this corner office and framed the fantastic view of the Hollywood sign added to my pleasure of coming to work every day. I always wanted to thank God for the overall fabulousness of my life.

But today, it was all that I could do to lumber to my desk. Flopping into my chair, I didn't even spin around and check out the view — another one of my morning rituals. All I did was lower my head into my hands.

It wasn't that I was upset. I wasn't, and that surprised me. I wasn't upset with my dad, probably because my mom wasn't here. Without her, I could focus on him. But this news still shook me.

"Wow."

My vocabulary had been reduced to that three-letter word. Just *wow.* I guess that summed up what I was thinking, all that I was feeling.

I dug into my tote for the letter once again, and this time I flattened it, as if smoothing out the wrinkles would make the words clearer. But as I reread it, nothing — not the words, not the message — had changed between Venice and Beverly Hills.

My father had still had an affair that had led to the birth of a child.

My sister.

Wow!

"Hey, Gabby, I just got an email from *The View* about Justus."

Regan sauntered into my office wearing a red dress that covered up everything but was so fitted it looked like it had been painted on her ample curves. If I hadn't been so off-kilter, I would've teased her and told her she wouldn't be able to wear that kind of outfit for much longer.

But I was still in zombie mode, so the only thing I did was look up and into the eyes of my best friend.

She paused. "What's wrong?"

I waved her in and then motioned for her to close the door. She pushed it shut, then rushed to the chair in front of my desk. "What's going on?" she asked with a frown.

I opened my mouth, but then I stopped. I

hadn't told Mauricio yet. But he was in class, and I didn't want to pull him away from his students. I'd tell him tonight, but even though he should've been the first one to hear this from me, I couldn't wait that long.

First, I took a deep breath, and then I exhaled, "You're not going to believe this."

"What? Something with one of our clients?" Then she held up her hands. "Don't tell me." She relaxed as she leaned back. "Something with Justus."

"No." I shook my head. "This is all about me. I mean, my dad. I mean, me and my dad." I paused, now understanding why my father had just given me the letter to read. It was too much to explain, so I did the same thing. "Here" — I slid the letter across my desk — "read this."

Leaning forward, she frowned at first, studying the envelope, then picked it up and slid out the letter. Then, as her eyes scanned the words, I could tell which part she was reading. First there was her frown of confusion, then her eyes widening with surprise, and when her lips parted, forming a wide O . . . well, I knew then that she had made it to the end.

And because she was my best friend who had been as close as a sister since we'd met in middle school and realized that we attended the same church, she did what I did — she reread the letter.

When she was finally able to raise her head, she looked at me with squinted eyes. "What?"

I nodded. "That's exactly what I said."

Then, after another moment, she added, "Wow!"

"That's exactly what I said."

"I mean . . . why would someone send this letter? Is someone trying to get money out of your dad?" It was like a light had been turned on inside of her, and Regan sprang up from her chair. "I'll get right on it." The lawyer inside of my friend rushed out hard. "I can't believe this . . ."

As she paced and ranted on about scams and shakedowns, I didn't say a word. All I did was slip the photo from the side pocket of my purse and slide it across the desk.

"Trust me," Regan continued before she looked down at the photo, "I'm going to . . ." And then, she stopped. She studied the photo for a moment, then once again her eyes opened wide. She just stared and stared and stared.

Then she fell back into the chair she'd been sitting in — she kinda dropped into the seat the same way I had.

When she finally looked up at me, I nodded.

She inhaled. "So . . ."

"It's true," I finished for her.

"It can't be."

"You wanna look at that photo again?"

She did and shook her head at the same time. "So what . . ."

"Does Daddy want to do?" Again, I finished her thought as if we were more than sisters, as if we were twins.

She nodded.

"Well, he wants to find Daisy . . . and Keisha. And so I'm going to find them."

"How?" She picked up the envelope and studied it. "There's no address, no phone number."

"I know, which is a little crazy. I mean, Daisy wrote the letter so my father could take responsibility for Keisha, but then she didn't give him any way to get in touch with her."

"Does he have an old phone number or something?"

"No, he had it once, but that was over twenty years ago. He said he lost it, probably on purpose."

When Regan finally sat back, I told her everything that wasn't in the letter. I told her about Daisy and how — as my dad put

54

it — she kept men company. I told her how she'd told my dad about being pregnant and how she was the one who brought up the abortion. "My dad wasn't having it, never believed it, but now . . ."

Regan glanced down at the photograph again. "Can you imagine if your father had believed her twenty years ago? How different would your life have been?"

I nodded, though it wasn't my life I was thinking about. If this had played out a different way — all I could think about was my mom. I could not even imagine a scenario where their marriage would have survived. How? An affair is one thing . . . an affair and a child makes it *a* thing — a thing that would be hard for any woman to overlook and for any marriage to endure.

But my mom hadn't known, and so she'd gone to her grave having loved and been loved by the same man for twenty-seven years.

"Well, I'm glad your dad wants to find her now." Regan nodded as she spoke. "Do the right thing."

"I agree. That's why I'm going down to White Haven . . . I guess."

I hadn't thought about that until this moment. It was like talking this out with Regan set my brain in motion. And I could think. I had to get down to Arkansas.

"No." Regan shook her head. "Let me go. I'm the attorney, I know the questions to ask, and I can probably get this done faster than you can."

"It's not going to be that hard."

She tilted her head and pursed her lips.

"I know I'm not a private investigator, but how big can White Haven be?"

"It doesn't matter. You won't know who to talk to, and even if you did, you wouldn't know the right questions to ask. Trust me, let me handle this."

"I don't know. I don't want you to leave your life right now."

She held up her hands; her question was in that gesture.

"Hello?" I pointed to her belly. "Have you forgotten?"

When I did that, she covered her stomach with her hand and smiled. "This baby won't be here for another six months. Certainly, it won't take me that long to find" — she paused, shook her head, then added — "your sister."

I sighed.

"Plus," Regan continued, "we have a lot going on right now. Have you forgotten about the pitch for Contour Jeans?"

I hit my forehead with the heel of my

hand. Of course I hadn't forgotten . . . at least I hadn't until after I'd read this letter.

Regan said, "You're the CEO; you're the face of our agency. You can't go to Arkansas, because my marketing presentations sound like my opening arguments in a drug trial."

"Ugh! You're right." I shook my head. "It'll just have to wait a week."

"Really? You think you and your dad can wait?" She stood, and in a few long strides, she opened the door and called out to Mattie, her assistant.

As I sat back, she asked Mattie to book a flight to White Haven, Arkansas. "Probably will have to fly into the nearest major city. Check and see if that's Pine Bluff." She told her to do a flight in the morning with an open return.

When she came back to my desk, I said, "You really want to leave tomorrow?"

She nodded. "This is one of those situations where sooner and better really do go together. I would have left tonight, but, if you don't mind, I want to review this with Doug."

"Of course. Will he be all right with you going?"

"Are you kidding me? First of all, this is for you and your dad, and second, I can bet that if my husband could get out of any of his cases, he'd be on that plane with me. He lives for digging up stuff like this."

She was right about that. Doug, who I'd known as long as Regan, was the brother I'd never had. They'd been together since our freshman year in high school, and from tenth grade, they dreamed of becoming two of Los Angeles's best prosecutors. Doug would want her down there. I breathed, "Okay." I couldn't keep the hesitation from my tone.

"Don't worry. It's not like this is a dangerous operation. I'll be safe, my baby will be safe, everything will be fine. I'll go down there and if I don't find anything, I'll come right back."

"And if you find them?"

"What do you want me to do?"

I inhaled. "Daddy would like them to come here."

"Okay, well, I'll find them, and if they agree, I'll bring them back. And at the very least, I'll be able to get a number or an email or something so that your father can be in touch with them."

I nodded. "If you can get them to come back here. At least . . . his . . . Keisha." I paused. "That's what he wants."

"Okay, then." She slammed her palm on the desk and said, "So, I'm going to work on Justus's calendar, speak to the producers over at *The View,* and then I'll head home. I really want to get my mind into this game. I want to call your dad first, ask him a few questions so that I'll know where to begin, and then there are a few things I want to research before I get on this plane."

"Like what?"

She shrugged. "I don't know. I want to make sure this isn't any kind of scam."

"How can it be a scam? You see that picture." I pointed to the photo she'd left in the center of my desk.

"Yeah, but Photoshop is a beast." She held up her hand as if she thought I was going to protest. "I just want to cover every single base. Remember, that's why you pay me the big bucks."

"Ummm . . . no. I don't pay you. We're partners, remember?"

She grinned. "No, we're more than that. We're sisters. So if you have a new sister . . . then I have one, too."

I pressed my hands over my heart. "I'm grateful."

She nodded and picked up the letter and picture. "Okay, let's get to work, and I'll let you know when I'm leaving."

I nodded, and before she stepped out of the door, I said, "Thanks, Regan."

"This is what sisters do."

Even after she was long gone, I still sat in place, letting one of her words echo through my mind.

Sisters.

Plural.

When I glanced at the clock on my desk, I couldn't believe it wasn't that far away from noon. Mauricio was probably in his office by now. I grabbed my phone, dialed his number, and then, the moment he picked up, I said, "Do I have something to tell you!"

# 6
## KEISHA

I limped into the bathroom, using my flashlight app, mad at myself for not getting home before dark. I didn't have any set hours at Beryl's since I was just an assistant, working primarily for tips. So I could pretty much come and go — whenever.

But since I still had that rent issue, I'd been trying to get home and settled in the house before dark. This way, I wouldn't have to turn on any lights that would give Mrs. Johnson a heads-up, even though that didn't stop her from banging on the door every single day.

But tonight I'd stayed at Beryl's because there were two late appointments in the book and I needed every dollar I could hustle together. So I hadn't left until after dark, and then I'd driven home with the gas needle hovering too close to trouble. I'd parked six streets away, then climbed the fence. And it was because it was dark that I cut my leg on a loose piece of wire.

Now my leg throbbed as I hobbled to the toilet, lowered the seat cover, then sat down before I leaned over and turned on the faucet.

But then . . . nothing.

What?

I pushed myself up. This time I turned on both the hot and cold water.

Nothing.

I twisted the knobs back and forth, then tried the faucet in the tub. Not a drip.

Stumbling back to the toilet, I sat down and sighed. There was no need for me to go into the kitchen; I knew what was up. Mrs. Johnson had probably turned off the lights, too, though I wasn't going to test it. The lights could have been a trick. She could have turned off the water and then thought that I would test the lights. I wasn't going to fall for that.

Ugh! Now what was I gonna do?

Rolling a wad of toilet paper in my hand, I pressed the paper hard against the cut on my leg. It was dumb for me to wear a skirt today, dumb for me to stay at Beryl's past dark, dumb for me to think that I was going to be able to sleep here much longer.

It was amazing to me that Mrs. Johnson hadn't already had the sheriff banging down my door, and if I didn't want to be dumb anymore, I needed to get out before the police really did show up. I just needed to face the facts of this situation — I wasn't going to be able to sleep here much past tonight.

I moaned with the thought of that. I was *really* going to have to sleep in my truck? That was my only option, because staying with Buck wouldn't work. Not with all of 'em people over there with him. And especially not with his father in one of those bedrooms. Whenever I was there, that house just wasn't big enough for me and his daddy. He always found a way to be up under me, and even now, the thought of that gave me the creeps. I wasn't going to give him another chance to touch me.

So I was back to my only choice — my truck, which was still better than sneaking around here every day until one night I came home and Mrs. Johnson had the locks changed.

My leg still throbbed, but I had a lot to do. I needed to pack up. Not that there was much for me to take, but there was enough that I didn't want to leave behind. I wanted to think about this carefully because this was my last connection to my mama.

That meant I had to do some planning. I

wouldn't be able to lug everything that I wanted to take with me over the backyard fence, so I'd have to get my car and bring it closer.

By the time I limped back into the bedroom, I had a full plan. I glanced at my cell phone. It was only eight fifty-seven. Mrs. Johnson was definitely home, probably peeking out her window.

Scooting back on the bed, I wrapped my mama's afghan around me and inhaled. Her perfume was still there. Really, her perfume was everywhere — in her pillows, in her closet, even in the fabric of the sofa from when she used to watch the TV in the front room. As I sat there in the dark, all I wanted right now was for my mama to come back and help me figure this out. But I only let that last for a moment. Because my mama had taught me never to wallow in anything. Just take care of business.

Looking at my phone again, I figured I could lie down for three or four hours since it was just a bit after nine. That would be a better time — when everyone was asleep — to pack and then be gone before the sun showed up.

I scooted under the afghan and snuggled against the pillow. I needed to get a couple of real good hours since these would be my last for a while. But when I closed my eyes, there were all kinds of thoughts in my head. I was thinking of my mama. And my father. And how I'd almost told her the other day that I knew about him. But I didn't because she was dying and so all I wanted her to have was peace. I didn't want her going to her grave having just found out that I'd known about my father since I was fourteen.

I wanted to push these thoughts aside so that I could really rest, because I needed a plan — desperately. Tomorrow at this time I'd be in my truck. How many tomorrows-in-my-truck would come after that?

I rolled over, and this time when I closed my eyes, my head wasn't filled with so many thoughts. There was only one thing inside my mind — and it was how I'd found out about my father.

There hadn't been a single day in my life since I'd learned the truth from Mrs. Burgess that I hadn't thought about my father. But I'd stopped asking my mama because she kept insisting I didn't have a daddy. Like I'd been hatched or something, as if I'd believe that for the rest of my life. But even though I couldn't get anything from my mama, I hadn't stopped searching for the truth.

Now, finally, I thought I'd found the way.

I held my breath as I pushed open the library door and then, I paused when I stepped inside. Today was my first day at Clinton High, and I was just figuring out where everything was in the building. Right now, I was supposed to be at lunch in the cafeteria, but I had snuck away to find this place.

I wasn't sure where I should look first — this library was sure different from the one in my middle school. On my left were rows and rows and rows of books. So many books and even standing at the front door, I could see that they were the new kind of books, not like the used books in my old school or even the library in White Haven, where I lived.

Turning to the right, I looked at the big square desk with an "Information" sign hanging from the ceiling above.

"May I help you, young lady?"

I didn't even hear the man walk up, even though he was standing right in front of me. The way he looked at me put a big lump in my throat. Like I wasn't supposed to be there.

My mama had told me to be careful. They were only busing in a few black kids to this new high school, so I didn't want to do anything wrong.

"I'm sorry," I whispered. "I just wanted to check out the library."

The man, whose pale skin looked more pink than white, lowered his head and looked at me over the rim of his glasses. "You one of the new freshmen?"

I nodded.

"You must like to read."

I nodded again, and then I wondered if that would be a lie even though I hadn't said any of the words out loud.

"So if you're a freshman" — he glanced up at the wall and I figured he was looking at a clock — "you're supposed to be in lunch."

"Yes, sir, but I wanted to check out the library 'cause I didn't know any other time when I could come here."

He nodded, and then he took his time looking at me. Like starting at my head and then going all the way down to my feet. The way he looked at me made me think big trouble was on its way. But for what? For coming to the library instead of going to lunch?

After a while, he said, "Okay, well, come on in." He turned his back, and I was glad he did, 'cause it gave me a chance to breathe. I followed him all the way inside, past all the big shelves and all the books. In the back, there were a few tables with a couple of students sitting down, reading from big textbooks.

When he stopped at one of the tables, I was looking around so much, I almost bumped into him.

He asked, "So, what kinds of books do you like to read?"

I didn't have an answer ready. "All kinds," I said. "But there was something else I wanted to do besides read."

He frowned.

"I want to do research."

"Oh!" He paused. "You have a research project already?"

"Yes, I mean, no. I mean, kinda." Looking away from him and out the window, I said, "I have a research project that I have to do . . . on my own. It doesn't have anything to do with school."

He nodded, and then his eyes did that slow stroll down my body again. After a moment that felt so long, he said, "Why don't you follow me? To my office."

That lump went right back into my throat, and all I could think about was trouble, trouble, trouble. I hugged my books to my chest as I followed him, past the front desk, then around to the side. The whole time I was thinking how was I going to explain this to my mama after she had told me not to get into any mess.

When he pushed open his office door, we both stepped into the tiny space. Really, maybe it wasn't all that small. It was just that it was crowded because of all the books. There were books every-where — stacked on his desk, on the floor, on the file cabinets. Even though he was kinda skinny, he had to squeeze past his desk to sit in the chair behind it. And then he said to me, "Sit down," and pointed to a chair in front of his desk.

I did what he told me to do, though I was still kinda scared. Why did he want me here? Was this like going to the principal's office?

When I sat down, he asked me, "So, what is it that you need to research?"

I released all of the air that I'd been hold-ing in. "I need to find somebody." But then I added quickly, "But, I don't mind. I can do the research myself 'cause I don't want to be no kind of trouble. I just knew that I could do research in the library." Then I looked over at the glass panel in his door, then down at the books in my lap, then up at the diploma on the wall that said that someone named Roger Stanley had graduated from the University of Arkansas at Fayetteville.

Finally, I let my eyes go back to him, and the man smiled.

For the first time since I came into his office, since I walked into the library really, I felt kinda like I could breathe. And the way he smiled made me think that maybe I could smile, too. And when I smiled, I knew there was something else I could do — I could trust him.

He leaned forward. "You never told me your name."

"Keisha Jones."

His new smile made me feel even better than before. "Okay, Keisha Jones. My name is Mr. Stanley, and I can help you do any kind of research you need."

"Really?" This was the first time ever that I felt I just might have a chance to find my father.

He said, "But I can't do it now." He looked down at his watch. "Because lunch for the freshmen is about to end and you're gonna have to get back to class."

He tapped his fingers on his desk like he was trying to figure something out. And my heart kinda fluttered. Even though I didn't go to church all that much, I did know how to pray. So as his fingers danced on the desk, I said a little prayer inside, asking God to let this man help me.

Then Mr. Stanley said, "I know what we can do. Why don't you come here after your last period?"

Dang! That wouldn't work.

When I bit my lip, Mr. Stanley asked, "What's wrong?" Before I could answer, he said, "Do you have to take the bus home?"

I nodded. He had to know that. I was a black kid. All the black kids in this school were bused in.

He said, "Where do you live?" Before I could answer, he asked, "Are you on the White Haven bus or the Pineville?"

"White Haven."

"Ah! That'll work, because I live in White Haven, too."

That made me frown. Really? I never saw too many white people in White Haven — well, not too many who lived there. Mama told me White Haven used to be all white long ago — that was how the town got its name. But now, the only white people I saw in White Haven worked there — in the bank, in the diner. There weren't even any white teachers in the school. I was sure there weren't more than ten white people who lived in White Haven.

And out of those ten, I'd never seen Mr. Stanley.

Still, he said, "So I can help you do research in here, and then I can drive you home afterward."

I moved to the edge of my seat. "Really?" But then I kinda sat back. Why was he being so nice to me? I had to ask myself that because my mama told me men were always nice — as long as you had something to give to them.

Well, I didn't have anything to give to Mr. Stanley — no money, no nothing. So he couldn't have been expecting anything from me. And then he explained.

"I'll do anything to help my students."

Now I understood, and I nodded. Coming to the library was the best idea I'd ever had. Standing up, I said, "Thank you, Mr. Stanley. Thank you so much."

My eyes fluttered open a little bit as I thought more about that day. I'd left the library with a big ole smile on my face, feeling hopeful, and now I had to blink a lot to hold back the tears as I remembered. I remembered that afternoon when I returned to the library and Mr. Stanley had me in his office once again. It really seemed like he was going to help me when I told him the

72

whole story — that I wanted to do research so I could find my father. He just listened to me. He didn't even ask me why hadn't I asked my mother. He just said he'd help me as if he understood everything I had been going through.

*I'll do anything to find my father.*

Once I told Mr. Stanley that, he'd asked me all kinds of questions he said would help him begin the research — like my full name, my mama's name, where I was born, and my birthdate. But then he asked me a whole bunch of questions that seemed kinda strange — like how much did I weigh and what kind of food did I like.

I had answered all of his questions honestly . . . until he asked about my mama.

*"What does your mother do?"*

*"What do you mean?"*

*"For a living? Where does she work?"*

*If this man really lived in White Haven, then he would have known. I couldn't figure out why he was lying, but it didn't matter because I was about to tell him a lie, too. "She's a hairdresser," I said, giving him the first thing I could think of because that was what I wanted to do when I graduated.*

*"Oh, she must work really long hours."*

*"Yeah, she does," I said. "She's hardly ever home."*

Pulling the afghan tighter around me I thought about how that had all played out in the months after I'd answered his questions. Mr. Stanley had done what he said — he'd helped me do what I'd wanted. He'd even given me a copy of my birth certificate with the name Elijah Wilson in the section for the father. He told me that it looked like my father lived in Los Angeles, and that he even had another daughter.

Mr. Stanley had told me everything . . . except for the price I'd have to pay for his help.

Glancing at my phone, I couldn't believe it was after midnight. In a way I was glad — now I had something else to think about besides Mr. Stanley. Pushing myself from the bed, I tiptoed through the back room to the front and moved the blinds as slightly as I could. The front house was totally dark. Mrs. Johnson was a schoolteacher, so she was probably asleep.

But I couldn't say that I trusted that, so I was going to stick to my plan.

Back in the bedroom, I started the task of trying to find — in the dark — all the things that were important to me. The little bit of clothes I had fit in one duffel bag. In the other bag were the things I wanted to keep from my mama. I stuffed her afghan and

74

her bathrobe inside. Then I went into the bathroom and got her perfume.

When I finished, I wished that I could take a shower, but I changed into sweatpants and a T-shirt, and now I was ready.

I thought about just carrying the bags, but they were too heavy, so I dumped them by the front door. I'd just go get my truck, then pull it into the driveway. I mean, what was Mrs. Johnson going to do if she woke up? She couldn't throw out someone who was already leaving.

Standing at the front door, I turned and looked at everything. From where I was, I could see the whole house — the front room and the back room, the tiny kitchen that didn't even hold a table, and the door to the bathroom. This was nothing but a shack, but I'd been happy here because I'd been with my mama.

The thought of that made me take those three steps to the sofa and sit down. With my mama gone, would I ever be happy again? I turned on my phone and did the first thing that I always did — I hit the Instagram app.

And then I did what I always did — I checked out the page of Elijah Wilson's daughter. Gabrielle only had one or two pictures of her father — that was all I remembered seeing since I'd started following her when I was fifteen and had gotten my first phone — from Mr. Stanley.

Instagram had just started way back then in 2010, but I still remembered the first time I saw Gabrielle, and I'd never seen anyone so beautiful. Definitely not in White Haven. She was tall and thin and looked like a model with the way she wore her hair and the way her makeup was always beat. And her clothes — she was always fresh, even though she had just graduated from college.

And then she got married, and then she started her business. And all the time, all I could do was watch how her happiness seemed to get bigger and better while my life stayed pretty much the same. Especially the life she had now. She was always hanging with celebrities, like my favorite singer — Justus.

I closed my eyes. What I would give to get to her. I'd sent her two emails, but she never answered. And I'd left a message with her assistant once, but she never returned my calls.

It was time for me to figure this out, figure out a way to meet Gabrielle Wilson. So she could lead me to our father. I didn't have an answer right now, but I would have a plan soon. I had to because finding my father was the only thing that I had left in my life.

# 7

## GABRIELLE

Using the remote, I muted the TV so that I could hear every word from Regan. When she finished, I leaned back against the headboard and adjusted my tablet so I was closer to the camera. "I can't believe you've found all of this out in just one day."

"This is what I do," my friend said with a shrug, the screen of the hotel's television behind her. "But there's no reason to celebrate." She wagged her finger in front of the camera. "All I have is this one fact."

"One fact that is huge," I said. At least it was huge to me. Fifteen minutes ago, I didn't know Daisy Jones was dead. It wasn't until Regan gave me this news that I realized how nervous I'd been about that part of this equation. I wasn't sure how I would've reacted to the woman who'd had an affair with my father. I was sure, standing in front of her, all I would have been thinking about was my mother. And with her in my mind, how could I be welcoming to Daisy Jones?

Now that wouldn't be an issue. Though I felt a bit of relief, inside I still said a little prayer for Daisy to rest in peace.

"Well," Regan began, bringing me back to our video call, "I don't have what's most important," Regan said. "I haven't found Keisha, but this is such a small town. It'll only take me a day or two."

"And now that her mother has died . . ." I paused and wondered. Would this make Keisha more or less likely to come to Los Angeles?

"I did find out that she used to live with her mother."

"Hmmm," I hummed. "In her letter, Daisy said they didn't have any other relatives, so now that she's gone . . ."

"Are you plotting something?" Regan asked me.

"No, I'm just thinking about the possibilities."

"Well, you know me. I'm a facts kind of chick. So let me do what I do and keep working."

I nodded and didn't hold back my smile. "Okay, do you need anything? Are you and the baby all right?"

She brought her face closer to the camera.

"Really, Gabby? Is this how it's gonna be for the next six months?"

"You were the same way when I was pregnant."

She smiled and when she leaned back, I could tell that she'd rested her hand on her belly. "All I need are your prayers."

"Those you always have."

"Then, between prayers and my skill set, I'm good. I'll check in with you tomorrow. Don't say anything to your dad yet. I don't want to disappoint him if I can't find her. Who knows? She may have moved away."

"As if the miles would stop you from tracking her down, but yeah, okay. I won't say anything." I paused. "Thanks again, Regan."

"No thanks necessary from family. Love you," she said.

"More!" I said, finishing our sign-off.

I tapped the tablet's screen to end the call just as Mauricio came out of the bathroom. My finger froze as did the rest of my body. Damn! My man was phine, spelled with a *p* for *perfection*.

All that moved on me were my eyes. I followed his topless torso as he strolled straight toward me.

"So, that was Regan?"

"Uh . . ." I stuttered. My words were stuck

in my throat, just like my eyes were stuck on him. Just. Phine. I blinked as I struggled to come back to life.

"Uh . . . yeah."

He paused at the edge of our bed. "So, do you really think she's going to find this woman?"

The way he said those words brought me all the way back to consciousness, and now I kinda, sorta forgot that my husband was standing in front of me half-naked. I didn't like the way he called my sister "this woman." But then, I guessed it was going to take some time for everyone to embrace Keisha. I couldn't blame Mauricio, since he hadn't been the one wanting a little sister his whole life.

I said, "She's going to find her. Regan's only been in Arkansas for a couple of hours, and she's already getting close."

Mauricio raised his eyebrows in question.

I said, "It seems that Daisy passed away . . . just recently."

My husband's eyebrows rose even higher. "Wow."

"Yeah, well, I got the impression this was expected. It seemed that was the purpose of her letter."

Mauricio pulled back the duvet and crawled in between the sheets. "So," he said.

"What about her kid?"

I winced. Now, my sister was just "her kid"? But all I said was, "She hasn't spoken to Keisha yet. She's trying to find out where she lives. Apparently, she moved from their last known address."

He nodded slowly.

That gesture and the frown that covered his face made me ask, "What?"

His eyes were straight ahead on the soundless television when he shrugged. "I don't know. I just wonder what will you do next?"

"What do you mean?"

"I mean what I said: then what?"

His tone was a little sharp, which surprised me. But then I thought, my husband — a professor of philosophy. His job was to be a skeptic. "Well, what's next? Daddy wants to meet her."

For the first time, he turned his eyes to mine. "So you're going to bring her here . . . from Arkansas . . . to meet Pops . . . and then what?"

"Why do you keep asking me that, Mauricio?" I twisted to put my tablet onto the nightstand and then turned my full attention to my husband. "Just tell me what it is that you're getting at."

He took a long moment to think before he spoke, just like the professor that he was.

"I just don't know if you and your dad have played this tape all the way through. You find her, Regan brings her back here . . . and then what? Is she here for a vacation? Or are you and your father thinking of something more permanent?"

It was my turn to pause. I said, "I don't think Dad's thought of that."

He nodded. "That's my point."

"But I don't understand why that is a point. I mean, why do we have to think so far in advance? We don't even know what Keisha will want. Shouldn't we play this by ear?"

He shook his head. "Not in situations like this. You have to have a plan because neither you nor your father knows anything about her. And the only plan you have so far is to open your door to this person . . ."

"She's not just a person, Mauricio," I snapped and folded my arms. "She's my sister."

Again, he did that eyebrow-raising thing that was beyond annoying now. "You don't know that yet."

Now it was my turn to measure my words before I said something that I would have to take back. "I showed you the letter. I showed you the picture."

"And even with both of those things, you

still need a DNA test."

"So you mean to tell me you can't look at that picture and know she's my father's child? She looks way more like him than I do."

"DNA tells the truth; our eyes often do not."

I squinted to show him my disapproval, but that didn't deter him.

Mauricio said, "I just think you need to be sure. Before anything, get the facts, do the science."

I pouted, just like our five-year-old. "Suppose she doesn't want to take a test. Should I force her?"

My tone, my body language were a stop sign, but Mauricio did not back up. "I would think she would want to, unless . . ." He shrugged as if that gesture made his words a complete thought.

"What?"

"She'd want to take the test unless she's running some kind of scam."

I opened my eyes so wide, I feared they might pop from their sockets. "Are you hearing yourself? This could be a scam? That began over twenty years ago? A scam where someone from a little town in Arkansas spent money to have plastic surgery to look just like my father so that she could scam him because" — I paused, just for the drama — "she will certainly become rich by scamming a man who owns a trucking company in Los Angeles." I shook my head. "Unbelievable."

And what effect did all of that have on my husband? All Mauricio did was shrug. "Say what you want, but I have to protect my family."

Okay, so how could I be mad at that?

He said, "I just want us to have a plan. For you and your dad to think this through."

"Okay, let me think . . ." I paused. "Father. Daughter. Sister. Sister. Thought completed."

He tilted his head and for the first time, he smiled. "I'm just trying to do my part. To play the . . ."

"Skeptic?"

"Whatever you want to call it, I know these relationships can be complicated, and I want you to be prepared in every way."

"Do you know what I'm prepared for?" I didn't give him a chance to answer. "I'm prepared for the love Keisha is going to give to us and we're going to give to her. She's going to adore us."

"Oh, really?"

"Of course. What's not to love? Between you and me and Bella."

He nodded a little. "Yeah, everyone loves Bella."

"Exactly. And then there's Daddy. The best dad in the world."

"You may think that, and I would agree. But she may not since she's an adult meeting him for the first time."

"That's not his fault," I pressed. "He just found out about her."

He gave me a small nod. "This is really important to you, isn't it?"

I scooted so I was fully facing my husband. "It really is, Mauricio. I don't know what it is, but I'm excited about meeting her. Excited about the possibility of her being part of our lives. Not only have I always wanted a sister, but I think this will be so good for Dad. Since Mom died, he just can't seem to find his way, except for work. Keisha will give him something else to do, someone else to love. She'll be good for him."

My words hung in the air as, once again, my husband was pensive. He said, "I hope this works out well for you, for all of us. I hope your childhood dreams don't turn into an adult nightmare."

I shook my head. "I don't understand why you're so negative."

Mauricio parted his lips as if he had a

ready response, but then he pressed his lips together as if he were trading the words he'd wanted to speak for new ones. He said, "I don't want to talk anymore."

I tilted my head. "Why not? You're making these statements as if everything is going to turn out . . ."

Before I could finish, his lips were on mine, and then his tongue danced with mine, and then that naked torso connected to mine. When he pulled his lips away, I wanted to demand that he come back. But he was gone just long enough to click off the television and then to blanket our bedroom in darkness.

When Mauricio kissed me again, I had no more thoughts about my father, my sister — I hardly had a memory of our daughter. My mind and my body were full and complete. I was filled with all of my love for my husband.

# 8
## KEISHA

My eyes fluttered open, and for a moment, I didn't remember my life. I tried to stretch, but then, when my leg hit the truck's door, my memory of who I was, where I was, what I was, all rushed back.

I moaned, feeling so stiff, and in my head, I added it up. Friday. Morning. That meant this was the third day I was waking up in my truck.

I scooted up off the back seat, then yawned as I peeked through the windows and scanned the Walmart parking lot. I'd been moving around, making a different spot my home every night, thinking that was the best way to make sure no one noticed me. I'd been thinking about this parking lot since the first night because it was well lit, so if anything jumped off, the light would have my back.

But the problem was Buck worked here and they always changed his hours and I didn't need him seeing me. He was already mad since I hadn't answered his calls or returned his texts. I knew he would want me to stay with him; it was just that I had enough drama of my own to figure out — I didn't want to deal with all that stuff going on in his house, too.

From the floor, I grabbed my cell phone. It wasn't even seven, but that was okay. Now I'd have an early start and make it over to Beryl's by nine. Today was going to be a big day. Friday mornings led to Friday afternoons, when folks got paid, and that led to Friday nights, when the ladies had to look good for their Friday night hookup. So they'd be packing the seats at Beryl's, and I needed that money. I needed the money for the plan — that I hadn't quite figured out yet.

Climbing into the front seat, I stretched once again, then revved up the engine. At least there was one thing I didn't have to worry about for a few days — I'd made enough in tips over the last few days to have a full tank of gas.

As I rolled out of the lot, a couple of cars were rolling in — the early-morning employees, I guessed. Maybe I needed to give up my dream of being a hairstylist and grab an application from here. I might make more money, and there was another plus to working at a superstore like this. I saw a movie once where a girl lived in a Walmart for a whole week or month, or maybe it was even a year. If I could live in the store and save some money, that would be dope.

There was only one problem with that, though. Buck worked here, and if he found out, he'd drag me home to his house, even with his daddy.

I made a left turn onto Central and then rode up three streets to the McDonald's parking lot, pulling into the same spot where I'd parked the last couple of mornings. I grabbed my backpack, then slid from my car. As I crossed the parking lot, I had to break through the cars already lined up for the drive-through. Inside, there were fewer people and I walked right up to the counter.

"Hey," the girl said to me as if we were friends. Maybe she thought we were since she'd seen me three mornings in a row. "You want your usual?"

I nodded. "A sausage biscuit and orange juice." Then I gave her three dollars and she gave me my change.

I paused, and before I could ask, she offered me the key. "Do you need this?"

"Yeah," I said and wondered if she knew

why I needed the key every morning.

But I didn't have any time to think about it or care about it. I was the town whore's daughter; I was used to people whispering in front of my face and talking about me behind my back. There was little left to embarrass me.

Inside the bathroom, I went into the handicapped stall, locked the door, and turned on the water in the sink. Then I stripped, lined up my toiletries on the counter as if I were home, and took a hoe bath, using my perfumed shower gel to cover all the hot spots, just like my mama taught me.

After that, I brushed my teeth, brushed my hair, keeping it in my ponytail, before I pulled my jeans and top from my backpack. Once I was dressed, I cleaned up my mess (another thing that my mama taught me) and then walked out of the bathroom, ready for my new day.

I glanced at my phone again — only about twelve minutes. I was getting better every day, knocking off eight whole minutes from when I'd first done this on Wednesday morning.

At the counter, I gave back the key and the girl gave me my order. And then I sat at the same corner table and like I did every morning, I rested. Not the sleep kind of rest, but the mind kind of rest where I wasn't thinking about anything except for how good this biscuit tasted.

But my rest only lasted about three minutes, because I really did have to think. I had to figure out a way not to sleep in my car for the rest of my life.

Pulling out my cell, I hit Instagram and then Gabrielle's page. She hadn't added anything since last night, but I loved that new picture. It was of Justus — and an announcement that he was going to be on *The View.*

Usually, I would spend all of my time looking at Justus's pictures, or any of the other celebrities. But today I scrolled through the photos, stopping only on the personal ones, especially of Gabrielle and her husband. They were always out, everywhere. And every time, they looked like they'd found their happily-ever-after, always holding hands, often kissing. Sometimes they looked more glamorous than her clients.

She was living some kind of life. A life that should have been mine, too.

I scrolled some more, back through what felt like hundreds of pictures (but was only three months) to the one Gabrielle had with her father taken on Father's Day. I clicked on the photo, then made the photo larger until Gabrielle's face was out of the screen and all I could see was her father's.

Her father.

My father.

Elijah Wilson.

I stared at his picture and in so many ways I felt like I was looking in a special mirror. The kind of mirror that kept the same face, just changed your gender. It was crazy how much I looked like him. I was the same brown like him, had eyebrows like him, and then we each had that mole right on the edge of our lips.

Gabrielle was closer to butterscotch than chocolate, had eyebrows that had to be penciled on, and then . . . where was her mole? She didn't get any of her looks from him. But I guess that didn't matter because what she got . . . was him. She was the one he claimed.

I stared and stared and stared until a tear trickled from my eye and I swiped it away with my fingertips. No, I would not cry. I just had to figure this out. This man was my father, and he needed to step up to that responsibility. Even if I was already twenty-two. He owed me; he owed me everything he had given to Gabrielle.

All I had to do was figure out how I was going to tell him that he had a daughter, then figure out how I was going to get him to believe me, then figure out how I was going to make him pay.

# 9
## KEISHA

The shop was poppin' like it was prom weekend or something. It wasn't even noon, and I'd already washed eight heads. And with one of the biggest tippers up as my next client, I was sure I was going to have a one-hundred-dollar-plus day.

"Okay, come on, Mrs. Whittle," I said to Beryl's oldest client. "I'm gonna get you started."

"Thank you, baby," Mrs. Whittle said as she rolled her walker down the center of the shop. When she got close to me, she whispered, "I was so sorry to hear about your mama, baby."

I stiffened.

She said, "I'm gonna give you a little extra today, okay?"

I nodded, not saying a word and not having any idea how Mrs. Whittle had found out about my mama. Yeah, some folks knew she'd been in the hospital and then in hospice. Not that anyone cared. The town's whore had no friends, 'cause even other whores were the enemy.

Mrs. Whittle took slow steps past me, and just as I turned to follow her, the bell over the front door rang. It was only reflex that made me check out who was walking in.

Then I stopped. Just so I could get a better look at the woman. I'd been working with Beryl for just a little more than a year, so I knew all of her regulars. Sure, she took walk-ins, but even then, I recognized most folks. There weren't but about fifteen hundred people who lived in White Haven. And I knew this woman wasn't one in that number.

But even if I didn't know just about everyone by at least recognition, I'd know this woman wasn't from White Haven. It started with her dress — it was one of those knits that I saw in the designer magazines. A dress that I wouldn't ever be able to afford, not even with a year's worth of tips. And her hair — neither Beryl nor anyone else in White Haven had anything to do with the way her curls bounced when she walked. Her hair even moved when she lowered her head and spoke.

But what was best? That big ole red bag she had on her shoulder. I'd seen that bag in all the magazines, and a lot of celebrities had it on Instagram. With the two *G*s on the outside, it was the kind of bag that let everybody know you had money — no, that you had *lots* of money. It was the kind of bag I hoped to carry one day.

So why would a woman who was wearing all of that, who looked like a movie star, be coming into Beryl's House of Beauty?

I had to get to Mrs. Whittle, especially if I wanted that tip. But if I could get just a little bit closer — I just wanted to hear what was going on. I pretended to be straightening out the magazines in the rack, but I still couldn't hear what the woman was saying to Adriana, the receptionist.

Then all of a sudden, both of them looked up and at me. Adriana pointed, then called out, "Hey, Keisha." Then she added a wave for me to come to her.

Even though she had called my name and was looking straight at me, I still kinda glanced over my shoulder to see if she was talking to someone else. Because there was no reason why that woman would want to see me. But Adriana kept waving. And the woman was looking up and at me, and now she was smiling.

What the hell?

But it was more than curiosity that made

me move toward the front of the shop. It was that when the woman smiled, I thought I knew her.

Then for a moment, I almost stopped. Because suppose this had something to do with my mama. Suppose my mama owed somebody some money. Or worse, suppose this lady was somebody's wife.

But it was too late for me to cut and run since I was just about all up on this woman. And she was still smiling . . .

"Did you want me, Adriana?" I asked the receptionist, even though I was looking this woman right in her eyes. Why in the heck did she look so familiar to me?

"Yeah," Adriana said. "This lady is looking for you."

The woman reached out her hand. "It's nice to meet you, Keisha."

The way she smiled, I could check one thing off my list — this didn't have anything to do with my mama. I shook her hand and gave her a side-eye at the same time. "Yeah."

She said, "I'd like to talk to you. Would you mind . . ." She paused and looked over my shoulder as if she were scoping out the shop. "Can we go outside to chat for a moment?"

Now my side-eye became a direct glare. "I don't know you; I'm not going anywhere with you."

My words, my attitude didn't faze her. She said, "I understand, but I have something important to talk to you about, and this" — again, she did that pause and that little glance around the shop — "might not be the best place."

I wanted to tell her she was wrong . . . except Adriana was sitting right here staring in my face, trying to get all in my business.

And I had a feeling that if I turned around, every single one of these heffas within ear- and eyeshot would be doing the same thing.

Plus, since this didn't have anything to do with my mama, I was starting to wonder something. This chick smelled like money, and with my current situation, there had to be a way I could use this to my advantage.

But I couldn't turn this into a pay-to-play in front of everyone. I couldn't tell her she'd have to pay for whatever information she needed from me within the range of any of these heffas' ears.

So I nodded, though I kept my arms folded as I stomped past this designer-wearing woman and marched straight to the door. I didn't even turn around to make sure that she was following me. She was.

When I stepped outside, I stopped right there on the sidewalk, faced her, and was ready to figure out a way to take her money when she said, "I'm Regan Givens."

Instagram. Gabrielle. Gabrielle's best friend. Regan.

She had no idea that telling me her name almost shut me down. I almost told her to get the hell outta here. But instead, I said, "So?"

She repeated her name and added, "I have to speak to you about something important."

It was a good thing I was Daisy Jones's daughter and I knew how to play poker, I knew how to turn the emotions on and off, even when my heart was pounding like it was giving me its final beats. But even with all that I'd been taught, it was hard to keep what I knew from my face. Hard to hide my question: What the hell was Gabrielle's best friend doing in White Haven talking to me?

She said, "I'm an attorney, and I have some information that may be important to you."

"Okay," I said, and I wanted to give myself a fist bump at the same time. Because I still stood as if her words didn't matter to me. "Just tell me what information you got."

She shook her head. "I'd like for us to go somewhere a little more private than" — she looked at the glass etching on the window — "Beryl's House of Beauty." Turning back to me, she added, "And this sidewalk."

I was ready to tell her that I'd go wherever she wanted. She had to know about my connection to Gabrielle.

But I kept silent, like I was thinking hard. Finally, I said, "There's a diner right down the road there." I was so cool, and I was more than collected.

Regan said, "Okay, do you want to jump in my car?"

I hadn't even noticed the car Regan pointed to and I had to do another one of those straight-faced moments. Because I sure did want to ride in a Mercedes.

But when I turned back to Regan, she would never have known that was my thought. "Nah, I got my truck right here. I'll meet you there. Since I know where it is, you wanna follow me?"

She said, "Are you talking about the Sizzlin' Griddle?"

I nodded, a little surprised that she'd heard of it.

"I had a cup of tea there yesterday," she explained.

Yesterday? How long had Regan been here? Had she been looking for me?

She said, "But I'll follow you."

"Okay, I have to run back in there and get my purse."

She nodded, then moved to her car, and I kept my steps slow and steady. My nonchalance continued, even when I walked into the shop. Even when Beryl asked me, "What did that siddity chick want?" all I did was shrug, grab my purse from the cubicle beneath Beryl's station, and turn back toward the door.

"Where you goin'?" Beryl asked me.

"I'll be right back," I said, thinking that whatever Regan had to say better be worth the tip I was about to lose from Mrs. Whittle.

I gave Regan a small wave before I jumped into my truck and then backed out of the strip mall parking lot. Thank God there was a red light right there because it gave me a chance to check out Instagram real quick. By the time the light turned green, I had Gabrielle's page open and had found a couple of the pictures I was looking for — yup, this woman behind me in that black Mercedes was Gabrielle's best friend.

I'd been dodging Buck, but I sure needed him now. I dialed his number and then hoped he'd pick up right away. And my hope came true.

"Yo, where you been?"

"I've been staying with Beryl," I said. That was the lie that I'd prepared for him.

"What's up with that? Why you ain't stayin' with me?"

I rolled my eyes. Buck knew my issues with his daddy, and this was why I hadn't told Buck anything — not about my mama finally dying, not about having to move out of Mrs. Johnson's back house, nothing. But I needed him to know what was up now. "I'll tell you everything later, but I gotta tell you this now, and I have to talk quick, so just listen."

"What's goin' down?"

"Remember Gabrielle, my father's daughter who lives in LA?"

"Yeah?"

Glancing in my rearview mirror, my eyes were on that black Mercedes when I said, "Well, her best friend is here and she was looking for me."

"Get out. Here in White Haven?"

I told Buck everything that had gone down at the shop, and then I said, "So what should I do?"

"What you should do is go and get that money."

Just another reason for me to roll my eyes. It was always about that for him. I mean, I was down for the money, too — that was the reason why I wanted to connect with Elijah. But we had to handle it right. "So what am I supposed to do? Tell her to turn over her wallet?"

"So you don't think that's a good approach?" He laughed. "Okay, boo, I got you. Just play this out. Listen to what she has to say."

Finally, he was being serious. "Should I tell her that I know about Gabrielle?"

"Nah, don't show none of your cards. See what they're playing with first. Find out what she wants, but don't say too much. Then let's hook up right after and we'll come up with a game plan."

"Okay," I told him when I was about a block from the diner. "I'll call you." Clicking off my cell, I checked the rearview mirror again, still not believing this was happening. Was this going to be the real connection to my father?

I wasn't going to have to wait too much longer to figure this out, because right then I made the left turn onto the gravel of the Sizzlin' Griddle, and then Regan parked her Mercedes next to me. I took a deep breath, then stepped out of my truck first, and when Regan slid out of her rental, she eyed my truck as I eyed her shoes. My 2002 Ford pickup told one story, and her red-bottom shoes told another. Now both of us knew a little more about each other.

I led her into the diner, and since it was pretty empty, I sat in the booth closest to the door.

"What are you gals having?" the waitress said, attending to us right away.

Regan looked at me and I didn't know if she expected me to order a full meal or what. But all I said was, "I'll just have an orange juice."

Regan said, "And I'll have a coffee . . . No," she held up her hand, "I'm sorry. Make that a cup of tea, please."

Once the waitress left us alone, I got right to the point. "So what do you want to talk to me about?"

Regan gave me that smile again. "Can you tell me a little about yourself?"

"Why?" I folded my arms. "I don't even know who you are."

"That's fair." She nodded. "As I said, I'm an attorney and I'm representing a client."

"A client for what? Someone's trying to sue me?"

"No" — she held up her hand — "definitely not. This could be good news, but I wanted to meet and speak with you first, so please talk to me."

I guessed she wasn't going to be moved,

so if I wanted to find out what she wanted, I had to tell her a little something. I shrugged. "I don't have a lot to say. I was born and raised here in White Haven."

Regan nodded. "So you work at the shop?"

"Yeah."

"Where do you live?"

I pressed my lips together. "I don't think I should be giving you that kind of information."

Then she gave me a look, like a pitying look, like she already knew I was living in my car. But I wasn't about to confess to my homelessness.

She said, "Okay, this is going to come as a shock to you. But I think you have a sister."

I raised my eyebrows, totally into the act of deception. "I don't have a sister. I was my mother's only child. She just died, so if there is someone trying to pull a scam on me, trying to get money from me, I just need to tell you . . ."

Regan held up her hand. "No, it's nothing like that. Actually, you're right. I believe you were your mother's only child. But you may have a half sister. You share a father."

Still in full acting mode, I narrowed my eyes. "I don't know who my father is."

"I know."

And then she went on to tell me the story

of my father, Elijah, and how he'd met my mother — facts that I already knew. At the end, she said, "And so your mother sent him this letter."

She moved too quickly for me to react, and before I could do anything, the envelope was out of her purse and the paper was unfolded in front of me. All I could do was stare, not touching it at all. I couldn't because right in front of me was Mama — well, maybe not my mama exactly, but there was a piece of her in the form of a slip of paper with her handwriting all over it. It was like she was still alive.

I read the letter, then blinked and blinked and blinked, because I didn't want to get into the real role and cry. But as I read the letter, it was hard to hold this all inside because my mama was trying to take care of me, even from the grave. Now I got it. Now I understood why my mama never told me about my father.

Regan whispered, "Is that your mother's handwriting?"

I nodded because I couldn't get any words past the rock stuck inside my throat.

"So that's why I think this is true. I think my best friend is your sister."

I read my mother's words again, then sat back in the booth. It was the tears in my eyes, the rock in my throat, and Mama's voice now in my head that was stopping me from thinking. I wasn't sure what I should do at this point. Should I just cry? Should I be happy? How should I play this? Because what I wanted to do was jump up and down.

So I didn't go with an act. I went with my gut. I said, "I can't believe this."

"I know . . . it's a shock. But now that this is out, what I'd like to do is take you to Los Angeles."

I had to pause and take in this moment. For all these years, for all the ways I'd been trying to scheme my way to get to Los Angeles, and now . . . this. Still, I was Daisy Jones's child, so I said, "To Los Angeles? But . . . I live here."

"Of course. I'm not saying for you to move there. Just for a visit. Just so you can meet them." She nodded as if she were trying to reassure me. "You wouldn't have to stay; we're just hoping this is something you'd want to do in person."

I sat there as if I were unsure even though I wanted to ask when was the next flight? "Suppose I go through all the trouble of making this trip and . . . these people aren't even related to me?"

"Well, if that happens, you'll get a free trip to Los Angeles and you'll have a chance to meet some really great people."

I nodded as if her words made sense, but I didn't say anything else.

"I know this is a lot for you to take in right now." Regan reached into her purse and pulled out a card. "So why don't you think about it. This is my cell." She jotted a number on the back. "I'm staying at the Holiday Inn Express."

I raised an eyebrow. That was the best hotel in White Haven.

"Give me a call tomorrow and let me know what you decide. No pressure. This is up to you. But I'll be heading back to Los Angeles tomorrow or Sunday."

I nodded and stayed silent just long enough for Regan to think that I was giving her offer some serious thought. Just as she began to slip out of the booth, I said, "Are you going to tell Gabrielle that you met me?"

Regan froze. I mean, she was halfway between standing up and sitting down, and it was like she was stuck in midair. But it was the look on her face that made me inhale. What had I done? So I asked her, "What? What's wrong?"

"Nothing." She shook her head, sat back down, and frowned. "I didn't realize that . . . I told you . . . your sister's name."

Her eyes were on me like a laser.

Damn. How could I have made a mistake like that? "Yeah," I began, and I frowned, too, like I didn't know what she was talking about. "You said I had a sister and you said her name." After a pause, I said, "How else would I know her name?"

After a moment, Regan nodded before she stood. "I guess, I just . . ." Then her smile went away. "You let me know. Of course, you don't have to worry about anything; I'll cover all of your expenses if you decide to come to Los Angeles."

I nodded, then watched her walk out the door and roll away in that fancy car.

By the time that Mercedes was out of my sight, I had made my decision — I decided I wasn't even going back to Beryl's. Why should I waste that trip?

All I was going to do was get in my car and figure out what I was going to take to LA and what I was going to leave over at Buck's. Because finally, I was on my way to having the life that I should have had in the first place. Maybe God did care about me after all.

# 10
## GABRIELLE

"Hold on," I said to Regan as her face came into view through my computer. "Let me close the door."

Actually, I was alone since it was well after seven, but I made this move just in case Pamela, Mattie, or anyone else walked back into the office.

When I bounced into my chair, I smiled into the computer's camera, ready for the update. "So, if you're calling me this late on a Friday . . ."

"Why are you still in the office?"

I frowned. That would have been a normal question from Regan, if I weren't sitting here so far on the edge of my seat I was about to fall off. "Ummm . . . 'cause I'm finalizing the Contour presentation? Remember, that's why I'm not down in Arkansas. And speaking of me being here and you there . . ." I adjusted the screen to make sure I had the best view of Regan's face.

She was inside her hotel room, but I could see she wasn't as relaxed as she'd been these last few days. That made me frown. No, Regan wasn't wearing any kind of look that said she had good news. "You didn't find her?" I asked, hearing the disappointment in my tone.

She hesitated, she nodded, and then she spoke ever so slowly. "I did."

"What?" Thank God for the desk that blocked me from slipping to the floor. "When?"

"Earlier today." She spoke with such nonchalance I wondered if we were having the same conversation.

"Earlier? How much earlier? And if you found her earlier, why are you just calling me now?"

She held up her hands. "If you're going to cross-examine someone, you have to give them a chance to respond."

"Sorry. But tell me . . . you found Keisha?" I just wanted to make sure.

"I did. I still haven't been able to find a home address for her, but I tracked her down at work and drove to the shop this morning."

"Shop?"

"She's a hairstylist," Regan explained. "At least, that's the assumption I'm making based on where she works."

I nodded. "So tell me everything. Please."

Regan took a breath, and then I had to hold mine as she told me about going into some shop called Beryl's House of Beauty, finding Keisha, and then talking to her in the diner. And then Regan stopped. I mean, she just stopped, like that was supposed to be the end.

I waited for a moment because I wondered if she'd done that only for effect. But when she said nothing else, I asked, "So, what did she say?"

"Well," Regan's voice slowed down again. "She was surprised."

"I can understand that. And . . ."

"And . . . that's it. She's going to think about it and let me know if she'll be making the trip to Los Angeles."

I felt my shoulders sink. "So she didn't agree to that right away?"

She shook her head.

"Ugh," I said, thinking that I still couldn't call my father with any kind of news. When he called me tomorrow, I'd have to tell him what I'd been telling him — that Regan didn't know anything yet. Especially now — I couldn't say a word because it would be worse if he knew we'd found her and then she'd decided that she didn't want to have anything to do with him. "Do you think she'll come to LA?"

Regan nodded. "Oh, she'll come. I'm sure of it."

"Okay, good." And then I waited for Regan to agree that everything she'd told me was all good. But my friend just stared into the camera, her eyes exposing her thoughts.

"What's bothering you?" I asked but didn't give her a chance to answer. "You found her, and you think she'll come." And then I thought back to Mauricio's warnings. "Do you think she's not my father's daughter?"

"Oh, no," Regan said with certainty. "She's your father's daughter all right. I mean, your father has to do a DNA test . . ."

I sat back in my seat. "Now you sound like Mauricio."

"Your husband is a smart man. No matter what, we still need the test, but I can tell you she looks more like your dad than you do. She's Elijah Wilson in drag."

The image of that took my angst about a DNA test away and made me laugh. "So then what's wrong, Regan?"

"She knew your name."

I blinked, trying to get those words to make some kind of sense. "What?"

She repeated her words, and then she went on to tell me about that part of their conversation. "I'm telling you, I didn't tell her your name."

"Well, you had to have. How else would she have known it?"

She paused. "I know, I guess, but if I'd told her, that would have been a rookie mistake. Because that would give her a chance to google you and find out about you." She shook her head. "No, that's a mistake, and I don't make many of those."

"True that. But maybe in this case, you're being more of a friend than an attorney. Maybe that's why you slipped."

"Being your friend over being an attorney is even more reason for me to protect you."

"Okay, I get it. You didn't want her to know my name, but even if she does, it's cool, Regan. I don't mind. Because what difference does it make? She is my sister. It's not like she can run some sort of scam on me."

"Maybe . . ."

I blew out a long breath, thinking Regan was about to take me into one of those conversations like I'd had with Mauricio the other night. "I don't understand what's bothering you. We have the letter, we have the photo, you met her and she's real . . ."

"And she looks like your dad."

"Exactly. So what's your concern?"

"No concern," Regan said as if she were burdened with all kinds of concerns.

"Great, then, I can't wait."

"Well, don't say anything to your dad yet; let's see what she says."

"If she says no, I'm coming down there myself."

"Like I told you, I'm pretty sure she'll say yes. I expect to hear from her tonight or in the morning, the latest, because she knows I'll be leaving soon."

"I'm so excited," I said to Regan and was a little surprised that my sister-friend didn't share my joy. And then I got it. For so long, it had been just me and Regan. From the youth program at our church to being in the same sixth-, then seventh-, then eighth-grade class, we shared the only kind of DNA that mattered — we shared DNA of the heart.

That was what was bothering Regan — it had to be. There was a part of her that thought she'd lose me, that perhaps thought she could be replaced because of that stupid blood-water cliché. I'd just have to find a way to let her know that, in the words of our middle school crush, MC Hammer, Keisha can't touch this. No one would ever be able to re-create the sister bond we had.

"Well, I'll let you know as soon as I hear from her," Regan said, bringing me back.

"Okay, I'll be praying."

"Yeah, do that."

That made me frown. Not her words — we were praying women, so that was something we said to each other all the time. But she said it now with a bit of urgency in her voice. Like the prayer was more for me than for her and that I needed it — for real. But then I shook that thought away and I told her, "Love you."

She finished with "More." And then she added, "Don't stay in the office too late. You have a husband and daughter to get home to," as if I needed that reminder — which I sometimes did. I loved Mauricio and Bella, but there was something about being behind this desk and making all of these decisions that made me lose track of my life. A behavior that so annoyed Mauricio.

Thinking of that made me click off the computer. I wouldn't be able to work much now anyway. My mind wouldn't be on anything beyond what Regan had told me.

Stuff was starting to get real. I had a sister, and I was going to meet her. How did I really feel about that?

Leaning back, I closed my eyes. And remembered a time when I was about five or six or seven . . .

*Mommy, all the girls in school have one and I want one, too.*

*My mother glanced at me as she handed me the spoon to mix the cake batter. "What are you talking about, sweet pea? A new doll?"*

*"Yeah, a real doll. A sister. All of the girls in school have a sister. And I want one, too."*

I opened my eyes at that memory, though my remembrance continued. I remembered the way tears had filled my mom's eyes. The only times I'd ever seen my mom cry were when she was happy — when we were watching movies, when she listened to a song, sometimes, she'd even cry during TV commercials. So when she started crying, I thought she was just as excited as I was about having a little sister.

But then I'd learned the truth. I was a teenager when I found out that my mom suffered from premature ovarian failure, a condition she developed right after my birth. I would forever be her only child.

I wallowed in that memory a bit longer. My mom had always told me if she were to have only one child, she was glad it was me because I was everything she could ever want. I used to believe those words were just things a good mother said.

Then I'd had Bella. And now it seemed that Bella would be the only child Mauricio and I would ever have. It was a disappointment for me, but now I knew what my mom meant. If she was going to be the only one, Bella was everything. Between my daughter and my husband, life couldn't be any more complete.

So my excitement about Keisha had nothing to do with filling any kind of void. My sister was my bonus blessing from God. And I wanted to be that same kind of blessing for her.

I scooped up my bag and grabbed the Contour file. Tonight, I'd work at home. Or maybe not. Just thinking about blessings made me want to be with my husband and my daughter and bask in all that God had given to me.

# 11
## KEISHA

The moment I hooked a left turn into the Holiday Inn Express parking lot, smoke began to rise from under my hood. I hated this truck, or this hoopty, as my mama used to call it. I eased into one of the spaces behind the hotel, then turned off the ignition, hoping it wouldn't take too long for the truck to cool off. I still hadn't decided what I was going to do with this thing. Sell it? Probably not, 'cause I'd end up owing somebody money. I'd just leave it right here because when I came back to White Haven, I'd have enough money to get me something nice. Maybe something even like the Mercedes Regan was driving yesterday.

After turning off the ignition, I glanced up at the hotel. I would bet any kind of money that Regan was staying on the top floor. My mama told me the rooms at the top cost the most. That was how she could tell if a man was really into (no pun intended) her. If he

120

spent money for one of the rooms on the top floor, then she knew she would get top dollar.

I glanced at my phone, it wasn't even seven yet. A little early, but I could hardly sleep last night, knowing I'd be spending the rest of my life in a bed, a real bed. Because once I got this money . . .

My phone vibrated, scaring me a little, and I checked out the incoming text:

Don't know why you haven't answered me, but I hope you're coming to work. You know today is Saturday, so it'll be bigger than yesterday, though you missed Mrs. Whittle. Let me know what's going on with you.

I tossed my phone onto the passenger seat. Beryl had reached out three times since yesterday, and the only reason she wanted me back there was so she could find out what was up.

Beryl and all of them heffas had probably talked about me for the rest of the day after I'd left the salon with Regan. But they'd never see me again. At least not in that shop. I might still have problems in my life, but now money wasn't going to be one of them. I had a feeling that God had finally remembered me and He was going to give me back everything.

Not only that, after I'd left Regan, there was too much that I had to do. I ended up hooking up with Buck, and putting everything that I was taking with me into one bag. The rest I was leaving with Buck. Then he and I hung out before we went back to his house last night. I would've slept in my car again, except he told me that his daddy was in Little Rock. So even though their house was filled with so many people it looked like a Fourth of July barbecue, I was able to find a corner in one of the bedrooms and sleep a bit, since Buck's bed was filled with a couple of his younger brothers.

Then, this morning, I got out of there before the sun or any of those people rose. I was wearing the same jeans and top I'd worn yesterday, but I figured that was a good thing. I needed some new clothes 'cause I didn't want to show up in Los Angeles looking like a chick who'd been living out of her car. So Regan needed to give me some money for that, and wearing what I'd worn yesterday would help with my argument.

That thought made me smile. A little money from Regan, a little more from Gabrielle, and the jackpot from Elijah.

"Yeah," I whispered. I didn't have it all worked out, but I figured after a couple of weeks in Los Angeles I'd have enough money to come back home and live like the queen of White Haven.

Checking my cell again, I exhaled when I saw the time. Seven was perfect, and so I opened my Messages app:

After thinking about it all night, I want to meet my father. I want to go to Los Angeles. Let me know what I have to do.

Then, once again, I tossed my cell phone to the other seat, and leaned back. Eight years after finding out my father's name I was going to meet him.

Eight years. I didn't want to do it, but that thought made my mind wander all the way back. I closed my eyes and squeezed them tight. Because I couldn't help but remember, yet I didn't want to cry:

I bounced into the library really happy. Because although it had taken a little bit of time, like three months, this morning, Mr. Stanley told me he was getting close.

"Meet me in the library after school," he whispered. "I have some really good news."

Since he had whispered that to me, I only nodded because he had told me before that no one could know he was helping me since teachers weren't supposed to help students this way. So I did my best to be discreet — that was the word he used.

But it was hard to hide my happy, and Mr. Stanley made me happy all the time. He was working so hard and he told me there were days when he wasn't even doing his work because he was doing my research. He was telling the truth, too, because every few days, he told me something new:

"You were born in White Haven Clinic."

That was the first thing he told me, like three days after he got started. I knew that. Mama had told me that she didn't have insurance and that was why I was born in the clinic instead of the hospital.

Then about a week after that, "Your mother was only eighteen when you were born."

I knew that, too. Mama always talked about that. She wanted me to go to school, get a good education, graduate from high school, and then get a job, not have a baby. She wanted me to have options she'd never had.

It had been a little information at a time, kinda like the water faucet in our bathtub — just drip, drip, drip. It was slow, but it was progress.

Now, when the library door closed behind me, I glanced around at the Thanksgiving decorations that hung from the windows and the walls. Then I did what I'd done just about every day for the last few months . . . I walked straight to Mr. Stanley's office.

Like every day, he was sitting in there waiting for me.

"Hey, Keisha."

After I said hello to him, I couldn't stop grinning. "So, you said you have something for me?"

He nodded, then motioned for me to sit down while he got up. This was another thing that Mr. Stanley did every day. Once I got there, he walked through the library turning out all the lights in the library part and locked the door. The first day, I'd been kinda scared. But then he'd explained that it was part of being discreet.

When he came back, he sat down, and now he was the one grinning. "As I've been looking for your father, I kinda found out a little bit more about your mother: where she works . . . and what she does for a living."

That took my grin away and I looked down at my books in my lap. I was hoping Mr. Stanley didn't have to know. That was one of the things I liked about being at Clinton High — nobody here knew me . . . or my mama.

He leaned across his desk and with his fingertips, touched my chin. "Lift your head up, Keisha."

I did what he said.

"You don't have anything to be ashamed of. Did you know the work your mother is doing is the world's oldest profession?"

I squinted, not understanding what he was saying.

He went on, "Way back, even in biblical days, there were women who" — he stopped as if he was trying to find the right words — "took care of their children by taking care of men."

I nodded, though I was surprised. Women . . . worked . . . just like my mama all the way back in the Bible? Even though it sounded like Mr. Stanley understood, I wanted to make sure that he did. "My mama is just doing what she has to do to take care of me."

"I know that. But with what she does for a living, it made it a little hard to find out . . . about your father."

My shoulders slumped. "I thought you said you had good news."

"Oh, I do." He held up his hands. "I have great news. I went down to the truck stop off the interstate and I talked to some of the men who know your mother and who have known her for a long time."

My eyes widened. "Did they know my father, too?"

"That's what I've been trying to figure out. That's what's taking me so long. But I got the names of a couple of men and I'm going to talk. . . ."

Before he said all of his words, I said, "No, wait!"

He frowned.

"I don't want you to talk to anybody because . . ." I stopped. How was I supposed to say this to him? "I just want to know my father's name."

"You don't want to talk to him?"

I shook my head. I mean, I hadn't really thought this all the way out. My mama would be mad if she knew what I was doing, because even though I was fourteen, she was still trying to convince me that I didn't have a father. "I don't know. I just want his name . . . for now."

He nodded and smiled as if he was trying to reassure me. "Okay, I'll get you a name. I'll be" — he paused — "discreet." He nodded. "I'll be discreet for you since you've been discreet for me."

"Okay," I said, feeling like I could breathe again.

"So, these are the names of the three men I'll talk to . . . and be discreet."

He turned the paper around and I read the names: John Smith, David Johnson, and Tim Black. My eyes were still on the paper when I asked, "Are one of these men my father?"

"I'm not sure," he said. "But I'm going to find out."

Mr. Stanley stood, but I didn't look up. I kept my eyes on the paper and wondered about John, David, and Tim. Was my real name Keisha Smith, Johnson, or Black? The thought that I could be looking at the name of my father made me start shaking a little.

Mr. Stanley took my hand and made me look up, then stand up. "What's wrong?" he asked. "Why are you crying?"

I didn't even realize that I was. "I guess I'm just happy, kinda."

"Ah, so these are happy tears?"

I nodded. "I'm just happy that you're helping me."

"I'm helping you, and we're getting close." He smiled, and then before I knew it, he put his arms around me and eased me into a hug. At first, I just stood there a little shocked because even though I was fourteen, I couldn't remember anyone ever hugging me.

And then he stepped back a little. I exhaled until he leaned down and kissed my cheek where it was wet. I froze again, and then even my heart stopped beating when he brought his hand up to my breast.

Oh my God! Now that he knew where my mama worked, did that mean he wanted me to do the same thing for him?

But even though I didn't want him to feel my breast, I didn't do anything. I just stood there because . . . I didn't know what to do.

I didn't say anything. He didn't say anything. He just kept his hand on my breast. Until he squeezed me.

That was when I jumped back and away.

His eyes got a little wide. "Is something wrong?"

What was I supposed to say? I mean, I didn't want to make him mad.

At first, I didn't say anything. I just looked down because I didn't want to look at him. So he said, "I'm sorry, Keisha. I didn't mean to hurt you."

"You didn't hurt me." My eyes were still on my sneakers.

He used his fingers to touch my chin and make me look at him, just like he'd done before. It took a long time before I looked up. He said, "It's just that since I've been spending all of this time with you helping to find your father, I discovered that I really like you."

Okay, what did that mean? I mean, I liked him, too. He was a good guy for helping me.

He said, "I was just thinking that maybe . . . you know . . ."

I tilted my head.

Then he said, "What about if we go out on a date?"

A date? Words came out of my mouth before I could even think about them: "My mama said that I can't date anyone until I'm seventeen."

"Wow," he said, sounding as if he was a little surprised.

"Yeah, she's real protective of me."

He nodded, though I could tell that didn't make much sense to him. Now I realized that for sure, he thought I did what my mama did. Maybe that was how he wanted me to pay him. I needed to set him straight.

"My mama wants me to focus on my education so that I can have options because she didn't have any."

"Okay." He nodded. "Well, I'm just talking about us going out to dinner. Didn't you tell me that your favorite food was hamburgers?"

"Uh-huh."

"Well, I know this place over in Lipton that has the best burgers in Arkansas."

I knew where Lipton was — it was like two towns over from White Haven. But I'd never heard anybody talking about their hamburgers.

He said, "That's what we'll do. On Friday. You'll be tired of turkey and dressing and we'll take a little road trip."

I didn't tell him that I wasn't going to have any turkey because my mama always worked on Thanksgiving. And I didn't tell him that I wasn't sure about going anywhere with him. I mean, he was older. I didn't know how old for sure, but he was old. He was over twenty-five, I thought. Because that diploma on his wall had a date of 2002.

He asked, "Have you ever been on a road trip before?"

I nodded. "One time. A long time ago. My mama took me to Hot Springs."

"Well, it's time for another trip. We'll have fun." He paused, and I shifted.

Then, he added, "And I'll have more information about your father."

Right away, I said, "Okay. We can go talk about my father on Friday," because that was what was most important to me.

I opened my eyes and had to look around the hotel parking lot to remind myself where I was. But opening my eyes didn't stop the memories. Mama had stayed home with me on that Wednesday, but just like I knew she would, she worked on Thursday and didn't come home until about ten in the morning on Friday. She had gone straight to bed 'cause it was the weekend, and sometimes, she worked all the way through till Sunday. That was why I wasn't worried about going on that road trip with Mr. Stanley. But all these years later, I sure wish I hadn't.

When I felt that tear on my cheek, I was mad. Damn! I had told myself I wasn't gonna cry. But every time I thought about Mr. Stanley . . .

The ringing of my cell phone made me jump. I stared down at the screen. I knew that number. My fingers were shaking a little when I answered the call.

"Yeah?" I said as if I didn't know who was

on the other end.

"Keisha? This is Regan. I got your text."

"Yeah . . . I thought about it . . . and . . ."

"Yes, I read what you said. So can you come over so that we can talk about it and figure everything out? I don't know how much time you'll need to plan this."

I wondered if I should tell her that I was ready to go now — except for the money I needed to go pick up some clothes.

She said, "What time do you want to meet up?"

"I can be there in five minutes," and then, because I didn't want to sound too pressed, I said, "My mama and I stay real close to your hotel. I mean now, it's just me, but. . . ." I stopped talking.

"Oh." She paused and in her silence, I heard her judgment, though I didn't know why. "Okay. Well, I'm getting up. We can go somewhere for breakfast."

"Okay. I can give you a little time."

"Give me about thirty minutes, okay?"

"Yeah," I said, then hung up because I didn't want to say anything else to Regan. I'd already messed up yesterday when I'd said Gabrielle's name and I could hear in what she said and didn't say that she wasn't sure if she could trust me.

I glanced out the window, looking up at

the top floor of the hotel. Then I leaned back. This time, though, I wasn't going to think about the darkness of the past. From now on, I was going to keep all my thoughts on the present and those people in Los Angeles. Because if I kept thinking about the past, then I'd have to remember all of those awful days during all of those awful years. And while Mr. Stanley made me cry, I didn't know what would happen if I thought about the other things. No, I couldn't let my mind go back to that. Not if I wanted to keep my sanity.

# 12
## GABRIELLE

On any other day, I would've pulled the pillow over my head and pretended not to hear the phone ringing. Because there was only one thing I did before the sun came up — all I did was turn over.

But this wasn't any other day. This was today, Saturday. The morning of the day after Regan had met Keisha. So the second the phone rang, I grabbed it, glanced at the screen, then peeked at Mauricio before I scooted my legs over the edge of the bed.

"Hey," I whispered as I pressed the phone against my ear, then rushed into the bathroom to grab my bathrobe. "What's up?"

"I'm sorry," Regan said. "I know it's early out there."

"No, it's all right." I stepped outside the bedroom. "I was getting up anyway." I scurried down the hallway, peeked inside Bella's room, then closed the door when I saw that my daughter looked like she still had a few more hours of sleep in her.

"Liar," my best friend said. "No way you were getting up."

I held in my laughter and excitement as I trotted down the staircase. "Okay, so I wasn't even awake, but I sure was waiting for you. Did you speak to Keisha? Is she okay? Is she coming back with you?" I settled onto the sofa in the living room.

Regan blew a long breath through the phone. "I can answer every question with one word — yeah. She called a little while ago. She's coming to Los Angeles."

I shrieked, then put my hand over my mouth, not wanting to wake Mauricio or Bella. "Oh my God. I can't believe it."

"I told you she was going to do it."

"I know, but I didn't want to get my hopes up."

"Speaking of hopes . . ." She stopped.

"What?" I frowned. Was there a wrench in this already?

"I don't know."

The way my friend said those three words made me sigh. "Are you still concerned about that name thing?"

"It wasn't just *a* thing. It was *something.*"

"Whatever it was, it doesn't change the fact that she's my sister."

"Yeah, but . . . how did she know your name?"

She sounded as if she were agonized by that question. "Really, Regan? What does it matter?" When Regan didn't say anything, I added, "Don't be the lawyer right now; don't be my business partner. All I need is my best friend."

"And as your friend I have some concerns."

I rolled my eyes. Regan was one steadfast chick.

She said, "Like the fact that Keisha just lied to me about where she lived."

"How do you know that?" I frowned. "I thought you didn't have an address for her."

"I don't. I could never find anything because the place where she used to live, the woman there told me that Keisha snuck out in the middle of the night, owing three months' rent."

"Well, I'm sure she and her mom didn't have it easy," I said, wanting to defend . . . my sister.

"Fine. I'll give her that. But then why did she just tell me that she and her mother lived just five minutes away from my hotel? The place that I found, the lady I spoke to — that's way more than five minutes from here."

"Maybe she's living with a friend."

"She said she'd lived there with her mother."

"Maybe she misspoke. You're making such a big deal out of a couple of little things."

Regan sighed — no, actually, she moaned, and I heard her judgment in that sound. "And what I've learned about a couple of little things is that they lead to serious situations."

Before I could ask her what the heck she was talking about, I heard some kind of banging. "What's that?" I asked.

"Hold on, someone's at my door." There were a couple of seconds of silence and then Regan whispered, "Ugh, I told her to give me thirty."

I sat up straight. "Who? Keisha? Is she there with you?"

"Yeah."

"Well, let her in," I said, raising my voice a bit.

I pressed the phone closer to my ear as if that would help me hear better, maybe even help me to get a visual. And then Regan's voice, "Hey, you're . . . early . . ."

"No," I whispered. Why was Regan saying that? I didn't want Keisha to feel unwelcome in any way. I needed to get my best friend straight about this.

And then, for the very first time, I heard my sister's voice. "Yeah, I'm sorry, it was just that I was so close. I can go back downstairs."

I didn't move. I didn't want to miss a syllable that she spoke.

Regan said, "No, come on in."

I closed my eyes and thanked God and Regan.

Then, "I'm talking to Gabrielle now. Here . . ."

In the couple of seconds between Regan's voice and Keisha's, my eyes widened, and I sprang up from the sofa. I wasn't ready . . .

"Yeah?" her voice sang into my ear.

"Keisha?"

"Yeah?"

"This is Gabrielle," I said, telling her what she already knew, but I didn't know what else to say.

"Uh . . . yeah. Hey."

I stood frozen, afraid that if I moved, I might miss a second of my first moments with . . . my sister. "Wow. I guess we really should have planned this. I mean, it makes sense that we would talk on the phone first, right?"

"Yeah, I guess."

She hadn't said much, but I heard so much. Her history, her life was in her voice.

It was in the raspiness of her tone; there was an edge, no warmth. I heard a girl who'd lived a different life from the one I was blessed to live, and now I wanted to know more about her.

I put as much heart into my voice as I could. "I'm really looking forward to meeting you."

"Me too."

At this moment, I wished I'd been some kind of journalist or attorney so I would know what to say next. So that I could stimulate our conversation and get more than two syllables from her at a time.

"Well, Regan is going to take care of everything for you, but is there anything you need before you leave? Anything I can do for you?"

There was a pause and then, "Yeah, I need some clothes."

"Oh." My head jerked back a bit with surprise. "Okay. Uh . . . I can arrange that. Regan can take you shopping."

"She doesn't have to take me," she said, with that edge. "I can go by myself. I just need a credit card."

"Oh . . . okay. Uh . . . let me speak to Regan."

"Okay."

"Keisha!" I shouted, hoping she hadn't

passed the phone to Regan. "I really can't wait to see you. And . . ." I held my breath for a second before I spoke my next words. "Our father . . . our father is looking forward to it, too."

"Okay," she said, though she didn't sound like she had any hope for the future.

Then, I heard, "Gabrielle?"

"Wow!" I whispered, not wanting to take the chance of Keisha hearing me through Regan's cell. "I just spoke to my sister."

"That's what we think. Still have to make sure."

"I know. The DNA test, and now that I know Keisha is coming, I'll talk to Daddy about that."

"Yup. Definitely going to do it and no worries, I'll handle it."

"Okay. And can you handle something else for me?" I didn't give her a chance to respond. "Keisha said she needs some clothes."

"I heard."

"She said she doesn't need you to take her shopping."

"Heard that, too."

"So, can you give her a couple of dollars?"

"I can handle that. I'm going to get everything together here and call you back with our plans."

"When do you think you're coming back?"

"I'm hoping tonight, but I'll talk to Keisha and then get back to you."

"Okay. And, Regan, thank you so much. I am forever grateful to you, my friend."

Her response to my words was only "I love you."

"More," I told her before I clicked off.

I kept the phone in my hand, feeling almost like that was the way to hold on to my sister.

My sister.

I had just spoken to the young woman that I was 99 percent sure was my sister.

It was weird — I'd sent Regan to find her, but I hadn't prepared myself for this moment. I hadn't been ready to speak to her and I wished to God that I'd had better words, stronger words, words that would have really welcomed her. But that was okay; it was the first time, and it was only over the phone. I'd be prepared for our first time standing face-to-face.

I had to get ready. I had to decide what we were going to do. Have a dinner? Take Keisha out to dinner? Have friends over, or should it just be me and Daddy first? What about Bella and Mauricio?

Or should we meet Keisha at the airport with balloons and a huge placard? Lots of cheers, overwhelm her with love?

"Take a deep breath," I told myself as I made my way back upstairs. There was plenty of time, especially since the sun was just beginning its rise.

The first thing I had to do was call my father, our father. I had to prepare Elijah Wilson to meet his second child.

# 13
## KEISHA

The moment I said good-bye and then handed the cell phone to Regan, I asked if I could use her bathroom. She nodded, then pressed the phone to her ear. I guessed she and Gabrielle were gonna do a little talking about me. Well, I was about to do a little talking about them.

I almost ran into that bathroom, and my fingers shook, making it hard for me to even lock the bathroom door. All this time, I'd been looking at her pictures, and now I had been on the phone talking to her.

I had talked to Gabrielle Wilson Flores.

Oh my God!

And she sounded nice. Way nice. The kind of nice that was going to work right into my plan. I had to tell Buck.

First, I turned on the faucet, then I pushed down the toilet seat and sat before I dialed his number; he answered on the first ring.

"Yo, you left and didn't say anything."

"I told you I had to meet Gabrielle's friend."

"Did you?"

"Uh-huh. I saw her, *and* I spoke to Gabrielle." I told him about the call.

"Yo, we're gonna get bank from this."

"I know," I said. "I asked Gabrielle for money to buy some clothes and she didn't even blink. She's gonna have Regan take care of it for me."

"That's what I'm talkin' 'bout. You think she'll let you use her credit card?"

"I don't know, but I'll try. Then, I'll head over to you. What time do you get to work?"

"I'm rolling into the lot right now. Come find me. I'll be in sporting goods."

"Got you."

I clicked off the phone, then turned off the water, and right before I left the bathroom I flushed the toilet just so Regan wouldn't be wondering what I'd been doing in here.

When I opened the door, though, I got a shock. Regan was standing right there. I mean, she was standing like her ear had been pressed to the door. Oh my God — had she been listening?

She stepped back, letting me move past her.

"Thank you," I said, wondering what this chick was up to. I crossed the room and stood in front of the window.

She said, "Did you wash your hands?"

"Huh?"

"I heard the water running for quite a while, then it stopped, then the toilet flushed." She paused. "So I was just asking . . . did you wash your hands?"

Dang! She was checking me like that?

"I don't know what you're talking about," I said, and then rubbed my hands together as if they were still a little wet or something.

She stood by the bathroom door, just looking at me and this time I saw her judgment in her stance. When she didn't say anything else, I spoke up, "Gabrielle said you would help me get some clothes. So, can I borrow your credit card?"

Regan had already been standing like she was a statue, but now she stood like she was a statue on ice.

"What?" I said, shrugging.

Now she squinted and looked at me as if I'd just cursed her or something.

"What?" I said again.

She folded her arms. But she didn't say anything.

So I crossed my arms, too, but I did say something. "Why are you looking at me like

I did something wrong?"

Finally, her lips parted. "You just spoke to the woman who could be your sister for the first time, and this is what you have to say? This is what you ask me?"

What in the world did she expect? "Yeah. I spoke to her and she asked if I needed anything. And I told her I needed some clothes if I was going to Los Angeles. I don't have anything to wear." I stared back at her as hard as she'd been looking at me.

For the first time, her eyes left my face, and she looked down at the jeans and top I was wearing. I was trying to keep my face tight, but I couldn't help it — I smirked. Because I could tell that she'd just noticed my clothes.

After she looked me up and down, she came toward me with this expression. Like she was so mad she wanted to fight. I wasn't worried. I was Daisy Jones's daughter; my mama had taken grown men down. I knew how to take care of myself.

But Regan didn't step to me at all. She stopped at the desk and opened that big ole red bag she'd been carrying yesterday. She pulled out her wallet. "Where are you going shopping?"

"Probably over to Walmart," I said, then

hoped she wouldn't say she was going with me.

"How much do you think you'll need?"

I shrugged. "I don't know. That's why I was thinking a credit card would be better than cash." She glared at me, and I added, "I won't spend that much. You can give me a limit."

She counted out some bills. "What I'm going to give you is this." She shoved the money into my hand, like I was a charity case. If getting money from her hadn't been part of my plan, I would've pushed those bills right back in her hand and told her what she could do with each of them one at a time.

But I had to remember my goal. I didn't get the credit card this time, but I would. Probably never from Regan, though, 'cause for some reason she wasn't feeling me. I didn't know why . . . I wasn't the one who'd come to them. But Regan still looked at me like I was some kind of fraud.

That was okay, though. Her last name wasn't Wilson.

So I took the money and said, "Thank you," then tucked the bills into my jeans without even looking at what she'd given me. "So do you know what time we're gonna leave today?"

She glanced at the clock on the night-stand. "There are a couple of flights leaving from Little Rock a little later. So it depends on you. What do you have to do today?"

"Nothing except go over to Walmart. It's not that far from here, over on Monument Drive."

She nodded. "Well, you go take care of that, and then we'll meet back here. I'm going to get dressed, pack my things, so I'm figuring we can leave any time this afternoon or this evening. I think the last flight leaves around six or so."

"Cool," I said. "So . . ." I wanted to just turn, cut and run, but I had to figure out which way Regan wanted me to act so that she would stop looking at me liked I'd just snatched her purse. "So I'll get going." Now I looked at the clock. It wasn't yet eight. "I'll be back by about two."

"Two?" She squinted. "I thought you said the only thing you had to do was go to Walmart."

Why was this woman checking me like I was ten and she was my mama?

"Yeah, that's all I have to do, but after that, I wanna say good-bye to a few people, let them know where I'm going." I paused. "Is that okay?" I wasn't really asking for her permission. I'd said it with such attitude —

my way of saying, *Back up, lady.* Now that I'd been introduced to Gabrielle, now that Elijah knew all about me, Regan was no longer a factor.

She nodded, but with the way she glared at me, I could tell she still didn't believe me. Whatever! It was too complicated trying to figure her out, so I just stomped past her.

I didn't even wait for the elevator; I took the stairs all the way from the seventh floor to the first, and when I got into my car, I pulled the money from my jeans and counted it — five twenty-dollar bills. Dang! I'd never had one hundred dollars to go shopping before.

I separated the money and put sixty in my right pocket and forty in my left one. Then I revved up my car and even though it started smoking, I didn't care. As long as it got me to Walmart and back, I'd be good.

As I drove, I imagined what it was going to be like in Los Angeles. Even though I was going there to take care of business, I was a little excited about going someplace outside of Arkansas. The biggest city I'd ever been to was Little Rock, and except for going to high school, I hadn't hung out there a lot.

But I knew a little about Los Angeles from

my tenth-grade geography class and all the stuff I saw on TV. I wondered if I was going to see movie stars, or other famous people. Would I run into some of my favorite stars from any of those *Real Housewives* shows? I wanted to meet those ladies because they were living the lit life.

There was so much in my head as I rolled into the parking lot, then rushed into the superstore, which on some weekends looked a lot like a club — Walmart was the place to hang out.

It was way too early for the Saturday-night club vibe, though. The store was almost empty as I weaved through the aisles, heading for Buck's section. I spotted him before I even got there. He was sitting on one of the bicycles, not doing anything that looked like work; just chillin'.

I shook my head. I had no idea how he was able to keep his job.

"Yo, boo, what's up?" he said before he hugged me, then kissed me like he wasn't at work and we weren't standing in the middle of this discount store. But when he stepped back, the first thing he said was, "So, did she give you her credit card?"

I looked my boyfriend up, then down. Even though he could be triflin', he really was fine. His best assets — he had two —

were his wavy hair and his biceps. Oh, and then there were all his tattoos (at least a dozen) and his gold grill, which had me from that first day when he'd said hello. I shook my head . . . yeah, he was fine.

Finally I answered his question. "Nah, I don't think she trusted me enough to give me her credit card, but she did give me some cash."

"How much?"

I reached into my pocket and pulled out two bills. "Forty dollars."

Buck took the money and checked it as if he thought maybe I didn't know how to count cash. "That's it?" He shook his head and made a sound with his teeth like he was disgusted. "Yo, she's cheap. How we gonna go to the bank with this?" He held up the two twenties.

"It's just the beginning." I snatched the money from him. "You didn't expect her to give me everything in her wallet the first time, did you? She don't know me like that. Plus, she's not Gabrielle and that's where I'm going to get the money. We just have to be patient and work this right." I tucked the money back inside my pocket.

"I guess." He shrugged and leaned back onto one of the bicycles. When he crossed his arms, his biceps popped. "So you still going with the plan? You're gonna get the credit cards?"

"Yeah," I said. "I'm gonna try."

"You get those numbers, 'cause Que got a new plan," he said, talking about his cousin. "He's getting out of drugs and into this. It's much safer. So you get the numbers and Que can turn that into some serious cash."

I didn't really want to be caught up in any kind of credit card scheme; I preferred cash 'cause there was no trail with dollar bills. That was something Mama taught me. She said all of her johns bought her gifts with cash so that their wives wouldn't find out. Still, though, I nodded. "And I'll get as much cash as I can. I'm hoping that even after I come back here, my father will send me money on the regular, and then we'll be set."

He sighed. "Maybe I should come to Los Angeles with you."

I laughed. "And how are you gonna do that?" I held up the money. "With this forty dollars? Or are you going to walk?"

"I'm just saying, with me there, I may be able to help you move things along. I might be able to help you get even more money. You know I always got you, boo."

Whenever Buck said that to me, I really did feel safe. He was the only person in my life, besides Mama, who could make me feel like everything was gonna be all right. I said, "No. Your being in LA won't help a thing. It'll just make them suspicious."

He nodded. "So, when are you leaving?"

I shoved the strap of my purse onto my shoulder. "Today, tonight. I think Regan is anxious to get back to Los Angeles."

"Whoa," he said. "So this is it? This is the last time I'm gonna see you?"

"Till I get back."

He nodded. "Okay, well . . ." He paused.

"What?" I frowned.

He took a deep breath, then looked away from me. "I was just gonna ask . . . since you going away and everything, are you gonna go over to the cemetery before you leave?"

My eyes widened.

"Don't get mad. I just wanna know. 'Cause, you know, I talked to your mama a little about that before she died, and she said I was gonna have to help you through because you still haven't gotten over what happened and . . ."

I punched him square in his chest. And over his moan of pain, I shoved my finger into his face. "Don't you ever bring that up again."

"What? I was just asking . . ."

"Don't you ever . . ." I shouted.

And then I heard, "Keisha?"

I whipped around, ready for a fight.

"Are you okay?" Regan asked.

Even though there were tears in my eyes and rage on my face, I said, "Yeah!"

"Okay," Regan said, looking first at me and then turning to Buck. "So . . . who's your friend?"

Buck took a step toward us, but I said, "He's nobody."

That made Buck take that step back.

I turned and glared at him. "Nobody. Just somebody I thought I remembered from high school." I hardly moved my lips when I added, "But I don't remember anything from high school."

And then I stomped away, praying the whole time that Regan would just follow me and not say a word to Buck, who, right now, didn't feel anything like my boyfriend. He felt like a traitor, an enemy of my heart who was trying to take me places where I wasn't strong enough to go.

By the time I got over to the clothes section, I'd calmed down a bit.

"Are you all right?"

I breathed. At least Regan was behind me. "I'm cool. I just wanna pick up a few things," I said, even though now I didn't want any clothes. What I wanted was to get on the plane and get out of White Haven.

"Okay," Regan said, giving me another one of those glances that let me know she didn't believe me. "Well, there are a couple of things I have to do, so I'll meet you back at the hotel . . . at two."

"Nah. I'll be back there as soon as I finish here. In like fifteen minutes."

She squinted and looked at me like I was a science project. But then she nodded. "Well, if you're heading back to the hotel now and you're ready to go, I'll change our plans."

Oh, no! "What do you mean?"

"We'll fly out of Fayetteville instead of Little Rock. It'll be a better flight."

I didn't know what she meant by that, but if it got me out of White Haven now, I was all for a better flight.

She stared at me for another moment, then nodded and walked away. I was glad my tears cooperated until she was gone because I didn't want to explain anything else to her.

When I walked into this store, I couldn't wait to go shopping. But I didn't care about clothes anymore. All I could do was think about what Buck had said.

Why did he ask me about the cemetery?

Why did he want me to go there when he knew that my heart would never beat again if I did that? Why did he want to take me back all of those years?

Shaking my head, I headed to the cash register. Now, all I wanted to do was get out of White Haven as fast as I could. And if Buck kept talking that way, I might never come back.

# 14
## KEISHA

I was still thinking about Buck, and the cemetery, and the reason why I could never go there as I followed Regan onto the airplane. We were like the third and fourth people to get on, even though there was a line waiting when we got to the gate.

Inside the airplane, we passed like only two rows before she said, "These are our seats. Why don't you sit by the window?"

I scooted across one big seat, sat down, then snuggled my butt into the leather. It kinda felt like the little leather sofa Buck had in the bedroom he shared with four of his brothers at his mama's house. With the way it felt, I was thinking this was gonna be a good ride — and then I got a glimpse of what was going on outside the window. There were men and women working all around the plane on the ground. That made me think . . . this thing was really about to go up in the air. Dang, maybe being back at

Walmart and talking to Buck about things I didn't want to talk about wasn't so bad, because now I had too many questions: like how was this big ole thing even going to get off the ground? And if it got into the air, how was it gonna stay there? Suppose it just fell down? Suppose it just ran out of gas? All of those questions crashing around inside my head made me moan out loud.

Regan said, "Are you all right?"

"Yeah." But that was all I said because this chick was always trying to read me. Like when I met her back at the hotel — she had all kinds of questions about Buck even though I had told her he was someone that I *thought* I knew but didn't. But like every other time, she looked at me like I was a liar.

So that was why I wanted to stay quiet. But I guessed Regan was still doing her best to catch me not telling the truth.

She said, "This is your first time on a plane, right?"

I thought about it for a second, wondering what she was really trying to find out. Then I nodded, though I didn't look at her; I kept my eyes on the window. That would give her the hint.

But this chick didn't catch my clue, and she had the nerve to say, "Well, you don't have to worry. Airplanes are safer than cars."

Now I had to look at her. Because I had to figure out what she was trying to say. "What do you mean?"

She shrugged. "More people die in car crashes than in airplane crashes."

"What?"

"You're more likely to die in a car than on an airplane." Then she smirked, looked down at her tablet, and pressed a couple of keys like she hadn't just been talking about all the different kinds of ways to die.

People were passing by us, loading up the plane, but I hardly noticed. All I could do was glare at Regan. She was trying to scare me. This chick was a witch.

"Would you like something to drink?" the flight attendant asked me, taking my attention away from Regan.

I shook my head, and Regan ordered a sparkling water.

Then Regan said to me, "You may want to lean back and try to go to sleep. It's a smooth ride; you won't even feel like we're moving, and I'll wake you up when they start serving dinner."

I did what Regan said, but only because I didn't want to talk to her. And it probably was a good idea, since it would be better if my eyes were closed when this big ole plane tried to get up in the air.

So I leaned back, and imagined what it was going to be like in Los Angeles. But as I tried to sleep and wanted to dream, my mind did what it did to me all the time. It made a left turn and took me back to hell. Maybe it was what Buck had said earlier that made me remember that Thanksgiving weekend in 2009. That weekend when I was just fourteen. That weekend that changed my whole life:

By the time it got to be noon on Friday after Thanksgiving, I was a little excited. I'd been stuck in the house doing nothing except watching TV since we got out of school on Tuesday, so I was ready to do something else. And that something else was meet up with Mr. Stanley.

Right before three o'clock, I stood at the opening to the park where Mr. Stanley dropped me off every day. This was the time Mr. Stanley had told me to meet him, and I didn't want to be late. Plus, I wanted to get out of the house while Mama was still asleep, before she woke up and started asking questions.

My heart was pounding with excitement, and started beating even harder when I saw Mr. Stanley's Ford pickup round the corner. But when he stopped and leaned across the truck to open the door, I didn't move. 'Cause right then, what happened on Tuesday with Mr. Stanley at school came to my mind. That picture was stuck — Mr. Stanley's hand on my breast.

He shouted out the window, "Hey, Keisha," and the way he smiled reminded me that he was my friend — who was helping me find my father.

So I hopped into the truck.

Mr. Stanley said, "Ready for some good hamburgers?"

"Yeah."

"Then let's get this road trip started."

When he grinned again, I relaxed a little more. It helped that I was in his truck because I loved riding up high, feeling like I was the princess of the road. With the windows open and the wind, I was sure that if I spread my arms, I would be able to fly. When I grew up, I was gonna have a truck like Mr. Stanley's.

When we hit the interstate, Mr. Stanley pushed a cassette into his system and I rocked to the music. I jammed all the way to Lipton with Drake and Beyoncé and Ne-Yo. It was a shock that Mr. Stanley liked the same music I did; it was a cool trip.

By the time we stopped in front of the

diner with big red letters proclaiming "Bubba's Burgers," I felt like Mr. Stanley was my best friend.

"This is it," Mr. Stanley said and turned off the ignition.

Inside, I thought red must've been Bubba's favorite color 'cause everything in the place was red: the floor, the chairs, the tablecloths, and the walls were red-and-white striped. "Wow," I said when we sat down and the lady handed us red menus.

"What?" Mr. Stanley said.

"This place is so . . . cool." That was the only word I could think of, because red was a color that made me feel happy.

"It's gonna be even better when you taste the hamburgers."

Mr. Stanley ordered two double cheeseburgers with french fries, and two vanilla shakes. When the lady walked away, Mr. Stanley got right down to business. "I talked to a couple of men at the truck stop."

"Already?" I asked.

He grinned. "Yeah, didn't I tell you I was gonna make this happen for you?"

"Yes." I squeezed my legs together, trying to hold in my excitement.

"I've narrowed it down to one man. His name is Elijah Wilson."

I repeated Mr. Stanley's words in my mind.

"Does that name mean anything to you?"

I shook my head. "Is he my daddy?"

"I don't know yet, but there's one thing you can know for sure — I'm gonna find out." He put his hand over mine.

For a couple of seconds, I looked down at our hands — his pale white one over my chocolate brown. Didn't seem like it was a good mix.

Right then, the lady came back with our hamburgers, and before I took my first bite, I knew Mr. Stanley had been right. These were the biggest hamburgers I'd ever seen, with a whole lotta stuff, like lettuce and tomatoes and pickles. But when I finally bit into it, I knew Mr. Stanley had been wrong — this hamburger was better than the best, if there was a word for that.

"Look at you." Mr. Stanley leaned over and wiped the hamburger's juices from my lips with his napkin.

I was a little embarrassed. "Sorry."

"Don't be sorry. I told you these were some good hamburgers."

For the rest of the meal, Mr. Stanley and I just talked — about school and how I wanted to be a hairdresser when I graduated.

He asked me, "Do you wanna get married one day?"

I'd never thought about that. I wasn't sure I even knew anybody who was married. "I don't know."

"Get out of here," he said. "As pretty as you are, I know you have a boyfriend."

"No." I shook my head. "I told you I can't date till I'm seventeen."

"Well, that never stopped the girls at Clinton. Lots of them have secret boyfriends. You can have a secret boyfriend, too, if you want one."

"No way." I shrugged. "I don't have a boyfriend nor a lot of friends. I kinda stay a lot to myself."

"I noticed that."

When we finished with the hamburgers, Mr. Stanley ordered dessert — two slices of cheesecake, even though I told him I was full. By the time we finally stood up to go back to White Haven, it was dark outside. As he walked up to the counter to pay the bill, Mr. Stanley said, "Why don't you go use the restroom."

I frowned. "I don't have to go."

"We have a long ride back, and it's harder to find a place to stop at night. So go on, just to make sure."

No one had told me to do that since I

was a kid. But Mr. Stanley probably knew what he was talking about.

It didn't take me long — since I didn't have to go — and when I came out of the bathroom, Mr. Stanley was already outside. He was in front of his truck, crouched down, looking at his front tire.

"What's wrong?"

"Damn it. I have a flat."

I leaned over his shoulder, but I couldn't see anything with the way Mr. Stanley blocked my view.

He said, "And I don't have a spare. I took it out when I was loading some timber for my friends." He slammed his hand on the hood. "Damn."

I stood there, not wanting to make him any more upset.

He shook his head. "I called Triple A." He held up his flip phone. "But they're talking 'bout it may take a couple of hours. Maybe not even till morning."

Not till morning? I hadn't told Mama where I was going, and even though she wouldn't be home, I needed to be. "They can't get here any faster? What are we gonna do?"

He glanced across the street, and when he did that, I did, too. He said, "We can sleep in there until someone can come and fix this."

I looked at the motel, then back at Bubba's Burgers. "Can we just wait in there?"

"They're 'bout ready to close." I sighed and he continued, "Don't worry." Then Mr. Stanley grinned the way he always did when he wanted me to feel better. "I'm gonna take care of you."

"But my mama . . . I didn't tell her I was coming over here with you."

"I'll call her. Tell her you're on a school trip or something."

"Okay." I nodded, even though I wasn't going to let him call her. But he didn't need to know that right now.

I wanted to sit in the truck and wait to be rescued, but I didn't want to sit out here by myself. So when Mr. Stanley started walking, I followed him across the four lanes to the motel. He told me to wait outside while he talked to the lady at the front desk.

As I waited, it began to feel colder and seemed even darker. And it felt empty, too. There were only two cars in this lot, and when I glanced across the wide street, everyone seemed to be leaving Bubba's Burgers. By the time Mr. Stanley came back outside, I was so ready to go inside.

"Our room is right down here."

Our room.

Just about four doors down, Mr. Stanley stepped in, and when he clicked on the light, the first thing I saw were two beds and a chair. I rushed inside and bounced down on the green flowered chair as if I were claiming that space as mine.

Mr. Stanley handed me the remote. "You can watch whatever you want."

"Thank you." When I flipped through a few channels, and found the best show on TV — *Martin* — I felt better. And it was one of those episodes with Sheneneh, so that made me feel doubly better.

I snuggled back into the chair while Mr. Stanley sat on the bed next to the window. After a couple of minutes of Gina, Pamela, and Sheneneh, I didn't even remember Mr. Stanley, I was cracking up so much.

Right when the second episode of Martin came on, Mr. Stanley said, "I'm going to check on the truck."

"Okay."

He said, "You should go ahead and sit on that bed." He pointed to the one by the bathroom. "It's more comfortable than that chair." And then he walked out of the room.

I waited a couple of seconds, then got up, crossed the room, and peeked out the window. It was so dark, I just turned away. For a second, I stared at the bed, then I did what Mr. Stanley said — I lay down.

By the time the third episode of Martin came on, Mr. Stanley still wasn't back. So I closed my eyes just during the commercial. But I guess I fell asleep. I could kinda hear the TV, but it wasn't until I felt something move behind me on the bed that I realized that I wasn't by myself. Was I dreaming?

Then the bed moved again and my eyes popped open. The room was dark except for the light from the TV. And then I felt Mr. Stanley behind me, lying next to me. His body was pressed against my back.

I wanted to run, but I stayed as frozen as I had the other day. I stayed that way, even when I felt his penis on my butt.

Oh my God! What was I supposed to do?

Then, when he put his hand on my breast again, I gasped, and that was too much. I had to get up.

But Mr. Stanley's arm stiffened like a vise and held me down. "It's okay," he whispered. "Be still. I'm not going to hurt you."

I squeezed my eyes shut as he moved his hand over my breast, but then, when he put his hand under my sweatshirt, I opened my eyes and blinked and blinked and blinked. His hands just kept moving up and down my skin, over and around my breast.

Martin and Gina laughed on the TV screen, and Mr. Stanley grunted like he was having trouble breathing.

We stayed that way for what felt like hours, but I know it wasn't that long because the same episode of *Martin* was still on when he moved his hand from under my sweatshirt, and then he tilted away from me. The bed moved again, and I stayed still even when Mr. Stanley went into the bathroom . . .

The way my head was turned, the first thing I saw when I woke up were the clouds below the airplane that looked like the softest of cotton. I couldn't believe we were already in the air, and for a second I wondered if the plane was even moving — maybe there was some kind of problem. But when I looked around and everyone else was just sitting there, I guessed everything was all right.

"Would you like dinner?" the flight attendant asked me and Regan.

It seemed like I'd woken up just in time. I chose the pasta, only because Regan asked for the fish. I tried to eat because I didn't want to think about Mr. Stanley anymore, but I couldn't seem to get him out of my head now that I was going to see my father. That was where I wanted my mind to stay — on Elijah Wilson. But the memory of the rest of that night seemed to want to play over and over.

When Mr. Stanley had gone into the bathroom, I had stayed on the bed, because I didn't know what to do. Even when he came out and said it was time to go, I didn't say anything. I didn't ask him how he knew his tire had been fixed. I didn't ask him why he'd touched me the way he had. I didn't do anything except follow him out of the motel and then across the four lanes.

Mr. Stanley didn't even check the tire. He just opened the door for me, then he got in on the other side.

The trip back to White Haven wasn't anything like when we'd come to Lipton. I didn't say anything to Mr. Stanley and he didn't say anything to me. There was no music, which was fine because all I wanted to do was think.

I was thinking how I was going to tell Mr. Stanley I didn't want to see him again. I didn't want to see him in school, I didn't want him to drive me home, I didn't want to be around him in any kind of way.

But then when he stopped the truck in front of the park, he said, "I'll have all the information you want about Elijah Wilson on Monday. So I'll see you after school."

I had all the words I'd wanted to say to him right on my tongue, but the only thing that came out of my mouth was, "Okay."

I blinked so that I wouldn't cry, especially not in front of Regan. But it was hard because that night was just the beginning of my horror. There was so much bad, but the thing was, there was good, too. Because Mr. Stanley had done what he'd promised. Because of him, I'd known about Elijah Wilson since I was fourteen.

When the flight attendant cleared my food tray, I had to fight to keep thoughts away from my horror and my hell. It seemed like I stared out that window for hours, but then a man's voice came over the loudspeakers, "Ladies and gentlemen, the seat belt sign has come back on as we begin our final descent . . ."

I leaned over to Regan. "What does that mean?"

"It means that in about twenty minutes we'll be landing in Los Angeles."

I turned back to the window. Everything outside was all dark now, the match to my mood. But I was hoping that would all change. I was hoping that in about twenty minutes, all of my thoughts of Mr. Stanley would be gone forever. Because now that I was going to meet my father, the rest of what happened with Mr. Stanley was the part that I really needed to forget.

# 15
## GABRIELLE

I peeked out the window and for at least the one thousand, six hundred and eighty-seventh time, I thought we'd made the wrong decision. We should have gone to the airport and met Keisha at baggage claim with balloons and signs and smiles that told her she was welcomed and loved. But now . . .

"Babe."

I jumped and turned around with my hand pressed against my chest. "You scared me."

Mauricio frowned. "Why are you so nervous?"

"I'm not," I said, crossing the room past him and once again fluffing the pillows on the sofa. Then I straightened the picture frames on the mantel before I shifted the flowerpots in front of our windows.

Before I could get over to the piano to adjust the seat, Mauricio held my arm. "I don't get why you're so nervous."

"Not nervous, anxious. We should have gone to the airport and we should have had Daddy here tonight, too."

"It was his idea to give her space tonight."

"Yeah," I began, pacing the length of the living room, "but I think he's just anxious like I am." I sighed, then bounced down onto the sofa. Holding my face in my hands, I did my best to steady my breathing, to steady my soul. But I didn't have a yoga exercise designed for meeting my sister. Feeling my husband hovering over me, I looked up.

Mauricio said, "It's going to be fine, you know."

I nodded, but then I said, "I just don't know how to do this. There's so much for us to make up."

"And you'll have plenty of time to do that."

Just as he said those words, both of us turned toward the bay window and the car lights that shined bright through the night into our living room.

"Oh my God," I whispered.

Mauricio peeked through the drapes. He said, "That's Regan," as if I didn't already know.

"Oh my God," I repeated. Anxiety had

stolen my strength; I didn't have any in my legs to stand.

Then my husband did what he always did. Without me speaking a word, he reached for my hand and lifted me up. "You got this and I got you."

He squeezed my hand, but then left me alone as he moved toward the door. Mauricio had gotten me up, but what was I supposed to do now?

The car lights disappeared and then I heard the slamming of the SUV's doors. I finally found the fortitude to follow my husband from the living room into the foyer. Regan (I assumed) had barely pressed the bell before Mauricio opened the door.

"Hey, you," he said to my best friend, and he pulled her into a hug.

My eyes stayed on my model-gorgeous-perfect-as-usual friend for only a moment; then moved beyond to the young woman who stood behind her. Regan had given me the dossier on Keisha: she was twenty-two, she was a hairstylist, and her mother had just passed away. But she hadn't given me any kind of physical description of the young lady, who looked as if she hadn't yet left her teens. She was dressed simply, in jeans and a white T-shirt with the words "New Yeah" written in gold letters. The simplicity of her clothes did nothing to hide her beauty. She had taken the best from our father — her brows were perfect frames for her light brown eyes, and the mole above her lip was more than a growth — it was really a beauty mark, God's stamp of approval for what He'd created.

As she stepped into our home, Mauricio said, "You must be Keisha."

"Yeah." She moved past him, her eyes scoping the space of our foyer.

I watched her check out the staircase that curved against the wall, then her glance rose to the chandelier above, before she studied the limestone floor that greeted our guests.

I stepped up, pulling her glance to me. "Hi, Keisha."

"Yeah. Hi."

Then, I had another one of those moments like when we were on the phone. I didn't know what to say, what to do. So instead of trying to figure it out, I just did what was in my heart. I pulled her into an embrace. I held her and tried not to squeeze too tight. Her arms, though, stayed by her sides.

After giving her (or maybe I was giving myself) a few moments, I stepped back. "It is so wonderful to meet you. I'm so glad you're here."

"Yeah."

"Why don't we all go on inside?" Mauricio said and cocked his head toward the living room.

I wanted to grab Keisha's hand and lead the way, but she followed my husband and I hung back. I glanced toward the door to make sure Regan was joining us, and her eyes were already on me. She gave me a smirk that was meant to be a message, and though my sister-friend and I were always in sync, I couldn't read her. It was probably me — I was the one out of step because my senses were discombobulated as I looked at Keisha. I'd have to get Regan's interpretation of her expression later.

Mauricio motioned toward the sofa and Keisha sat down, though she sat so close to the end, if the arm weren't there, she would have fallen off. My husband sat in the chair across from the couch, and I settled in the middle of the sofa, feeling like I was miles away from my sister.

Regan stood behind Mauricio, and once we were in our places, we all stared at Keisha. She shifted beneath the heat of our stares and silence, and I felt terrible; it was like we were treating her as if she were a lab animal under a microscope.

I said, "So . . . how . . . are you?"

She shrugged. "I'm good."

Then there was more silence until Regan said, "I hope you good people won't mind, but it's late and I have a husband waiting for me."

Keisha's eyes were squinted when she said to Regan, "You married?"

"Yes, I am."

"Wow. I can't believe that." Now Regan narrowed her eyes, but Keisha stayed strong beneath the fire my friend sent her way. She glared right back, then said, "I mean, you never said anything about having a husband."

"Why would I?" Looking at me, she said, "So anyway . . ."

This time, I got my best friend's message. Not only in her expression, but in that exchange between her and Keisha. There was no semblance of warmth; something had happened between the two.

Even though I needed to understand what was going down, there was no way I was going to get up and leave Keisha alone just so I could talk to Regan. Anything she had to tell me would have to wait.

Again, my husband did one of those things he'd always done. Without a word from me, he stood up. "I'll walk you out, Regan."

"Okay," my friend said, though her eyes

were still on me. "Keisha's bag is in the car, so" — now she turned to Mauricio — "you can bring it in."

As they turned toward the door, I pressed my hands together as if I were going to pray. "Thank you," I told Regan. "Thank you" — I glanced at Keisha — "for bringing my sister home."

Regan gave me a long look, then chased that with a slow nod before she followed my husband out the door.

When we were alone, I turned to Keisha. Why I waited for her to speak, I didn't know. But after a few seconds, I told her, "I'm so glad you're here."

"Yeah, you said that."

"Oh . . . kay." I dragged the word out. "So, how was your flight?"

She shrugged. "It was long."

I nodded. "Yeah, but I was glad when Regan was able to get you two on a direct flight."

I saw the question in her eyes, but I wasn't sure what she was asking until she said, "What's a direct flight?"

For just a moment, I hesitated. "It's a plane that goes straight from one city to another without you having to change and take a second plane."

"Oh," she said. Then, her eyes took a

journey, soaking in the sight of our living room before her gaze rested on our piano. She said, "You play that?"

I smiled. "I do." I tilted my head. "Do you know how to play?"

"No, I don't know anybody who knows how to play the piano."

"You know me." She looked as if she had no idea what I meant by that. I said, "And maybe I can teach you."

She shrugged, but didn't give me another word to work with. So again I had to figure out what to say. And again I just reached into my heart. "Keisha, I'm really sorry about your mother."

Her eyes turned back to me and she gave me such a frown that for a moment, I wondered if Regan had messed up that intel totally. Was Daisy alive? If I bungled this part up, if her mother hadn't died, that certainly wasn't the way to start a relation-ship.

I said, "Your mother . . . she passed away . . . right?"

She nodded. "Yeah, she died. Not that long ago."

I breathed. "I'm really sorry."

"Oh. Yeah." After a moment's thought, she added, "Thank you."

Then the silence that hung between

strangers came back, and I wished I'd had a list of talking points. "Are you hungry?"

She shook her head. "I ate on the plane."

"Oh, that's right. You were in first class, so they did serve a meal."

She shrugged.

"What about something to drink?"

She shook her head and yawned.

"Oh, my goodness," I said. "You have got to be tired." I glanced at my watch. "It's after midnight for you."

She frowned as she reached into her purse, then glanced at her phone before she held it up for me to see. "It's not midnight; it's only ten."

"Yes, here." I rested my hand over hers. "It's ten here. But with the time change — we're two hours behind you." She frowned and I added, "You're on central time, and this is Pacific time."

She glanced at her phone, then back at me before she shrugged.

At that moment, all I wanted to do was wrap my arms around Keisha. What had her life been like that she didn't know what a direct flight was or understand time zones? Those were two little things I took for granted, and now I wanted to teach her everything that I knew.

"Since it's so late, why don't we do this:

I'll take you up to your bedroom, you'll get a good night's rest, and we can start this all over in the morning."

She tilted her head. "I'm staying here?"

That question surprised me. "Yes."

"I thought I'd be staying with . . . uh . . ."

The way her eyes shifted, I could tell she was hunting for a word. She said, "Elijah. I thought I'd be staying with him."

"Oh, no. I thought you'd be more comfortable here."

She frowned. "What's wrong with his house?"

"Nothing. That's not what I meant. I just mean you don't know him."

And without taking a breath, she said, "I don't know you either."

That made me bust out laughing. One thing I was never going to have to wonder was what Keisha was thinking. "That's true." And then, for the first time, I spoke to her as my little sister. "But another thing that's true is that I wanted you here with me. I know this can't be easy and I'm sure you're going to have lots of questions. I want to be here, close by, so that you know you have a big sister who's going to help you through all of this." After a pause, I added, "And having you close, I know you'll help me, too. Okay?"

I'd given her my best; I'd given her my heart. And what she gave me in return for those words was another shrug.

I said, "So we're going to his home tomorrow afternoon and we'll spend the day with him. Is that all right with you?"

She shrugged, and right then I thought it was a good thing that my self-esteem was healthy. Because talking to Keisha could give me a complex.

"Okay." Mauricio's voice came into the living room before he did. He stood at the archway, carrying a duffel bag. "I'm going to take your bag upstairs to your room, Keisha."

"Perfect timing," I said. When I stood, Keisha did, too. "Keisha's tired, understandably," I told my husband. "So we were going up, but I want to give her a tour around so she'll know where everything is."

Mauricio nodded, gave us a grin, and then moved toward the staircase. But before he was up two steps, he stopped, turned back. "Keisha, we're glad to have you here. Welcome to our home."

"Thank you." And then she smiled. "Thank you very much."

That made me raise my eyebrows a bit. Six words and a smile? My husband had gotten far more out of my sister than I had.

Keisha and I watched Mauricio trot up, and then I led her through the foyer to the dining room. "I just want to show you around because I want you to know that this house is your home, too. So you don't have to ask me for anything, unless you can't find it. But if you get hungry in the middle of the night, just come on down." From the dining room, we moved into the kitchen.

"Wow," she said when I clicked on the light. "I never saw a kitchen like this."

I watched as her fingers trailed along the black granite countertop, and then she paused. "You have two ovens."

I nodded. "It's a double oven, but I don't do as much cooking as I'd like." I paused. "But maybe we can do a little cooking together."

For the first time, I got my own smile from Keisha. "Yeah, maybe." My own smile and her first positive word — *maybe.*

From the kitchen, I led her down the three steps into our sunken family room and watched her eyes widen at all of the blessings I often took for granted. It was fun seeing my world through Keisha's eyes — the way she sat and reclined in one of the six theater-style seats we had in the family room; next the way she marveled at the hundreds of books that lined three walls in our library; and finally the way she said, "No way," when we walked into our work-out room.

"You have your own gym in your own house?"

"Well, I wouldn't call it a gym. Especially since it's not very big."

"It's big to me."

I soaked in Keisha's appreciation. "I'll save the backyard for tomorrow." I led her up the winding staircase. "Up here are the bedrooms and our home office."

"You have an office in your house, too?"

"I do," I told her. "I have my own business and Mauricio's a professor, but sometimes we bring work home, and we work in there. But I'll show you that tomorrow, too, and of course, you'll meet . . ."

"Babe," Mauricio interrupted me right when Keisha and I got to the top of the staircase, "did you put clean towels in Keisha's bathroom?"

"Yeah, her room is completely ready," I said.

I led Keisha to her room as Mauricio went into ours. When Keisha stepped inside, she stopped, and I wondered if there was something wrong. But then I realized that like downstairs, she was just taking this all in —

the platform canopied bed, the armoire, the dresser, and the forty-two-inch flat screen hanging on the wall.

The burgundy-and-white room was so plain, so regular to me; I hadn't had much time to design it. But once again, Keisha made me pause. Appreciate all that I'd been given.

I was having another one of those moments — when I just wanted to take her into my arms and let her know she was going to be fine now. After a few moments, I crossed the bedroom. "Your bathroom is here."

It took her a moment to follow me and she peeked in before she stepped in. "I've never seen a bathroom attached to a bedroom before, except in a hotel."

"Well, this is your bathroom; there are fresh towels and here's a basket of soaps and shower gels you can choose from."

"I brought my own shower gel."

"That's okay. You can use your own or what's here. Whatever you want, Keisha; it's up to you."

She nodded and gave me another smile, which this time warmed my heart. We stepped back into the bedroom, and I handed her the TV's remote. "I'm going to leave you alone now. But if you need anything, I'm just right down the hall, okay?"

"Yeah."

I waited a moment, then hugged her again. Her arms still stayed at her sides. When I stepped back, I said, "Get some sleep, and I'll see you in the morning."

"Yeah," she said.

I walked out, closed the doors, then stood in the hallway. This wasn't exactly the way I imagined it, though the fantasy I had in my head wasn't anywhere near realistic. I'd imagined that Keisha and I would have stayed up all night, sitting in the middle of her bed, chomping on popcorn and sharing secrets as sisters. I'd imagined a slumber party filled with laughter and hugs, something that I shared with Regan.

"One day," I whispered as I trekked into my bedroom. "One day."

# 16
## KEISHA

I felt like I was one of those people who took pictures of celebrities. No, I felt like one of those celebrities. No, I felt like one of those big celebrities, like a Real House-wife of Atlanta. No, those chicks were fake; Gabrielle was the real deal. I was a Real Housewife of Beverly Hills.

Pushing back the heavy drapes, I peeked out the window. I never asked what part of California Gabrielle lived in . . . was I in Beverly Hills? The thought of that made me squeal. Nobody in White Haven was ever going to believe this.

I kicked off my sneakers and socks, then began at the door. I took a panoramic picture of the whole room before I walked to the bathroom and did the same thing. Next, I took shots of the bed, the TV, and the dresser and that matching piece of furniture in the corner. Just as I got ready to sit down, I jumped up and walked to what I was sure was the closet. When I opened it, a light automatically came on.

"Whoa," I said as I walked inside. The closet was empty, but with hangers on the bars on both sides, somebody could hang a whole bunch of clothes in this joint.

Shaking my head, I went back into the bedroom and decided to take a picture of the drapes because I'd only seen curtains like this on TV. They were burgundy and thick and heavy. I was thinking they were velvet, but based on everything else in this house, they were probably some kind of expensive, specially made material that I'd never heard of before.

Once I had all the pictures I wanted, I sat on the bed, but I popped up and took a picture of the cover because I had never felt anything like it; it was like cotton-ball soft.

Dang! Who was Gabrielle? Did she really have it like this? I mean, yeah, I could tell from Instagram that she was rich, but this was more than rich. This was . . . like, Beverly Hills rich.

I swiped through all the pictures I'd taken and couldn't wait to send them to Buck.

Buck.

Did I want to send these to him? I was still mad, and he needed to recognize.

First, I sent a text:

I'm mad at you.

Less than a minute had passed when my phone vibrated.

Why you mad? Where you at?

I smiled. He wanted to know where I was? I could show him better than I could tell him. I sent picture after picture, not giving him a moment to respond. He did, though, right after I sent the last photo. He responded, but not with a text. My phone rang. I didn't answer it the first time, and Buck did what I expected him to do — he called right back.

This time, I jumped down from the bed and scurried along the carpet, which tickled my toes, but inside the bathroom, the tile was so cool under my feet. Even though I wanted to just sink into the bed and talk to Buck, I didn't want to take the chance of Gabrielle or her husband hearing me talking. So I closed the bathroom door and sat on the edge of the oversize tub.

I pressed "Talk," then said, "Yeah."

"Yo, you done hit the friggin' lottery," Buck said.

Though I grinned, I wiped the smile from my face so that I could say, "The first thing you need to do is apologize."

"What you talkin' about, boo?"

He put that *boo* in there because he heard my attitude. "You know what I'm talking about, Buck."

"What? The cemetery?"

I pressed my lips together, thinking that Buck was lucky I wasn't standing in front of him, or else again, I would've tried to punch his heart out since he kept slashing mine.

Then he said, "Yo, I'm sorry. But I just think . . ."

"We won't have no problems, Buck, if you stop trying to think for me."

"But your mom and I talked about it before she died."

"I'm gonna hang up."

"Yo! No, boo. All right. I won't talk about it."

"You better not."

"I won't, but you did hit the lottery. You know that, right?"

I leaned toward the sink and fingered a burgundy hand towel that had some letters sewn into the fabric. That towel was as thick as a blanket.

"Yo, Kesh," Buck said. "I'm trippin' off these pics. Your sister got it like that?"

"She got it beyond that." I glanced at the mirror that covered one wall. "Buck, the pictures don't even tell the whole story. You should see their house."

"Do a video call. Show me."

For a second, I stared at my phone. Sometimes, my boyfriend . . . "I can't do that."

"What? They got you on lockdown? You can't walk around their house?"

"I can go anywhere I want, but what would I look like walking around with you on the phone? I'd look like I was casing the joint or something."

"Yo, I guess that wouldn't be a good look."

"No, it wouldn't be." I stood up. "But later on, I'll get some pics for you. You're not going to believe this place." I told him about the tour I'd taken — everything from the theater seating in the family room to the gym.

"Yo, a gym in their house?"

"That's what I said. I bet we could fit ten of your mama's houses into the downstairs alone."

"Yo!" was all Buck said. And then he asked, "You think it's bigger than Que's triple-wide?"

I rolled my eyes. Really? Was Buck trying to compare his dope-dealing, credit-card scamming cousin's trailer to this? Everybody in White Haven thought Que's place was a mansion. But all Que had was a tricked-out trailer parked in his grandma's front yard.

"This is a whole 'nother level," I said, wanting to break it down for Buck. "Ain't no storm coming and blowing this place away."

"What kind of cars do they drive?"

"I don't know about them, but Regan, the girl who was with me in White Haven? Well, she drives a SUV . . ."

"That's all?"

I smirked a little before I said, "A Mercedes SUV."

"Yo, I didn't even know they made SUVs. Boo, this is it for you. So, they nice?"

I shrugged and thought about it. "Well, Regan is a witch, but Gabrielle seems cool, and her husband, he's fine for real, so easy on the eyes."

"Yo, he better not be hittin' on my girl, or I'll have somethin' for him."

Inside, I laughed. Buck couldn't even stand in the same room with Gabrielle's husband. But all I said was, "He's not black, though."

"She married a white dude?"

"Nah, he's Puerto Rican or something. I don't know. They're both nice, I guess. But I'm not here to make friends. I just want to meet my father, get paid, and get out."

194

"Yo! That's why you're my boo. You're keeping your eye on the prize. So let's do this game plan."

"No," I said as I leaned against the sink. "Let me get settled first. I'm gonna meet my father tomorrow."

"So we'll put together the plan tomorrow?"

I blew out a breath. I wanted to get the money as much as Buck, but I was smart enough to know I couldn't just grab the cash and bounce. "Just give me a little time," I told him. "I've got to get to know these people, get them to trust me."

"They probably have all kinds of credit cards," Buck said as if he hadn't heard anything I'd just said. "You can probably get her to give you one of her credit cards tomorrow. Tell her you need to buy some stuff."

I massaged my temple, trying to press away the ache on the side of my head that came courtesy of Buck. "I'm telling you, I can't just ask her for a card. You gotta give me a minute and then I'll get you ten credit cards."

"All right, but yo, this is gonna be good, right, boo?"

"Yeah, it is. But I'm tired, so I'll speak to you later."

195

"Okay, hit me up in the morning."

I clicked off the phone, then walked back into the bedroom. Pressing my ear against the door, I didn't hear any sound. They were either already asleep or these were some good walls.

Moving back to the bed, I climbed onto, then sank into, the softness. I couldn't help but sigh. I'd never been in any kind of bed that made me feel like I was floating. After a moment, I sat up. I'd seen rooms like these before — in my celebrity magazines. But I never thought I'd be staying in a place like this.

My eyes moved from one end of the room to the other. I hadn't even been here for . . . what was it? An hour? Definitely not two. And already I knew that there might have to be a change of plans. Because I was beginning to think that getting the money and then going back to White Haven wasn't enough.

Cash would just last for a little while . . . what I wanted was this kind of life.

When I opened my eyes and saw that big-screen TV hanging on the wall, my mind couldn't make sense of it. And then I remembered, I wasn't balled up in my mama's bed, I wasn't tucked in the back seat of my truck, and I wasn't even hovering in some corner in Buck's mama's house.

I was sleeping in Gabrielle Wilson Flores's home.

Rolling over, I looked up, but I couldn't see the ceiling because of this canopy.

"Wow." That was all I kept saying last night as I unpacked my few clothes and hung them in the closet. I only used ten hangers and that made the closet seem even bigger, but still, it felt like my clothes and I really belonged here.

I picked up the phone from the nightstand and checked the time — it was just a little after six. What was I doing up so early? I was wide awake, though, and what I really wanted to do was get up and walk around the house since it would be light soon. I wanted to do that before Gabrielle or her husband woke up.

I'd been washing up in McDonald's bathrooms for too many days, so, I took my time in the shower. Like everything else in Gabrielle's house, this wasn't any kind of ordinary shower. It felt like a light rain pouring over me. If water could be soft, this was it. Once I got out, though, I took care of my business quickly, the way I'd been doing at McDonald's. Since I was meeting my father today, I'd decided to wear jeans — well, that was all I had — but I'd put on a regular white T-shirt so I wouldn't be so casual. I mean, I didn't want him thinking I was just some chick without any kind of class.

Glancing at my cell phone once again, I figured I'd have plenty of time to check out the house before anyone woke up. It was just about seven and now with the light coming through the windows, I'd be able to get a good look at this place.

But the moment I opened my bedroom, my plan was ghost. It was the aroma that hit me — the smell of bacon that came swirling up the staircase. My stomach growled, and my mouth watered.

These people were up this early?

Glancing toward one end of the hallway, I walked in the other direction toward the steps. At the top, I could almost reach out and touch the chandelier that was high above my head when I walked into the house last night. Slowly, I walked down the stairs, taking in the front of the house in the daylight. Everything was white and clean and expensive. All I kept thinking was that I could live like this.

Then, right when I got to the bottom . . .

"Mommy, I want three pancakes today."

I froze.

What was that?

I heard Gabrielle's voice, a little softer. "Let's start with one, Bella, and then if you want another, I'll give it to you."

"But I know I want three already."

"Bella . . ."

Bella? Who was Bella? I scrolled through my memory, trying to recall any mention of a Bella on Instagram. But there was nothing in my mind because I hadn't seen anything about a little girl. That, I would have remembered.

"Mommy," the girl whined.

I leaned against the wall. There was a little girl here . . . did she belong to Gabrielle? Of course she did — the girl had called her Mommy.

Closing my eyes, I fought hard not to allow the sound of that voice to take me back. I breathed in a load of oxygen, trying to keep myself in the present. But still, I couldn't figure out how this had happened. Why didn't I know Gabrielle had a little girl? If I had known, I wouldn't have . . .

"Keisha?"

My eyes popped open, and I stared into the eyes of Gabrielle's husband.

He said, "Are you all right?"

I swallowed, I nodded, and tried to think of a good lie for why I was lurking at the bottom of the staircase. But I didn't have to do that because he came up with an excuse for me.

He said, "Were you looking for us? For the kitchen?"

I took a deep breath because I needed even more oxygen just to say, "Yeah, I got down here and wasn't sure . . ."

"This way" — he motioned with his head — "to the kitchen. Gabby was on her way up to see if you were awake."

He walked and I followed only because I couldn't figure out a way to tell him that I needed to go upstairs and pack and get back to White Haven. When he stepped into the kitchen, I did, too. And then I didn't see anything except for the little girl sitting at the table.

It took her a couple of moments to notice me, and when she did, she grinned, jumped up, and ran over to where I was standing.

I wasn't that tall, just about five three, five four or something like that, but she had to lean her head back to look up. "Are you my auntie?" She didn't wait for me give her an answer; she wrapped her arms around my butt because that was as high as she could reach. It was only my reflex that made me hug her back. But that same reflex took me too far back and reminded me of far too much.

In a few seconds, so many memories passed through my mind, and there was only one way I would survive. I turned and ran like I was fleeing the scene of a crime. I dashed through that kitchen, then made a left and took the staircase two steps at a time. Gabrielle's husband thought I didn't know where I was going, but he was wrong. I found my bedroom and closed those doors behind me.

I had to pause for a moment because I felt so dizzy.

Gabrielle had a daughter?

That became a mantra in my mind.

Gabrielle had a daughter!

I sank onto the bed just as there was a knock on the door. I expected the door to open and for someone, probably Gabrielle, to walk in. But nothing happened. And then another knock.

I frowned. "Come in?" I wasn't sure if that was what I was supposed to say. I mean, this was their house. They could go wherever they wanted.

The door opened and Gabrielle peeked her head inside. "May I come in?"

"Yeah."

Last night, she had left the door open when she brought me into this room, but now she closed it behind her, and I knew I was in trouble. It looked like this money train was coming to an end before it even began its journey.

She sat next to me on the bed, then when she reached for my hand, I jumped a little, but settled down when she only held me.

"Are you okay?" she asked.

I had to think quickly because the truth wasn't an option. I nodded. "Yeah."

She was quiet as if she thought I was going to say something else. When I didn't, she said, "What happened?"

I took a breath and decided to start with the truth. "I didn't know you had a daughter."

"Oh, yeah." She shook her head a little. "She was asleep when you got here last night, and I think I was getting ready to tell you about her and . . ." She looked up at me. "So . . . did Bella upset you?"

"Bella." I said her name, really liking it. "No, she didn't upset me." This was where the truth had to stop. "I was just surprised, and seeing her . . ." I had to think, think, think . . . I said, "Seeing her . . . made me think . . . of my mama."

"Oh," Gabrielle said with plenty of pity in her voice.

"Yeah," I said, keeping the story going. "Seeing . . . Bella just reminded me of all the happy times I had with her."

"I'm so sorry."

I pulled my hand away from Gabrielle and stood up. "Yeah . . . umm . . . my mama and I didn't have a lot of money, but you know . . ." I folded my arms across my chest and shrugged. "My mama did everything she could to make me happy." This story didn't have anything to do with what was going on with me right now, but it was the truth.

Gabrielle nodded, and then she stood up. Facing me, she said, "A mother's love doesn't come with a stack of dollar bills. I can tell your mom loved you by the way she raised you. I don't even know you very well, and I can see you're a kind, gentle, loving person. That all came from your mom. That all came from love."

I nodded and swiped away a tear, pissed at myself for crying, though I wasn't sure if I was crying for Mama or. . . .

"You're going to miss your mom," Gabrielle said, stopping my thoughts, "but I promise it will get easier as time goes on. You know how I know?"

I shook my head.

She said, "Because my mom passed away, too."

My head jerked back a little bit; I didn't

know — she hadn't put that on Instagram. For the first time I realized I hadn't thought about Gabrielle's mother at all.

She said, "My mom passed away seven years ago, and when it happened, I wasn't able to breathe for the first year. But then one day, I was able to not cry for at least an hour, and then the next day, I was tear-free for two hours, and it kept going that way. Then finally, I got to the day when I was able to do something more than cry."

I looked at her, waiting for her to finish her story.

She said, "I got to the day when instead of crying, I smiled." Putting her fingers on my chin, she kept on, "And one day, you'll think about your mom and you'll smile, too."

I nodded.

"But until then, I'm here. You have a family, Keisha, and we're all here for you, okay?"

I nodded again and she put her arms around me. I hadn't cried too much about my mama because crying wasn't going to bring back what God had taken away. If I'd thought crying would help, I would've cried me a river, as my mama used to say.

But since she couldn't come back from being dead, I didn't cry. For some reason, though, now I did. I was crying for my mama, and I was crying about all the stuff I couldn't talk to anyone about.

The more I cried, the tighter Gabrielle held me. And when I realized that she wasn't going to let me go, I lifted my arms and held her, too.

# 17
## KEISHA

Balancing the plate and glass in one hand, I took a deep breath before I stepped into the hallway from my bedroom. I listened for voices, but when I didn't hear anything, I took the same path that I had this morning, down the steps, pausing at the bottom. Then, I took a deep breath hoping that would give me courage, before I turned toward the kitchen.

When I saw the space was empty, I exhaled relief and set my plate (still about half-full, though I'd eaten all the bacon) and the glass on top of the spotless counter. When Gabrielle had brought that plate up to me, she'd told me to eat and then lie down for a little while. And I did. Not because I was tired and not even because I was upset. It was because I needed the time to get myself together. If I was going to stay and play this gig out, I had to find a way to deal with Bella.

"Hi."

I froze, but just for a second, and then I turned and faced the little girl.

This time, I didn't freak out. But as I studied her, it was hard not to feel a little queasy. I settled down fast, though, because she was really cute. It was her pigtails and bangs that swept across her forehead that made her so adorable. What was most interesting to me, though, was that she didn't look all that much like Gabrielle or her husband. And for a moment, I wondered if she was adopted . . . until I saw . . . that mole on her lip!

Oh my God!

I pressed my hand against my mouth and peered at her longer. This was beyond interesting . . . it was weird. This little girl looked more like me than Gabrielle. Her eyebrows weren't as thick as mine, but they were thicker than Gabrielle's, and she was a shade darker than her mother, too, closer to me.

"Mommy said that you had to rest." Bella interrupted my inspection. She tilted her head. "Did your tummy hurt?"

Inside my head, I imagined that I was calm so that my words would come out that way. "No. I was just tired because I traveled on an airplane yesterday."

"I've been on an airplane before."

"You have?"

She nodded. "Lots of times." And then she said, "You're my auntie, right?"

"Yeah, I think so."

"I'm glad," Bella said. "I have some aunties, but Mommy said they're not *really* my aunties, so I think you're my favorite one 'cause you're real."

Those words made my shoulders relax. "Oh, yeah?" Then, for the first time since I'd arrived in California, I smiled. Like, really smiled. And if I thought about it, this was probably the first time I'd smiled since my mama passed away. All because of Bella. "How do you know I'm your favorite when you don't even know me?"

"I don't know you, but I don't have to know you to like you."

Now I crouched down and looked into the eyes of the best person that I'd met in California. "Well, you know what? I like you, too."

She grinned and then wrapped her arms around my neck. Tears once again came to my eyes, but not for the same reason as this morning. Bella just made me happy.

"I see you've met our little girl."

When Gabrielle's husband walked into the kitchen, I stood. And then, I couldn't help it — I looked him up and down. Somebody was going to have to come up with a new word for *fine,* because that wasn't enough to describe how this man looked in his black turtleneck and jeans.

Once again, Bella interrupted my inspection, this time of her father.

She said, "She met me before, Daddy. Remember before she got sick?"

"Oh, yeah," he said as he lifted her into his arms. Looking at me, he asked, "Feeling better?"

I nodded. "Yeah." And then I had a question for him. "What's your name?"

He frowned as if he didn't understand, but I didn't know why. He'd never said his name to me, and the only one who called him anything was Bella . . . and this man was fine, but I wasn't going to call him Daddy.

"Mauricio," he said.

"Mauricio," I repeated. "I've heard that name before." I squinted, trying to remember.

"It's a Spanish name," Bella schooled me.

I did what I did every time she spoke — I smiled.

But before I said anything else, Gabrielle came in — wearing her own black turtleneck and jeans. The only difference between her and Mauricio was that she had on a pair of fierce, black thigh-high boots. She looked fresh.

"I just checked to see if you were awake." Gabrielle stepped right into my personal space. "Feeling better?" she asked, just like her husband.

"Yeah."

She looked at me the exact same way that I'd been looking at Bella. "Good. So, are you up to this? Going to see our . . ." The way she paused, I could see she was trying to figure out what she should call Elijah.

I gave her a break and said, "Yeah. I want to meet him."

"Good." Her smile told me that she was relieved I'd given her that answer.

"Well, then" — Gabrielle turned to Mauricio — "we're ready."

"We're going to Grandpa's house?" Bella said.

"Yup," Mauricio told her. "So let's meet back here in five minutes ready to walk out the door."

He carried Bella out of the kitchen, and when Gabrielle followed him, I saw the red bottoms on her boots. I sighed. Yup, those were fire. But since I didn't need anything besides my cell phone, I just sauntered over to the family room. Sitting in one of those leather chairs, I thought that this was better than anything I'd sat in inside the movies. I didn't turn on the TV, but I imagined watching some of my favorite shows in here. What would *Love & Hip Hop* look like on this big-screen TV? Or what would even be better — *The Real Housewives of Atlanta* or *The Real Housewives of Beverly Hills* . . .

I popped up in the chair. That was it.

Mauricio.

He looked just like that guy on that show with the same name.

Wow!

Leaning back, I crossed my legs, closed my eyes, and went back to dreaming. I imagined myself in a house like this with a husband like that.

"Keisha?"

My eyes sprang open.

"You ready?" Gabrielle asked me.

I nodded and tried to keep the smile off my face as I pushed myself up, grabbed my cell phone, and followed Gabrielle into the garage. The SUVs that were parked side by side didn't surprise me — a Lexus, a Range Rover.

Mauricio stood at the door of the Range Rover, tucking Bella into her car seat. She waved at me and I waved back as I made my way to the other side.

When I opened the car door to climb in next to her, Bella said, "Hi, Auntie."

I raised my hand to give her a high five, and she did the same, then giggled, and I giggled, too. I was still chuckling as we rolled out of the garage . . . and then I looked up at their house and all of my laughter stopped.

"Wow!" I meant to say that word inside, but it came out of me — twice. I pressed my nose against the window so I could see more. I'd thought the houses across the street were mansions, but two of them made one of Gabrielle's house.

"This is the biggest house I've ever seen in my life," I said. "How big is it?"

From the front seat, Gabrielle glanced over her shoulder. "It's not that big. Just six bedrooms and six and a half baths."

"Six bedrooms?" I bounced back against the leather seat. "You don't call that big? But there are only three of you."

Gabrielle shifted in her seat so that her body half faced me now. "Well, there're kinda four of us now, right?"

She grinned, but then I caught a quick glance of Mauricio through the rearview mirror. And his smile was upside down. He didn't look happy about what Gabrielle just said. What was his deal? Why was he frown-ing?

But then I forgot all about him because when we turned onto this wide street, there was nothing but water on one side of me. "Is that a beach?" I asked.

"Yes," Gabrielle said. "That's the Pacific Ocean, and this is Santa Monica Beach."

"You live right by the ocean?" I did that pressing my nose against the window thing again.

"Yup. Santa Monica, which is the city where we live, is a beachfront town."

As we rolled down the street, I kept my eyes on the ocean. I couldn't see a whole bunch because there were trees and grass in between the street and the water. But it was still one of the coolest things I'd seen.

"We don't live that far from my dad," Ga-brielle said. And then she added, "I mean, our . . . I mean, Elijah." She twisted in her seat so that she faced me even more. "Our father, Elijah, doesn't live too far from here. He lives in Venice and depending on traffic, only takes about ten to fifteen minutes from door to door."

I nodded because I didn't have anything to say about that, but there was something else I did want to know. "So what kind of business do you have?"

"A public relations agency," she said, not having any idea that I already knew that.

What I didn't know was my next question. "Do you make a lot of money?"

"Well, I do fine," she said, as if she wasn't at all upset by me asking. "I've been really blessed. Regan and I started this business about five years ago, and we have a couple of big clients, like Justus. Have you ever heard of him?"

"The singer?" I asked, playing my part.

"Yeah," she said. "I went to high school with him right here in Venice and —"

"Babe," Mauricio interrupted, "what time did you tell your dad we were going to be there?"

Gabrielle frowned, but turned her attention to him and answered. As she changed the subject and talked about the dinner her father had planned, I sat back and peeped Mauricio's game. Why was he checking me like that? Seemed like he wasn't that different from Regan and I was gonna have to watch him while he thought he was watching me.

I'd let him think he'd won this round. I sat back and listened to Gabrielle chat about Elijah. But I was gonna get what I needed to know — believe that.

It didn't even take us fifteen minutes

before Mauricio rolled his Range Rover into a driveway and parked behind a Ford Explorer. With just a quick glance through both windows, it was easy to see that this neighborhood wasn't anything like where Gabrielle lived. Here, the houses were small, much smaller. And they were close together, too.

Checking out the house in front of us, my eyes paused. And I stared at the man standing on the porch.

"Grandpa," Bella belted out and kicked up her legs.

My heart raced, though I didn't know why. I guessed it was because I'd spent this morning recovering from seeing Bella rather than getting ready for meeting Elijah.

But I sucked in air and pushed down all the anxiousness I felt. All I needed to focus on was the fact that I had a plan and I had a purpose.

So I jumped out of the car like it wasn't any big deal and I waited for Gabrielle to do the same. She smiled at me, then took my hand, like I was her kid or something. I didn't pull away, though, 'cause I felt stronger holding on to her. As we walked up the driveway, the man stared at me as hard as I stared at him.

He came to the edge of the porch, and

right where the steps began, Gabrielle and I stopped. He was close enough now for me to see the water that glazed his eyes. And by the time he stepped down and met us on the driveway, a tear had crept down his cheek.

Standing in my space, he raised his hands, and I did my best not to flinch as Gabrielle stepped aside.

"Keisha." He whispered my name right before he held my face in between his hands.

I tried to stand still, but I squirmed under the warmth of his touch.

He said my name again, and then another tear fell from his eye.

"Daddy," Gabrielle whispered. "Let's go inside."

It was like he was getting himself out of a trance the way he blinked and blinked, then nodded. But he still held my face and I wondered how was I supposed to walk with him holding me like this.

It wasn't until he let me go that I realized I'd stopped breathing. So it was good that Gabrielle held my hand again 'cause this was more emotional than I'd thought it was going to be. I was trying to keep this just about business, but I felt some kind of way — my heart was still beating a little faster, and my stomach was kinda fluttering.

Maybe it was just something that happened to everyone when they met their father.

Stepping inside the house, I tossed aside all of those some-kind-of-way feelings and took my mind straight back to business. As soon as we walked through the door, we were right in the living room. And from where I stood, I could see the kitchen. It was kinda like the shack behind Ms. Johnson's house, though this certainly wasn't a shack. It was a house — a real house, but a house that could fit in the entryway of Gabrielle's.

And the size wasn't the only difference. Gabrielle's place was filled with furniture that looked like it came straight out of a designer showcase. Everything was white or cream and sparkling clean. But Elijah's home was set up and filled with the kind of furniture that I was used to. He had a long, dark brown sofa that was clean but kinda dingy from use and a matching recliner. There was no piano in this living room, just regular tables at the ends of the couch that each held ordinary lamps.

Before I got here, I still hadn't decided how I was going to play this whole trip out. But one thing I knew right now was that if I were going to cash a check, it wouldn't be written by Elijah. It would all have to come from Gabrielle and that was going to be tough for two reasons: Regan and Mauricio.

But then there was Gabrielle, too. My plan had been to lean on Elijah's guilt; Gabrielle wouldn't have any regrets; I wasn't her responsibility. There was a lot that I had to work out.

Finally, Elijah said something besides my name. "Come in. Come into my home."

Still holding Gabrielle's hand, I followed as Elijah moved to the sofa. I wasn't really feeling sitting so close to him, and then Bella saved me.

"Grandpa!" She ran into the house, almost pushing me over to get to Elijah.

He lifted her up a little, kissed her cheek before he sat her on the sofa, then sat down beside her. That was when I sat down, too. It was much better with Bella in between us and Gabrielle still on the other side of me.

But though Elijah wrapped his arms around Bella, his eyes stayed on me. He didn't say anything until Mauricio sat in the recliner right next to us.

Elijah said, "So . . . Keisha."

I nodded, then shrugged, 'cause what was I supposed to say when someone just kept calling my name?

He said, "I'm so glad to meet you."

I thought about my plan, I thought about

my money, and that was why I said, "I'm glad to meet you, too."

I didn't even realize Gabrielle was still holding my hand until she squeezed it. I guessed she approved of my words.

He said, "Forgive me if I keep staring at you. It's just that . . ."

I knew what was coming because from the moment I saw that first picture of him, I thought we looked alike, too.

"It's just that . . . you look like my mother."

My eyes widened.

He said, "You look just like your grand-mother."

"She does, Daddy," Gabrielle said. "And that means she looks like you. 'Cause you look like Granny, too."

He chuckled, a laugh that came from his belly, like the Santa Claus I used to see at the malls. Not that I ever believed in any kind of Santa Claus. How could I believe in a dude who never came down my chimney?

"Well, I guess you're right," he said. It was like the chuckle made him relax, because he leaned into the couch's cushions, then rested his arm on the back. "So, I know you haven't seen much, but how do you like California so far?"

I shrugged. "It's cool."

"We haven't had time to see anything," Gabrielle jumped in. "But we'll take her to all the sights."

"Can we take her to Disneyland?" Bella asked. Before anyone answered, Bella continued, "Disneyland is the best place on earth. Did you know that?"

"No," I said.

"Have you ever been to Disneyland?"

I shook my head.

Bella poked out her bottom lip like what I'd just said was the saddest thing she'd ever heard. "Everybody should go to Disneyland." She leaned forward and pleaded, "Mommy, we *have* to take her."

"We will. We'll take her there and everywhere else she wants to go."

Bella clapped. Elijah laughed. Gabrielle smiled. But when I looked at Mauricio, his face was blank — well, maybe *blank* wasn't the right word, 'cause he stared at me as if he were trying to see into my soul.

Then Gabrielle turned to Elijah. "Is everything ready for dinner?"

He nodded. "It is. They delivered the whole spread about twenty minutes ago." He motioned toward the kitchen. "A whole Sunday soul food dinner. Y'all ready to eat?"

"I am." Bella clapped again, and this time, even Mauricio took a moment from his case study of me and laughed.

"I'll get everything set up." Gabrielle stood. "Keisha, you want to help me?"

I didn't, but I didn't want to be left behind either, not with Elijah, who kept staring at me because to him I looked like his mama, nor with Mauricio, who kept staring at me because to him I must've looked like some kind of thief. So I dumped my phone on the couch, stood and followed Gabrielle into the kitchen, which (like the living room) didn't look anything like what she had at her house. Elijah's appliances were like the refrigerator and stove that my mama and I had in Mrs. Johnson's shack — old and shabby.

"So let's check out what we have," Gabrielle said, turning to the five pans of food on the counter by the sink.

When Gabrielle uncovered the foil, and the aromas of catfish and chicken, macaroni and cheese, and collard greens and yams scented the air, I was shocked. This was the same food that I ate down in White Haven. I didn't know what I'd expected, but I was sure surprised (and happy) to see some fried catfish.

Gabrielle showed me where all of the dishes were, and together we laid out the plates, the glasses, and the utensils. I had just finished folding the napkins the way Gabrielle showed me, when she stood back and said, "We work well together, don't we?"

I shrugged. I mean, we hadn't done all that much, but if it was good for Gabrielle, then it was good for me.

"Okay, everyone." Gabrielle walked back into the living room. "If you're ready to eat, we're ready to serve."

"Yay," Bella cheered as she leaped down from the sofa.

But just as Elijah and Mauricio stood, the doorbell rang, and Gabrielle rushed to open it.

She said, "I was hoping you guys would make it," to someone that I couldn't yet see. "Talk about being right on time."

"That must mean we're about to eat."

I heard her before I saw her, and I groaned. Really? Regan? On top of Mauricio?

She stepped into the house followed by some man, and all the good feelings I'd had inside went outside. Why was she here?

I hung back, leaning on the wall that separated the living room and kitchen, and watched as everyone greeted Regan and the man (whom they called Doug) like they were movie stars.

When Bella shouted, "Auntie Regan," I

wondered if I was still her favorite. And then when she hugged Regan and the man like she didn't want to let them go, I doubted that I was.

Regan didn't look my way, though I knew for sure she'd seen me when she walked in. I sighed but then perked up a little when Elijah said, "This is the first time I have a chance to congratulate you two." He hugged Regan, then slapped Doug on the back. Elijah continued, "This makes me happy. Another grandchild."

His words made me frown. Was Regan having a baby?

Those words seemed to bring me back to Elijah's memory. "Keisha" — he motioned with his hand — "come over here." He didn't wait for me to walk to him. He came to where I was standing, and now he was the one who took my hand. But it wasn't like when I walked with Gabrielle. Elijah had to kinda yank me along because I never walked willingly to the enemy.

Before I even got there, the man everyone called Doug reached out his hand to me. "Hey, Keisha, I'm Regan's husband."

I shook his hand, but since he wasn't on my side, I didn't say anything.

And then Regan stepped up to me. "Good to see you," she said.

Instead of calling her a liar, I just glared at her.

She didn't seem fazed, though. All she did was look around at everyone and say, "I'm so glad we're all here." She reached into her tote and pulled out a large envelope. No one said anything as she handed it to Elijah. "I found some of the best clinics in West LA for paternity testing. And these will give you results quickly." Then Regan looked at me and smiled, a shots-fired kind of smile, aimed at me.

A paternity test? Was this about me? But why would she want me to take a test when these people found me?

My eyes moved to Gabrielle, and then to Elijah.

His eyes were almost as wide as mine. "What's this?" Now he looked at Regan. "I didn't ask for this. I don't need this."

"Oh" — Regan began as if she were surprised — "I thought Gabrielle talked to you."

"No, I didn't." She snatched the envelope from her father's hands. "And I don't want to talk about it now." She glanced at me before she tucked the envelope into her purse.

"Well, I want to talk about it." I folded my arms.

Now all eyes were on me and I didn't care. Right now, I wanted to punch somebody — that was how mad I was.

"We don't need to talk about this right now," Gabrielle said. She glared at Regan. "We were just getting ready to sit down and have a family dinner, together for the first time. So this is *not* the time."

Regan held up her hands. "I'm sorry. I was just thinking that since everyone was here and this is something that you need to take care of right away . . ."

"Right away, but not right now," Gabrielle snapped.

"What? You don't think I'm his daughter?" I challenged Regan and Gabrielle. "You think I'm running some scam or something?"

Gabrielle said, "Nobody thinks that, Keisha."

But Regan raised her eyebrows as if she wasn't sure.

I said, "Look, I didn't come to all of you." My eyes went around the circle where we stood. "You all came to me. But if you don't want me here . . ."

"Nobody is saying that." Elijah stepped closer to me. "I don't need any kind of test. I know you're my daughter. And my God" — Elijah looked at me — "she looks like my mother." He turned to Regan. "I don't need a test. Keisha is my daughter."

"Pops" — Mauricio stepped forward — "I know this is not the most comfortable thing to talk about, and maybe this wasn't the best time, but Regan is just looking out for you."

Regan and her husband nodded.

Mauricio said, "This is good for you and Keisha."

"How is it good for me?" I asked.

"Because it's good when everyone knows for sure," Mauricio said.

"So y'all weren't sure before you sent her" — I used my thumb to point to Regan — "to come and interrupt my life?"

Now Regan crossed her arms on her chest. "Your life?"

I knew that was another shot fired. Like she was saying I didn't have any kind of life for anybody to interrupt. "You know what?" For the first time, I moved. I searched the space for my phone. I'd left it on the couch, but it wasn't there. "Where's my phone?" I almost screamed.

"I'm . . . sorry . . ." Bella's voice was soft. "Here it is." She held it up to me, her lips trembling like she was afraid. I hated that — how could I be her favorite if I scared her? And I wanted to crouch down and tell her everything was okay.

But I couldn't, because it wasn't. And all I wanted to do was get out of there. Maybe even get out of California.

I was careful not to snatch the phone from Bella, but that was as far as I could go. Once I had the phone in my hand, I stomped toward the door.

Gabrielle and Elijah spoke at the same time.

"Keisha," he said.

"Where are you going?" she asked.

My hand was already on the doorknob, but I had to pause with Gabrielle's question. I didn't know where I was going, I only knew I had to get out of there. Turning back to face them, I blinked over and over. Because I couldn't let them see me cry — not even mad tears. And especially not Regan.

Gabrielle rushed to me. "I know you're upset, and I'm sorry. But you don't have to be. We're not going to talk about this" — she paused and turned around to the others — "right?"

Regan pressed her lips together as if she had something to say but was trying her best not to say it.

"I just want to leave," I said.

"No," Gabrielle said.

"Why?" Elijah asked.

"Because my mama taught me not to stay anywhere I'm not wanted."

Elijah said, "You're not only wanted here, Keisha, you're welcomed. This is where you belong. I don't want a test. I don't need a test. I am and want to be your father."

"Well, there are certain people who don't want that."

"That's not what we're saying," Mauricio piped in. "We want to do a test as much for you, Keisha, as for Elijah. Don't you want to be sure?"

Looking at Regan, I said, "She told me everyone was sure."

"I never said that," Regan said in a tone that was *really* calling me a liar.

"I just wish everyone would calm down," Gabrielle said. She looked at each one of us. "Let's eat and forget about this."

Regan said, "That's fine with me. We can forget about this . . ."

I narrowed my eyes.

She continued, "Until tomorrow."

"I'm out," I said.

"Regan!" Gabrielle shouted.

I reached for the door again, and this time I couldn't hold my tears back. Regan was trying to mess this all up for me. I wouldn't sit down and break even stale bread with her.

Gabrielle said, "Keisha, please wait."

"I don't want to. I just want to go back to your house," I said, finally getting the door open and stepping out onto the porch. That was when I let it go, just let the tears flow.

Gabrielle and Elijah followed me outside. When Elijah looked at me, I held my hands over my face.

"I'm sorry for all of this," he said. "I'm gonna shut it all down. You don't have to worry, Keisha."

I swiped the tears from my cheeks and shook my head. "I just want to go," I said, crossing my arms and planting my feet. "I can take a cab." I didn't have any money, but at this point, they owed me at least enough cash to catch a ride.

"No, you're not taking a cab." Gabrielle sighed. "I'll take you home."

"Thank you," I whispered.

"Just let me get in there, get my purse, and get Bella." She gave me a long look, then shook her head.

Even though we were alone, I still couldn't bring myself to look into Elijah's eyes, so I kept my gaze on his feet.

He stepped closer. "Keisha." With his fingers, he lifted my chin and held my head up so that I had to look at him. "I wish you would stay."

"I can't."

After a moment, he nodded. "I really want to spend time with you, get to know you because I am your father."

I took a deep breath and nodded. "Maybe . . ."

"What?"

"Maybe I can see you . . . tomorrow."

He smiled. "I'd like that. And you know what?"

This time, I was the one to say, "What?"

"It'll just be you and me. And we'll leave all of those clowns in there behind."

Even though I was crying, I laughed. And then, for the first time in my life, my father hugged me, and I did nothing to stop him.

# 18
## GABRIELLE

I peeked through the open door of Keisha's room and smiled as I watched Keisha and Bella leaning back on the pillows in the center of the bed. My daughter was reading to my sister and I marveled that a day that had been filled with so many tears for Keisha was nothing but laughter for her now.

"Bella." I stepped inside and they both looked up. "You haven't given Keisha a break since we came home."

"But she likes being with me, Mommy," Bella told me. "And I don't want her to be by herself."

Keisha laughed. "And I don't want to be by myself." Then to me, she said, "It's all right. I love hanging out with Bella."

"Okay, but" — I glanced at my watch — "it's almost bedtime."

"Ah, no," Bella whined and snuggled into Keisha's side a little more.

Keisha looked down at my daughter. "What about if I help you get ready for bed?"

"Yay," Bella cheered as she wrapped her arms around Keisha's neck.

I crossed my hands, pressing them over my heart.

Keisha said, "Come on, let's go, and then we can read a little more in your room."

"Okay." Bella climbed down before she grabbed Keisha's hand and the two scurried past me.

With Bella taken care of, I went into my bedroom and clicked on the television. I'd never expected this kind of ending when I'd carried a crying Bella away from her dad and grandfather. By the time I hooked her into her car seat and jumped into the driver's seat of Mauricio's Range Rover, I had two hysterical humans in my back seat.

But with a stop by Bella's second-favorite place — In-N-Out Burger (and it turned out Keisha loved hamburgers, too), I was able to dry all tears. Over burgers, fries, and three chocolate shakes, we cried, but now the tears were from laughter at Bella's silly knock-knock jokes.

"Knock, knock."

"Who's there?"

"Who."

"Who *who*?"

"That's what an owl says."

She had a dozen that were just as silly, but it was wonderful because Keisha (and Bella) were still laughing when we came home. And that gave me a chance to apologize to Keisha again. But then it gave her a chance to tell me that if I wanted her to take the test, she would.

She hadn't waited for my answer. She'd just taken Bella's hand and gone up to her bedroom.

Just thinking about that made me warm in all kinds of ways. But then my blood turned cold when I heard the beep of the alarm as the front door opened. I jumped from the bed and rushed down the stairs just as Mauricio locked the door.

He faced me, but it still took him a moment to say, "Hey, babe."

I rolled my eyes and then walked past him, marching into the kitchen, knowing he would follow.

"Okay," he said. "You're upset."

I reached into the refrigerator for a bottle of water. "How was dinner?"

"You were the one who told me to stay."

"Because you didn't seem like you wanted to leave."

"I didn't." He shook his head. "I wanted

to talk to your father about this, Gabby."

"Why? Why is a paternity test so important to you?"

"Because we have to know. Do you know your father is talking about changing his will?"

I leaned my head back, a bit surprised since he hadn't mentioned that to me.

"See," Mauricio said, responding to my reaction. "He just told us, and I'm not going to let him do that without knowing one hundred percent that Keisha is his daughter."

I folded my arms. "None of this is necessary."

"Is this you talking or Keisha?" He narrowed his eyes. "If everything is cool, why is Keisha so against it?"

When he made me mad, Mauricio made me mad to new levels of madness. Especially since he was standing there all smug. "She's not against it." I stayed silent just to let those words sink in. And it worked; the smirk faded from his lips. I continued, "She said she'd do it if I wanted her to."

"Oh." He grabbed his own water. "Well, that's good, but I still think there's more going on with her. She has some ulterior motives."

"What?" And then I lowered my voice, not

wanting to take any chances of Keisha overhearing us. "What are you talking about?"

He'd followed my lead and kept his voice at a whisper. "Why was she asking you all of those questions?"

I frowned. "What questions?"

"In the car this morning . . . she was asking you how big the house is and how much you make."

I hardly remembered what Mauricio was talking about. "She's curious. She's never been anywhere. She wants to know everything. What's wrong with that?"

"I'm just saying, I'm going to feel so much better if we know for sure before we open more than our home to her. I'm concerned about opening our hearts."

"Whatever," I said. "She's going to do it, so this is no longer a thing."

"Good," he said.

"Good," I said, feeling like a teenager as I mimicked him, then stomped away. I kept my steps heavy even as I climbed the staircase. I wanted Mauricio to know he had pissed me off.

At the top, I turned toward Bella's bedroom and paused at the door, peeking in and my warm heart returned. I watched Keisha kneeling beside Bella's twin bed, her hand rubbing my daughter's hair as Bella slept.

"You're so precious, Bella," Keisha whispered.

She was so good with my daughter, and I looked forward to Keisha and Bella really bonding. I had a feeling it was going to be good for both of them.

She said, "So precious."

I smiled.

"So precious, my precious daughter."

Now I frowned.

"My precious daughter, my baby, my love."

Why was she saying that? I stepped into the room, then stopped. The way she stroked my daughter's hair, I could tell she was having a moment.

So I began to step away. But what was this moment about? I backed up and turned to my bedroom.

For the rest of the night, I couldn't get Keisha's words out of my mind — not when I was awake, and not even while I slept.

# 19
## KEISHA

I looked at myself in the mirror, then turned off the bathroom light before I strolled back into the bedroom. One of the *Real House-wives* shows was on, but it wasn't Atlanta nor Beverly Hills, so I really didn't care.

I rolled onto the bed, then put the TV on mute because I needed the quiet to think.

Yesterday, Regan had tried to blow my world up, but it had still turned out to be a pretty good day once Gabrielle got me out of there. Between some good hamburgers and then hanging out with the best person in California, I thought it would all go down smooth from here. I thought that today, my second full day in California, would be even better than yesterday.

But something had gone left. Something was weird. And that something weird was Gabrielle, who showed up to my room first thing this morning:

The knock made me sit up straight in the bed. It sounded like the police were at the door.

I said, "Come in," although Gabrielle was already stepping into the bedroom. She didn't wait the way she always did before.

"I'm sorry, I didn't mean to wake you."

"That's okay." As I pushed myself up, I checked out the black pantsuit she wore. It was designer for sure. But one thing she wasn't wearing was a smile.

Her eyebrows were tight, almost coming together when she said, "I just wanted to let you know that I'm taking Bella to school, and then I'll be going into my office."

"Oh. Okay." I was a little surprised; she wasn't acting like she wanted me to go with her. She wasn't even acting as if she liked me.

"I'll be back."

Even though her face was still in a frown, her words made me feel a little better. "Oh, okay. I'll get ready and maybe I can go with you."

She paused, looked down, then raised her eyes to stare straight at me. "I'll be back because I'm going to make an appointment with one of the clinics."

I didn't blink.

"For the test. The paternity test."

I stayed still.

"You're still fine with it, right?"

"Yeah." I was glad that my voice wasn't trembling since everything else inside of me was.

She stood there as if she thought I was gonna get up and give her a hug or something. But I stayed in that bed and stared and didn't breathe until she said, "I'll be back in a couple of hours."

When she'd left the room, I had tried to figure out what was going on. Yeah, I had told Gabrielle I would take the test, but I'd only said that because I thought she was on my side. I didn't think that she would *make* me do it.

What happened? It had to be Mauricio; he'd told her something. What had he talked about with Elijah, Regan, and her husband after we left? And if Mauricio was acting this way, was Elijah doubting me now, too? Had Elijah and Gabrielle joined the side of Regan and Mauricio? Did I have four foes and no friends?

The creaking sound of the garage door lifting up snatched me back from my thoughts. I jumped from my bed, ran to the window, as Gabrielle's Lexus rolled into the garage.

I backed up and paced from the window to the door and back again wondering what I should do. I'd have a much better idea of how to make my moves if I knew what had changed with Gabrielle.

And then, "Keisha?" she yelled up from downstairs.

I grabbed my purse, my cell phone, my sweater, took a deep breath, and then stepped into the hallway. She was already halfway up the staircase.

She said, "Are you ready?"

"Yeah." I tried to read her, but all she gave me was a nod before she turned around.

When I followed her through the kitchen, she asked, "Did you eat breakfast?"

I shook my head because I hadn't even thought about food. I hadn't thought about anything except trying to figure out why Gabrielle had turned on me.

My mind stayed on that until . . . I got inside her SUV. When I sank into that soft leather seat, my thoughts were put on hold. Because this car? Was fire! Not only was everything in this joint leather with wood that looked like chocolate candy, but with the push of one button, I felt like I was a passenger in a spaceship.

But once we backed out of the garage and the car was quiet, I went right back to wondering. As Gabrielle drove, I thought about it so much that I finally just came out and said, "Are you mad at me?"

Even though she kept her eyes on the road, I could tell my question made her frown — or at least frown a little more than she'd been doing. "No." She glanced at me for a second. "Why would you think that?"

I shrugged as I looked out at the ocean. "You seem kinda quiet. Like something is wrong."

"No." Then, with one hand, she reached over and squeezed mine. "I just have a lot on my mind. Business."

There was only one kind of business that concerned me. "The paternity test?"

She was quiet for a moment, then said, "Are you concerned about the test?"

"No." I said that as strongly as I could just so she would know. "It's not like I lied about anything. You guys came to me so I'm not concerned about it. It's just that . . . yesterday you seemed like you were on my side."

"I was then, and I am now."

"So why do you want me to take the test? I mean, you said that I look like Elijah and he said that I look like his mother."

241

"I don't have any doubts," she said. "But I want to make sure that no one else has any either. I want everyone to not only look at you and know, but have the science to back that up." She squeezed my hand again. "This is as much for you as it is for everyone else, okay? It's a good thing, I promise."

I nodded, but I didn't have too much time to think about what she'd just said because about a minute later, she swung into a small parking lot with a sign: Beach Cities Lab. By the time she pulled up next to a truck and turned off the ignition, she was back to being serious. So I opened my door and slid down the leather seat. But when I looked up, there was Elijah.

He closed the door for me. "Hi, Keisha." He hugged me before I could say anything, then added, "I hope you're feeling better . . . after yesterday."

"Yeah."

Gabrielle came from around the front of her car. "Hey, Daddy." After a hug for him, she said, "So, y'all ready for this?"

Elijah and I nodded and Gabrielle led the way — she was in front of me; Elijah was behind me. Inside the clinic, I moved right to the chairs lined against the wall as Gabrielle and Elijah walked to the receptionist.

As I watched them, it became harder to breathe. I mean, I knew what this test was going to say; I'd known about Elijah Wilson for years before he'd ever heard my name. But still . . .

Then I looked down at Elijah's shoes. And that made me laugh. He actually had on a pair of Timbs. Really? That old man had on Timbs with his jeans. Just looking at his Timbs made me forget . . . until Gabrielle and Elijah came toward me.

Gabrielle said, "This isn't going to take much time." She sat on one side of me, and Elijah sat on the other. It was funny the way they always put me in the middle. I didn't know if they were trying to protect me or gang up on me.

Gabrielle kept talking. "All they're going to do is take a swab of your cheek and then a swab of Dad's."

I frowned. "Like a cotton swab?"

She nodded. "To get cells from inside your cheek."

"And then?"

She shrugged. "That's it."

That seemed like too simple a thing for all of this trouble. I said, "I hope they don't charge a lot if that's all they're going to do."

Gabrielle and Elijah laughed even though I wasn't trying to make any kind of joke.

"Well, we could have done this at home through the mail," Gabrielle explained. "But this way, we'll have the results faster . . . in two days."

"Yeah," Elijah said. "We'll get this behind us."

Gabrielle nodded at his words. I just shrugged because I didn't think this was going to make any difference for Regan and Mauricio.

"Ms. Jones." A lady wearing a lab coat nodded when I stood up, then asked me to follow her. I did what she told me as if this were no big deal, even though it was probably the second-biggest deal since I'd been born.

She led me into a room, had me sit in a chair while she ripped open this little tinfoil-looking package, told me to open my mouth, and then in less than a minute, I was walking out just as Elijah was going into another room.

Ten minutes after that, we were back in Gabrielle's car, and this time she was smiling the way she'd smiled yesterday. Another ten minutes, and we parked on the street in front of a restaurant that was right on the beach.

I got out of the car feeling kinda excited. I'd never been to a beach before.

"We can go on in and get a table," Gabrielle said as she hit the fob of her car. "Daddy will be here in a minute."

Gabrielle told the hostess that we wanted to sit on the deck, and she led us through the entire restaurant before we stepped outside.

"Wow." It felt like I could reach out and touch the water.

While Gabrielle sat down, I walked to the ledge, inhaled and took in the fragrance of the Pacific. Right now, it smelled better than any of my mama's perfumes.

"Hey, Daddy," Gabrielle said.

I didn't want to turn around, but I did. Then, Elijah pulled out a chair for me to sit down, and even though I didn't want to, I did that, too.

He said, "This is my favorite restaurant, and I wanted you to see it."

This girl who looked like she was way younger than me came out with the menus; I read over mine, but I couldn't figure out any of this fancy food: spinach pappardelle pasta, Dungeness crab enchiladas, seared crab cakes. On the other side of the menu was the one thing I recognized, but not even that was regular: it was an eight-ounce Angus sirloin cheeseburger. At least I would recognize the beef patty and bun when it came out of the kitchen.

I told the waitress that I wanted the cheeseburger — and Gabrielle and Elijah stared at me as if I'd just broken the law.

"What?"

"This place is called the Lobster House." Elijah asked me, "Don't you like seafood?"

"I like fried catfish."

Gabrielle said, "Would you like to try something different?"

*No.* What was wrong with a cheeseburger? I shrugged, and I guessed Gabrielle took that as a yes.

She told the girl, "Get us two lobster rolls."

When Elijah said, "Make that three," the waitress took our menus and went away.

Gabrielle said, "If you don't like the lobster roll, then we'll order the cheeseburger for you. But I have a feeling you're going to love it. Everyone does."

I didn't bother to ask her what a lobster roll was. I guessed I'd see soon enough. For a little while, we just sat at our table not saying anything. It felt like we were supposed to be quiet here, just looking at the waves hitting the sand.

"This is so cool."

Elijah said, "Your mother always dreamed of going to the beach."

My eyes had been on the ocean, but now I faced him. "How do you know that?"

"She told me a long time ago."

"Wow." I knew this man was my father, but I'd never thought about him with my mama. I mean, yeah, I knew they'd been together — like that — but I'd never spent a whole lot of time thinking about my mama with Elijah or any of the other men. I certainly never thought that she did any talking.

"Keisha . . ."

When he said my name like that, I knew something serious was about to go down.

"If you have any questions about your mother . . . and me, I want you to feel free to ask, okay?"

I shrugged. I nodded.

He waited another moment before he asked me, "Is there anything you want to know?"

It sounded like he wanted me to ask something, so I asked the first thing that came to my mind: "Did you like her?"

He leaned back in his chair and repeated what I'd said. Then, "Yeah, I did like her." He smiled. "That's a good question, Keisha. Because I didn't know Daisy well enough to love her, but I did like her. She got me through some trying times on the road."

I nodded, and then another question came to my mind. "Did you know about me?"

He slowly nodded, but right when he parted his lips, Gabrielle reached all the way across the table and put her hand over his. "Daddy, maybe this should wait until . . ."

"Until when?" he interrupted her. "Until we get the results? I don't need those, sweetness. She's mine."

*She's mine.* Going back in my head, I tried to remember if anybody had ever in my life said that about me.

Elijah said, "I didn't know about you. But . . . I did know that your mother was pregnant."

I tilted my head. "So if you knew she was pregnant, then you did know about me, right?"

He raised his hand. "Let me explain. The last time I saw your mother, she told me she was pregnant, but I didn't think that had anything to do with me. I'd only passed through White Haven five or six times, and I knew what your mom . . ."

When he took too long to finish, I said, "Did for a living?" and completed the sentence for him.

He nodded. "So when she told me she was pregnant, and that I might be the father, I . . ." He stopped again.

"Didn't believe her." I said what he didn't want to say.

It took him a moment, but he nodded again. "Keisha, if I had known then . . ."

"When did you find out?"

He squinted as if he were thinking back. "How long has it been? Two weeks maybe. I gave your mom's letter to Gabby so that we could find you. Your mother didn't leave a good trail, not a phone number or any way to reach her."

"She was in a hospice; she didn't really have a phone." He nodded and I could tell he wanted to know what had happened but was too polite to ask. So I told him, "She died from complications from HIV." Now I nodded. "Folks don't know people still die from AIDS, but the problem with Mama was she didn't get treated for a long time, so her immune system was shot — at least that's what the doctors told us. She ended up with every infection in the world, poisoning her blood, but it was her heart that killed her. It just stopped. It was too weak to go on."

He put his hand over mine. "I'm sorry."

I shrugged. "I'm sorry, too. 'Cause my mama was a really good person."

"From the short time that I knew her, I could tell that she was. No matter what . . ."

Then he snapped his mouth shut like he was sorry for something he was about to say.

So again, I finished for him, "No matter what she did for a living?" I didn't let him answer. "I'm not embarrassed by that. People tried to embarrass me my whole life, calling my mama a whore. And yeah, she was. But I know that what makes you good is not what you do but who you are. And who my mama was, was a great woman who loved and took care of me."

I looked at Elijah and then over at Gabrielle, and without saying a word, I asked them if there was anything else they wanted to know about my mama.

At first they didn't say anything, but then Elijah glanced at Gabrielle and said, "Well, what do you think?"

It wasn't until then that I realized Gabrielle had tears in her eyes. This time she was the one to reach for my hand. "I think . . . I'm really proud to have you as my little sister."

When she leaned over to hug me, that put a few tears in my eyes, too.

# 20
## KEISHA

I hoped Gabrielle didn't live too far away from this restaurant, because this here lobster roll was the truth and I wanted one every single day.

"So you like it?" Gabrielle smiled.

This time when I nodded, I nodded for real.

"Do you want another one?" Elijah asked.

Even though I did, I shook my head. I'd figure out a way to come back here.

"So yesterday, when I asked you about California, you hadn't seen all of this" — Elijah waved his hand toward the ocean — "right? What do you think now?"

"I can't believe the beach is like right here in front of me. I've never seen a beach in person before."

"Did you travel much out of White Haven?"

I nodded. "We'd go to Little Rock and Pine Bluff sometimes. Especially since the bigger malls were there."

He asked, "Have you ever traveled outside of Arkansas?"

I shook my head. "Not until I got on the plane with Regan."

He nodded. "So what do you do down there in White Haven?"

Okay, this was like the third question, which meant he was leading up to something. That made me put my guard up, though I kept a smile on my face.

"I don't do too much," I said, being careful. "I spent the last year taking care of my mama. She had just died when Regan got there."

Elijah shook his head a little. "In her letter, your mom said you didn't have any relatives."

This wasn't a question, but he was still fishing for information. "We didn't. But that was cool. It was just me and Mama; we took care of each other."

I guessed that was a good answer, 'cause that made Gabrielle and Elijah smile.

He wiped his face with his napkin, then rested both of his arms on the table. "Keisha . . ."

Seemed like I was about to find out the real reason for all of his questions.

"I really want to get to know you," he said.

He paused like he wanted me to say something. So I said, "Yeah."

He took a deep breath. "What do you think . . . what would you say if I were to ask you to stay in Los Angeles?"

I frowned, not understanding what he was getting at.

He added quickly, "Not permanently — I mean, I'd love you to live here permanently, but if you don't like it and you miss home, you should definitely go back. But if you're able to, I'd like you to give us, to give Los Angeles a chance. I'd like for you to think about living in Los Angeles for a while."

From the moment I got here and saw how they were living, this thought had been in my mind. I didn't want to tell him that, though. So I said, "But in White Haven, I'm working . . ."

He waved his hand. "You can find a job here."

"You definitely can," Gabrielle piped in. "Because if you take Daddy up on this offer to stay, not only can you live with me, but you can work with me, too."

"Oh, sweetness" — Elijah grinned — "that would be great."

I needed to understand exactly what she was saying. "Work with you?"

She nodded like she'd just gotten a new

toy or something. "I have my own business. We started talking about it the other day, but it's a PR firm and I'm doing pretty well."

Elijah chuckled, and I knew what that meant. "Pretty well" didn't describe how Gabrielle's firm was doing. She had top entertainers and corporate clients. She'd been in *Essence* as one of the 40 Under 40. She was making bank.

Gabrielle said, "And not only are we doing well, but we're still bringing on new clients, so I could certainly use you there right by my side." Her grin was so wide she looked like that beaming-face all-teeth emoji.

I swallowed, and then I took a sip of water because my throat was so dry. Gabrielle wanted me by her side? I'd come here to get the money, and now she was offering me the life.

Maybe God was truly trying to give everything back to me.

"I think this is a great idea," Elijah said. "I hope you'll consider it."

"Come on," Gabrielle added, still with that emoji face. "If it's the test you're worried about, the three of us know what the results will be."

They kept talking, one and then the other,

trying to convince me.

After a couple more rounds, I finally said, "Yeah."

"Yeah?" Gabrielle and Elijah said together.

I nodded and as Elijah leaned over to hug me, Gabrielle squeezed my hand.

I was in.

We stood in front of Gabrielle's Lexus and the way Elijah looked at me, I knew he expected me to hug him. But I just stood there, so he hugged me.

Leaning back, he put his hands on my shoulders. "So, I'm going to see you soon?"

"Yeah."

He grinned. "That's your favorite word, isn't it?"

I had to press my lips together so that I wouldn't say that again.

Elijah hugged Gabrielle before he trotted away from us . . . in his Timbs.

I guessed I was smiling when I slid into Gabrielle's SUV, because she glanced at me and said, "You're happy."

"I am." And then I added, "It must've been the lobster roll."

And together, Gabrielle and I busted out laughing.

She slapped on her sunglasses and when she pulled the car away from the curb, she said, "I took the rest of the day off, but I have to run a couple of errands. Do you want to go with me or head home?"

It didn't even take me a second to consider. "Can I go back to your place? I wanna check out what clothes I have since I'm going to be working with you."

She nodded. "Okay, but don't worry about that. We're pretty casual at work, and anything you need, we'll go shopping. You wouldn't mind that, would you?"

I leaned to the side so that I could get a good look at her as she drove. Was she kidding me? What girl didn't like to shop? Especially to all the expensive places where I was sure she'd be taking me. By the time we rounded the driveway to her front door, I was already imagining all the new designer outfits I'd be wearing this time next week. And shoes, too. Oh, and boots — I couldn't forget the boots. I wanted a pair of those over-the-knee boots she'd worn yesterday. I wanted a pair in black, and maybe even blue to wear with my jeans.

Gabrielle left the SUV running as she jumped out, then trotted up the two steps to her front door to unlock it for me. As I walked up behind her, she said, "While I'm out, I'll get a key for you."

Was she talking about a key to this house?

"Okay," I said.

As if this were something she did every day, she gave me a hug, then waved to me over her shoulder. "I'll be back in a couple of hours. Right after I pick up Bella. Mauricio will be home at about that time, too."

I waved back, then stepped inside and closed the front door behind me. I leaned against it for a moment, just taking in this view. This was only the second time that I'd walked in through the front door.

Walking into their house this way — it really was impressive, it was majestic. Like this house was built for a king and queen.

My eyes roamed over the staircase and then up to that chandelier that looked like it had a hundred lights and a thousand crystals.

I closed my eyes and tried to take myself to a place in the future, but a time that was not too far away. I imagined when I'd have this house — or one just like it.

Opening my eyes, I wanted everything in *my* house to be the same — the staircase, the chandelier . . . I looked to the right — I wanted a living room with soft white couches and chairs just like Gabrielle's. Oh, and a piano. I wanted a white piano, too.

As I roamed through the first floor, I imagined that this really was my home, and as I went from room to room, there was nothing I would change. I wanted to keep that mahogany dining room set that I only knew was mahogany because I'd seen it in one of the designer magazines. I'd keep the kitchen exactly the same, too — everything sparkling white with all of these stainless steel appliances, especially the dishwasher — I'd never had a dishwasher.

I paused in the family room. Maybe instead of six chairs, I'd have ten. And in the gym, I would have more than just an elliptical machine and treadmill, I'd add a bicycle and a couple of weight stations. Oh, yeah, I could really see myself in a house just like this. Especially now that I was going to be working right by Gabrielle's side.

Turning back to the staircase, I ran up the steps because there was one room that I really wanted to see. But when I got to the top, I paused. I wasn't sure if I should do it — I didn't want to be caught. But then, Gabrielle had just left; she wouldn't be back for a while, so I had plenty of time to sneak a peek.

Their bedroom was all the way down on the other end of the hall, making it almost feel like it was in a different part of the house — it was like a suite. That's what the Beverly Hills housewives called it. There were double doors to their bedroom, too, and again I paused before I took a breath, then pushed them open wide.

For a moment, I just stood there. This place looked like a showroom — none of the housewives on any of the shows could ever compete with this. It didn't even look like anyone slept in this room.

The first thing that struck me was the color — everything was a soft gold. In magazines, they called it bronze. Everything was a shade of that color, from the tufted bed to the cover and the dozens of decorative pillows that lined the headboard. Even the chandelier was a bronze circular fixture that hung high above the bed.

The next thing that I loved were the three floor-to-ceiling window panels that covered one wall of the bedroom and welcomed in the sun.

"This is incredible," I whispered as I turned and saw my reflection in the antique floor mirror. Ever since I'd seen one of these in a magazine, I'd wanted to have one.

This room was everything I thought it would be, but now what I really wanted to see was Gabrielle's closet. I spun around in a circle, but there were no doors, only the one that led to the bathroom. Where in the world did they keep their clothes?

But I forgot about the closet when I stepped into their bathroom. The only word I had for this room was — *drama.* Almost everything was the same color as the bedroom — from the bronze tiles on the floor to the gold counter that held their double sinks. And then the towels that hung on the rack — all that soft gold.

It was hard to decide what I liked best — I guessed it was the huge glass shower, which seemed big enough to hold a party. But then I saw the window that stretched across the wall and looked right out onto the ocean.

I stood in the center and turned in a circle. Yup, my bathroom was going to be just like this. It wasn't until I faced the mirror that I noticed the doors — two, one on each side of the sink. When I pushed one door open, a light came on, just the way it did in the closet in my room. But this closet didn't look anything like mine.

The bedroom I was staying in was larger than any bedroom I'd ever been inside, but I was pretty sure my bedroom could fit inside this closet and there would be room left over. And while I had only used about ten hangers, it seemed like Gabrielle had hundreds of hangers in here, and there was something hanging on each one.

I walked in, thinking this looked like the first floor of Kohl's . . . no, this was better than Kohl's. Because none of Gabrielle's clothes had come from a department store. I could tell everything in here was all the way designer.

It was organized like a store, too. All of her clothes were lined up, by blouses and pants and dresses — all set up by color. On the other side were all things casual — jeans and leggings and sweatshirts.

And then in the back — there were the gowns. She didn't have just one or two — there were dozens: black and white ones, red and green ones. So many.

I couldn't help it — I lifted one of the red ones and gasped. This was the gown that Gabrielle had on in her Instagram profile picture. I looked at the label — Vera Wang.

Wow!

I caressed the beads, stroked the silk. Then I closed my eyes and imagined the day when I'd have on a gown just like this.

It was because of the picture in my mind that I hung the gown back up, then stripped out of my jeans and top before I slid into the dress.

I zipped it up, and all I could say was, "Oh my God!" I had never felt anything this good against my skin. Turning around, I searched for a mirror, but except for the small one on the vanity against the back wall of the closet, there wasn't one where I could really see what I looked like.

Lifting up the dress, I stepped slowly through the closet into the bathroom and back to the bedroom. When I stood in front of the mirror, all I could do was stare. The gown was way too long, but besides that, it was so perfect. I twisted to the left, then turned to the right, going back and forth, not believing how I looked — like a queen.

I closed my eyes and thought about Gabrielle's Instagram time line: the parties, the premieres, the awards shows where she had worn gowns like this. In my mind, I pushed Gabrielle's image aside. And now I was the one walking down that carpet. I was the one wearing the dress . . .

"Keisha!"

My eyes popped open, and through the reflection, I saw Mauricio standing behind me. I took in his blue suit, his blue plaid bow tie, and the deep frown that creased his forehead. I blinked, hoping that the images in my mind had just twisted in some kind of crazy way. But when he moved closer to me, I knew this wasn't an illusion.

"What are you doing?"

I wanted to turn around, but I was stuck

in my fear.

"Keisha."

When he said my name the second time, there was nothing I could do but face this man who was my foe. By the time I did a full turn, the tears were pouring from my eyes, and it wasn't an act. I was so pissed at myself.

"I'm . . . I'm . . . so sorry."

He looked at me like he was a little bit confused and a little bit angry.

I said, "I just had never seen . . . I've never had . . . I've never been . . ." Then I sobbed. Like, I cried straight from my chest with the sound effects and all. "I was just looking for . . . a sweater or a jacket. Because I don't have many clothes and when I went into Gabrielle's closet to borrow one, I saw this, and I . . . I . . ." I held my face in my hands, hiding my tears from him.

Too many silent moments passed, and I cried harder because I was sure I had just blown this whole gig. Just hours after Gabrielle had made me that grand offer.

I couldn't see Mauricio, but I felt him moving closer until he was right in front of me. I stiffened, waiting for him to grab my arm and snatch his wife's dress right off me.

But then, Mauricio, the enemy, put his arms around me. And now when I sobbed,

263

it was from relief more than fear.

"Come over here," he said. He led me to the chair in front of the window and told me to sit down. Then he said, "Keisha, look at me."

I raised my head and was really a little shocked. There was so much care in his light brown eyes.

"It's okay." His voice was so soft.

"I was just trying . . ."

He held up his hand stopping me. "It's okay. Just let it be this one time unless you talk to Gabrielle first, okay?"

I nodded.

He said, "Because I'm sure she wouldn't mind you trying on her clothes. Just ask her."

"Okay," I whispered. I looked down at my hands. "Can I ask . . ." I paused and slowly raised my eyes. "Please don't tell Gabrielle. She's been so good to me, and I don't want her to be mad."

"She wouldn't be. She'd understand the same way I do."

"I know, but I just" — I wrung my hands — "I just want to do everything right."

"No one's perfect," he told me.

"I know, but please."

He nodded, but he didn't say okay. All he said was, "Why don't you go and change

264

back into your clothes. Gabrielle and Bella will be home soon."

He stood, then as he made his way toward the door, I called out to him. When Mauricio turned back, I said, "Thank you."

He nodded, and when he smiled, I added another thing to the list of all that I was going to have soon. I figured Buck and I would get married eventually. But if that didn't work out, one day, maybe I'd have a husband just like Mauricio.

# 21

## GABRIELLE

I edged the SUV right to the curb in the long line of vehicles dropping off kids to school. Glancing back, I asked Bella, "You want Auntie Keisha to walk you to school?"

"Yay," my daughter cheered.

For the first time since yesterday, I saw a grin on Keisha's face, too.

I said to her, "You just have to walk her to that door." I pointed. "Bella calls it walking to school."

Keisha laughed. "Okay." Then she hopped out and helped Bella, who was already halfway out of her car seat.

"Bye, Mommy." Bella waved, then blew me a kiss.

I did the same, then watched as she held Keisha's hand and skipped up the walkway.

There was a smile on my face, but inside, I felt my frown, the one I'd had since I'd heard Keisha in Bella's room Sunday night.

*"So precious, my precious daughter . . ."*

I was squinting so hard I felt a headache coming on. So I pushed down my shoulders, loosened my grip on the steering wheel, and repeated in my head the explanation I'd come up with — everybody loved Bella. Who wouldn't want her to be their little girl?

But as Keisha walked back toward the car, I tensed again. It wasn't her; I adored this young woman already. It was just her words; I was really bothered by what she'd said.

When she slid back into the car, I gave her a smile, but she didn't return the gesture. I waited until I eased into traffic before I spoke. "Are you okay?"

She looked straight ahead and gave me one of her normal answers — she shrugged.

"You seem kinda quiet since I dropped you off at home yesterday."

Her eyes stayed forward, but her lips began to move, then she shook her head.

"Okay," I said. "I just want you to know you can talk to me about anything. I'm always here, Keisha. You're not used to having a big sister, but what that means is that I look out for you. And, there will be times when you have to look out for me."

That made her turn her head. "What can I do for you?"

"What do you mean? You can do lots of things." I thought for a second. "You already do so much. Like with Bella. You've only been here for a couple of days, and the two of you . . ." I paused, shook my head, but made sure that Keisha saw my smile.

Now, Keisha smiled, too. No, I couldn't even call it just a smile. Everything about her brightened. Truly, it was like her aura lit up the car. "I love being around Bella; she makes me happy."

I nodded. "I can see that." Another pause, another thought. "Have you ever wanted to have any kids?"

That brightness dimmed so fast, her aura had turned to midnight. Now I had even more questions, but this was not the time. I just had to tuck this away, right next to what I'd overheard on Sunday.

The darkness in the car didn't lift until I swerved into the lot, rolled up to the second level, and parked in my designated space. Keisha was still quiet, but at least now she wore a little smile as we walked toward the garage elevator and then finally into the lobby of the Wilshire Boulevard building.

"Wow," Keisha whispered. Her eyes were as wide as Bella's at Disneyland as she looked around, taking in the men and women dressed in suits, moving around the lobby and in and out of the Starbucks entrance. "I feel a little underdressed."

I glanced at the jeans she wore along with the navy blazer she'd borrowed from me. She looked cute, chic, but we were going to have to get her away from just jeans.

Inside the elevator, Keisha watched the floor panel as we ascended and then when we stepped off, I felt her excitement.

"Wow," she said again when we stood in front of the glass doors of my office. "Your name is on the door."

I laughed. "Well, Regan and I can do that since we own the business." When I pushed the door open, I stepped aside so Keisha could enter first. And then, like on Saturday night when I gave Keisha a tour of my home, I saw my office through her eyes.

"Good morning." Pamela jumped from her desk and came around to greet us.

I'd called my assistant last night and filled her in on the details of Keisha. Before I could make the introduction, my assistant (who could have been a perpetual high school cheerleader by her looks and demeanor) greeted Keisha with glee and a hug.

"I'm Pamela, and it's so nice to meet you."

When Pamela released her from the embrace, Keisha said, "Yeah."

"Mattie isn't here yet," I told Keisha as I led her into my office. "She works for

Regan, so you two will be working closely together, too."

I pushed open my office door and paused as I always did before I stepped inside.

Keisha followed me. "Is that the real Hollywood sign?"

I laughed. "Yeah. We'll figure out a time to take you up there."

Her eyes were as wide as her grin when she turned from the window, and now her gaze digested my office. "This is different from your house. There's a lot of color here."

"That's true. Mauricio and I love neutrals — we love that Zen feeling at home. But here, I wanted my office to be bold with color."

"Every color," she said, taking in the wall that had been painted green, then my oversize red cube desk and the yellow chairs in front of it. "It's really . . . kinda funky."

That word made me laugh. "Well, let's get you settled." Stepping back out into the reception area, I paused as Mattie came in. "Oh, Keisha, this is Regan's assistant."

Like Pamela, Mattie hugged Keisha and then I led her through the rest of the office, introducing her to our two PR associates and showing her the conference room, before I knocked on Regan's door.

"Come in," she said, then held up her hand letting me know that she was finishing a call. "Okay, Thursday is good. I just have to check with Gabrielle and I'll have Pamela or Mattie call you back." She paused. "Now, Justus . . ."

As soon as she said his name, Keisha gasped.

"Be on time," Regan continued. "We have to get you prepped for *The View.*" She hung up, then looked up. And her smile was as fake as those Persian rugs sold on every corner on La Brea Avenue.

"You were talking to Justus?" Keisha sounded as if she were almost hyperventilating.

"Uh . . . yeah." Regan's tone was far from warm. "He's one of our clients." Regan turned to me. "So you're giving her a tour?"

I nodded before I added, "A tour and a job." And then, because of the way Regan's stare turned to a glare, I turned around and rushed Keisha out of there. Because I didn't want to hear the words that came along with that expression. At least I didn't want to hear them in front of Keisha, and the challenge with my friend was that she had no filter.

"So," I began once we stepped from Regan's office, "that's it. That's everyone and everything."

"Wow. I thought you'd have more people working here."

Inside my office, she sat down as I rounded my desk. "Well, we all work hard, and it is going to be a relief having you here with us." Placing my arms on my desk, I leaned forward. "I'm so happy about this, Keisha. I hope you are, too."

She nodded, and I was just glad she didn't shrug.

"All right." I reached for the phone. "I'm going to have you work with Pamela first." I buzzed Pamela's desk, asked her to join us, and once she got settled next to Keisha, I said, "This is an exciting time; we're growing some more. So, Pamela, if for the next week, Keisha can shadow you, that will be great. A week with you, and she'll know everything."

"Okay," Pamela said.

Keisha shrugged, but at least she was grinning.

"And then," I said to Pamela, "Regan and I will talk to you about what you'll be doing next."

"That's great," Pamela said. "Whatever, you know that I'm in. I love working here."

"What a coincidence. 'Cause we love having you work here."

"Okay, well, the first thing you and I have to do" — Pamela turned to Keisha — "is get ready for Justus coming in this week. We're prepping him for media and whenever he comes into the office, it's a big deal."

I said, "I think Regan already set it up for Thursday."

"Welp." Pamela jumped out of her seat. "Let's get started."

"I'm ready," Keisha said, and I gave her a thumbs-up as she popped up and followed Pamela.

Pamela closed the door, leaving me alone the way she did every morning. I swiveled my chair and faced the view. And gave thanks to God for all of His blessings — which included Keisha.

I liked to do this bit of meditation for about ten minutes before I dived into my day. It was a part of my routine that everyone knew about and everyone respected. No one came to my door until I opened it.

Which was why I was a bit startled when after just about a minute, there was a quick knock and then Regan barged into my space.

"Excuse you," I said.

She closed the door behind her, stood over my desk, and folded her arms like she was about to give me a serious scolding. "Do you want to explain this job that you gave to Keisha without talking to me?" Her head moved in all kinds of ways with her words.

"This is about my dad. He really wants her to stay in Los Angeles."

"Get to the part where she's now working here."

"That is the part. If she's going to stay in Los Angeles, she needs a job. So why wouldn't I hire her?"

"Because hiring is permanent."

"Well, we're hoping that she'll stay in LA permanently." My eyes widened a bit when Regan growled and I further explained, "It's perfect timing. You and I just talked about making Pamela an associate."

She held up her hand. "You know I don't have a problem with promoting Pamela. This isn't about her."

"Well, when we promote her, I'm going to need an assistant. I was going to have to hire someone, so why not Keisha?"

Regan blew out a long breath, then sat down. "Gabby, I think you and your dad are moving too quickly."

Now I was the one who growled. "If this is about the test, we'll have the results tomorrow."

She shook her head and leaned forward as if she needed to get into my face to deliver her message. "This is about more than those test results. I don't trust Keisha."

"Why? What happened with the two of you down there in White Haven?"

"We haven't had a chance to talk since you stomped out of your dad's house."

I rolled my eyes.

"But the thing is, Keisha's shady." Regan held up her hand and began counting off her fingers. "First of all, she knew your name."

"Really? You're going back to that?"

"She lied about where she lived."

"You don't know that for sure. She could have been staying with someone and said that's where she was living."

"And I caught her talking to this guy in Walmart . . ."

I raised my eyebrows. "Oh, that's shady for real, 'cause you know, those Walmart customers . . ."

"He wasn't a customer; he worked there," she said, my sarcasm doing nothing to abate her anger. "They were in a heated discussion when I walked up, and then she lied about knowing him."

I sat back and waited for more. When she said nothing else, I said, "So these are the reasons why you don't trust her? This is your evidence?"

"You want proof?" She paused. "Well, this is it — I have the gift of discernment, and I know when something's not right."

"Okay, I'll give you that. But all of your doubts will go away tomorrow."

"What I'm talking about, Gabrielle, has nothing to do with DNA." She shook her head as she pushed herself up. "This has nothing to do with her father. She wasn't raised by the same people who raised you. She's different, and you need to be careful."

Regan stomped toward the door, but before she opened it, she looked over her shoulder. "Don't say that I didn't warn you."

And then she sailed out of the office as if she had just rested her case.

# 22
## KEISHA

I'd only been in Los Angeles for five days, but in many ways I felt like I'd been here forever. Already this felt like my life — the house and now the business. It was just my second day in the office and I was learning so much. Gabrielle was right: I'd be able to begin working by her side in just a week.

I imagined the clients I'd be talking to. She probably wouldn't start me off with Justus, but my plan was to make myself so valuable that quickly, she'd put me in charge of the important clients. Maybe one day, she'd even decide that she didn't need Regan. That would be the day to sing Hallelujah! Because it wasn't getting any better with Gabrielle's best-witch, my new name for her best friend.

As I sat next to Pamela in Gabrielle's office, Pamela pulled out her tablet. "Okay, let's go over your schedule," she said to Gabrielle. Then to me, she added, "This is probably the most important thing for Gabrielle because she doesn't keep track of anything."

"Hey, I can hear you," Gabrielle said, and we all laughed.

"Seriously, Pamela is right," Gabrielle told me. "She is my brain when it comes to where I'm supposed to be."

As Pamela reviewed Gabrielle's schedule for the next two days, I couldn't wait for the day when Pamela would be doing the same with me. I wanted her to be in charge of all of my appointments. And then I wondered, where would my office be? It didn't look like they had any extra space, and I couldn't imagine them wanting to move away from this one. There had to be a way to make more space, I figured.

"Keisha is going to need one."

I blinked. Damn, my mind had wandered so much I didn't know what Pamela was talking about.

Gabrielle said, "Yes, definitely, I agree. You have to have a tablet."

I breathed. "Yeah, since everything is done digitally."

She nodded. "We may have to get you a new phone, too, because we sync everything."

"That's fine," I said. "Whatever you need

I'm willing to do."

"Okay," Pamela began, "so do you want to have a full lunch spread for tomorrow, or just light sandwiches?"

"Who's coming in with Justus?" Gabrielle asked.

"I don't know; I sent him an email, but I can call him." She tapped something on her tablet.

"Do that," Gabrielle said. "Find out and then we'll make a decision. I want to do that before noon."

My legs started to tremble. Pamela was going to call Justus while I was sitting right there? Oh my God! What if she let me talk to him? She had to let me; this would be my first opportunity to prove what I could do.

"Excuse me."

The tap on Gabrielle's open door and that voice made me push thoughts of Justus aside and turn the same way Pamela and Gabrielle did.

A black man in a brown UPS uniform stepped inside. "There was no one out there" — he held up a manila envelope — "to sign for this delivery."

"Oh, my goodness." Gabrielle jumped from her chair so fast it almost fell back. "I'll sign."

He handed her the envelope, and after she looked at the front of it, she took a deep breath. She signed the tablet, handed it back to the UPS guy, and thanked him.

The way she looked at me made my heart thump. And then when she said to Pamela, "Would you mind leaving me and Keisha alone for a moment?" I knew what she held in her hand.

Pamela nodded without asking any questions, but when she closed the door behind her, I had one for Gabrielle.

"Is that it?"

It was like she was moving in slow motion when she sat down and nodded. She stared at the envelope, and I stared at her.

Until I said, "Are you going to open it?"

She looked up. "Do you want to?"

I shook my head right away.

Gabrielle said, "These results are addressed to you, so you can open it."

"No, you do it."

Then Gabrielle waved her hand in the air. "I don't know why we're being dramatic about this; we know what this is going to say." She ripped open the envelope, and I felt like I was sitting in the living room of Mrs. Johnson's shack watching *Maury.*

Gabrielle yanked the paper out, glanced at it for just a second, and her smile told the whole story. While she was looking down, she was smiling; when she glanced up, she was beaming. "You are my sister."

Even though I knew it all along, even though Gabrielle and Elijah kept telling me that they knew it, too, with all the drama that had been happening between Regan and her stank attitude toward me, and even Mauricio's suspicions, I didn't know if one of them would try to change the results like what happened on TV sometimes.

Gabrielle said again, "You are my sister," and tears were in her eyes. She rose from her seat, but I stayed still. She had to take my hand and lift me up in order for me to move. She hugged me, and this time, I hugged her, too, for real. She stepped back for a moment and said again, "You are my sister."

"Yeah."

That made her crack up. Like really laugh out loud. It was because she sounded so silly that I laughed, too.

"We have to celebrate," she said.

"Yeah."

"And the best way to celebrate?" She wasn't really asking me a question, so I didn't say anything. She said, "Shopping. We have to go shopping. Oh my God." She finally let me go and went back around to her side of the desk. "Now that we know you'll be staying here . . ."

She paused and I hesitated for only a moment before I nodded.

"Good," she continued. "You look great, but I want to take you shopping."

"Okay."

"If we can, we'll do that tonight."

"Okay."

There was another light knock on the door and Regan peeked inside. "Sounds like there's a party in here."

I snatched the letter from Gabrielle's desk and shoved it into her face. It wasn't the most subtle thing I'd ever done, but I couldn't wait for Regan to see.

I watched her eyes move as she read the words.

"Well," Regan said.

"Well," I mimicked her and folded my arms.

Gabrielle moved in between us as if she thought our next move might be one of us throwing an uppercut.

"Keisha" — Gabrielle turned to me — "why don't you call Daddy?" She nodded as if she wanted me to know she wasn't making a suggestion.

"Yeah," I said. I held out my hand toward Regan, and when she handed me the letter,

I did everything I could not to snatch it from her. I would have done that if Gabrielle hadn't been standing right there.

Turning back to Gabrielle, I said, "Okay, I'll call . . ." I paused. "I'll call . . . Elijah." Gabrielle felt like my family, but Elijah . . . not yet. Even though I'd searched for him all this time, I wasn't feeling it.

Looking at Regan one more time, I stepped out of the office, then told Pamela that I was going downstairs for a minute.

On the way down in the elevator, I read the paper. It was weird; I expected the page to be filled with words — something that just said: *Elijah Wilson, you are the father!*

But instead, the paper was loaded with dozens of numbers that I didn't understand. There was something that was the combined paternity index, but then there was the number that I did understand: probability of paternity — 99.9998 percent.

Wow! We couldn't get any more sure than that. By the time I walked out of the building, I was imagining what this 99.9998 percent meant — I was going to have this life for sure. I was going to have everything that Gabrielle had, all because she and Elijah were related to me.

When I stepped outside, I wondered if this was the best place to make the call. The streets here were so noisy between the cars and the buses, the horns and the brakes. Still, I leaned against one of the columns in front of the building, pressed the number, and wasn't surprised when he answered right away.

"Yo, what's up? Why don't you answer my calls no more? You too good for me now that you're in California?"

Three seconds and I was already sorry that I'd called Buck first. I mean, I really did care for Buck because of all that he'd done for me, but . . . "Are you going to let me say anything or are you gonna keep asking questions?"

"Yo, talk to me."

"It's just that you always call when I'm around them."

"Them who?"

"Gabrielle and Elijah, who do you think? But I snuck out to call you 'cause I got some news." I filled him in on what had been going on since I'd last spoken to him on Saturday, particularly the DNA results.

"Yo, congratulations, boo. You're in the money now for real. When can you send some cash my way?"

I couldn't be mad at Buck 'cause that had been the plan all along. But now that Gabrielle was bringing me into her company,

Buck and I didn't have to go this route. In a couple of months, he could move out here, we could get our own place, and by Christmas, we'd be living large with all the money I'd be making working alongside Gabrielle. I could probably even hire Buck by then, too.

"There's been a change of plans," I told him.

"What you talkin' 'bout?"

"I can't explain it all right now, but, Buck, what's going down here is better than the little bit of cash we could get from them. I'm tellin' you, trust me. This is life-changing."

"Life-changing?" He paused as if he had to think about my words. Then, "All right. I'm willing to listen. When can you talk?"

"Maybe tonight or tomorrow, but I promise you, you'll be happy."

"Okay, I trust you, boo. I'll be waiting; hit me up."

And then, I told him what he'd always told me. "I got you."

He laughed. "That's what I'm talkin' 'bout. That's my boo."

When we hung up, I was feeling pretty good. I did want to have Buck's back 'cause even though he worked every nerve in my body sometimes, he had always taken good care of me.

The thought of all that Buck had done took my smile away. He'd done a lot, but what was most important was that he'd saved me from Mr. Stanley.

Wow. I hadn't thought about Mr. Stanley since I'd gotten off the plane on Saturday. It was like all the miles between White Haven and Los Angeles had erased all the memories. So I didn't know why I was remembering him now. Maybe it was because today was a full-circle moment that started with Mr. Stanley and ended with this paper in my hand. Yes, Mr. Stanley had started it when he promised me the name of my father and he'd come through, even though I'd learned later that he hadn't done all the research he'd said. All he'd done was go down to the County Clerk's office. But whatever, he'd still given me the name of my father on that Monday after Thanksgiving. A Monday that had changed my life in so many ways.

I leaned back fully on the column, and though I faced the street and was bombarded by the sights and sounds of the morning, the city around me became silent as my mind took me back, year after year after year, until I was once again in 2009:

I glanced at the clock on the gym wall. The last bell of the day rang more than fifteen minutes ago, and that meant I was ten minutes late for Mr. Stanley. I had always been so anxious to see him. Every day. But not after what he'd done to me in that hotel room on Friday.

Over the weekend, I couldn't stop thinking about it. I'd been surprised; I'd been confused. Then I closed my eyes, really remembered, and now I was ashamed. Because even though I'd been afraid and didn't understand why Mr. Stanley had done that to me — there was a part of it . . . that felt kinda good. So if it felt good, did it have to be bad?

Grabbing my backpack from the bleachers, I climbed down, then made my way into the hallway. It was pretty empty; kids shot out of school as soon as the bell rang.

My heart was beating fast as I made my way to the library. Inside, I took the same steps I'd been taking for the last two months; I walked around the information counter and right into Mr. Stanley's office.

He looked up and smiled, the way he always did. Then, without saying anything, he got up when I sat down, and walked out into the library. As he got rid of the kids, I hugged my backpack as if it would keep me safe and stared at the plaques on Mr. Stanley's walls. As the minutes ticked by, I wondered, did I really want to stay? Should I just leave and never come back? What was finding my father going to do anyway?

I stood up at the exact moment that Mr. Stanley came back.

"Where are you going, Keisha?"

I shook my head. "I was . . . just . . . to . . . the bathroom." I sat down. "But I don't have to go anymore."

He squinted as if he knew I was lying but couldn't figure out why. After a couple of seconds, he took his seat behind his desk and smiled.

Every other day when he'd done that, when he looked at me that way, it would make me feel kinda tingly. 'Cause he was helping me get to the one thing I wanted so bad. But today I felt the opposite of tingly . . . I felt . . . dirty.

He said, "Well." Then he paused as if that would increase the drama, but all it did was make my heart hammer harder. "I promised you this information."

When he said that, my heart calmed down a bit and I moved to the edge of the chair.

He opened a folder, lifted what looked

like some kind of document, and then slid it across his desk.

I looked down but kept my hands away from the paper. I just read the bold letters at the top: Certificate of Live Birth.

The first line — the child's name — there was my name: Keisha LaVonne . . . only, there was a mistake — it said Keisha La-Vonne Wilson.

Wilson?

Now my eyes scanned the different lines faster: my date of birth, the time I was born, my sex, and my address. I got down to the line that had my mother's maiden name: Daisy Jones.

And then there it was on the bottom under father's name: Elijah Abraham Wilson. With his date of birth, though the line for his birthplace was blank.

"Elijah Abraham Wilson," I whispered. That was the name that Mr. Stanley had given me last week — without the Abraham. I raised my eyes. "That's my father's name?"

He nodded. "That's the official document," he told me. Then he shook his head. "Whew! It took a lot to get this. I did everything because I was doing it for you."

"I'm so . . ." I wasn't sure what to say. Was I happy? Was I grateful? Was I a little scared?

I was all of that, so all I said to Mr. Stanley was, "Thank you."

He nodded, but he wasn't smiling. He stood, came around and took my backpack from my lap, then set it on his desk. By the time he reached for my hand, I was shaking and my heart was stomping through my chest.

When he pulled me up, he said, "I'm happy I was able to do this for you, Keisha. I know how much you wanted to find your father."

"Yeah."

"And I was the one who found him for you."

"Yeah."

"So now that I've done this for you, are you willing to do some things for me?"

I blinked, and my senses came back to life. Cars whizzed past, and the rumbling of the tires where the rubber met the road filled my ears. It took me a second or two to realize that this was today and not eight years ago. I needed to forget Mr. Stanley, but it was hard. Because from that day, that man shaped my life.

After he found my father, he didn't want me coming to his office anymore. Now he took me to his home every Wednesday after school.

He didn't live in White Haven like he had told me, but I was sure he didn't remember that lie, or maybe he just didn't care. He lived right outside of Little Rock, about thirty minutes away from White Haven. But I never said anything about that. I never said anything about anything. I just did what he told me when I got to his house. All the kinds of things that I was sure my mama did with her johns.

"Keisha?"

I looked up, blinked, and tried to focus through the sun that blinded me. But then she came into view, and I groaned.

"What's wrong?" Regan asked in a tone that sounded like she was more nosy than caring.

"Nothing."

"Well, why are you standing out here crying?"

It might sound crazy, but I hadn't even known that I was. I swiped the tears from my cheek and then looked down at the paper that I still held. "I'm just . . . happy, I guess."

She gave me that look again, the one where she told me without saying a word that I was a liar. But I didn't care; there was nothing Regan could do to me now.

And I told her that — not in words. I told her that when I pushed myself off the column, turned my back, and stomped away from her like she was just some stranger on the street.

I hadn't called Elijah, but I'd do that later. Right now, all I wanted to do was get away from Regan and the memories of Mr. Stanley.

# 23
## KEISHA

Rolling over, I grabbed my cell and hit the button to turn off the alarm. Only it didn't stop chirping.

"Ugh!" I pushed myself up and studied the face of my new phone. Finally finding the side button, I silenced my cell, then bounced back onto the bed.

A new cell phone . . . just one of the things that Gabrielle bought for me last night when we did our celebration shopping. I chuckled a little (though it wasn't funny) at the thought of calling it a celebration. Yeah, we'd done some shopping, but it turned out not to be any kind of party for me.

It had started out like a celebration because once I'd come back upstairs from talking to Buck it had been festive for the rest of the day. I'd ended up calling Elijah from Gabrielle's office, using the excuse that I didn't have his office number. He'd been thrilled about the test results and Gabrielle told him we would all celebrate together this weekend because last night was reserved for the sisters.

Then she'd taken me and Pamela to lunch and when we returned, Pamela and I'd spent the entire afternoon planning for Justus and his entourage and the meeting this morning. I didn't even realize it when the clock had struck five, but Gabrielle had closed up her office and was standing over Pamela's desk.

"You ready to rock and roll out of here to do some serious retail therapy?"

I nodded, I shrugged, I grinned, and told her, "Yeah."

She laughed, and we almost skipped out of the office. When we got in the car, I was glad Gabrielle had to take a business call, because that gave me time and space to just think. I wanted to imagine where Gabrielle was taking me.

I almost didn't need a car — I could have floated straight to Rodeo Drive. I only knew about that street because Gabrielle had posted a couple of pictures of her and Regan one day traipsing in and out of Burberry and Christian Dior and Jimmy Choo. That day, Gabrielle and her best witch looked like they had their own reality show; they had looked better than the Kardashians.

Or maybe Rodeo Drive was too far away and Gabrielle was taking me to the Beverly Center — another mall I only knew through Instagram. It wasn't as upscale as Rodeo Drive, but it still had stores like Louis Vuitton and Gucci.

But just as Gabrielle ended her call, she angled her SUV into the parking lot of a place that I hadn't seen on social media. "This is the Westfield mall," Gabrielle said before I even asked. "Back in the day when I was a teenager, it was called Fox Hills."

She sounded excited, but I wasn't. I didn't see the names of any designer stores on the outside. But there had to be some; Gabrielle only shopped in the best places.

But then . . . we entered the mall. And then . . . Gabrielle said, "It's been a while since I've been here, but I think Old Navy is down this way."

Even now, as I remembered those words, I sighed. It was just as unbelievable now as it was last night. Still, I'd followed Gabrielle only because I was in such shock and didn't know what to say. She was taking me to Old Navy? She might as well have been taking me to where I *used* to buy all my clothes — Walmart.

But when we got into the store, Gabrielle

changed her mind. "This is too casual," she said. "Let's head down to Macy's."

We bounced out of there; I was still in my shock state, but at least Macy's was a little better.

When we walked inside that store, Gabrielle had asked me, "What kind of clothes do you like?"

I'd wanted to tell her that I liked everything in her closet, all the clothes she wore in her pictures. But I just shrugged, and I guessed that gave her permission to take over.

We'd come home with bags and bags and bags of pants and tops, suits and dresses. Gabrielle had bought me three pairs of shoes and two pairs of boots. She'd actually spent more than a couple of thousand dollars, which would have sent me to the moon — a week ago. But that was before I'd come to Los Angeles. Before I saw how Gabrielle was really living.

Rolling onto my back, I stared up at the canopy. Why had Gabrielle decided that Old Navy was good enough for me when she wore Vera Wang gowns? Why had she settled for Macy's when she carried a Gucci purse?

At least, she had bought me a red Coach bag and a pair of Privé Revaux sunglasses, which I loved. But still, I had only one pair of the designer glasses — Gabrielle had a dozen.

Maybe Gabrielle didn't think of me as her real sister. Maybe there was something else that had to happen before she thought I was designer-worthy.

Glancing at my new cell phone, I checked out the time. Gabrielle had bought me the top-of-the-line iPhone and the iPad to go with it, though that was all work. But at least that was something.

Finally rolling from the bed, I stepped into the closet and stared at the space. This closet was halfway full now, and for that alone, I should have been glad. And I would have been if . . .

I sifted through the pants and tops and I chose the mustard velvet jeans and the black blouse with the huge bow. With the black boots that were a great knockoff of the Louboutins that Gabrielle had, I figured this outfit was enough to get Justus's attention.

I hopped into the shower, hoping that the gentle water would help me get my mind right. No matter what, whatever I wore today I would look better than yesterday. Really, today, I would look better than any day in my whole life. So I should be satisfied with that, I guessed. It was just that I didn't understand why I couldn't have what

Gabrielle had.

By the time I stepped back into the bedroom and glanced once again at the outfit that I'd laid out on the bed, I felt better. The things that were most important were that I was in Los Angeles, I was working with Gabrielle, and today, I was meeting Justus. And, I was sure the next shopping spree would be much better than last night.

So I had a lot to be grateful for and that was where I was going to keep my focus.

"Well, look at you," Pamela said when Gabrielle and I walked through the door. "You look fabulous."

I gave her half a smile, though I wasn't sure if Pamela meant what she said or she was just trying to be nice. I did have to admit that although I wasn't wearing anything like the designer navy polka-dot shirred-waist dress that Gabrielle had on, I did feel good.

Gabrielle grinned. "She looks great, doesn't she?"

I smiled back and hoped that my smile wasn't too fake.

As Gabrielle went into her office, Pamela said, "Well, let's get to work. We don't have much time."

Rushing into the conference room, I set

up the agenda booklets in front of each chair. While I did that, Pamela led the caterers inside and set up the breakfast spread along with the coffee and tea dispensers. Within an hour, we were ready, and within seconds of us telling Gabrielle and Regan that everything was good, this burly dude (who wasn't that much taller than me) busted through the door.

"Hey, Smokey," Pamela said.

And then right after him . . . came Justus.

Oh my God. The photos I'd seen of this man didn't do anything for him. He was finer in real life, though I wasn't sure what I liked best about him. Was it that he was so tall — at least six three or maybe more? Or was it his chestnut-colored complexion, which was covered by a closely cropped beard? Yeah, that beard was sexy, but couldn't compete with those lips. Since I'd come to California, I'd been doing a lot of imagining. And right now, all I could imagine were what those lips could do to me. Until his light brown eyes looked straight at me.

I rushed over to him. "Oh my God, Justus, it is so nice to meet you. Can I take a selfie?"

Before he said a word, I grabbed my phone from the top of Pamela's desk and held it above my head, but then he backed up and away from me.

"Yo, Gabby, babe, what's up?" Justus held up his hands like he was surrendering to the police. "You know I don't do this when I come in here." His voice was gravelly, like he was sleepy and cranky. "This is supposed to be a fan-free zone."

Gabby rushed over and hugged Justus, and I frowned a bit at the way he held her. With his eyes closed and everything. It didn't look like any kind of business hug to me.

After a long moment, Gabby stepped back. "I'm sorry," she said. She turned to me. "Keisha is . . . *new.*"

I raised my eyebrows. She wasn't going to introduce me? As her sister? As the *new* person working with her side by side?

She said, "Come on in. We're ready to begin." She nodded to Pamela to lead them into the conference room.

Pamela grabbed her tablet, then stepped in front of Smokey. He followed, then Justus and the two other dudes who were behind Justus did the same.

I took a deep breath. That was certainly a diss, but maybe Gabrielle was going to make the introduction and announcement inside the meeting. I guessed that was the most appropriate place. When they were all inside, I grabbed my tablet, then walked toward the conference room. But as I was stepping in, Gabrielle was stepping out, and she stopped me.

"Uh, Keisha, you're going to be out here" — she pointed to the front of the office — "while we're meeting."

"What?"

Her frown matched mine. As if she didn't understand my misunderstanding. She said, "We don't need the assistants in the meeting, just the associates."

Before I could ask her what that had to do with me, Justus called out, "Gabby, babe, you know I don't drink this bootleg coffee. Can you get your girl to make a Starbucks run? You know what I like." He grinned.

She nodded, then turned back to me. "Okay, you're going to cover the phones, but Mattie can cover you while you get coffee for Justus. Get him a venti caffè latte with two shots, protein powder, and mocha drizzle." Then she said, "Oh, wait. Money."

She rushed out of the conference room, down the hall to her office. And just like last night, I followed her because she had sent me once again into that shock state.

Grabbing her purse, she pulled out her

wallet and then her credit card. "Here, use this." Then, she rushed away from me, but after a couple of steps, turned back around. "Oh, and tell them to make Justus's drink extra hot so that it will still be hot when you get back. And get something for yourself, if you want."

She grinned, but even after she dashed away from me, I stood there with my mouth open. It wasn't until I heard the conference door close that I moved with slow steps to the outer office, past Mattie, then through the doors to the elevators.

First last night and now today. Gabrielle didn't have to send me any more clues — she didn't see me working by her side; she saw me as her assistant.

Inside the elevator, I had to blink back real tears. So if I was nothing to her, then what had been the purpose of the test? Why in the world did she have me take it if she had no plans of ever claiming me? Had this week just been about humiliating me? So much for thinking that God was restoring anything.

My head was down when the elevator doors parted; I stepped out and bumped right into someone.

"I'm sorry," I said, trying to sniff back my tears.

"Keisha?"

Looking up, once again, I stared into the eyes of Mauricio. And just like two days ago at his home, he questioned me. "What's wrong?"

I shook my head, and then he held my elbow and led me away from the view of others. Standing against the wall, he asked me again what was going on.

I said, "Nothing. I was just . . ." I paused and measured my words. "I have to get Starbucks for Justus and —"

"Oh," Mauricio said, as if those few words explained everything. "Justus is here?"

The disdain in his voice was like a tissue that wiped my tears away. Now my curiosity trumped my being pissed.

He said with a sigh, "If I'd known that, I wouldn't have dropped by to surprise Gabby." Then, "So they sent *you* to get his coffee?" Before I answered, he shook his head. "Listen, don't let that guy get to you. He's an ass." Right after he said that, he pressed his lips together, almost as if he wanted to say more, but couldn't. "Forget I said that. He and I have never gotten along, but . . ." He stopped again. "Look, do you need any help getting the coffee?"

I shook my head. "No, they have coffee up there. He's the only one who wanted something special, so I can carry up one cup."

"Well" — he glanced at his watch — "so much for my surprise. I'll head back to the school. You good?"

I nodded.

He put his hand on my shoulder. "Just ignore Justus, okay?"

Then he strolled away. As he moved toward the parking garage elevators, I headed to the other side of the lobby to the Starbucks.

I'd come down in the elevator so sad, but now I had a clear understanding. Gabrielle wasn't going to share her life with me, so that just meant that I had to do what I had to do — I had to take what I wanted. If I wanted this life, I had to grab it.

I didn't know everything that I was going to do, but Mauricio had just given me some information and ammunition. And I was going to use it.

I stepped up to the counter, gave the barista Justus's order, and then passed him Gabrielle's credit card. When he gave me the card back, I looked down at the numbers.

I stepped to the side and, as I waited for Justus's drink, I pressed Buck's number on my new cell phone. By the time he answered, I had all the numbers on Gabrielle's credit card memorized.

"Yo, boo, what's up?"

"Remember that plan I thought I had?"

"You *thought* you had?"

"Yeah, well, I don't have it anymore. We're back to your plan and I have a credit card for you."

"That's my boo. Okay, what you got?"

I gave him the number and I didn't even ask Buck what he and Que were gonna do. I'd just let them do their thing and then I was gonna figure out how to do mine.

# 24

## GABRIELLE

Standing in front of Keisha's bedroom door, I heard her voice, though muffled, and wondered who she was talking to.

I tapped on the door and waited for her to invite me in. When she paused for a moment, but then kept talking, I tapped again, this time with a bit of a heavier hand . . . and I didn't wait for Keisha's invitation, which felt like it wasn't going to come. I pushed open the door and peeked inside.

Keisha was kicked back on her bed, one leg crossed over the other. She raised her head from the pillow. "Hold up," she said into her cell. Then to me, she said, "Yeah," without any kind of smile, without any kind of warmth.

I stepped inside the room and glanced at the television that was on mute. Keisha had the TV tuned to one of those reality shows about housewives; it was the kind of television that made me cringe. Facing her, I said, "I just dropped Bella off to the birthday party at Chuck E. Cheese."

Even when I mentioned Bella's name, Keisha's face stayed void of any emotion.

"So," I continued, "I was thinking you and I could do something. I mean, since this is your first Saturday here and it's kinda warm outside."

She rolled over now and looked at me as if she was suddenly interested.

I said, "I was gonna call Regan and maybe we could all go out to lunch. I know you like the beach, and there are lots of restaurants on the beach."

She only blinked.

"Or we could go walk on the beach. And talk."

"Nah, that's okay. I'm not hungry, and I don't feel like exercising." And then, she kicked back once again and returned the phone to her ear as if I weren't there. I was being dismissed, I supposed.

I obliged and stepped from the room. But I stood there staring at the closed door, trying to figure out what had happened. What happened to the relationship that was blossoming between us?

As I moved toward the staircase, my mind scrolled through the past days. The DNA results on Wednesday, everything had been better than fine. And then . . . then what? Yes, she'd been a bit subdued when we'd gone shopping, but I thought that was because she was concerned about how much money I was spending. She'd kept looking at the price tags and I'd kept assuring her that money wasn't an issue. But really, her attitude had changed since then. From Wednesday night.

I sauntered to the patio door, opened it, then only closed the screen behind me. Mauricio glanced up from the newspaper (yes, an actual newspaper) that he was reading. He looked nothing like a college professor today. No sports jacket, no bow tie. Just a T-shirt and sweats. Really, he could have passed for one of his students.

"What's up?" he said. "Bella's settled in at the party?"

I nodded, then slumped into the patio chair across from him. "Yeah."

He grinned. "Don't tell me you have Mommy separation syndrome."

"No, not Mommy." I shifted the chair so that I faced him. "Mauricio, have you noticed anything about Keisha?"

He frowned a little, then shook his head. "Like what?"

"I don't know. She's been . . . a bit cold, and I can't figure it out."

"Oh." He leaned back. "Well, I know she was upset on Thursday."

I tilted my head in question.

He said, "I came by the office to surprise you and bumped into her coming off the elevator. She was upset. About getting coffee for Justus."

I paused trying to understand. "Why would she be upset about that?"

"Oh . . . I don't know," he sang. "Maybe because she never expected to be the coffee girl?"

"She's not a coffee girl; she's my assistant. That means helping me with everything. I would've gone and gotten his coffee myself if the meeting hadn't been starting."

Lowering his head, Mauricio mumbled, "I'm sure you would have."

I crossed my arms. "What does that mean?"

He held up his hands. "Look, these conversations never end well. I don't want to fight about Justus."

"Just say what you were going to say." The edge in my tone was sharper than intended, but Mauricio was right. Conversations about Justus were the bane of our marriage; his offense was always sharp and my defense always had a bit of a bite.

"All right." He closed the newspaper. "I

meant that when it comes to Justus, he's the only one who matters." Before I could call him a liar, Mauricio continued, "You drop everything for him."

"He's our firm's biggest client."

"He's also your ex."

Leaning back and away from him, I said, "Really, Mauricio. Are you going to bring up the fact that I dated him . . . in high school . . . every time we talk about Justus?"

He shrugged. "I'm talking about someone you considered marrying . . ."

"Not seriously."

"And then you started your business because of him."

"You say that all the time as if you never knew my plan was always to have my own company. That's why I got my MBA, and if I hadn't gotten my MBA, I would never have met you."

He shrugged again.

I squinted. "This cannot still be about him giving Regan and me the money to start Media Connections."

"Correction: he gave *you* the money."

"Correction: Regan and I own that firm together."

He held up his hand. "See what I mean? We will never agree. But I can tell you this

— as long as he doesn't respect me as your husband, he gets no love from me."

I pouted.

"But going back to how this conversation started — think about what you asked Keisha to do when he came to your office."

I shook my head. "It can't be that. Pamela and Mattie have been sent to get him dozens of cups of coffee."

"And neither one of them is your sister."

"She's not my sister in the office." I paused and tightened my arms across my chest. "And when did you become such a Keisha fan? Just last Sunday you were insisting that she have the DNA test."

"I was never against your sister. I wanted the test; the results are in, and now she's family. Family who wants to fit in, Gabrielle. And you sending her out for coffee won't help her to feel that way. For God's sake, I found her the other day in your closet, trying on your clothes."

"What?" I frowned.

"Don't make a big deal about it." He pushed his hands down as if he were trying to lower the temperature of the discussion. "Really, it was nothing and I hadn't even planned to mention it. But she was trying on one of your dresses, imagining, I'm sure, that she was like her big sister. And she probably didn't feel anything like her big sister the other day with Justus."

"I gave her a job because she's family, because she's my little sister."

"You gave her a job to carry Justus's coffee."

I glared at him and he stared right back at me. If I'd been ten years younger, I would have told Mauricio that he made me sick. If I'd been fifteen years younger, I would have stuck my tongue out. And if I'd been Bella's age, I would've told him he made me sick, stuck my tongue out, and told him to kick rocks. But since none of those acts were appropriate for a thirty-two-year-old woman, I just glared at him a little longer, said a couple of good curse words in my head, then pushed myself up from the chair and stomped away.

I snatched the screen door back, stepped inside, and almost bumped right into Keisha.

"Oh, I'm sorry," she said. "I was just coming to look for you."

I paused and wondered how long she'd been standing there. "That's all right." I thought about what Mauricio had just told me and I wondered if Keisha and I needed to talk about this — the clothes in my closet and the coffee.

But before I could say anything, she said, "I'm sorry" again.

"About what?"

"I've been mad at you."

I gestured with my head and led her into the kitchen. She sat at the counter and I stood across from her. I said, "I can tell you've been upset, but why?"

She sighed. "This is going to sound silly."

"Nothing you say will sound silly to me. Remember, I'm your sister." Then, after a pause, I added, "Silly."

That made her smile. Still, it took her a moment to say, "I wanted to meet Justus."

I paused for a moment because this wasn't about clothes; this wasn't about coffee. Mauricio thought he knew everything, but I couldn't even be mad at him because clearly, I didn't know anything. I pressed the heel of my hand against my forehead, feeling like the biggest dummy around. What twenty-two-year-old didn't want to meet Justus? Especially a twenty-two-year-old who was my sister. "Ugh. I'm the silly one."

"No, you're not. It's just that he's my favorite, and I thought I'd get a chance to at least meet him."

"You're right. I should've introduced you. It's just that sometimes when I get into that space, I get into business mode —"

"I noticed."

"And I don't think beyond that. I'm sorry, Keisha. And the next time he comes in, I'll introduce you." Her smile was so wide it brightened the kitchen. "So all is forgiven?"

Then Keisha did something she'd never done before. She slipped down from the chair, walked to the other side of the counter, and hugged me. It was the first time she'd ever done that, and I squeezed her tight.

Stepping back, I said, "I'm glad you came to me."

"I'm glad, too."

"So, do you want to go out and do something?"

She nodded. "Yeah. Let's go walk on the beach."

"Perfect."

As we trotted up the stairs to get our phones and purses, I told her I'd meet her back downstairs in ten. Before she stepped into her bedroom, I asked, "Who were you talking to earlier?" I didn't ask to be nosy. It was just that I wanted to know everything about Keisha.

But that darkening thing happened again. It was something that came all over her and made me step back a little. She did answer me, though. She said, "Nobody, really."

And then she walked into her room and closed the door.

# 25
# KEISHA

I peeked into the hallway and heard Gabrielle having her normal morning debate with Bella. So I shut my door as softly as I could and tiptoed into my bathroom. I was dressed and ready to go, but the bathroom gave me cover to make this call. I hadn't been discreet when I talked to Buck on Saturday; I didn't even care when Gabrielle had barged into my room.

But once she asked me who I'd been talking to, I decided I did need to be careful if I was going to make this work.

Closing the bathroom door with one hand, I tapped Buck's name on the screen with the other, and he answered so fast, I wasn't sure if his phone actually rang.

"Yo, boo, what's good?"

"Where you at?" I asked. "Work?"

"Nah, I quit."

"What?" I pushed down the toilet seat and sat. "Why?"

" 'Cause why I gotta work for the white man when I have this plan with you?"

Every time I talked to Buck I felt more confident that we could pull this off, but I wasn't sure that he should've quit his job even if he did have this whole plan.

When I'd told him how Gabrielle had promised to have me working by her side, then how she'd flipped on me and now I was nothing but an assistant — the same title I'd had with Beryl, Buck had gone off.

*"Why she think she can treat you like that?"*

I'd calmed down because I had to keep him calm. And once he settled down, he told me not to worry about getting mad.

*"If she don't want to share, boo, just take what should be yours."*

That was exactly how I felt. Why shouldn't I have everything that Gabrielle had? The thing was, I didn't have a plan — but Buck did.

*"Take her down at home, take her down at work, blow up her world. And when she steps out, you'll step right in. How hard could it be to do her job anyway?"*

When Buck had first said this, it sounded good, but I didn't know how I could make it all happen. But then, I thought about it, and slept on it, and thought about it. And it became so clear. I could take her down at work — that would be easy enough . . . as her assistant. And at home — there was this thing with Mauricio and Justus that I could figure out. There had to be a way to cause so much confusion and chaos that she'd be out at work, out at home, and I'd be the one to have it all after that.

*"So what I'm gonna get outta this?"*

When Buck had asked me that, I was all in with his credit card scam. Not for me, but for him. My plan was to get this life, but I would help him out, too.

*"All you gotta do is give me the numbers, I'll do the rest."*

"So, boo." Buck's shout through the cell brought me back to now. "Ain't that right?" he repeated. "No need to be hustling for Mr. Walmart when I can be hustling for myself."

"I'm just not sure you should've quit Walmart. I don't know how long the credit card scam is going to last. Once they see the fraudulent charges, they're going to report them, and then you and Que won't be able to use the card anymore."

"So? They got more than one card, don't they?"

"And you don't think it's gonna look weird that they have fraudulent charges on all of their cards?"

318

"Look, you're worrying about things that Que already got worked out. Trust me, have I ever let you down, boo?"

I sighed, but the thing was, he never had.

He said, "You made up with her, right?"

"Yeah." Buck had overheard the way I'd spoken to Gabrielle on Saturday, and he told me I'd needed to fix that. "She doesn't have any idea what I'm planning to do."

"Good. 'Cause playas never let the other side know their moves," he said as if he were schooling me.

There was a quick knock on my bedroom door, and I stepped out of the bathroom.

Gabrielle shouted, "Keisha, I'll be ready to leave in about ten minutes."

"Okay," I told her, and then I whispered into my cell, "I gotta go."

"Got ya. Stay strong, boo. I'm in your corner all the way, all the time. Call me if you need anything."

I clicked off the phone and held it close to my chest. There were times when Buck made my head throb, but there were other times when he did the same thing to my heart.

Moving to the bed, I grabbed my Coach bag and stuffed my cell phone inside. Then I sat down and thought about Buck. For so long, he'd been trying to take care of me.

Buck and my mama. Just the two of them. And Buck had been there for me at a time when Mama couldn't even be.

This was a rough bus ride home. It was always that way. Even though it was 2010, there were so many roads in White Haven that were still not paved.

But that wasn't what made the ride so rough today. It was the words that kept jumping around in my head. Looking out the window, I saw nothing, not even the trees. The tears in my eyes blurred every-thing. The tears had been in my eyes from the moment Mr. Stanley had dismissed me.

I'd gone into his office just like I did every Wednesday. We never left for his house until all the school buses and all the teach-ers had left. But today, when I walked through the library and then into his office, I changed the routine a little bit. I spoke before he even looked up and smiled.

"I think I'm pregnant."

He bounced from his seat, then went around me and closed the door to his of-fice. Facing me, he crossed his arms. "Why do you think that?"

It was hard for me to say the next words to a guy, but I had to so that Mr. Stanley would believe me. "I missed my period. For two months now." When he didn't say anything else, I said it again to make sure that he understood. "So I think I'm pregnant. I don't know for sure, but I looked it up on here." I raised the cell phone that he had given me for my fifteenth birthday. "On the Internet, they said if I missed my period for two months, I was probably pregnant."

He squinted, he frowned; he looked like he was gonna be sick. I got that — I'd been feeling sick, too. It took him a long time to speak, and when he did, what came out was, "It's not mine." That was it. Then he walked out of his office like he always did.

His words shocked me. What did he mean by that? It had to be his baby. I'd never had sex with anyone else. I lowered myself into the chair where I always sat and waited for Mr. Stanley . . . just like I did every Wednesday.

Today, he came back faster than normal. But he didn't have the smile on his face that was always there. This time, he stood in front of me and crossed his arms. "I think we need to end . . ." He shook his head. "You don't need to come to my office anymore. In fact, you should leave right now. So that you can catch the bus, or you'll have to walk home. Our business is finished."

There were so many words in those sentences that scared me, but all I did was focus on catching the bus. Because White Haven was more than twenty miles away from Clinton High; it would take me till tomorrow morning to get home if I had to walk.

Without saying another word to him, I dashed out of the library, then prayed the whole time that I would make the bus. I did; I was the last one on, and since there were only nine of us who were bused in from White Haven, I got my regular seat by the window.

I was glad I sat alone. No one would see my tears. What did Mr. Stanley mean when he said the baby wasn't his? What did he mean that our business was finished?

I was still asking myself those same questions when the bus made it back to White Haven. The driver made only one stop when we hit town — on the curb in front of Walmart. All of us had to walk the rest of the way to our homes.

But when I stepped off that bus, I wasn't thinking about going home. All I could do was stare at the big store in front of me.

I'd told Mr. Stanley I thought I was pregnant because I didn't know for sure. I'd missed my period, yes, but on the Internet, it said that could be because I was pregnant, but it could be because of other things, too. That was why I'd told Mr. Stanley. Because I thought he was gonna help me figure it out like he helped me figure out my father.

But it seemed like I'd have to do this by myself. So the first thing I had to figure out — was I pregnant?

I slung my backpack over my shoulder, then traipsed from the street, through the parking lot. The whole time, my eyes were on the big store sign.

When I stepped inside, though, I just stood there. Where would I find pregnancy tests in this big ole place? I knew they had pregnancy tests; there were lots of commercials on TV about them. So I just began to wander through the store — I walked toward the sign that said Health and Beauty because those tests had nothing to do with beauty, but this sure 'nuff was about my health.

The store wasn't all that crowded — I guessed people didn't hang out in Walmart in the middle of the week right before dinner. I turned into the section and was a little surprised to see the pregnancy tests right there. There were a bunch of them, all in boxes that were so pretty you wouldn't mind leaving them out on the shelf at home. But when I picked one up, my eyes almost busted out of my head.

This was almost ten dollars. I mean, it was only seven, but that might as well have been ten. Especially since all I had in my pocket was two dollars.

Dang. I wanted this test, but how was I gonna get five more dollars? Mama didn't have it; Mama never did. And not only that, she'd ask me why I wanted the money.

I could knock on some doors and ask anyone if they wanted me to babysit or do some chores. But even before I finished thinking about that, I knew that wouldn't work. None of the ladies where I lived ever let me babysit or do anything. I guessed they didn't want me around their kids or their men. I guessed they thought I was just like my mama.

There was only one way I was gonna get this test. I looked up one end of the aisle and then turned the other way. Then holding my breath, I opened my backpack and just before I was about to stuff the box inside, someone grabbed my arm.

I didn't look up — there was no need to; I was sure it was the police. And another reason why I didn't need to look up — I was going to die from a heart attack anyway.

"Yo, what you doin', girl?"

When I raised my eyes, the guy who was holding me didn't look like a policeman. I mean, he didn't have on any kind of uniform, but he didn't even look like an undercover cop either. Maybe he just worked here — he looked like he was old, like twenty or something.

Still, I said, "I'm so sorry. I shouldn't have done this. I won't do it again."

"Shhh . . . girl, I'm not the po-lice. But if you trying to get this out of here, you sure gonna get caught. They got these things in them that will set off the alarm the moment you walk through the door."

"Oh." I didn't know what kind of thing he was talking about and I was too scared to ask.

He took the box, glanced at it, then brought his eyes back to me. "You pregnant?"

I snatched the box from him. "None of your business."

He grinned. "I'm just asking 'cause I was gonna try to help you. You want this?"

Now I had what my English teacher called a dilemma — I didn't want this dude in my business, but I needed this test. "You work here?"

"Nah, I wanna get a job here, but you can't if you're not sixteen."

I frowned. "How old are you?" I'd thought he was so much older.

"Oh, so now you wanna get all in my business." When he grinned, I sighed like I was in love. It was his gold grill. All the tough guys had started wearing those things . . . I just loved them.

"Umm . . ." Damn . . . I'd forgotten what he'd said and what I was supposed to say back.

He saved me when he said, "Look, I'mma get this for you. Just meet me outside, okay?"

I had a whole bunch of questions — like how was he going to do it and why did he want to help me? But I needed that test, and this guy with the wavy black hair and gold grill was gonna get me what I needed . . .

He'd met me outside, gave me the bag with the box inside, and then he walked me home. I never knew if he had stolen it or bought it, but as we walked, I did find out that his name was Buck, he went to White Haven High, and he was fifteen, like me.

When we got to my house, Mama hadn't left for work yet, so Buck had told me what to do with the test like he was an expert. And then he'd given me his phone number and told me to call him after I'd finished.

Just about two hours after that, Mama was gone and I did what Buck told me to do: took the test, called him, cried, and asked Buck what was I gonna do.

"Don't worry, boo, I got you."

That was what he'd said then; that was what Buck said always. And he followed his words with action. That was why no matter how many times he made me want to punch his heart out, he'd always have mine.

There was another quick knock on my door, and I pushed myself off the bed. "I'm ready," I shouted out to Gabrielle as I grabbed my purse and the white denim jacket I was going to wear with the black flounce miniskirt.

Before I stepped out of the room, I paused and looked at myself in the mirror inside the closet door. The boots really set this outfit off. I looked good, and now I had to be good. I had to take care of business.

It was time to go, time to put this whole plan to work.

# 26
## KEISHA

Bella jumped into my arms from her car seat, and I set her down on the ground.

"Bye, Mommy," she shouted out the way she always did, then we skipped up the walkway to the front door of the Dalton School.

Since we'd been doing this for two weeks now, I didn't flip out at all of the white kids jumping out of Bentleys and even limos. It was just this life — the kind of life my kid should have.

My kid.

Looking at Bella, I smiled, then crouched down so that we were eye to eye. "You have a good day today, okay?"

She nodded, then leaned over and gave me a hug.

"I love you," I told her.

"I love you, too, Auntie."

I held her, keeping her inside my arms for another moment. Then I said, "You can call me Mama."

Bella leaned back. "Mama?"

I nodded. "Don't you want to call me that?"

She frowned, then looked over her shoulder; I was sure she was searching for Gabrielle.

"That's different from Mommy," I told her.

"It is?"

"Uh-huh. That's why you can call me Mama. But you know what?"

She shook her head and her eyes got wide like she thought I was going to tell her something special.

I said, "Let's keep this between just you and me, okay?"

She nodded.

"Just call me Mama when we're by ourselves, okay?"

She hesitated for a moment, then nodded slowly.

"Okay." I kissed her cheek, then waited for her to say something, but she stepped away and took the hand of one of the kindergarten assistants who met us at the door every day. I watched her go inside and smiled. It might take a week, maybe two, but she'd call me Mama.

Turning back to the car, I wasn't quite

sure how I was gonna make Bella part of the plan, but that little girl was gonna be mine, too. Maybe it was just as simple as making Gabrielle lose everything and I would be there to take care of Bella. Or maybe it would take more.

I didn't know yet, but I knew I'd know soon.

When I slid back into the car, Gabrielle smiled. "Thank you," she said the way she did every morning.

I clicked my seat belt, and at the same time, her phone beeped. Gabrielle frowned as she read a message. "I have to call my bank." She tapped in a number, then set the call on Bluetooth before she eased from the curb.

I pretended to be looking at my own phone as the automated voice answered and told her to press one for this or press two for that. She tapped a couple of buttons before a real woman came on and asked Gabrielle what kind of help she needed.

"I received a notification from the fraud department."

The woman asked for some identification that I made note of: the last four digits of her Social Security number, and her phone code. After all of that, the woman told Gabrielle, "Yes, we noticed some activity that we suspect is fraudulent. There's a charge here for eighteen hundred dollars."

What shocked me most was Gabrielle didn't freak out. If I had a credit card and someone told me there was that kind of a charge on it, I would've been screaming. Rich people problems, I guessed.

But as if the woman had just told her about the weather, Gabrielle said, "My husband and I share this card, so can you tell me what the charge is for?"

"The purchase was made from a retailer called Motor Sports in Boston."

"Oh, no, that doesn't belong to us."

"That charge has already been paid, but you won't be responsible for it. And since your card has been compromised, we have to cancel it."

"All right." Gabrielle sighed.

"We'll send new ones; you'll receive them in about seven business days."

"Thank you so much."

As she gave more information to the woman, I opened my Messages app and texted:

Credit card canceled. Stop NOW.

Then I closed the app and sat back. It seemed like this was the only charge they'd

331

made that delivered a fraud alert, but knowing Buck and Que, they'd charged more than $1,800.

"That is really something," Gabrielle said as she clicked off the phone at the same time as she turned into the parking garage on Wilshire Boulevard. "I can't believe people do that." She shook her head. "Just get a job."

I chuckled; I'd pass on her advice to Buck.

She chatted all the way up to the office, and all I did was smile and nod. I wasn't listening — my mind was on what I was setting in motion today . . . would it work?

Once we were in the office, I sat at Pamela's desk — that was the way I thought of this space. Everybody called it mine since Pamela was now sharing an office with one of the other associates after she'd been promoted. But while they all saw me as an assistant, I saw myself sitting right in Gabrielle's office.

I gave Gabrielle a couple of extra minutes beyond her normal fifteen before I knocked on her door. "You ready?"

She nodded, and I settled in front of her with my tablet. Gabrielle was right — once she came into the office, she went straight into business mode. But she always focused on the big picture rather than the details, and that was what I was hoping she'd do today.

She said, "For the next two days I'm going to need you to do quite a bit of research for me."

I nodded.

"There are three new clients I want to pursue in the coming months, and I want you to get me everything you can find about them."

I took notes and listened to Gabrielle with half of my brain. Because my thoughts were already on the next part of this meeting.

Then Gabrielle said, "Okay, let's go over my calendar. Anything for today?"

I inhaled as I looked. "No, just your lunch with Regan tomorrow. That's it."

She frowned, looking down at her tablet, then up in the air like she was trying to remember something. "I thought . . . hmmm . . . didn't I have something for tomorrow?"

As if I were checking my tablet again, I looked down. "Nope, you're free." And just because I wanted to take her focus off this, I jumped from my chair. "Okay, so I'm going to get started because I want to do a lot of cross-referencing with this research."

"That's great," Gabrielle said. "I'll be working on a more detailed marketing plan for Contour, so I'll be right here for much of the day."

I scooted from the room, and then once I stepped back to Pamela's desk, I exhaled. When Pamela had told me that I'd be in charge of Gabrielle's calendar because she remembered nothing, that hadn't seemed like too big a deal. But today, it was.

"Everything okay?"

I looked up and across the massive space to the other side of the outer office. Mattie hardly ever said a word — Gabrielle's best witch kept her assistant totally busy, so Mattie always had her head down, always working.

But now her nosy butt was in my business when I didn't need her to be. I said, "Yeah, I'm good."

"Okay, I was worried. There's a flu going around, and you look a little pale."

What did she mean by that? I was black; I couldn't be pale. "I'm fine." I opened the browser on the desktop and then typed in the name of the first company Gabrielle had given to me. But I knew I was going to have a hard time concentrating because my thoughts were totally on tomorrow.

After about an hour, I gave up, thinking a break would help me get focused.

"Hey, Mattie, I'm going . . . down to Star-bucks."

"Oh, would you mind getting me some-thing?"

On my face, I had a smile, but in my head, I was rolling my eyes. Did everyone think I was their coffee girl? But I took her money — she was lucky she didn't give me her credit card — and took her order for a chai tea latte.

Then I rushed away from the office, feel-ing excited about what was going down.

I was beginning to spend more time in this bathroom than any other place in this house. But it was just that I couldn't take the chance of being overheard. Especially not with this call.

I dialed the number and then did my best to put a smile in my voice, so he wouldn't hear me trembling.

"Keisha?" Elijah answered the phone as if he couldn't believe my number had popped up on his cell.

"Uh, yeah, Elijah. It's me."

"Hey, sweetheart, how are you?"

If there was anyone I didn't want to hurt in all of this, it was Elijah. From the mo-ment I'd called him and told him the results of the test, from the moment we'd gone to his house last Sunday, from the moment he'd hugged me that day and told me he was so glad I was now officially his daughter, he had started calling me *sweetheart.* He acted like he loved me already; he acted like he loved me always.

"It's so good to hear from you. I was going to call and ask if you wanted to do something this weekend. Go out to dinner, maybe?"

"Uh . . . yeah, that would be cool."

"Good. I'll choose another great restaurant for you." He paused. "So, is everything all right?"

"Uh . . . yeah. It is. But . . ."

"What is it, sweetheart?"

"Well, I don't know if I should really be calling you."

"You can always call me. For anything."

"Uh . . . yeah. Well, it's about Gabrielle."

I heard the frown in his voice when he repeated her name. And then I began to spin my story. "I was hoping you could do me a favor and call her and get together with her in the morning."

"Why? What's wrong?"

"Nothing's wrong, and she's been really great with me. You know she gave me a job. But I heard her talking to Mauricio . . ." And then, I paused. His name had just come out — I hadn't planned to include him, and right away, I was scared that this could be a bad move. Suppose Elijah called Mauricio? But there was nothing that I could do now.

I picked up my story. "I think she's feeling a little left out."

"Left out of what?"

"Well, all the attention has been on me, and . . ."

I paused as he laughed. "Trust me," he said, "Gabby is fine. She was really happy to find out that you are her sister."

"I know, but . . ." I paused. How could I convince him? "I would just feel better if Gabrielle felt better, too."

Now I heard his smile. "You're thinking about your sister."

"I am. Everybody has been making such a big deal over me, and I just want you to do something special with her."

"You know what? That's a good idea. Okay, I'll give her a call . . ."

"No. Uh . . . I mean, yeah. I was hoping you could just have her over to your house tomorrow morning for coffee or something."

"Well, that won't work." His voice was so stern, so sure. "Gabby will never leave her office. She's always so busy."

"No, that's why I'm calling you. I checked

her calendar. I'm her . . . assistant." I paused as I looked up and into the mirror. And in my reflection, I saw how much disdain I had for that word. "I'm her assistant," I repeated. "You know that, right?"

"Yeah. Isn't that great?"

With those words, Elijah moved from being one of my favorites. How could he think a second-rate position like that was what I deserved? I told him, "So, she's free in the morning, but she has a really busy schedule for the rest of the week, and I think this will help her to start her day off."

"Well, I had something I had to do in the morning . . ."

Oh, God! Why wouldn't he just do what I asked?

"But you know what?" he said through my silent moaning. "I'm going to do it. I'm going to call her first thing in the morning. And why don't you come with her?"

I rolled my eyes. Really? "That won't work. I want you to give her all the attention."

He chuckled. "The two of you . . . looking out for each other already."

"I'm trying."

"I love it, sweetheart. Well, consider it done."

"Thank you, Elijah. And one thing — I

want to look out for Gabrielle, but don't tell her —"

"Oh, don't worry. This will be my idea and our secret."

That almost made me want to put him back on my favorites list. "Thank you."

"You're welcome, sweetheart. So, I'll see you this weekend?"

"Yeah."

"Looking forward to it. Love you."

Speaking as fast as I could, I said, "Okay. Bye." And I clicked off my phone, hoping he didn't notice that I couldn't say "I love you" back. I guessed that I could say it, but I didn't want to be so fake.

I leaned against the wall and closed my eyes. Everything was in place. Now I just had to hope and wait.

# 27

## GABRIELLE

"Okay, Daddy. Your timing is perfect. I don't have to be in the office early, so Keisha and I will drop by." Even though he didn't sound anything like he had just a few weeks before, I couldn't help but wonder why my father wanted to see me. Again . . . a call in the morning. Again . . . he was calling from home. The last time, I'd ended up with a sister.

Today, would I have a brother?

That made me chuckle. But then that chuckle went away when my father said, "Uh . . . would you mind if it's just the two of us, and not Keisha?"

Even though I frowned, I said, "Sure," and dragged the word out as if it weren't monosyllabic. After my, "Okay, I'll see you in about thirty minutes," I hung up the phone but held my cell in my hand.

"What's up with Pops?" Mauricio asked as he stepped from the bathroom and made a path straight toward me. He stopped right in my personal space and handed me his bow tie.

Tossing my phone onto the bed, I turned my attention to Mauricio's collar, though the frown on my face was deep.

My husband stepped back and, with his fingertips, lifted my chin so that my eyes were on his. "What's going on?"

"I don't know. Just weird." I went back to folding and tucking the tie. "Daddy didn't say much. And you know what happened last time he summoned me to his home early in the morning."

"Yeah." Then he grinned, and I knew he was about to say something smart. He said, "Maybe this time you'll get a brother."

"That's exactly what I thought."

"That great-minds thing isn't just a cliché. Anyway, let's just do what we did before. I'll take Bella to school, and you and Keisha can go to your dad's."

I tilted my head. "This was another thing that was weird. He wanted me to come alone," I said, with my voice lowered. "That's why I'm a little worried."

"Oh." There was surprise in his tone. "Well . . . instead of worrying, why don't you just get over there. I'll drop Bella off at school and Keisha at your office."

I exhaled a little bit of relief. "Thanks, babe." I wrapped my arms around his neck, and he smirked.

I knew what his smugness was about. It had been days since we'd argued about Justus, but even though we'd made up, we hadn't *made up.* There was still a bit of distance between us, space that always remained whenever it came to my longtime friend and high school boyfriend.

Mauricio said, "Is this an apology?"

My answer: I kissed him with a fervor that was meant to leave him breathless, wanting, and imagining what would happen tonight. When I stepped back, I used the tips of my fingers to wipe my lipstick from his lips, kissed his cheek, and left him standing there watching me wide-eyed and wide-mouthed.

Oh, yeah, tonight was gonna be one to remember.

But first I had to deal with my dad.

"So, have you had enough?" my father asked me.

I lowered my eyes to my plate, which was filled with just the bones of two devoured chicken wings and the leftover syrup that hadn't been sopped up by the waffle I'd chowed down.

When I looked back at my dad, I said,

342

"Okay, you've fed me good; now you have to talk to me." I pushed my plate aside. "Daddy, what's going on?"

"Why does something have to be going on?" he asked as he lifted my plate from the table. "Can't I just have breakfast with my beautiful daughter?"

"Of course you can." I pushed my chair back and stood next to him as he piled our dishes into the sink. "But you never do because you're always at work by six. So if you're not at work . . ."

He chuckled and shook his head. "You think you know me, huh?"

"I do. So I'm figuring . . . last time, I got a new sister, and today . . ."

"All right." He laughed and faced me. "I guess I have to tell you the truth."

That made my heart pound a little faster. Was this about Keisha? Had he found out more news? Was this good or bad?

The questions rolled through my mind, and I pressed pause. My dad was standing right here.

He leaned against the sink and folded his arms. "It was really nothing, sweetness. I just wanted to check in with you. See how things are going. Because the last time I called you here, I turned your life upside down."

I breathed, a bit relieved but still questioning. "What do you mean?"

"Well" — he shrugged a little — "one morning I call you and tell you I have another daughter, and a week later, you have a new sister, a new assistant, and a new roommate."

I laughed. "That about sums it up."

He said, "So, how are things going and . . . do you think Keisha plans to stay?"

I nodded. Now this made sense. "Well, first, you didn't turn a thing upside down. I love having a sister. Keisha's a cool kid."

He chuckled. "I don't know if she sees herself as a kid." He returned to his seat at the kitchen table, and I followed him.

"I know, I really like looking out for her; that's why I call her a kid. But you're right . . . she's no kid because she's really stepped up in the office. She's a quick learner, she knows all things digital, she works hard, goes the extra mile . . . she's a joy. So while I like looking out for her, she's helping me quite a bit."

"Good." His voice suddenly got softer. "And, uh . . . what about at home? I'm sure you and Mauricio didn't plan to have another mouth to feed."

"Well, that's not a problem." I laughed. "But if you're asking how is it having

344

another person in our house, that's been really cool, too. Especially for Bella."

That made my dad's face light up. "Bella likes having her there?"

I nodded. "But the thing is, Keisha loves having Bella there. Once we get home, the two of them spend all of their time together." And then . . . Keisha's words came back to my mind: *So precious, my precious daughter.*

Daddy said, "What? What is it?"

I shook my head to not only tell him that it was nothing, but to shake those thoughts away, too. Why did her words keep coming back to me?

"Is there a problem?"

After a final shake of my head, I turned to my dad with a smile. "No, it truly is wonderful, and while Keisha is a gift to you, she's been a gift to me, too."

He grinned as he stood and pulled me into a hug. "Now, if it ever gets to be too much, she can come and stay here with me. Although this" — he paused and glanced around the kitchen — "is nothing compared to that mansion where she's living right now."

"We don't have a mansion, but this is all you need to know: She's fine. I'm fine. We're fine. It's wonderful."

He nodded. "Well, now that I got all the information I needed, I'm sure you're itching to get out of here."

"I love you, but I am." From the back of the chair where I'd been sitting, I lifted the jacket to my suit, then grabbed my purse from the sofa.

He said, "I told Keisha that I wanted to get together this weekend."

"Okay, we'll do that. I'll arrange something." I gave my dad a kiss and rushed out the door.

Though I'd enjoyed my time with him and those chicken and waffles were the truth, I still had the feeling there was more to this morning meal. Maybe he just needed this assurance — that everything was cool with his daughters.

His daughters.

I was glad I could report that all was better than well.

Inside my car I put on my sunglasses, hit the button to call the office, but then clicked it off and instead thought about the conversation I'd had with Keisha the other day. There was something else I wanted to do right now. In two seconds, I had the plan in my head, then as I dialed the number, I grinned, just thinking about the look that would be on Keisha's face when I carried this out this weekend.

# 28
## KEISHA

The moment Regan opened her office door and stepped out, I lowered my head and pretended that I was searching for something on my phone.

Gabrielle's best witch was almost stomping as she led the two men from the Chancellor Corporation into the outer office. She paused when they were between where I was sitting and Mattie's desk.

"Mr. Flynn, Mr. Williams, once again, I'm so sorry. I can't imagine what happened to Gabrielle." She looked over her shoulder at me as if this were my fault.

My face was solemn as I held up my phone, indicating that I was still trying to reach Gabrielle.

Mr. Williams said, "Well, the good thing is that we're leaving with the numbers." Turning back, he looked at me. "Thank you, young lady."

He smiled, Regan glared, and I beamed.

My plan . . . had worked.

While Regan walked the men to the elevator, I sat back, inhaled accomplishment, and exhaled relief. Through the glass panels, I watched Regan shake the men's hands, then she marched back toward the office with fire in her eyes and brimstone in her steps.

She pushed the door open with such force it rattled, and that made me sit up straight. Especially once she came straight for me.

"Have you been calling Gabrielle?"

I held up my phone so that she could see Gabrielle's name under my recent calls. "What do you think I've been doing?"

"Let me call her myself," she said as if I were inept.

Just as she picked up the phone on my desk, Gabrielle sailed into the office. "Good morning," she sang.

Regan slammed down the phone and faced her. "Where have you been?"

"What? Didn't Keisha tell you?"

They both turned to me. "No," I said, ready with this answer. "You didn't tell me anything," I reminded Gabrielle. "All Mauricio said was that you had an appointment. I didn't know anything else." That was the truth. Mauricio had only told me that he would be driving me to the office. I guessed he didn't want me to know that Gabrielle and Elijah were getting together without me.

Regan turned her glare back to Gabrielle as if she was now giving her permission to speak.

Gabrielle said, "I'm here now, but if you have to know, I was having breakfast with my dad." She looked from Regan to me, then back to her best witch. "What's going on?"

"You just missed the financial meeting with the Chancellor Corporation. Remember, the follow-up they wanted to have before they made the decision about which PR firm they were going to choose?"

"Oh my God." She pressed her hand against her chest. "That was this morning?"

Regan nodded, and they both turned toward me.

"I'm so sorry, I don't know what happened, but somehow the calendar didn't sync correctly when I got this new tablet. Everything from Pamela's didn't download to mine."

"What?" She shook her head as if she was confused.

"That's why I didn't tell you about the meeting." I continued my explanation. "Because it's not on my calendar or yours. It's like the cloud wiped it out or something."

"Oh my God." Gabrielle exhaled as if she were just getting the full understanding. "I missed the meeting?"

Regan nodded, and I waited for her to say something. But when she didn't fill Gabrielle in, I did.

"But I was able to step in and give them the numbers." I stood up. "I remembered that you'd worked on them sometime last week, so I went into your computer, got the numbers, and printed them out."

"Really?" She frowned as if she didn't understand how I was able to do that. "Well, why didn't anyone call me?"

Regan glared at me and once again, I held up my phone. "I did, like a dozen times. And it would ring a few times and then go to voice mail."

Gabrielle grabbed her phone from her purse, tapped the screen, and said, "I don't have any missed calls."

Another glare from Regan, but her scowl didn't scare me. I held out my phone. "You can check it."

When Regan grabbed it from me, I was a bit surprised, but then, I was even more amazed when she *and* Gabrielle studied my call log.

"Ugh," Gabrielle moaned. "I see what

happened. You were calling our home phone."

I gave her a blank look. "It says cell."

"Yeah, I guess when I put in my numbers when we were buying your phone at the store, I must've mixed them up." She took the phone from Regan and handed it back to me. "My fault," she said to me, and then she turned to Regan. Regan folded her arms, and her stare stayed hot. As if she still thought I was to blame. After a moment, she said, "Well, they got their numbers, and that was what they came for." She shook her head, glanced at me, then said to Gabrielle, "Can I talk to you in my office? Go over what I told them?"

Gabrielle nodded, and then, as she moved past me, I mouthed, *I'm sorry.*

She nodded and smiled as if she was trying to assure me that all was well. She didn't have to tell me that — this, I already knew.

When Regan closed, or rather, slammed her office door, Mattie whispered, "That was intense."

I nodded, kicked back my chair for a moment, and then sauntered into Gabrielle's office. I closed the door behind me, then let my eyes drift from one corner of the room to the other. This office with the big red block desk and the yellow leather butterfly chairs wasn't like anything that I would have designed, but I'd be able to work it.

I still hadn't figured out this company situation yet because Regan and I didn't like each other — I certainly didn't want her for a partner. But I'd figure out how to get rid of her later. Today proved that I was going to be able to pull this whole thing off. There was not a bit of this situation that I didn't plan out — down to switching the numbers that Gabrielle had put into my phone. I'd done more than just cover the bases, I'd wrapped each one up in silk and satin.

Moving toward the oversize purple chair behind her desk, I sat down, but then I popped up and locked the door before I returned to where I'd been. I snuggled into the chair, then swiveled so I faced the windows.

This view was everything, this was Los Angeles, this was just a moment away from being my life.

The way this was beginning to go down, I wondered if this way had been God's plan all along. Maybe God was looking out for me and He believed that since I'd lost so much, He was going to give me this new life. I'd just have to work for it.

I laughed. I was thinking about God, giving Him credit . . . something that I'd never thought I'd do again. I'd been doubting Him for such a long time — since I was fourteen, really. Since I'd met Mr. Stanley. And when Mr. Stanley deserted me when I was fifteen, I knew for sure that God had left me, too.

That had been such a devastating year, a horrible time. And even now, as I remembered, I could still feel that pain.

I was pregnant.

And I had no idea what I was going to do. When I first suspected it, I thought I'd be able to handle it — because of Mr. Stanley. He'd been there for me and I'd been there for him, too. Doing all kinds of things with him on Wednesdays.

Now that I was pregnant, though, it had all changed. When I used to pass him in the halls, he wouldn't say anything, but he would give me a wink or a smile on the sly. But now he didn't even look my way. His eyes never wandered toward me . . . and when they did, it was as if he saw me by accident, but then he treated me as if I were invisible.

I was far from invisible, especially the way every day my belly protruded even more. It was still a secret, though. No one knew except for Buck, and I was so grateful for my new friend.

From the day I'd met him in Walmart, Buck had stayed by my side. Every day, he met me at the bus stop and walked me home. On Fridays, he'd stay at my house, sometimes all night, since Mama never came home till the next day.

And every day when I saw Buck, we had almost the same conversation:

"What am I going to do? I can't have no baby."

"I know. But I got you, boo. We'll figure this out."

"How?"

"Well, there are people who take care of these things. You can get an abortion."

"But they don't do abortions down at the clinic anymore," I said. "All of those churches got that place closed down."

"I know. But there are still private doctors who do them."

"Yeah, and those doctors cost so much money. I've checked."

"I told you, I got you. I'm trying to round up some money now. My cousin Que just got in the game."

I knew what he meant by that — his cousin was selling drugs. They were some

of the biggest moneymakers in White Haven.

He said, "I asked him if he could lend
me the money, but he's putting all of his
money back into his business. He said
he'd see what he could do, though."

I nodded, though I had no hope.

"No matter what happens, you not gonna
be by yourself. I'm gonna be here for you."

"I'm gonna have to tell my mama soon."

"Don't say nothing yet. Not till we figure
out which way to go. Just keep wearing
your big clothes."

I did what Buck told me, wearing sweatshirts, even when the temperature was
above eighty. Like Buck said, it worked at
home. Not that Mama didn't care about
me, but she had to work so much, she
didn't have time to check out what I was
wearing or notice how much weight I was
gaining. When we were home together, I
just kept on my bathrobe.

Then, on one of the regular days when
Buck walked me from the bus stop, I
paused and kissed him at the end of the
driveway when I saw Mama's car parked
there. But while I was kissing him, he
wasn't kissing me.

His eyes were wide open, and then he
said, "I think that's your mama."

I whipped around and saw Mama standing on the porch with her hands on her hips. There was only one time when she stood that way — that meant trouble.

I didn't even turn around and say anything to Buck; I just rushed away from him and scooted up the walkway. "Hey, Mama."

Her blond hair swung behind her back when she said, "Keisha. LaVonne. Jones."

That was the second bad sign — my full name. She glared at me and then her eyes rose over my head and I knew she was looking at Buck.

Dang! I should've told him to get out of here, to run all the way to wherever he was going. But I wasn't going to turn around now.

I was shaking, but I had to ask, "Mama, what's wrong?" My voice trembled along with the rest of me.

"Are you pregnant?" she asked me.

I was stunned . . . How did she know? I looked down at my belly, wondering if it was sticking out that much.

That was the only answer Mama needed. "You *are* pregnant." Then she glared over my head once again. "You've been having sex with that snotty-nosed boy over there?"

I gulped, trying to think of how I was going to tell her about Mr. Stanley. But before I could get the words out, I heard footsteps on the pavement. Two seconds after that, Buck stood by my side.

"Yeah, Ms. Jones. I'm the baby daddy."

I turned to Buck with wide and wild eyes. What was he talking about? I had never told him about Mr. Stanley — he had never asked. But we sure 'nuff knew that Buck wasn't the father. We had just started kissing.

Looking straight at my mama, Buck kept talking. "I just want you to know, Ms. Jones, that I'm gonna take care of Keisha and our baby."

Mama's glare softened — just a little — as if she already liked Buck. And then she said, "Well, you two come on in the house. We have a lot to talk about. And one of the things is that school said you can't come back there."

Now I was so shocked I couldn't move at all. At least, though, I knew how Mama had found out.

But Buck said, "Yes, ma'am," to Mama, then took my backpack from me, grabbed my hand, and pulled me into the house, into the living room and then, onto the sofa.

Mama marched in behind us, sat across

from us, and folded her arms. But that didn't scare Buck. He talked as if this were really our baby — telling Mama his plan about going to the clinic to get me and the baby some care, and how he was gonna find a job, probably at Walmart as soon as he turned sixteen, and then, he'd take care of both of us.

By the time Buck finished, Mama's arms were down by her sides, and she was leaning forward, smiling, and asking Buck when she was gonna meet his people.

Her final words to Buck that day were, "Well, all right now, you're stepping up. I like a man who steps up."

"Yes, ma'am," Buck said. "That's what I'm trying to be. I'm trying to be a man."

I swiveled the chair away from the window. Buck had told my mama he was gonna be a man, and even though he was only fifteen, he'd been more of a man than any who had been in my life. He'd taken responsibility for a baby that didn't have anything to do with him. And when he started really loving me, I was able to start loving that baby.

The more Buck said that he was my baby's daddy, the more I believed it, too.

Until like five months later, when I popped the baby out of me. It hadn't been all that bad, and Buck and Mama had been in the hospital room watching it all go down and all come out.

When the nurse handed the baby to Buck, he had cooed over her like he'd never seen anything so beautiful. "Nzuri. That's your name," he said without ever talking to me about a baby's name. I hadn't thought about it really.

But that name sounded pretty, and I really liked it when Buck explained to me, the baby, and Mama that Nzuri meant *beautiful* in Swahili. I didn't know where Swahili was, but the name was fine with me.

Buck had given our daughter her name, but that was just about all he could give her. Because without his DNA, he couldn't give her the charcoal tone of his skin. And because of that, and because of Mr. Stanley, Nzuri came out of me as yellow as the rubber duck that was in the crib that Mama had already set up next to my bed at home.

Mama hadn't really seen the baby until Buck handed Nzuri to her. Even now, I shook my head remembering the look of shock or horror (I could never tell which) that passed over Mama's face. She looked down at that baby, then looked up at me and Buck, and she only had one thing to say: "Oh, lawd!"

The rattling knob on Gabrielle's door brought my mind back to now, and that was a relief. It ripped my thoughts away from Mr. Stanley, but even more important than that, it took me away from Nzuri — and all that happened with her.

Now there was a knock and, "Keisha?"

I jumped up and dashed to the door. When I opened it, Gabrielle peeked in before she stepped in.

"Why was the door locked?" She gave me a real hard side-eye glance.

"I don't know. I didn't even realize it. I'd just come in here to make sure all the calendars were synced. I'm still trying to figure out what happened this morning."

She moved toward her desk and waved her hand. "That's okay. It was probably like you said — when we got your new phone, it didn't sync everything properly."

I nodded.

"From now on, we'll just double- and triple-check, because I cannot have another disaster like that." She paused. "But thank you for getting those numbers together and giving them to Regan."

"You're welcome." I turned, but before I could step out of the office, Gabrielle said, "I have a question, though. How did you get into my computer?"

Slowly, I turned and faced her. Giving those numbers to Mr. Flynn and Mr. Williams had not been in my plan. That had come to me this morning, and I wasn't even sure if it would work — since I didn't think I had the pass code to Gabrielle's computer.

But when I'd come up with the idea, I walked into her office and tried one code — the last four digits of her Social Security number.

And it worked.

People were so predictable. That was something that Buck taught me.

I said, "I just hit the mouse; it was unlocked."

She frowned. "I shut it down last night."

I shook my head. "It was on this morning, so . . ." And then I added, "Remember we rushed out of here because Mauricio asked you to pick up Bella?" I shrugged. "Maybe in the rush . . ."

She looked down at her computer. "Yeah, maybe." Then glancing at me, she said, "Well, thank you for having my back."

She smiled when she spoke; I didn't. I said, "Always. I'll always have your back. Just like you have mine."

I spun around and walked from her office, already planning my next steps in my head.

# 29

## GABRIELLE

After the morning I'd had, what I needed was some comfort food. So when Regan asked where I wanted to go for lunch, my expression told my best friend that the Hot Dog Shack was my eatery of choice today.

Since it was just a few blocks up Wilshire, that was another advantage. We could take a walk, something I never did in Los Angeles, and I could walk out some of this tension, while enjoying the cooler September temperatures.

We took the leisurely stroll, arriving just a smidgen before the lunchtime rush, and ordered our specialty hot dogs. Later, we exited to their courtyard and chose one of the red-and-white-checkered-tablecloth tables far away from the counter, where a crowd would congregate in just minutes.

The wrought-iron chairs scraped the bricked ground as Regan and I scooted closer to the table. Then, as the sun beamed over us, we bowed our heads, said silent prayers, then dug into the chili-and-cheese dogs, which were too decadent to eat more than once every month or so.

After I took that first bite, I closed my eyes and savored the treat. "I deserve this," I said after a long sigh of pleasure. "Today has been a day."

"And it's just noon."

"Thanks for not canceling on me."

At first the way Regan frowned, I thought she had no idea what I was talking about. "Why would I do that?" But then, just as quickly, she added, "Just because I have a business partner who doesn't take her job seriously?"

I chuckled, but Regan didn't crack a smile, and I tilted my head. "You don't think that . . ."

Now she grinned. "I was kidding. Well, about part of it. About not taking things seriously . . ." When she stopped, her smile went away, too. "Are you sure that there was a problem with your calendar syncing?"

I threw my hands in the air. "What else could it be?"

"I don't know." She slowed down her cadence. "It's just such a coincidence that the meeting wasn't on your calendar *and* you weren't in the office. Think about it —

any other day, you would have been sitting right there when the Chancellor people came in. But *today* . . . when it wasn't on your calendar . . . your father just happened to call you to come over . . ."

"Oh, so now you're a conspiracy theorist, and my dad is involved in this plot to keep me away from the office so that . . . what? Is he planning some kind of takeover?"

After a moment, she shrugged. "How is your dad?"

"He's good." I popped a french fry into my mouth. "He just wanted to check in and make sure everything was fine with me and Mauricio since Keisha is living with us. I think he was beginning to feel a little guilty about being the one who wanted her here, but she's staying at our place."

"That's a good point. And?"

"And what? Are things good with Keisha being there?" I answered before Regan had a chance to. "We're fine. I love having her there, and she's not the reason why Mauricio can sometimes be a jerk."

Regan raised an eyebrow. "A jerk? Oh, tough language." She laughed. "What's going on?"

I took another bite because I was going to need a little energy to talk about this. "Mauricio and I are good now, but for a few days, the air was sure salty between us. And you'll never believe why."

Her eyebrows furrowed together.

I waited several beats before I said, "Justus."

She leaned back in her chair. "Again?"

"That's almost exactly what I said. This time, it was over me asking Keisha to get Justus coffee." When Regan frowned, I filled her in on all that Mauricio had told me.

"Wow. A cup of coffee caused all of that?"

"No, it wasn't about coffee, it wasn't about Keisha, it was all about Justus. It just seems like any time Justus's name is mentioned, the conversation goes left."

She nodded, though it took Regan a moment to say something. Then finally, "What is it with Mauricio? He knows you love him, so what is this jealousy about?" She shook her head. "It's not attractive, especially on a man."

"He's never recovered from Justus telling him that if he'd come back to LA two weeks before our wedding, there would have been no wedding." I sighed. "You know how Justus is. He says crazy things like that to get under Mauricio's skin, and I don't know how to stop it. I don't know how to stop Justus, and I don't know how to stop Mauricio from getting riled up every time."

"Is this rivalry between them ever going to end?"

"There is no rivalry. I loved Justus fifteen years ago. I've loved Mauricio since I met him in grad school. Mauricio is the man I married. Forever."

"Yeah, well . . . and Justus is the man who financed our business."

"Now you sound like Mauricio."

"I'm just sayin', maybe I can understand your husband a little. I mean, it's like he's never going to get rid of this man who's a major Hollywood star, who still acts like he's in love with his wife."

I groaned. "It's not like that. But anyway, Mauricio and I made up all the way this morning, and I'm going to put an exclamation point on that tonight."

She laughed and we bumped fists.

But then, after a few bites and chews, Regan got serious again. "You know . . ." She stopped, then waved her hand. "Never mind."

I shrugged, refusing to ask Regan what she was going to say, and that was the key to get my best friend talking.

She said, "This is all Keisha's fault."

I was waiting for the rest of it, and when she said nothing else, I laughed. "Wow, I know you don't like my sister, but you're blaming her for Mauricio and me getting into it about Justus?" I didn't give her a chance to respond. "That's a stretch, don't you think?"

She put her hot dog down and leaned back. "Well, actually, from what you just said, she is to blame for your disagreement. At least indirectly. And that's what I mean. She may not be the cause of any of this directly, but what do your missing a very important meeting this morning and your fight with Mauricio have in common?"

I gave her the coldest, blankest stare I could muster.

And how did she respond to my expression? She said, "I rest my case."

I slapped my hand on the table. "You have no case. You're just crazy."

As if I hadn't spoken, Regan said, "Keisha is the common denominator in both of these situations." She sounded like she was giving a closing argument. "She had some part in this."

"Now you're stretching your crazy."

My words did nothing to stop her. "Maybe, but there are people out there who are just bad luck, and I think your sister is one of them. She's a bad, bad omen."

I leaned back. "Wow," I said, adding a couple of syllables to the word. "Do you want to take back what you just said?"

"No," she said without any hesitation. "In fact, I want to double down. There is just something that is not right about your sister. I don't know what it is, but before you and I started Media Connections, you know I prosecuted some shady folks, and she . . ." She tossed her napkin onto the table. "I know this is tough to hear, but I'm worried about you and your dad. I don't trust that girl. Like I said, she's a bad omen."

"So you're saying my sister is evil?"

Because of my tone, I expected Regan to really pause now and roll back her words. But not only did she not take them back, she doubled down — again. This time, though, she didn't say anything. She spoke through her expression — an if-the-shoe-fits-your-sister kind of glare.

Now it was my turn to speak without words. I glared right back, then pushed my chair from the table, scraping it loudly along the ground.

"Gabby." Regan called my name as I marched away from her. "Come on."

I didn't even turn around and it was a good thing I didn't. Because if I had, I would have cussed my best friend out. I would have cursed her with words that hadn't even been invented.

So since I already had enough on my plate to repent for, I just kept walking, hoping that by the time we saw each other once again, I didn't still want to punch her right in the nose.

# 30
## KEISHA

"I wanna go with Mommy and Auntie Keisha." Wearing her tutu and red hat, Bella stood in the middle of the kitchen, her arms crossed and her eyes spitting smoke.

"We talked about this, Bella." Gabrielle stood at the dishwasher, unloading the breakfast dishes while Mauricio sat next to me, the newspaper spread before him on the counter. Gabrielle continued, "We're going to a grown-up lunch."

"So?" She stuck her bottom lip out farther than I thought possible. "I'm grown-up."

While both Gabrielle and Mauricio frowned, I thought this was hella funny. She was exactly like I imagined Nzuri would be.

As quickly as that thought came, I shook it away. I wouldn't be able to breathe if Nzuri was in my mind.

Slipping from the bar stool, I knelt in front of Bella. "You want to go to a grown-up lunch, but I wish I were going to a little-girl lunch." I sighed as dramatically as I could.

She tilted her head. "Why?"

"Because little girls have way more fun at lunch."

She squinted, doubting my words.

I said, "At a grown-up lunch, I have to eat Brussels sprouts, broccoli, and liver with lots of onions . . ."

"Yuck!" Her nose creased.

"But at a kids' lunch, there's hamburgers and french fries and ice cream and maybe even a toy, like at McDonald's."

There were three pairs of wide eyes on me, though only one pair was filled with joy.

"McDonald's!" Bella cheered. "We never go to McDonald's. Can I go to McDonald's?" She turned to her parents and pressed the palms of her hands together. "Please?"

Gabrielle and Mauricio took matching deep breaths, and then he spoke. "Sure," he said, though he sounded like he still hadn't exhaled. Now he knelt down. To Bella he said, "We'll have lunch" — he cringed as he continued — "at McDonald's."

Bella and Mauricio cheered together, and I glanced at Gabrielle, who rolled her eyes, but then she smiled and nodded.

Gabrielle said, "After lunch, why don't we

come back here and watch lots of movies with lots of popcorn."

There were more cheers from Bella, and Mauricio gave her a high five.

He said, "Yay, Bella day!"

Now we all cheered.

Bella hugged her parents, then me, before Gabrielle and I rushed out. Gabrielle made plans for us to meet Elijah at noon, and really, I didn't know why Bella couldn't come with us. I was sure Elijah would want to see her as much as she seemed to love being around him.

But I asked no questions — I didn't even ask where we were going. I just hopped into the Lexus and went along for the ride.

As I rode, the streets looked familiar and it didn't take long to figure out we were somewhere in Beverly Hills. As much as Gabrielle came to this part of Los Angeles, I wondered why she and Mauricio didn't just live up here. I got living by the beach; that was cool. But Beverly Hills? Living here would be lit. And then, I had a new thought — when I took Gabrielle's place, that would be the one change I'd make. I'd live in Beverly Hills: me and Buck . . . and Bella.

That thought made me smile so hard as Gabrielle made a turn onto Santa Monica Boulevard, and then, a few blocks up, she slowed the car. When she stopped, I glanced up at the name of the restaurant: Crustacean.

Gabrielle gave the keys to the valet, and when we walked to the front door, Elijah stood waiting.

He hugged us, then said to Gabrielle, "The room is ready."

Room? What kind of restaurant had rooms? But I didn't say anything, like always. I just watched, like always.

The hostess greeted Gabrielle like she knew her, and then the woman led us up the staircase. We weaved through the maze of tables before the hostess stepped aside so that we could . . . enter a room.

I stepped inside, took one look across the table in the center, and shrieked.

With my hand over my mouth, I mumbled, "Oh my God," a million times as I took a couple of quick steps toward Justus. But then I drew back, remembering what happened before.

But this time, *he* came to *me.* "Hey, sweetheart." And then *he* pulled *me* into a hug.

Before he let go, he kissed my cheek, and I swore I would never wash my face again. While I stood there with my palm pressed to where his lips had been, Justus gave

Elijah one of those brother-brother hugs, and then he turned to Gabrielle.

"Come here, beautiful."

I stepped aside, not to give Gabrielle any extra room, but to watch the two. Just like the other day, Justus held her tight and held her close. He hugged her like Elijah wasn't even standing there.

When his lips lingered on her cheek, I knew something was going on.

Justus's arms were still around Gabrielle when he turned to me. "So, what's up?"

I pressed both of my hands over my heart. "That's what I wanna know."

"Well" — Gabrielle smiled at Justus like he was her man — "I called Justus, told him about my sister, and he arranged all of this." She spread her arms wide.

"Yeah," Elijah said. "Then they called me. I hadn't seen Tony in a little while —"

"Tony?" I frowned.

Justus chuckled. "Pops still calls me by my government name."

Elijah said, "That's not your government name. That's the name your mama and your daddy — God bless their souls — gave you." He shook his head. "Gabrielle says that same nonsense."

They laughed, but I didn't, and when Elijah noticed, he led me to the table like he wanted to make sure I was included.

As he pulled out a chair for me, Elijah said, "I've been knowing this boy since he was six." Then he sat next to me. "Coming to my house, knocking on my door all the time asking if Gabby could come out to play." Elijah shook his head at the memory.

Gabrielle and Justus joined us, and they chuckled at Elijah's words.

Justus said, "Yeah, I knew back then she was gonna be my wife."

Elijah laughed, Gabrielle sighed, and I made more mental notes, because this plot was surely thickening.

"But what I want to talk about" — Justus turned to me — "is you. When I heard that Gabby had a sister I couldn't believe it." He slapped Elijah's back. "Pops, you been holding out on us."

This time I smiled along with Gabrielle and Justus, but the smile faded away from Elijah.

Elijah's voice was soft when he said, "I didn't know about Keisha. If I had, she would've been in our lives." His eyes were on me as he finished with, "But now, I'm going to make these years up to her."

"Well, all right," Justus said. As if his words were some kind of cue, the door opened and a guy wearing a white jacket and a chef's hat came in. Now, I'd seen chefs on TV, but I didn't think they dressed this way for real.

He must have been a big-time chef, too, because everyone (except for me) greeted him like he was the celebrity. He shook my hand and then hung around Justus's chair asking silly questions like: *Hasn't the weather been great? And how 'bout them Dodgers?*

I didn't say anything after hello because he wasn't the one I wanted to talk to. When the chef finally left with promises that the food would be out soon, I got right to it. "So you guys have been friends for a long time?"

Justus said, "Yup, we grew up in Venice, went to the same schools, and our folks were friends."

Elijah and Gabrielle nodded.

"So, how did you become Justus?" I asked. "I mean, Elijah called you Tony."

Gabrielle jumped in, "Oh, I can explain that — when we were in middle school, Justus started writing all kinds of rhymes. That's all he ever did in class, in the library, when we were doing homework. This guy never even studied."

"Why did I have to study when I could get the answers from you?"

They all laughed together again.

377

Justus said, "Seriously, though, rapping, singing was something I've wanted to do my whole life; I got lucky on the acting part."

"Not lucky, son," Elijah said. "You're blessed."

"True dat." Justus turned back to me. "So, Keisha, tell me about you."

What was I supposed to say about my life that would compare to his? I said, "I grew up in Arkansas."

They waited for more, but when they realized that was all they were gonna get, Justus nodded.

He said, "Well, if you had to discover a new family, there aren't people better than these two." He pounded his fist against his chest. "These are my peeps, and I love them." He spoke to me, but looked at Gabrielle.

The chef returned with a couple of waiters and filled the table with all kinds of dishes I'd never heard of, like Buddha rolls, seared ahi tuna, wok egg noodles. After Elijah blessed the food, we ate, and I listened to them share their good-ole-days stories.

Gabrielle talked about when they tricked a substitute teacher in middle school into sitting on a chair covered with glue.

"What?" Elijah frowned. "I didn't know about this."

Gabrielle and Justus busted out laughing. Then together, they said, "Oops."

Then Justus shared his memory. "I took Gabby to both proms — our junior and senior."

Pointing back and forth between them, I said, "So y'all were boyfriend and girlfriend?"

They nodded together as if they were still in sync.

Elijah laughed. "Let me tell you something, Keisha. When these two didn't get married, it shocked the whole neighborhood, especially me. The first time he asked me if he could marry my daughter, they were thirteen. Then he asked me about thirteen thousand times after that."

Through his own laughter, Justus said, "And she said no then, and every time since."

As if she had to defend herself, Gabrielle said, "He was never serious."

"How you gonna say that?"

"Not that it matters," Elijah said, with more seriousness than laughter in his tone this time, " 'cause she has a husband now."

They laughed, but Elijah had shut down that part of the conversation. The talk turned to Justus: his appearance on *The View* and the success of his recent movie, *Last Man Standing.*

"I'm getting serious offers," he said. " 'Cause you know black actors don't sell internationally. But *Last Man . . .*" He shook his head. "We tripled the domestic box office overseas."

Elijah said, "Son, I'm so proud of you."

With a nod, Justus dipped his head a bit.

Elijah glanced at his watch, then tossed his napkin onto the table. "As much as I'd like to hang out, I gotta go. Choir practice." He looked back and forth between me and Gabrielle. "Y'all coming to church?"

After Gabrielle nodded, I did, too. It had been a long time since I'd stepped foot in a house of worship, but at least I could go to make Elijah happy and to thank God for my plan and for having me sitting here with Justus.

He hugged us, but the moment he walked out, Gabrielle said, "We need to get moving, too."

"Wait." Justus held up his hand. "I need to talk to you — a little business. Something important."

Gabrielle pushed her plate aside, then glanced at me.

That made me burn. Was she going to

treat me like that again? What was she going to do this time? Ask me to wait on the street?

Justus glanced at me. "Nah, Keisha can stay. I want her to."

"Okay," Gabrielle said. "What's up?"

I was pissed that this guy I'd just met thought more of me than Gabrielle, but I kept that smile because her treating me as if I were not worthy — those days were coming to an end.

"You know I finished my first children's book in that series and my literary agent got an offer."

"Congratulations, you're building your brand," Gabrielle said. "This is gonna be great for you."

Justus nodded. "The thing is, they're not offering me all that much up front. They're not convinced I can sell a children's book."

"What are they talking about?" Gabrielle and I said the same words at the same time.

He looked between the two of us. "Sisters." Then he got right back to his business. "They don't think children are gonna want to read a book from me."

Gabrielle said, "Have they forgotten about LL Cool J and Will Smith?" She pulled her tablet from her purse. "I need to get some sales numbers so your agent can show these people."

"I guess they're thinking they've never seen me in that kind of environment."

I said, "Well, why can't we do something so they *can* see you that way?"

Both of their glances shifted to me.

"I don't know, but maybe we can put together some kind of family event where you can greet people, sign autographs, and maybe even talk about your children's books. Get everyone excited. And if we do it live on social media, it will get you publicity across the country."

When their stares became blank, I wanted to shrink under the table. Why had I said anything? I shouldn't be so anxious — I had to learn a little more before I could step into these shoes.

But then Justus gave me a slow smile and Gabrielle did, too.

That made me want to continue. "You'll get a big crowd because the kids may not know you, but the parents will be the ones buying the books anyway. They'll drag their kids there as long as it's a family event."

As I spoke, Justus kept nodding. He waited until I finished to say, "Where have you been all my life?" Turning to Gabrielle, he said, "That's brilliant."

She nodded. "It is." And she beamed at me.

"You better watch out, beautiful. I might start a new PR firm with your sister. Call it Keisha's PR."

They laughed. Or rather, Justus chuckled, but Gabrielle folded over in a full-out belly laugh. As if that was either the funniest — or dumbest — idea she'd ever heard.

She spoke no words, but I heard her thoughts: *This girl just came out of Arkansas. She's my assistant, barely my sister.*

I said, "If you think it's a good idea, why don't we do it?"

Justus nodded. "The thing is, we're in negotiations now. It won't do me any good in two or three months."

"What about two or three weeks?" I asked. "I can think of lots of ways to promote this so in three weeks, we'll have so many people, we'll have to turn some away."

He squinted. "Tell me more — what're you thinking?"

I paused; he'd asked me, but I needed Gabrielle's support, so I deferred to her. "I don't know," I said, even though there were a million ideas jumping inside my head. "What do you think?"

"My concern is pulling something off this

quickly because of what's on our plates right now."

"I can do it. I can work on it full-time." And then I rolled that back. "I mean, in between all the other work you have for me. As long as you tell me who to call, what to do. I can get this done and get it done well."

Gabrielle said, "I don't know . . ."

"Nah, let's do it." Justus overruled her and pointed his thumb toward me. "I'm with her. In fact" — he pulled out his phone — "let's do some planning right now so that on Monday when you hit the office, you can get to running."

I exhaled relief when Gabrielle scooted her chair closer to the table. She said, "Keisha, I hope you're ready."

Then we all leaned in. And with our heads almost touching, we brainstormed: on the date, the venue, what we would call the event, how we would advertise. As we talked, I had to press my legs together and hold my hands together, just to keep myself together. I couldn't stop shaking. I was sitting here with Justus, planning an event for him. Justus talked to me like I was the one in charge.

With this idea, my plan for getting this life was just put . . . on . . . lock.

We were so intense, so focused, the heavy

knock on the door startled all of us. The guy, Smokey, who was with Justus the other day, peeked inside.

"Boss man, you about ready? It's almost five."

"Already?" Justus said.

Gabrielle glanced at her watch. "Oh, shoot. We have to get home." She turned to me. "Remember, Bella day."

"How is that little girl who was supposed to be mine?"

Gabrielle rolled her eyes. "Would you stop?" She pushed back her chair.

But I got another idea. "Justus, would you mind taking a picture with me? I mean, it would just be between the two of us. I won't post it all over social media. But it would mean a lot."

"Sure," he said. "I'm not worried about that. We're family now, and family looks out for family."

We stood and the picture party began — selfies with me and Justus, then the three of us, then with Justus and Gabrielle. I took some candid shots of them — the best one: Gabrielle buckled over with laughter as Justus tickled her and kissed her at the same time. Good stuff.

It took Gabrielle too long to realize how much more time had passed, and when the dude knocked on the door again and said it was six, Gabrielle shrieked.

"We really have to go."

After Justus hugged her and gave her a kiss (which I had a feeling would be much different if I hadn't been standing there), Justus turned to me.

"I'm gonna give you my number, my email — heck, the key to my house." He laughed; I didn't. "We'll work this to make *Justus's Family and His Friends* the event of the fall. You in?"

I grinned. I didn't get the hug and kiss that he'd given to Gabrielle; I got a fist bump, but that was good enough — for now. Justus was too old for me anyway, and what I needed from him had nothing to do with sex.

He walked us outside but didn't wait for the valet to bring Gabrielle's car. Instead, he hopped into a Cadillac SUV that was waiting, and then he got out of there before people recognized him.

It wasn't until he drove away that I realized this had been the best day of my life.

# 31
## GABRIELLE

Once again, I was seeing the world through Keisha's eyes and her excitement was contagious. We giggled and chatted all the way home. I often forgot that Tony was Justus — when we were hanging out, he was just my friend. It was always fun, though, to see others react to him. Well, by *others,* I didn't mean Mauricio.

I pushed thoughts of my husband aside and went back to the moment when I came up with this idea. I'd wanted to make up for that horrible faux pas at the meeting because I never wanted Keisha to feel less than in any way.

"I just can't believe it," she said for the gazillionth time. "Thank you, Gabrielle." She'd said that lots of times, too. "I promise, I won't let you down."

"I'm not worried," I told her. "We'll work together closely on this. Actually, events are Regan's responsibility, but she'll be fine working with you."

Her excitement had been palpable, and now the darkness that washed over Keisha was just as apparent.

She said, "Regan doesn't like me."

I said, "That's not true." Then I ducked, hoping the lightning strike would miss me.

But while it seemed the wrath of God wasn't coming down on me just yet, my lie didn't make it past Keisha. She gave me one of those lean-back, side-eye glances that said two words: *Yeah, right.*

I wasn't going to be able to leave it there, so I added, "Regan doesn't know you, so the three of us working on this will help. She'll see how wonderful you are and how hard you work, and all will be well."

This time, Keisha said, "Yeah, right," outright just as we turned onto our street. When I pulled into the garage, before I even turned off the ignition, Keisha jumped out, a fireball of bliss.

Inside, the entire downstairs of the house was dark. There was light, though, from the family room, and I was glad Mauricio hadn't waited for us to get Bella day started.

Keisha and I tiptoed inside, and only Mauricio looked up. He smiled, then after glancing at Bella (whose eyes didn't leave the screen), he stood and came to the back.

He kissed my cheek. "You're late," he said. "Shopping?"

Before I could say anything, Keisha jumped in, "Oh, no. We were hanging out with Justus."

Now, I hadn't planned on lying to my husband, though if it had been just me, maybe I would've let him believe that it was shopping that had me coming home later than planned. Because what I tried to do, always, was avoid this — the darkening of my husband's eyes, the stiffening of his shoulders, the fading of his smile.

Keisha carried on, "We had lunch and then just hung out talking and planning and taking pictures. We took pictures for almost an hour. Here, look!"

Before I could stop her, she had the pictures on her phone in Mauricio's face, and I wanted to choke her. But how could I? She had no idea my husband reverted to our daughter's age whenever Justus's name was mentioned.

And because she didn't know, she turned up the heat. "Oh, this is the best picture," she said, not noticing the flames in Mauricio's eyes. "I had no idea they used to go out."

Mauricio paused as if he was making sure she was finished. When nothing else bubbled out of her, Mauricio asked Keisha, "Can you stay here with Bella?"

She was so into her joy, she didn't notice the throbbing vein in his forehead or the deepness of his voice. She just said, "Sure," and bounced into the room.

Mauricio marched out; he didn't have to ask me — I followed. He didn't stop in the kitchen; he went into the hall, hooked a right, passed through the foyer, and stepped into the living room.

He faced me with his arms crossed. "So another brush-off of your husband and daughter for Justus."

I tossed my purse onto the sofa and sighed. "That's not what happened."

"You told me you were having lunch with your dad."

"We did. Dad was there and I didn't mention Justus because of this." I waved my hand toward him.

"Because of what? Me questioning why you didn't come home when we said we'd make this an afternoon for Bella?"

"We never set a time."

He looked at his watch. "Well, when you left at eleven thirty and said you'd be gone a couple of hours, I didn't think you would be coming home after six."

"It was just like Keisha said: we had

lunch, then got caught up with business. He has this book he's writing and . . ."

He held up his hand. "It's always about business — Justus's business. This dude keeps getting in the middle of our lives."

"Don't you think that, once again, you're overreacting?"

"No."

"Because when you thought Keisha and I had been out shopping, you were fine. But now it's an issue."

His lips barely moved. "This man is trying to come between us."

"He's not. He's just being a friend who sometimes jokes too much. But he's never made a move on me, never propositioned me in any way."

Mauricio chuckled, but there wasn't any kind of amusement in the sound. "He doesn't have to come at you with sex; he can have you any time he wants with his money."

His words knocked me back. "You are going low with that."

"It's the truth." He raised his arms before they flopped to his sides. "Any time you need money, you go to him."

"Now you're just making it up as you go. The only time I talked to Justus about money was for my business. And that's because he wanted me to represent him."

"And what about Bella's birthday? I didn't want to spend that kind of money, and then all of a sudden, Justus is knocking on our door with a check."

"That was his idea. He knew it was her fifth birthday and he wanted to do something special. What you don't seem to remember is that I've known this man for practically my whole life. And what I don't understand is why we always have these kinds of discussions about Justus."

He glared at me. "You just don't get it." And that was the end. He said nothing else, just stomped out of the room.

I watched him walk away, then listened to him march up the staircase before I slumped onto the sofa. Holding my face in my hands, I moaned. I didn't know what to do, and what was worse was that I didn't know how this was going to end.

# 32
## GABRIELLE

It was cold in this car. Not the physical temperature, but the mental one, the emotional one — the air was as frigid, as solid as ice.

Without turning my head, I peeked at Mauricio. He wore the same expression he'd had since we'd awakened this morning. Actually, he'd gone to bed with it last night. His stare was hard, his lips set in a tight line.

The last words my husband had spoken to me were the ones he'd left me with last night: *You just don't get it.* That was it, unless I counted his grunt after I'd reminded him about church this morning.

"Mommy."

Bella's voice was soft. I twisted and took in my daughter's wide brown eyes. My child, always the ebullient one, sat stiff, her fear as palpable as the tension in this car, and I wanted to lift her from her car seat and hold her in my arms until she was scared no more.

I understood her fear; Mauricio and I had always done this part of our marriage well. Bella never saw any disagreements between us. But while she hadn't seen what happened, she could feel it. Everyone could.

Except . . . Keisha.

Turning around, I watched Keisha for a moment. Her eyes were on the sights that flew by as Mauricio sped up Venice Boulevard. The smile on her face was the sign of her oblivion. I was almost sorry I'd introduced Keisha and Justus because she hadn't stopped talking about him.

If there was a Sunday when this family needed to be at the altar before the Lord, today was that Sunday morning.

I closed my eyes and prayed inside: *Dear Lord, please have a word for me.*

That became my mantra as Mauricio pulled into the parking lot of Hope Chapel. This Inglewood church had been my spiritual home since I was in high school, and Pastor Ford had been the only pastor who'd constantly been in my life. She'd been my and Mauricio's premarital counselor, then she'd officiated over our wedding. She was there for me as I lived through both ends of life — the death of my mom and the birth of my daughter.

As we stepped across the parking lot, I wondered if talking to Pastor Ford might be a good option. Maybe she could help me see what I was missing with Mauricio.

Just as I pulled open the heavy wooden door, Mauricio said, "I'll take Bella to children's church."

I nodded. "I'll save you . . ."

He stepped away as if he didn't care what I had to say. Keisha bounced inside and I followed her into the humming sanctuary, which was charged with Sunday-morning electricity.

I hugged the ushers, took a program, then walked down the left aisle to the section a few rows from the front. Keisha passed over me as I kept the aisle seat free for Mauricio.

The moment we sat, I felt a hand on my shoulder, then glanced up and into the eyes of my father. There were tears in my eyes when I jumped into his arms.

After our embrace, he stepped back. "What's wrong, sweetness?"

I shook my head. "Nothing. It's just we haven't been here in a few weeks and you know how much I love Pastor Ford . . ."

He stared at me for a little longer, then leaned over and hugged Keisha, before he went to his place on the podium with the praise team.

I bowed my head to pray again, but before I could get a word out, Mauricio eased next to me. It was a shame that I felt relief; it was just that I wouldn't have been surprised if he'd decided to sit somewhere else this morning. That was how dysfunctional this whole situation was to me.

"This is the day," my father's voice boomed through the church's speakers, "that the Lord has made."

Everyone in the sanctuary sprang to their feet. And together, we finished the scripture: "Let us rejoice and be glad in it."

"Hallelujah," my father led the church in praise.

Around me, people raised their hands, shouted out their gratitude to the Lord. But my arms remained by my sides, and my eyes stayed straight ahead until I peeked at Mauricio; his stance was the same as mine.

*Dear Lord, please have a word* . . . and then I changed up my prayer . . . *for us.*

That was my new mantra as the praise team sang song after song exalting our God. I tried to sing, but no sound came from me. I was weary from this battle with Mauricio.

Through praise and worship, then the welcoming of the visitors (and all the people who came to greet Keisha), then through the announcements, I struggled to keep my smile. There was a warring in my spirit that I couldn't calm.

Then, Pastor Ford glided into the sanctuary and stood at the pulpit with her head bowed until the only sound in the sanctuary was the soft music from the keyboard. Just watching her, feeling her silent prayers, made my spirit settle.

Finally, she began, "You know, I pray all week as I reflect and meditate to receive God's guidance for the word He wants me to bring. I was ready to speak this morning, but as I walked into this atmosphere, the Holy Spirit spoke to me."

"Amen," a few people murmured.

Jackie, the minister of music, still played the keyboard softly. "You know how sometimes you go to church and the pastor is talking directly to you?"

"That's me every Sunday, Pastor," someone from the back shouted, and the sanctuary filled with laughter.

Pastor Ford chuckled, too, but then, she returned to the solemnness she'd carried since she'd walked to the altar. She gestured for the music to stop.

When the church was void of any sound, Pastor said, "Today, I have this word for somebody, or maybe it's for more than one somebody."

"Amen."

"Today, we need to have a little talk about envy."

There were many more "Amens" this time.

I tapped the Bible app on my tablet, waiting for Pastor Ford to send us to scripture.

She said, "But I don't want to talk about envy alone." She held up her finger. "I want to talk about envy *and* jealousy. Because often, we confuse the two. It's not that one's better than the other, but you must know the difference so you can know how to pray. Because, you see, this is what you must know: attacks of envy, attacks of jealousy cannot be fought in the flesh. It's spiritual warfare, and you have to know which fight you're having before you get into the battle. Not knowing what you're fighting is like taking a knife to war when the devil has an entire militia."

"Amen!"

"So, what's the difference between envy and jealousy? And I want you to really get this." She paused. "Envy is between two people, and jealousy involves three." She stopped again as if she wanted us to digest those words. "To take it further, envy is a reaction to the lack of something — you don't have something that someone else has, and you want it. Jealousy is the reaction of losing something that you don't want to lose. And that some*thing* is usually some-*one*."

There were murmurs inside the church, and even I shifted. Was this what Mauricio and I were battling? Was my husband . . . jealous?

I shook my head. No, couldn't be. But when Pastor told us to turn to Proverbs 14:30, I couldn't get to the scripture fast enough.

Pastor read from the New King James version of the Bible, "A sound heart is life to the body, but envy is rottenness to the bones."

As Pastor spoke, I read the scripture again. I couldn't remember how many times I'd read Proverbs, but I didn't recall this scripture, though I wasn't sure how anyone could forget these words.

Pastor said, "Rottenness to the bones. Do you know what *rottenness* means?" Over the whispers of the congregation, Pastor continued, "When something is rotten, it is decomposing or decaying. Having some-thing rotten in your life has happened to all of us. You leave something in your car or in your refrigerator. And later, when you open that car or refrigerator, you have to step back."

When Pastor took a couple of giant steps away from the pulpit, members laughed once again. Though I didn't; this was serious to me.

She continued, "So you *know* the smell of decomposition. And if you know that smell, then you know the smell of envy."

"Preach!"

With my hand, I covered my nose. As if the smell of envy was close by.

Pastor Ford said, "That is what envy does to you. It turns you rotten down to the bone. Your bones, the very foundation of your physical body. You smell to everyone you come in contact with."

"Dang," Keisha leaned over to me and whispered. "Glad that's not me."

I nodded and turned my attention back to the pastor.

She said, "So now that I've made you uncomfortable" — there were a few chuckles — "let's talk about jealousy. We're going to stay in Proverbs. Turn to chapter twenty-seven, verse four." Before half of the church got there, Pastor read, "Wrath is cruel, anger is overwhelming, but who can stand before jealousy." She strutted away from the pulpit. "Commentaries make the meaning of this scripture clear. Wrath and anger are like storms — they rage, but they end. But jealousy?" She moved closer to the front row. "When jealousy is inside of you, it stays and stays and stays. You may be able to hide it for a minute or a month. But it will rear its head always."

I opened my notes app and tapped out the message Pastor had just delivered. When I glanced up, Mauricio was doing the same. As he typed, he nodded, then he glanced back at Pastor.

"Like I said, this message is for somebody or more than one somebody . . ."

As she said that, I felt Mauricio's eyes on me.

"But this is what I know. Both of these emotions bring battles that must be fought *and* can be won."

Mauricio reached for my hand.

"These are human emotions, but you are children of God. So fight! Fight with the armor He has given you. Then claim your victory."

There were fresh tears in my eyes when I gazed down at where my hand was intertwined with my husband's. I guessed we were in a battle. But this is what I knew for sure — we would fight and we would win. Because God had brought me and Mauricio here today. And He had changed Pastor's message just for us — we were the somebodies.

I squeezed my husband's hand as a tear dripped from my eye.

The temperature in the car had changed, though the ride home was still silent. Mostly because it was just me and Mauricio, as Keisha and Bella had stayed behind to have lunch with Dad.

I'd been surprised Keisha had agreed. I had a feeling, though, it had more to do with her hanging out with Bella than spending time with our father.

Driving home now, Mauricio's lips were no longer fixed in that tight smile. He'd relaxed, and that was a relief to me.

Still, after Pastor Ford's sermon, I needed to talk to him. I wanted to assure my husband there was no one I would ever love the way I loved him.

That thought made me cover his hand that rested on the console between us with mine. He gave me a quick glance, a small smile, then returned his eyes to the road. The temperature in the car warmed even more.

About twenty minutes later, Mauricio pulled into our garage. When he slid from the car, he said, "I'm going to check the mail; I didn't do it yesterday."

I sauntered into the house, then waited for him in the kitchen. He was already sorting through envelopes when he stepped inside and I watched his eyes narrow as he stared at one.

"What is it?" I asked.

He tore open the envelope, scanned the paper, and glanced up. There weren't tears in his eyes, but there were tears in his voice. "Just my test results. My sperm count." He inhaled.

I wanted to rush to my husband and hold him. I knew the difficulty of this disorder for him. That was why after a lot of prayer and as much studying, he'd enrolled in this experimental case study to see if, with a new drug, his sperm count would increase. But unless he responded to these treatments, we'd never have another child. We did have the option of traveling that uncertain road of in vitro fertilization. But neither one of us wanted that emotional and expensive roller coaster ride.

The way he studied me, I knew he was going to ask the same question he did every time his results came in. "Any regrets?"

I tilted my head. "How could I have any when I have you and Bella? The two of you . . . you're all I need."

He nodded, though I still felt the ache the results left him with each time. He dropped the rest of the mail onto the table, then stood on the opposite side of the island facing me.

At the same time, we spoke:

"Gabrielle, I wanted to talk to you."

"Mauricio, I wanted to talk to you."

We chuckled, looked down, then glanced up, our moves in rhythm.

I said, "You first."

He nodded. "In church this morning, Pastor Ford's message . . . it was deep."

"That's what I wanted to talk about, too."

He said, "I heard her, but I'm not jealous. I really searched my heart and that's not what we're fighting."

"Okay. Because I wanted to tell you that there is no need for you to be jealous. You will never lose me to anyone or anything."

He didn't move, as if he didn't quite believe my words. "It's not about losing you, it's about priorities. When I look at our lives, there is hardly anything that goes on with me that can get in the way of you and Bella. But that's not the same with you. There are too many times when Bella and I come behind" — he paused as if he wanted to say the right thing — "Media Connections."

I nodded, even though I didn't agree. I wanted to acknowledge that I heard him. "You and Bella are my priority. But I'm a new entrepreneur with a business that's just five years old. I'm far from eight-hour days."

"I get that. And that's why I'm willing to always help out. I just never expected it to be like this."

I rounded the island, then hooked my arms around his neck. "You are the kindest, gentlest, most loving man I know." Then my lips spread into a slow smile. "And I can't forget the finest. The only man I can see through my eyes, inside my heart, and in my life . . . is you. I love you with everything in me."

"I love you, too."

"And I'm going to work on this. I'm going to make sure you and Bella always know how important you are to me."

His arms tightened around my waist. "I think this is what lawyers call a deal." He pressed his lips to mine, and before I even parted my lips and welcomed him in, I sighed.

Our tongues danced a slow waltz, and I could have stayed like this for the rest of my life. My passion was rising, rising, rising, and I pulled back breathless.

I said, "I'm trying to figure this out."

"What?"

"Well, I've told you how much I love you" — I tapped my finger on my lips as if I were in deep thought — "but I think it's time to show you."

Now he squinted as if he were wondering about this, too. "How many rooms are in this house?"

"Counting all the bathrooms, I'm not sure. Something like ten, eleven, twelve . . ."

"Stop there. Twelve's enough. I can think of a dozen ways and a dozen places" — he began to unbutton my blouse — "where you can show me."

This time when our lips locked, for the next three hours, they hardly parted.

# 33
## KEISHA

Gabrielle stepped into her office and closed the door the way she always did. I rounded Pamela's desk and took what I knew for sure now was my temporary place. Setting my purse down, the first thing that I went for was my phone. I had a message:

Morning, boo. Call me later.

That made me grin. Buck and I had talked last night till like two in the morning. He was as excited as I was about the best weekend of my life.

*"Yo, boo. We're gonna be living large in LA."*

Buck was right about that because as it was all coming together for me, it was falling apart for Gabrielle. When I talked about Justus on Saturday night, Mauricio was like those volcanic rocks in the saunas I'd seen when Mama and I had taken a trip to Hot Springs — he was steaming, and I just kept pouring on the water.

It seemed, though, that by the time Bella and I had come home yesterday, Gabrielle and Mauricio had some kind of truce. I hadn't expected that, but I'd set up enough trouble between them, and now I could stir up more with what I'd found out yesterday.

I adjusted Pamela's computer monitor so no one would see the screen, then I typed: low sperm count.

In the two seconds it took for the information to load, I thought about last night when Gabrielle asked me to move the mail from the kitchen table so we could set the plates for dinner. There was lots of mail, but only one envelope was open. It was the word "sperm" on the unfolded page that made me stop.

I'd only had a few seconds to scan it: Addressed to Mauricio . . . low sperm count . . . then dozens of numbers I didn't understand. With Gabrielle only feet away, I couldn't study my discovery, so I tucked the mail behind the canisters on the counter.

But when I'd snuck downstairs after everyone was asleep, the letter and the rest of the mail were gone.

So now I had to research on my own. Dozens of sites popped up, all of them having to do with . . . male infertility. I sat back and stared at the screen. Was this a problem for Mauricio? Did this mean he couldn't have children? Was Bella even his?

*"How is that little girl who was supposed to be mine?"*

That was what Justus had said to Gabrielle on Saturday. Was Bella . . . his daughter? I had questions with no answers. But what I did know was this was something I could use.

Just as I clicked off the screen, the postman walked in, nodded the way he did every morning, and placed the mail on Mattie's desk. I gathered the stack addressed to Gabrielle.

Skimming through the letters, one envelope — with a generic return address — made me pause. I felt through the paper . . . credit cards.

Rushing back to Pamela's desk, with great care I lifted the lip of the envelope so I'd be able to reseal it. There were two credit cards inside, and I laid both on the desk, grabbed my cell, opened the camera, took a picture of the front, and just when I snapped a photo of the back . . .

"What are you doing?"

My head jerked up, and there was Gabrielle's best witch looking down. She'd slithered in like the snake she was without making a sound.

"What are you doing?" she repeated, now sounding like a growling dog.

"I was taking a picture of this credit card."

She snatched it from the desk.

I said, "Hey, that's not yours."

After she scanned the card, she said, "And apparently, it's not yours either."

"I never said that it was. It's Gabrielle's, and I was going to show her an app that stores credit cards safely."

"That doesn't even make sense."

"Well, the good thing" — I snatched the card back — "is that I don't have to make sense to you. You can ask Gabrielle if I have permission to do this."

My bet was that she wouldn't do that, at least not right now, because she couldn't take the chance of being wrong in front of me. I won that bet when after another moment of her glaring, she rolled her eyes, then rolled her big ole hips down the hall. She seemed to be getting fatter by the day; I looked much cuter when I was pregnant. I shook that memory away and returned to my task.

Dang . . . I needed to be more careful, and now I'd have to find some kind of app for Gabrielle. In the meantime, at least I had one credit card for Buck.

When Gabrielle opened her door, I stood and tapped on it. "Are you ready?"

She waved me in.

I put the mail on her desk. "Your credit cards came, and I've been researching apps that can guard your numbers, and even detect fraud faster than the bank. We'll go over those later."

"That's great, Keisha." She grinned. "You're turning out to be a wonderful assistant."

It was hard for me to even give her a fake smile when she used every opportunity to belittle me. Why did she always have to say I was her assistant?

To stop the boiling in my blood, I said, "I'd like to review some things for Justus's event before your conference call this morning."

Just as I sat down, her cell phone rang.

Gabrielle glanced at the screen. "Speaking of," she said before she answered. "What's up, Justus?" Then, "She's with me now. Let me put you on speaker." Another pause. "Okay, you're on."

"I haven't been able to stop thinking about this since Saturday. So, what I want to know is . . . what have you accomplished so far?"

I stiffened.

Gabrielle rolled her eyes. "Really, Justus."

He laughed. "But that's how serious I am about this. So can we meet this morning?"

"Sure," Gabrielle said. "As long as you come in after eleven."

Every good thing I'd been feeling faded away fast. Because if Justus came to this office, that would give Gabrielle another excuse to shut me down and lock me out.

Justus said, "Nah, I'm waiting on a delivery. So I was thinking you could come over here."

"I can't this morning," Gabrielle said.

"I wasn't talking about you; I was talking about Keisha."

His words made Gabrielle sit back in her chair, but to me, they sounded like a new song.

"Oh," Gabrielle said. "When you said you . . ."

"You already told me all that's on your plate. I just want to lay out a few things I've been thinking about and get it down in a plan before I leave for New York tomorrow."

"I didn't realize you were going out of town."

"Going to have a face-to-face with my literary agent. Tell him what's up."

"Well, then you and Keisha need to meet. I'll have her Uber over."

"Nah, I'll send Smokey." He paused. "How soon can you be ready, sweetheart?"

It took me a couple of seconds to realize he was talking to me. "I'm ready now."

"Bet. Smokey will call up when he's downstairs."

After a few good-byes, Gabrielle hung up, and I had to press my legs together to stop that shaking thing that happened to me with Justus.

I said, "I promise you, I'll be able to handle this with Justus."

"Handle what with Justus?"

I didn't even turn around; just the sound of that witch's voice sent my blood back to boiling.

"I'm glad you're here, Regan." Gabrielle waved for her to come in. "I was gonna call you last night, but we were so busy."

"What's up?"

I had a feeling that I wasn't going to have to worry about the credit card situation for a minute. Because once her best witch heard this . . .

"Keisha has come up with the most fabulous idea to support Justus with his literary career." She motioned toward the other chair and Regan sat next to me.

Gabrielle went on to tell Regan the details that we had to this point. She ended with,

"Keisha's on her way over to Justus's place now."

Regan turned her body around so that she faced me, and then just as dramatically, she swung back to Gabrielle. "Ah . . . events for our clients, especially the major ones, are my responsibility."

"Of course, but this just came up, and with everything that we're both doing, I thought it was a good idea for Keisha to get this started."

Regan shook her head.

"It's not a big deal," Gabrielle said. "Justus loves it, and he likes working with Keisha."

After a few moments of way too much silence, Regan said, "Keisha, would you mind leaving us alone?" She spoke to me, but her eyes were hard on Gabrielle.

I didn't move. It was bad enough that I was Gabrielle's assistant. I wasn't about to jump when the witch said so.

Even when Gabrielle nodded, I took my time standing. I'd only taken two steps when Regan said, "And close the damn door."

I almost stopped to tell her that she needed to find better words and a better way to talk to me. But then I kept going because this was part of the plan. By the time I finished, maybe even Regan would be gone and I could just work for Justus. With him as my only client, it would still be enough for this life.

Sauntering to Pamela's desk, I went back to my phone, found the picture of the credit card, then texted it to Buck along with a message:

For you, boo.

Then I waited for Smokey to arrive, and it felt like I was waiting for my future.

# 34
## KEISHA

I had never been in this part of California, but the signs said we were in Bel-Air. Everyone in the world knew about this place; this was where the Fresh Prince lived.

But what I didn't know about Bel-Air were the houses. Not that I could see any; they were all behind big iron gates. Bel-Air was like Beverly Hills on steroids.

Finally, Smokey turned the tricked-out SUV into a short driveway with a gate that had a big *J* in the middle. He eased to the side, pushed the button to lower his window, then pressed numbers into a keypad.

It was magic in Bel-Air. The gate parted. Smokey eased the SUV forward, then drove up a narrow, winding road that was flanked by trees.

It didn't take too long to get up the hill where a huge fountain with water sprouting out of the trunk of an elephant stood. Smokey rounded the fountain, and my mouth opened as wide as my eyes. I had never — not in any magazine, not on any TV show — seen a house this big. *This* was a mansion.

I jumped down from the SUV, then followed Smokey up three steps to the front doors, which were tinted glass. Before Smokey could even ring the bell, a man wearing a real butler's uniform opened the door. That made me think of the Fresh Prince again, and I wondered if every house in Bel-Air had a butler.

"Yo, Ed," Smokey said to the man.

"What's up, Smokey?" He turned to me. "Come in, Ms. Keisha."

I stepped inside, but then all I could do was stand at this front door and stare at this massive space. This place made Gabrielle's house look like a toy box. She only had one staircase; Justus had two, one on the left and the other on the right. And he had two chandeliers *and* marble floors.

"Hey, sweetheart."

I glanced up to where Justus stood above us wearing jeans and a white wifebeater. But he was so high up, his voice echoed down. My hello was a grin — and I hoped I didn't look too silly.

He did a sexy trot down the stairs. When he got to the bottom, he pulled me into a hug, then told me to follow him. He said to Ed, "Bring us some drinks and snacks."

As I walked behind him, I tried not to stare at his arms; his biceps bulged more than Buck's and he had tats, too, which was so sexy to me. Yeah, Justus was older, but he was the kind of older that was kind of fine.

He led me into a room where two walls were completely covered by floor-to-ceiling bookcases. One looked like it held thousands of books, and the other was filled with statues and plaques. I knew what some of them were: a Grammy, an Oscar, and a boatload of NAACP Image Awards.

"Sit over here." He directed me to a brown leather sofa that faced the opposite wall, where two huge flat-screen TVs hung. Both televisions were on, though muted — one on CNN and the other on ESPN.

When I sat down, the leather reached out and hugged me. Dang, I'd thought Gabrielle's furniture was lit.

Justus sat at the other end of the long sofa and stretched his arm along the back. I didn't miss the way he stared at my legs, and I was glad I'd worn this black denim mini with my ankle boots.

"So," he began, "ready to get working?"

"I am." I pulled my tablet from my bag.

"I've been thinking about this all weekend, too. I want you to know, Justus, I'm going to do a good job, so that any time after this if you need me . . ."

He laughed. "Slow your roll, sweetheart. Gabby's the one who works with me."

"Of course. I was just saying if anything happened to her . . ."

He frowned.

"I mean if she got sick or whatever, I want you to know I could step right in."

"I see that, sweetheart. You're loaded with ambition, aren't you?"

"I am." I gave him a grin and again hoped that I didn't look too stupid.

"So, how do you like being in California and staying over there with Gabby and her husband? It's working out?"

"Well, they certainly have enough room for me."

He nodded. "So things are good?"

I bit my lip to stop myself from speaking. Justus was fishing, and I had something for him to catch, but I needed information, too. I had to play this, though, like I wasn't trying to start trouble.

"Yeah, it's good," I finally said, "but I don't know how long I'll be there."

He frowned. "What do you mean?"

I hesitated, more for affect than anything.

"Well, they argue a lot, and I have a feeling they didn't argue much before. I think it's because of me."

He shook his head. "Nah, I know Gabby, and when she told me about you, she was thrilled. If they're having problems it's because of that punk she married."

I laughed. "I have a feeling he'd call you the same thing."

His eyebrows rose to the top of his forehead. "Oh, really?"

"Yeah, when we came home from hanging out with you on Saturday . . ." I shook my head, letting that gesture finish my sentence.

"He had a problem with that?" He chuckled. "Yeah, that clown knows what time it is. I just hope Gabby comes to her senses."

"You think they'll break up?"

"Oh, yeah," he said with such certainty. "He'll give her a reason; he probably has already."

I shrugged. "You may be right. I mean, with all the arguing and the fact that he has a low sperm count and can't have kids and . . ."

"Wait!" he shouted. "Hold up."

When he leaned forward, I put my hand over my mouth. "Oh my God. I shouldn't have said that."

"That came out of nowhere."

"It was just that we were talking about the reasons they could break up and that could be a reason and . . . Oh, God," I moaned.

He said, "How do you know this?"

I shook my head.

"Come on; I won't say anything to Gabby."

Still, I hesitated, but not for too long. "I read a piece of paper by accident. A test he's doing, a drug he's taking. Please don't tell Gabrielle."

He held up his hand. "No worries. I told you I won't." Then his gaze left me and was on the televisions. "So" — he nodded — "Mauricio is shooting blanks." He chuckled, then with the remote, clicked off the televisions. Facing me, he said, "Okay, sweetheart, let's do this."

With a nod, I agreed. But really, with what just happened, my work today was done. It was clear Justus hadn't known about Mauricio's condition. But he showed no signs of suspecting that Bella might be his.

Still, she could be, I just had to figure it out. And then . . . I had a thought. Maybe there was a way that I could let somebody else figure it out for me.

# 35
## GABRIELLE

As I edged my car from the garage, I wondered if I really wanted to do this. Even the sun was just waking up, so no one should be dressed and out already.

But I needed to do this, so I set the car into drive, made a left and headed north. I yawned my way through the streets of Santa Monica as the sun made a lazy ascent to the horizon. Finally, I hooked a right, then drove into the Venice Beach parking lot.

Even though it was Saturday and the clock had just ticked to seven, the lot was filled with cars that belonged to the group of the fifty or so people already on the edge of the beach.

I peeked through the cluster of men and women and spotted Regan right away — the only member of the LA Road Runners with hips. I wondered how much longer she'd be doing this, but I was sure it would take a doctor's order to make her stop.

Jumping from my car, I trudged through the sand, snaking my way through until I stood next to Regan.

Her eyes were on the young women demonstrating a hamstring stretch. I got into the formation, stretching one leg in front of the other. It took a moment for Regan to notice me — with a double take.

I continued through the stretching exercises as if this were something I did on the regular.

Regan kept her eyes forward, but after about the fourth stretch, she turned to me with her hands on those hips. "What are you doing here?"

I lifted my hand, then stretched to the left. "Well, my best friend has been avoiding me," I said, looking at her from my view, which had her almost upside down. "For a week, she's been working from home, she won't return my calls, and she only responds to my work-related texts."

Regan shook her head.

I said, "So I really had to talk to her, and this seemed like the only way." Mimicking the young woman in front of us, I put my hands on my hips and leaned back; I guessed this was a stretch for my core, but when I tried it, I lost it and tumbled backward until my butt hit the sand.

"Ouch!"

With another shake of her head, Regan extended her hand and pulled me up. "So, this was the best you could do?"

"If you were running, you had to talk to me." I wiped the sand from my butt. "Kinda like having a captive audience."

"But you don't even run to the bathroom when you have to go bad."

"I was willing to run today." I did a little jog in place, stretched my neck to the left, then the right, did a couple of uppercut moves that made Regan frown — and I was ready to go.

"Really?" She threw up both of her hands and began to walk away from the running group.

"No, don't leave." I had to trot to keep up with her. "Let's run."

"You look like you're preparing for a boxing match with a kindergartner," she said.

So instead of running, I walked by her side. We strolled along the edge of the ocean, right where the sand greeted the waves. It wasn't June, but still that Los Angeles gloom had settled over the beach, sure to burn away once the sun hung higher.

After minutes of silence, I said, "How did we get here?"

"I drove."

I chuckled. "How did we get to the place where best friends don't even talk to work an issue out?"

"I can't even tell you."

"I can't remember us having a fight before," I said.

She glanced at me but gave me no words.

I continued, "If I'd known you were going to be upset about this event with Justus, I would never have agreed to it."

She stopped so suddenly that when I did the same, I stumbled.

"You just don't get it." When Regan said that, I remembered Mauricio saying the same thing to me about Justus. "It's not the event. That's a great idea, and I'm glad Keisha came up with it. The challenge is, you keep making these decisions without me. This is supposed to be *our* business, Gabby."

"It is." I couldn't believe she was reacting this way over one thing.

"You haven't been treating me that way. First, you brought Keisha in without discussing it."

"I brought her in as my assistant. Why would I talk to you about that?"

"Because to this point, we've discussed everything. You interviewed Mattie before I hired her."

"But Keisha's my sister. I didn't think you'd have a problem with that."

"It's still *our* business. And then, the major thing I do for Media Connections — you make a decision to have your sister handle it *and* handle it for our major client. Again, decision without me."

She flopped down onto the sand, and I did, too. We hugged our knees to our chests and watched the ocean's waves onrush the earth before the tide returned to the sea.

Regan said, "Now it's my turn to ask, how *did* we get here?"

I shook my head. "It doesn't make sense. Just like the arguments I've been having with Mauricio."

She glanced at me through the corner of her eye. "More arguments?"

"We're in a good place right now, but last weekend?" I shook my head. "It was ugly."

"About Keisha?"

"No," I said with a little edge. Why did Regan always take it back to her? "Again about Justus, and it's getting more intense and more often."

"You're gonna have to do something."

"But what? Short of closing Media Connections — and that's not going to happen — I don't know what to do." I kicked up some sand. "I've calmed him down, but

Mauricio has to understand what I do with Justus is all business. He's gonna have to be an adult."

Looking straight ahead, Regan said, "Is that what you want me to do about Keisha?"

"Our situation is different. If I'd seen this the way you do, then I would be begging for your forgiveness. But what I can do now is promise that I won't decide what I'm having for lunch without you."

"I'm not trying to be petty. I just wanted you to be aware."

I nodded. "And you know what I want? I want life to go back to the way it was just a month ago. No fights with Mauricio, no fights with you, no fights with Bella and her tutu, no credit card companies calling about fraud, no new ideas from Keisha, no . . ."

"Wait," Regan said. "What about your credit cards?"

I waved my hand. "Just regular stuff. Someone got ahold of one of my credit cards and charged up a storm. When they first called me it was only eighteen hundred dollars."

"Wow."

"But they ended up getting away with almost five thousand." I shook my head. "I don't know why folks do that."

"Yeah," she said, dragging out the word.

"You know, I meant to tell you . . ." She stopped.

"What?"

Regan gave me a long look as if she was trying to figure out something. Finally, she said, "You know what? I'll figure it out myself because I don't want to be another burden, so" — Regan twisted her body to face me — "I accept your apology."

I grinned. "I haven't apologized yet."

"But you were about to, right?"

"Yeah." And then we leaned forward and hugged. "I'm really sorry, Regan."

"I know. And I love you."

"More."

She stood first, then pulled me up and with our arms around each other's shoulders, we plodded through the sand, making our way back to the parking lot. Sister-friends once again. Sister-friends for always.

# 36
## KEISHA

It had been thirteen days since Justus had given Media Connections the go-ahead. And because of me, Media Connections had pulled this off.

That was my thought as Mauricio turned off Crenshaw Boulevard and pulled in front of the valet stand, since street parking was limited in Leimert Park.

I'd never heard of this area, but Justus was insistent; he'd wanted his event in this predominately black community, which was sort of a cultural hub. I'd been here four times during our planning, and though it was a cute little area, it was so far from Bel-Air, and I wasn't talking miles.

As the valet attendant trotted toward us, I slid out of the front seat, then opened the back door for Bella. She jumped down and into my arms.

"Thanks, Mama!"

I grinned, but then looked to the other

side of the SUV, making sure Mauricio hadn't heard her. Bella had started calling me Mama, even though I'd told her not to do it when we were out. So far, no one else had heard her, though I had an explanation ready if anyone did — I would say I'd been telling Bella stories of my mother, my mama.

As Mauricio gave the keys to the valet, my thoughts were on the day when Bella wouldn't have to hide and she'd call me Mama everywhere, all the time.

When Mauricio came around to our side, Bella grabbed his hand, then mine, and walked between us.

As we entered the festival under the big banner: "Justus's Family and His Friends," I stopped so that Bella and I could take a selfie.

Mauricio said, "You're excited, huh?"

"I am. I worked hard on this."

"I know you did. That's why I was surprised that you didn't leave with Gabrielle earlier."

I shook my head. "No, I wanted to hang out with Bella."

"Yay!" she cheered, her answer for almost everything.

Then Bella's attention turned to the festival in front of us. It was a street fair that had gone beyond a celebration for children. We had tons of stations set up to entertain kids and lots of information about Justus's upcoming children's books, but we also had tables set up for voter registration, colleges, and even a few banks were in the mix.

All of it sponsored by Justus. All of it planned by me.

"I wanna do that." Bella pointed to the face-painting table.

I glanced at Mauricio, he grinned, and Bella skipped to the table.

Mauricio said, "I can take her if you have to find Gabrielle or do something else."

"No, I told you. I really want to hang out with Bella. Gabrielle is taking care of Justus; my part is done." I helped Bella climb into the chair, then stepped back, standing shoulder to shoulder with Mauricio. Bella kicked her heels up in anticipation, and Mauricio and I laughed.

As the artist leaned over Bella, Mauricio said, "I'm gonna check out what's over there." He pointed to the next table. "I'll be right back."

A moment after he stepped away, a woman with a head of hair that looked like fresh snow nudged me. "So cute. Is she your daughter?"

Without any kind of hesitation, I said, "Yes."

Then the woman glanced at Mauricio. "And your husband?"

I gave her another nod.

She pressed her hands over her heart as if she were looking at the most precious picture. "You have a beautiful family."

"Thank you."

When she walked away, I sighed. This beautiful family picture belonged to Gabrielle, but there was no reason why it shouldn't belong to me. Especially since if God hadn't intervened, I would have a little girl just like Bella.

The thought of that took me to a place I didn't want to go. But sometimes I didn't have control, and so my mind wandered . . . back to that day . . . in 2011: the beginning and end of my beautiful family.

"Say cheese."

With Buck's arm around me, we said, "Cheese," as I held Nzuri.

Mama clicked the camera, which one of her johns had given her last Christmas.

"Okay, my turn." She handed the camera to Buck, positioned herself on the sofa, then said, "Three generations of Jones girls: me, my little girl, and my grandbaby."

It was Buck's turn to snap away. "Y'all look so pretty in all that pink."

Mama beamed. She had saved money to buy these dresses so that we'd match in the photos. Today, Nzuri was four months old and we were taking her first pictures. Even Buck matched — almost. He said his red tie matched our faded red dresses 'cause real men didn't wear pink.

"I'm so excited," I said, holding Nzuri up when Buck took the last photo. Lifting her above my head, my baby giggled and wiggled in my arms.

She made me laugh out loud. Four months, but I felt like Nzuri had been in my life forever. My world was this little girl. Then I looked over at Buck and Mama trying to figure out something with the camera, and I changed my mind — my world was this little girl and Mama and Buck.

I loved Nzuri and Mama, and I really liked Buck, too. I saw him every day, and sometimes, his mama and daddy came to see the baby, though I wished his daddy would stay away. He looked at me the same way Mr. Stanley had.

I pushed his daddy and Mr. Stanley out of my mind and only thought about Buck. He had gotten that job at Walmart, but making not even five dollars an hour didn't leave him with a whole bunch of time or money. Although any extra he had of both, he gave to me and Nzuri.

We were making it, though, especially since we didn't need a babysitter — I'd never gone back to school. There was no reason since all I wanted to be now was Nzuri's mama.

"Okay, let me get into this kitchen and get dinner started. You staying, Buck?"

"Yes, ma'am."

Mama laughed, and I grinned. When had Buck ever said no?

Mama said, "I'll have this ready in about an hour."

"Uh . . . Mrs. Jones." Mama paused right before she got to the kitchen. "Can you watch Nzuri? I want to take Keisha for a walk."

"I don't wanna go nowhere." I never wanted to go out. And why would I when I could play with and take care of Nzuri all day?

But Mama said, "Good! That girl never leaves this house." Looking at me, she said, "Go put Nzuri down. Look at her already asleep."

This was the part about babies that was funny to me. One minute, Nzuri was laughing, and then she'd be sleeping.

"Come on," Buck said. "Let's go. Just for a little while."

It was hard to say no to Buck since he never asked me for anything, he just gave me everything. So I took Nzuri to the bedroom and laid her in the crib, which was still right by my bed because even at night, I didn't want to be too far away.

Leaning over the rail, I kissed her pudgy cheek. She was still as yellow as a banana, but she was my baby. I never thought about her daddy because nobody ever asked me about Mr. Stanley. Not even Mama. I guessed once Nzuri was here, it didn't matter.

Looking down at her, I sighed. She was a miracle that had been in my belly when I was fifteen, and she'd come out — so perfect — when I was sixteen.

"I'm going to give you everything, Nzuri," I said. "Everything, even my life." I stroked her blond hair. "I will always take care of you."

It still took me a couple of minutes to break away, but finally, I went back into the living room.

Mama said, "So where y'all going all dressed up?"

"We just gonna go for a walk. To the park. We'll be right back."

"Glad you dragging her out of here."

Buck and Mama laughed. I didn't. I wanted to run back into the bedroom and give Nzuri another kiss. But the way Buck held my hand, I knew he'd never let me do it.

Once we were outside, the air did feel good. We strolled up the street not saying a word, just holding hands. The park was about seven blocks from my house, and when we got there, I sat on one of the two swings and Buck stood behind me.

"See?" He pushed me into the air. "Aren't you glad you got out?"

I nodded. The April breeze cooled my skin, and I closed my eyes, imagining that I could fly.

He said, "I can't wait for Nzuri to get bigger so I can bring her here."

I laughed because I could see her doing the same thing, flying high on this swing, then running in the grass. "She's gonna love this. She's such a happy baby."

"She don't have no reason not to be happy," Buck said, pushing me even higher. "We take care of everything for her."

"That's true." I laughed with him.

Thinking about Buck out here with Nzuri made me a little serious. "Buck?"

"Yeah?"

I waited a couple of seconds. "Why'd you do it?" I asked the question that had been on my mind, but I'd never asked before.

I didn't even have to explain — he knew what I meant. I could tell by the way he halted the swing; then he sat on the other one, his eyes away from me.

After a while, he just shrugged. "Why not?"

"But you're not her daddy."

"Nobody knows that."

I leaned back in the swing and gave him a side-eye. "Everybody knows that. Half the people don't think I'm her mama, she's so white."

He laughed, but then got serious again. He kicked up some dirt. "I don't know. When I saw you in Walmart, I just felt like" — his eyes rose up — "I wanted to take care of you." He stood up from the swing. "Then after I'd been around for a while, I wanted to do it all the time. Now we have Nzuri. Now I love you. I love both of you."

He took my hand and helped me to stand. "I love you, Keisha."

He may have been waiting for me to say it back, but when I didn't, it didn't seem to matter to him. 'Cause right there in the middle of the park, he kissed me deep.

437

Buck and I had kissed a lot, but that was all we'd done. Because I was already pregnant when I met him and once Mama found out, she told us not to do anything to hurt the baby. Then, after Nzuri was born, I never wanted to go anywhere or do anything that didn't include my baby.

But now we were out, we were alone, and I guessed it was time. Buck didn't say anything when he led me to the back side of the park and found a soft spot on the grass. He laid me down, lifted my dress, and lowered his pants. And right there, we had sex.

It turned out that the grass was soft, but the ground wasn't. That didn't matter, though, because being with Buck was the opposite of being with Mr. Stanley. Everything about Buck was the opposite. My skin never matched with Mr. Stanley's, but even though Buck was black-black, he was a better match for me. And Mr. Stanley never talked to me, and the whole time, Buck told me how much he loved me.

By the time we finished and Buck gave me a kiss that felt like forever, I loved him, too.

After we fixed our clothes, we sat on the swings for a little while longer before we strolled back down the streets. I couldn't wait to see Nzuri; even though she wouldn't understand, I wanted to tell her she would always be safe because it would always be me, and her, and her daddy.

But when we turned to my street, I slowed down a little because what I saw didn't make sense: a fire truck and an ambulance.

I began to run and Buck did, too. But since I was running to get my baby, he couldn't outrun me. Right as we got to the house, Mama stepped out with Mrs. George, the next-door neighbor, holding her up by her arm.

"Mama." I was so out of breath. "What happened? Where's Nzuri?" I didn't wait for her to answer. I dashed into the house, thankful that it wasn't that big, and into the bedroom I shared with my baby.

The crib — was empty.

"Nzuri," I screamed as I ran through the house searching every room. I kept calling her like I expected her to walk out and say, *Hey, Mama,* even though she wasn't old enough to utter a single word or take a single step.

When I couldn't find her, I charged back outside, and now Buck was holding Mama. Dashing over, I ripped them apart. "Mama, where's Nzuri? Where's my baby?" I yelled.

Mama wept, but through her tears, she shook her head. "She's gone, baby."

"She's gone? Where did she go?"

"She died."

I whipped my head from side to side. "Babies don't die."

Mama shook her head, Buck nodded, and I released a wail that went all the way to heaven, or maybe it was to hell, I didn't know. It was a shriek that could be heard into eternity, then finally took me out and made me see nothing but darkness . . .

I shook my head to rid that memory and blinked back my tears. This was why I never thought about Nzuri, never looked at any pictures of her, never visited her in the cemetery. Because any thought of her took me back to that darkness that was so black, so heavy, it strangled me and one day would keep me there forever.

So I fought hard to keep thoughts of Nzuri away. But sometimes that darkness inched back, sneaking up. It lurked around me now, making me remember how I fainted that day. How later on, Mama told us she'd gone into the room to check on her, and Nzuri wasn't yellow anymore, she was blue. How the doctors told us she'd died of something that was a syndrome. A syndrome that made healthy babies go to heaven.

Sudden infant death syndrome *and* God had taken Nzuri from me.

Mama and Buck had buried my baby together because I couldn't do it. But after they had that funeral, Mama was never the same. She didn't work too much, so we never had any money and had to keep moving from one house to another. Then Mama got sick, and over the next six years, she got sicker every day. By the time we moved to the back of Mrs. Johnson's house, I knew the end was close for Mama. And I had to live through the death of someone else I loved.

But while it was the end for Mama, that really was the beginning for me. Because right after that, Regan came to White Haven . . .

"Mama!"

The sound of her voice made me squeeze my eyes together and hope that I could thrust away the darkness. When I opened my eyes, right in front of me was the light.

*Babies don't die.*

Bella said, "Look at my face."

I crouched down. "You look so pretty."

"I know."

I laughed. It was true — babies didn't die. How could they? They weren't old enough for God to be mad about anything. So babies *couldn't* die. They just took over new bodies. At least, that was what I thought now when I looked at Bella. She was the light that Nzuri was supposed to be.

Pulling her into my arms, I squeezed her as tightly as I could. Nzuri . . . Bella . . . the two were almost the same to me.

# 37

## GABRIELLE

I checked out the spread in the greenroom inside Eso Won, a bookstore that had been a decades-long neighborhood staple. For the five hours I'd been here, there had not been a single blip. The streets were merry with the festivities, and Justus (with his entourage) played his part, moseying through the crowd taking pictures, signing autographs.

Yet anxiety coursed through my veins.

Because Mauricio and Justus were within twenty miles of each other. And my greatest fear was at any moment, those twenty miles would be twenty feet.

Angst gripped me, even though I had spoken to both of these grown men and each had made a pledge to me:

Justus: *"I got this. I'm not trying to mess up anything today. This is all about me. No worries."*

Mauricio: *"I won't do anything to mess up*

*this day for you. It's all about you. No worries."*

Two men, so similar, so different. I had hugged one and kissed the other, praying they'd keep their promises.

The moment I stepped out of the bookstore, I heard, "Mommy."

Bella wasn't yet in my view, but her voice calmed my spirit. Seconds later, I saw my daughter barreling toward me, and then she jumped into my arms.

"Look at my face," she said.

"Oh, my. You're even more beautiful than you were last night. How did that happen?"

She giggled and I hugged Keisha, then kissed my husband.

"Hey, Gabrielle!"

I glanced at one of the photographers we'd hired for the day.

"Perfect timing," the young woman said. "I'd love to get a couple of shots of you with your family."

"Definitely." I held Bella, then inched closer to Mauricio on one side and Keisha on the other.

The woman looked through her lens, then lifted her head with a frown. "I'm sorry," she said to Keisha. "I just want the family, for now."

"She is family." I reached my hand toward

Keisha and pulled her even closer to me. "She's my sister."

"Oh," the photographer said before she lowered her eyes back to her camera.

After a couple of shots, I said, "I'd like to get a few pictures with my husband in front of the step-and-repeat banner."

The photographer nodded, and I reached for Mauricio's hand. When he took mine and squeezed it, the anxiety eased right out of me. In front of the banner, Mauricio and I posed and laughed and held each other, giving the photographer some spectacular candids.

Then I heard, "Gabrielle, would you mind if our photographer took some pictures as well?"

Glancing over my shoulder, my smile faded when I saw Veda Laurelton. What was she doing here? This certainly wasn't a big enough event for the *National Intruder*'s senior editor to show up. There was only one reason she showed up anywhere — she was digging for dirt.

But even though I wanted to tell her to go find a new hole to crawl into, I smiled. Because as a publicist I knew all publicity was good publicity.

"Veda, I'm surprised to see you."

"I'm sure you are" — she gave me the

same plastic smile that I wore — "since we didn't receive the press release for this."

"You didn't?"

She shook her head. "But I'm here now, so would you mind?" She pointed to the photographer standing beside her.

I nodded, then turned my back as Mauricio wrapped his arms around my waist.

As the photographer took a photo with a bright flash that was not necessary in this daylight, but that blinded me for a moment, Veda said, "What do you think about the post that appeared on our blog this morning?"

I turned and faced Mauricio for a different pose, ignoring Veda. Did she think I spent any time reading their blog?

She rephrased her question: "What do you have to say about the report that Justus is the father of your daughter?"

My jaw dropped, and my arms did the same.

"What?" Mauricio and I shouted together.

Flash! The photographer took another photo of us standing with our mouths agape.

"Your daughter?" Veda and the photographer turned toward Bella, who stood just feet away, holding Keisha's hand. "Justus is her father, correct?"

Bella and Keisha stood stiff, wearing

matching expressions of confusion. The only relief I had at the moment was seeing Regan and Doug stroll up behind them.

"Regan," I shouted, "please take Bella over . . ." I stopped. It was hard to think when I couldn't breathe.

"To the jumping station," Mauricio finished.

Regan frowned, but she and Doug did as we asked, taking Keisha with them, too.

Now Mauricio and I were the ones who wore matching glares. I said to Veda, "You need to take your lying —"

"Don't be mad at me," she interrupted before I could curse her out. "Let me pull it up on my phone."

I had no idea why Mauricio and I stood there, but Veda found the post in less than ten seconds and read: "According to an unnamed source at Media Connections, Justus is the father of his publicist, Gabrielle Wilson Flores's, five-year-old daughter, Bella, and —"

"You better take this garbage out of here." Mauricio stepped right up in Veda's face, and I was afraid at that moment, he had no regard for the fact that she was a woman.

"I'm just doing my job." She shrugged. "Would you like to make a statement?"

When I saw that vein throbbing in my

husband's temple, I grabbed his arm to save Veda's life. To Veda, I said, "That post is a lie, and if you don't get out of here, I'm going to have you removed." Now I took my husband's hand and dragged him away to the station serving lemonade. Oh, how I wanted something stronger. I picked up two plastic cups, then pulled Mauricio to the side.

We sipped the lemonade as if it were wine and after a few gulps, I said, "I have no idea what she's talking about, but I will find out. I think she made it up."

His breathing was still shallow. "She didn't. Someone leaked that fake story."

"Who would do that?" I shook my head.

"Who would do what?"

For a moment, I closed my eyes and wished I could grab Mauricio's hand, click my heels three times, and my husband and I would disappear to Tahiti or Dubai or Bali — it didn't matter. Because Justus was about to be the water on the grease fire that simmered inside Mauricio.

But because I couldn't ignore him, I faced him, hoping I could get Justus to go back to wherever he came from.

Before I had a chance, Mauricio stepped forward and spoke up. "It was you, wasn't it?"

Justus raised an eyebrow. "I don't know what you're talking about, bruh, but you better back up."

"You're the one who planted that fake story."

"What fake story?" Justus's face was creased with confusion.

By the way he responded, I knew Justus wasn't behind Veda's lie. But Mauricio had fired the first shot, and Justus wasn't the type to back down or go away.

And neither was my husband.

But I had to convince him, for the good of this world, to just leave this alone. "Babe" — I pressed my hand gently on my husband's chest — "let's go . . . get Bella." Our daughter's name was supposed to be the balm.

"Nah. Don't walk away," Justus said, the determined agitator. "Let's handle it." He threw up his hands like he was ready to rumble. "What're you talking about, fool?"

"Justus!" I growled his name. "Back up."

He held up his hands but glared at Mauricio. "What? Your woman gotta speak for you now?"

"No." Mauricio stepped right into Justus's space. "I'm doing the talking, and you better have a good answer."

Oh, God!

"Why did the *National Intruder* walk up in here asking me and my wife if you were Bella's father?"

When that sly, slow grin spread across Justus's face, I knew I only had seconds.

Justus said, "Maybe that's a good question since everybody knows you're shooting blanks."

The time to stop trouble had just expired. "What?" I screamed in shock *and* fear.

"Yeah," Justus said to Mauricio. "We all wanna know — who is that baby's daddy, 'cause it ain't you, right?"

"You better . . ." Mauricio growled.

"I better what? Look, don't be mad at me just because I'm the only man standing here."

Justus's chuckle wasn't even all the way out before Mauricio hooked a right shot to his jaw, which knocked Justus back but didn't knock him down. It was only shock that made Justus hesitate, and then when he charged my husband, it was all over.

I gave Bella an extra hug because she looked so scared. "Daddy's going to be fine, okay?"

She nodded, but there were tears in her eyes. "I wanna stay with you and Daddy."

I shook my head. "Please go home with Auntie Regan and Auntie Keisha. We'll be home soon."

As Regan took her hand and led her from the greenroom, Bella kept her eyes on us, looking back the whole time until they were out the door.

While Doug stood over Mauricio, Keisha said to me, "Is there anything I can do?" Then her eyes lowered to Mauricio sitting on the sofa.

"Just go home with Regan and Doug and take care of Bella. She's going to need you."

Keisha hugged me, then she said goodbye to Mauricio. He didn't speak, just raised his hand, acknowledging her. After sharing a few whispers with my husband, Doug stood, hugged me, then followed his wife, my daughter, and my sister.

When we were alone, I closed the door, then crossed the room and sat next to Mauricio. Like him, I leaned forward, my arms resting on my legs. The only difference: I wasn't holding an ice pack to my left eye.

"Why did you tell him?" Those were the first words Mauricio had spoken to me.

"I didn't." Though I was pissed at having to even answer this, I did because what was most important right now was assuring my husband. "You know I didn't tell Justus. I've told no one. Not even Regan, and I share everything with her. But this, your condition, has been just you and me. You know that."

He nodded. "So why would he even think to plant a story like that?"

"I don't know. And the thing is, I don't think he did it."

"Nah, he did." The volume of his voice rose. "This has his name on it."

"Why would he plant this story? How would it help him?"

He shrugged. "He has one of two reasons. To get under my skin."

"Well . . ."

"Or because he suspects it's true."

If, at that moment, Mauricio had punched me the way he had tried to take out Justus, that would have caused me less pain than those words. "What are you saying?"

Slowly, he faced me, and now . . . he didn't say anything. At least not with his mouth.

I shook my head and fought hard to stay calm. "How could you accuse me of this?"

"I'm not accusing you. I'm asking about Justus."

"But when you ask about him, you do realize what you're saying about me, right?" I cried. "Are we really in this place where you're questioning whether you're Bella's father?"

Again, he used his silence to slash my heart.

"Oh my God." I cried out to the Lord over and over.

"Well" — his tone was so matter-of-fact in the middle of my pain — "I do have a condition."

"But the doctors explained that to us. We may have had a dozen if we'd tried when you were twenty-one, but why are we even talking about this? You know you're Bella's father. Forget about looking at her; all you have to do is look at me."

Mauricio held my gaze for a long moment before he turned away. I had to stand so that I could breathe. I folded my arms and leaned my head back, trying to return the tears to my eyes.

"I can't believe this," I said.

"Neither can I."

"You don't trust me."

"It's not that." He shook his head. "Look at this from my side. How did Justus find out?"

"I. Don't. Know. Maybe he knows the doctor, maybe he knows someone at the clinic — hell, maybe he knows the man who delivers our mail."

We stayed in our places, and as time ticked by, I regretted its passage. Because in this place, time healed nothing; time just deepened our divide.

Finally, Mauricio said, "So what do we do now?"

I shook my head.

"I have a suggestion." He spoke as if he'd had a plan for a while. "I don't know how we continue with Justus in our lives."

I swiped at the tears on my cheek.

"I just can't do it, Gabby."

I nodded. "I'll do my best from this point. I'll keep you two apart."

His eyes narrowed. "That's the solution to you?" He didn't give me a chance to respond. "I'm talking about you not representing him anymore."

"Mauricio, we've had this discussion. He *is* Media Connections. Without him, I don't have a business."

"That's not true; you've done a great job building your business."

"But without Justus . . . without his business, without his investment, our business won't survive. And it's not just about me. There's Regan and the associates, not to mention Keisha and Mattie. So many people will be affected if I close the business."

"Again, I didn't say anything about closing. I think you can make it," he said. "Move out of your Beverly Hills office; that will save a fortune. Move to . . . Culver City."

With my fingertips, I massaged my temples. "I have a PR firm. This is all about image."

"Then" — he shrugged — "I don't have anything else for you. I just know that you have to either get rid of him or get rid of the business."

"It's the same thing. Why would you ask me to do this?"

He lowered his head and sighed.

I eased back down onto the sofa and put my hand on his shoulder. "Mauricio, all you need to know and believe is that I love you."

Slowly, he raised his gaze to mine. After a couple of seconds, he uttered just two words: "Prove it." Then he pushed himself up.

And as he walked away, I knew he was doing more than just walking out of this room; my husband was actually walking away from me.

# 38
## KEISHA

I paced the length of my bedroom with all kinds of images in my mind. I wished that Gabrielle had let me stay so I could see everything. It was already better than anything I could have planned. The melee at the festival — my God!

I bounced down onto the bed. The press release had worked. Not that I'd had much hope, especially since I'd sent it from a fake email. I wasn't sure that anyone would answer, and definitely not this soon.

The creaking of the garage made me dash to the window. It was just turning dark, but there was enough light to see the Range Rover.

Mauricio.

I doubted that Gabrielle was with him since she'd driven her own car this morning. What should I do?

Gabrielle and Mauricio thought I was with Regan. But the moment I got in the car with her best witch and the husband, I'd told them to bring me home. There was no way I wanted to sit in her house and watch her clean her broom. It was no surprise to me when Regan obliged me.

But now — should I let Mauricio know I was here? Should I talk to him? Maybe console him?

Moving to the door, I paused, then sat back down.

No, talking to him wasn't a good idea. What would I say?

But then . . . there had to be something. Mauricio liked me. Jumping up, I reached for the door, but the moment my hand touched the doorknob, once again, I sat back down.

I needed to just let this play out.

All of the questions kept me inside my bedroom as I heard Mauricio's footsteps on the stairs. Then there was silence when he reached the landing, and the carpet quieted his steps. But as I pressed my ear to the door, I could feel when he passed by.

I counted the seconds that it would take for him to get to their bedroom, then I peeked out. The moment he turned on the light, I eased my bedroom door closed.

The question was still in my mind — what should I do? But before I could think, the garage opened again. I rushed over just in time to see the Lexus roll inside.

Now I knew for sure — I was going to stay in my room, let them think they were alone so I could see how this played out.

Returning to the door, I pressed my ear against it and heard the same sounds: Gabrielle on the stairs, then silence, though I felt her passing by.

"Mauricio," she called out.

I kicked off my shoes, then eased open my door and slipped into the hallway. Pressing my back against the wall, I edged inch by inch closer to their bedroom. My heart hurt my chest the way it pounded — I wasn't sure if it was fear of being caught or the excitement of what I might hear.

"What do you mean by 'prove it'?" Gabrielle said. "What will walking away from my business prove?"

"It will prove you decided *not* to walk away from your marriage."

I gasped and covered my mouth.

"I don't want to walk away from my marriage, but I want to keep my business."

"You can't. Not if you want to keep me. Because I refuse to be constantly disrespected by that jackass. If his planting that story isn't proof to you, then . . ."

Now I pressed my hand to my chest. Mauricio thought Justus had planted the story?

Mauricio's voice floated once again into the hallway. "He's trying to destroy us, and I can't give him the room to do that."

There was silence, so much that I began to step back toward my bedroom.

But then Gabrielle said, "What are you doing?" Then, "Where are you going?"

I stopped.

Mauricio said, "We need a little time and space."

"This isn't the way, Mauricio."

"It's the only thing I can do right now. I need room to think; you need room to decide."

"Walking away has never solved anything," Gabrielle said with tears in her voice.

"Well, staying here sure won't either. Because while I don't want to fight, what's more hurtful is looking into your eyes and knowing this is even a choice for you."

I heard Gabrielle sob, and I did a quick side-step move back to my bedroom. Closing the door behind me, I stood there for a moment, just listening.

I felt a little tinge in my heart, a soft ache. Gabrielle was crying. I hadn't really thought about this part.

Then their voices were in the hallway.

"Mauricio, please."

There was silence in the space where his response should have been. Then I heard their footsteps on the stairs. When I was sure they had cleared the steps, I tiptoed out of my bedroom.

"I'll give you a call tomorrow." Mauricio's voice came from around the corner. "Kiss Bella for me."

The door from the house to the garage opened, then closed. I crept halfway down the stairs, but paused when I heard Gabrielle sobbing.

Turning back, I moved as fast as I could without making a sound, returning to my room. Sitting on the edge of the bed, I'd expected to feel jubilant. With her marriage falling apart, I was one step closer to getting what I wanted. Everything was coming together, right? So why did I now suddenly feel so wrong?

Grabbing my cell, I tiptoed across the room. Talking to Buck would help me get my mind back on track. He'd help me remember my objective, and he'd help me get to the finish line.

Stepping inside the bathroom, I closed the door behind me.

# 39
## Keisha

I was up. I was dressed. I was ready. And it wasn't even seven yet. I peeked into the hallway, and one of the double doors to their bedroom was open, but the house was silent.

Closing my bedroom door, I decided to wait at least a little while longer. When I reached for my cell, I didn't go into the bathroom. There was no need. I had a feeling Gabrielle would sleep through this whole day if I let her.

I dialed Buck's number, and like last night, it went straight to voice mail. This was weird. I'd expected Buck to be blowing up my phone, knowing that yesterday was Justus's festival. But Buck hadn't answered last night, and I didn't bother to leave him another voice mail. Instead, I sent him a text:

Where are you?

Not even five seconds passed before my phone vibrated:

Can't talk right now, but got a ?. You got any more credit card numbers?

Why was he asking me that right now? I shook my head. Que was probably pressing him. That was cool because in a few weeks, Buck would be out here with me and that credit card scam would be behind us.

I texted back:

No, call me so I can tell you what happened. Big news.

His text came back:

Okay.

I waited for him to text something else, but that was it. He must have been distracted, though I didn't know what he had going on this early on a Sunday.

Tossing the phone onto the bed, I turned on the TV and flipped through the channels, but all that was on were those TV preachers. So I muted the screen, then sat, just staring, just thinking.

I wasn't sure which part of my plan was

done — was Gabrielle's marriage ruined or was she about to lose her business? Maybe it was both. So now what did that mean for me? I had to get in touch with Justus. I had to let him know that I could take over — and after what I'd pulled off yesterday, he'd believe me. Except for the fight, the family festival had been beyond flawless.

The clock took its time ticking off the minutes, and after about fifteen or so, I couldn't wait anymore.

Stepping from my bedroom, I moved down the hallway and tapped on the door to Gabrielle's bedroom. Then I peeked inside.

"Gabrielle?" I whispered.

She didn't move, and I stepped in. Tiptoeing to her side of her bed, I stood over her. The duvet was pulled almost to her head, but I could see her eyes; she was in a deep sleep, which didn't surprise me. When Nzuri died, sleep was all I wanted. Maybe that was how Gabrielle felt right now.

Leaving as quietly as I came, I closed both of her bedroom doors, then stood in the hallway, not really sure what to do next. Dang, I really wished I could talk to Buck.

I returned to my bedroom and grabbed my cell. Maybe I'd get something to eat, and by then, Buck would call. But as I got to the bottom of the stairs, the doorbell rang.

Peeking through the side glass panel, I groaned. What was the best witch doing here? And then I remembered . . . she had Bella. Placing my cell on the table, I swung open the door, and my smile was wide as the best person in California stood in front of me.

"Hey." I knelt down. "Are you okay?"

She nodded, but her eyes were puffy, like she'd been crying a lot, and I pulled her into a hug.

Finally standing up, I told Regan, "You can leave now."

She shook her head, stepped in, and closed the door behind her. "I'm not going anywhere."

It wasn't her words that made me frown; I was so used to her being rude. But there was something in her tone. More disdain than normal.

She asked, "Where're Gabby and Mauricio?"

Before I answered her, I said, "Bella, can you do me a favor and go up to your room? I'll come up in a minute, okay?"

She nodded, then after she took a couple of steps, she turned back and hugged Regan. I wanted to snatch her away from that witch, but I stayed still and pretended to smile.

At least Regan had enough grace not to say anything until Bella was up the stairs. Then she turned to me. "Are they in the kitchen?"

I smirked. "If they were, don't you think they would've been out here by now?" I folded my arms. "They're not home."

And for the first time, Regan said out loud what she'd been saying to me with her eyes from the moment she'd met me. "You're a liar." Then she moved toward the stairs.

I jumped in front of her. "Where are you going?"

"Move out of my way, Keisha."

"Who's gonna make me, boo?"

She squinted as if she didn't understand my English. "What?"

I shook my head. "I told you, they're not home, so you're not welcome in this house."

She laughed right in my face. "What did you just call me? Was it *boo*? Let me tell you something . . . boo . . . I'm more welcome in this house than you will ever be. In fact, when I finish telling them what I know, you'll be out, taken away in handcuffs preferably."

Her words distracted me — that was the only reason why she got by. But I recovered quickly and charged up the steps, nudging her out of the way. I was younger, and I wasn't pregnant, so I made it to the top first, and this time, I blocked her path completely. "You're not going anywhere," I spat.

"You think this is gonna stop me from telling Gabrielle and Mauricio that you are nothing but a dirty little liar and a thief?"

My eyes narrowed.

She chuckled. "You don't have anything to say now, huh? Well, I have a lot to say. A lot to tell them about what you've been doing with their credit cards."

I swallowed.

"And a lot to tell them about what you told Justus."

There was no way for me to swallow again because the lump that filled my throat came quick and was like a plug that threatened to stop me from breathing.

"Oh, yeah, I spoke to Justus, and I've been speaking to the police for a couple of weeks. And, add on what I know about the *National Intruder* . . . It is over for you. Get out of my way."

It was because she pushed me that I pushed her back. That was the only way to stop her from what she was about to do, the only way to stop her from ruining my plans.

But when I did, I pushed her with a force that was filled with every emotion Regan brought out of me. I pushed her so she would know how much I hated her.

And then time stopped.

That was how it felt at first when Regan's eyes widened with shock and fear just before her arms flailed in the air.

She fell backward.

Then time moved, but it crept forward so slowly as Regan tumbled, tumbled, tumbled.

Down every step.

Hitting.

Each.

One.

Hard.

I watched, incapable of moving, not even able to do so when she landed at the bottom, headfirst.

Still I stood and stared. Still I stood and listened to her moans. Still I stood, until . . .

"Auntie Regan!"

Now I moved. "Bella," I whispered, facing her.

"What's wrong with Auntie Regan?" she whimpered.

"Nothing." I looked down the steps and said the first thing that came to my mind. "She's asleep."

"No, she's not," Bella said and jerked her arms from my grasp. "I'm going to get Mommy."

She darted around me, but I was faster. Before she got to Gabrielle's room, I grabbed her.

"Let me go!" she screamed.

I muffled her cries with my hand over her mouth. "Please, please, Bella. Please," I kept saying as I tucked her under my arm, then carried her like a sack down the stairs. I kept my eyes raised, not wanting to see the sight at the bottom.

Bella cried and kicked; it was hard to smother her screams, but I tried. All I could do was pray that Gabrielle wouldn't hear anything. Not until I could get away.

At the bottom, I paused. The only way I could get to the front door was if I stepped over Regan.

"Auntie Regan," Bella cried.

That was when I looked down. That was when I saw . . . all the blood.

Regan's eyes were glassy as she held out her hand. "Help. Me," she gasped.

I closed my eyes; I needed to think. I needed a plan.

To get away. "Help. Me."

Regan's whimpers assaulted me more than the screams coming from Bella.

"Help. Me."

I hated Regan. And if I let her, she would tell Gabrielle everything. I had no idea how she'd found out, but I knew that she knew enough.

"Help. Me."

The plan began to formulate in my mind. I could take Regan's purse; the keys to her car and her money would be in there. That would be enough until I could get in touch with Buck. That would be enough for me and Bella for now.

Stepping over Regan, it was hard to balance myself as Bella squirmed. But I made it to the other side.

Leaning over, I reached for Regan's purse, which was still on her shoulder.

But then.

The blood.

It was staining her dress. Between her legs.

Regan's baby.

"Help. Me."

I couldn't breathe. I couldn't think. No . . . that wasn't true. I could think, but all I could think about was the baby. And Nzuri.

And . . . "Auntie Keisha, let me go."

Bella.

With a sob, I lowered Bella to the floor, then grabbed my cell from the table.

I had one final thought before I did what

I had to do: *Babies don't die.*
I glanced down at Regan and called 911.

# EPILOGUE:
## KEISHA

*Six Months Later*

The hardest part of everything was that Regan's baby died.

Really, that was the only thing that I cared about: Regan's baby died, just like mine.

From the moment I made the call that day, and then sat on the staircase and watched and waited, I knew. It was because the stain on Regan's dress kept getting deeper and deeper. When her eyes finally closed, I was sure she was dead, too.

Even then, I didn't move. I stayed in place as Bella ran up the stairs and woke up Gabrielle. She'd stumbled out of her bedroom and then staggered down the stairs right as the paramedics arrived.

It was too late, though. That was what I told all of them.

"Her baby's dead," I'd said to Gabrielle and the men she'd let in the door. "Babies do die."

"Keisha!"

The shout of my name took me away from my memories. From where I lay on the bottom cot, I didn't have to turn my head much to look up at Beth.

She said, "Today's the day, huh?"

I blinked, which to Beth meant I'd not only said yes, but had given her permission to continue. And she did. "You don't have to worry," she said as if I'd told her I was afraid. "Sentencing is nowhere near as bad as a trial."

Then she lowered herself onto the edge of my bunk and continued like the expert that her three sentencing hearings made her. "All you gotta do is listen to the victims' statements, and then anyone who wants to ask for leniency on your behalf. And then the judge will say how much time you're gonna get. Okay?"

I blinked, and she patted my hand as if she were my lawyer. When I blinked again, she held out her fist and I bumped mine against hers just so she'd leave me alone.

She grinned, pivoted, then strolled right out of our cell, probably headed to the rec room to watch TV, which is something I didn't do much. I never felt like fighting over what was on. Most of the women here were older, so they liked shows like *The*

*Golden Girls* and *Murder, She Wrote.* I passed on all of those — I preferred my TV stars alive.

I sighed, but it was good because this was one of those few times when I was alone in this two-woman cell that held three cots. That was why I often stayed behind whenever Beth and Monica ventured out; this was the only time I could breathe.

But that wasn't the reason why I'd stayed behind today. I'd stayed because I was waiting for my sentencing. Today, I'd find out how long I'd be in prison.

I looked up and was reminded of the canopy that was on top of my bed at Gabrielle's house. That was the only thing this cot had in common with that bed that had been mine. Here, the ceiling was blocked from my view, too — by the bunk above me.

I closed my eyes and breathed deeply, over and over. Preparing for what I had to face. My cell mate had been right. Everything Beth said, my attorney, Mr. Steele, had told me.

When the women in here heard that I was being represented by Theodore Steele, they all swooned — and it wasn't just because of his looks. He was the best, they said. I wasn't surprised. Elijah had hired him, and that was how my father rolled.

My father.

I hated that Elijah was paying for this expensive attorney. Hated that he kept putting money on my books. It was too much, but I'd never told him that. Because whenever he came to the jail, I refused to see him. I refused to see Gabrielle and Mauricio, too. There was no way I could face any of them, not after all I'd done.

At least they'd stop trying to see me now. They'd have to. It had been too easy for them to make the trip to downtown Los Angeles, where I'd been since the day the police had taken me from Gabrielle's home — in handcuffs, like Regan promised.

After my sentencing today, I'd be moved. Probably to the Central California Women's Facility out in Chowchilla. That four-hour drive would certainly deter Elijah and Gabrielle from coming to see me now. At least that was what I hoped.

I wasn't sure how I felt about leaving this place I'd called home for a little over six months. I'd gotten to know the facility, the people. It was crazy that I felt comfortable in a jail; I wasn't sure how I'd feel about a prison.

But then I thought back to my beginnings here. That day when it had all happened,

*I didn't know what to expect back then either . . .*

I was scared, but not so much for me. Even though I sat in the back of this police car with my hands cuffed in front of me, I was more scared for Regan. The Lord knew that I didn't like that lady, but having to go through this — I didn't even wish this on *her.*

But once the police took me inside the precinct and sat me down in this room, the fear that filled me up was all for me.

"I'll be right back," one of the detectives said before he left me alone in a room that looked like we were shooting an episode of *Law & Order.*

This was the first time that my heart really pounded. Oh, how I wished that I could talk to Buck. He would calm me down, tell me what to do; he'd say, "I got you, boo."

But I was afraid that he might be in trouble, too. Regan knew something about what I'd done with the credit cards — suppose she knew about Buck, too?

Even though there was a chair in the room, I didn't sit down. I just walked from one wall to the other, trying to figure out what was going on. There was too much to imagine — first Regan and then the credit cards. What was I going to do?

I had no idea how long I waited in that room; I just knew it was long enough for my fear to flip to crazy. The room was small, and it was getting smaller. And hotter. Just when I started thinking about banging on the door, it opened and a black man came in. He didn't look like a policeman; he didn't look like anything because he looked like he'd just come from a run on the beach, dressed in a sweat suit.

"Keisha?"

I didn't say yes; I didn't say no. I just stared at him.

He said, "My name is Theodore Steele." He held out his hand. "Your father, Elijah, asked me to come here for you."

"Is he here?"

He shook his head. "Not yet. He's on his way."

"I don't want to see him."

"Well," Mr. Steele said as he sat down and then motioned for me to sit in the chair across from him, "you can decide when he gets here."

"I already know."

"Okay." He leaned back in his chair. "Well, we have other things to talk about."

"Do you know anything about Regan?"

"The young lady who fell down the stairs?"

I nodded, but I didn't correct him. There would be plenty of time to tell him that I'd pushed her.

"I don't have anything on her yet. And we have to talk about her, about what happened . . . and we have to talk about those credit cards."

Now I pressed my lips together. I'd talk about Regan, but the credit cards? No. Because of Buck.

Mr. Steele said, "Do you know someone by the name of Bobby-John Hansen?"

I nodded, even though I didn't mean to. It was just that I was so surprised when he said Buck's real name.

It seemed that I didn't have to say too much. Mr. Steele knew a lot more than I did. He knew about Buck and Que and what they'd been doing. Seemed like the feds had been onto them for a while. I wondered if they had given the police my name or if Regan was the one.

After Mr. Steele told me everything he knew, I said, "It doesn't matter. I want to plead guilty."

He shook his head before I had even finished. "No, you don't have to do that. I'm good at what I do, Keisha. I can get you off."

"I don't want a trial. I don't want nothing. I don't even want Elijah to have to pay you."

"All right." But the way he said it, I had a feeling he would keep trying to change my mind. "We have to wait probably until tomorrow for you to be charged, and then bail will be set."

"I don't want bail either."

This time, his eyes got wide. "Keisha, I don't know why you're doing this, but you don't want to spend any time in this place."

We debated back and forth a few times, and then Mr. Steele gave up.

"Okay," he said. "You have to stay here at least for tonight. We'll see how you feel tomorrow about bail."

He said that with kind of a smirk in his voice. Like after one night I'd be begging for bail. But Mr. Steele didn't know me. He didn't know what I'd been through. He didn't know that my life had prepared me for a time such as this.

I opened my eyes . . . it was hard to believe that I hadn't left this place since that day. I'd celebrated Christmas and New Year's and even the dates of the birth and death of Nzuri.

And now it was coming to an end.

"Keisha."

I rolled off the bed at the sound of the CO's voice.

"It's time to head over to the court."

I'd done this twice before, so I knew the ritual: the handcuffs, the shackles — only because we would be leaving the building. Like the other times, I was alone in the van and there was little that I could see from the barred windows. Inside the courthouse, I changed my clothes. It was the only time I was allowed out of my prison uniform.

In less than an hour from when the CO came to my cell, I was walking beside two sheriffs.

When they led me into the courtroom, I sighed. This was just what I wanted to avoid. All of the faces I didn't want to see were there, staring back at me: Elijah, Gabrielle, Mauricio . . . and then there were Regan and her husband, all in the front row.

Before I'd taken two steps, Gabrielle jumped up, but I averted my eyes away from hers. I was led to the table where I'd sat with Mr. Steele the last time — when I'd pleaded guilty to the charges of assault and voluntary manslaughter.

Yes, I was a murderer. Fetal homicide for the death of Regan's baby. They'd dropped the credit card fraud charges against me. I guessed going after a murderer was better for their records.

When the sheriff left me in the custody of my attorney, Mr. Steele shook my hand. "How are you?"

I blinked and he nodded. In this system, a blink was considered communication, it seemed.

That was all I wanted to give him because if I turned and talked, I'd be able to see Gabrielle and Elijah from the corner of my eye. So I just blinked, then turned and faced the front of the courtroom, right in time for the bailiff to tell us, "All rise."

Even as I stood, and then waited for the judge to hit her gavel, I felt the heat of the stares behind me. From Elijah and Gabrielle, I felt their pleas for me to turn around, just once.

And then there was Regan. I knew her stare that bore into my back was one that would send me straight to hell if that were possible.

My eyes stayed steady on the judge. All I was doing was waiting for Regan to get up, give her statement, and ask the judge to change the law so that I could be sentenced to death. I wasn't even mad at her for what she was going to say. That was what I would've asked if I'd had anyone to blame for my baby.

The bailiff spoke, "The case of the State of California versus Keisha LaVonne Wilson."

Wilson. I didn't even hear anything else from the bailiff nor the judge. I only focused on that word: Wilson. I'd never used that name before. Never had a way to do it because of Mama. And I never had a need because one of Mama's johns had gotten me my driver's license since Mama said she'd lost my birth certificate. I never told her that I had a copy, never told her all she had to do was go to the County Clerk's office.

So now, for the first time in my life as I sat in court for being a murderer, I was a Wilson.

My attention returned to the judge just as she asked the prosecutor if there would be any victims' statements.

"Yes, Your Honor. Regan Givens."

I held my breath and kept my eyes forward as I felt the movement behind me. This was going to be tough to listen to, but I wanted Regan to have this time. This was the only thing I could give her.

The podium that was set up for Regan to speak was a little bit in front of the table, so it was hard for me not to look at her. As she settled her notes on the podium, I noticed that Regan looked thinner than when I last saw her . . . and that made me sad.

"Thank you, Your Honor, for this opportunity." Regan paused. "I met Keisha Wilson a little more than a year ago. She's the sister of my best friend, Gabrielle Wilson Flores. Keisha and I have never had a relationship. We were adversaries from that first day we met.

"When I look back, however, I realize that both of us were protecting our territories. I wanted to protect my best friend, and Keisha was doing what she knew how to do — she was taking care of herself. So those were two worlds that would always collide; they could never exist on the same axis.

"I'm sure if Keisha and I had found any kind of common ground, any room for a relationship, what happened would have never happened. And for that, I accept some responsibility."

My eyes widened at her words.

"And not only would that day back in October of last year not have happened, but I may have been able to have an influence on her after I found out the other things she'd been doing. I may have gone to Keisha before I went to the police. I may have tried to save her instead of punishing her." She paused. "And so what I'm asking from this court is leniency and the understanding that I never gave her."

"What?" I said those words under my breath, but Mr. Steele still touched my arm, quieting me.

Regan continued, "I'm asking for the court to take into consideration everything about Keisha Wilson, how she was raised, and most important" — she turned and faced me — "how she was a mother who lost her baby."

I swallowed. I didn't know they knew about that pain.

Regan faced the judge again. "There is something that happens to you when you lose a child. A piece of your soul dies, and without help, without love and the right support, I'm not sure you can ever be right again.

"Keisha needed help, and I don't think she ever received that. So while my husband and I grieve, we pray for Keisha every day, we have forgiven her, and we pray she will forgive herself. And because of that, we know we can look forward to a better time in our lives." She paused before she added, "Thank you so much, Your Honor."

When she turned, her eyes paused on me

for a moment, and all I could do . . . was blink.

I pressed my hand against my chest, grateful that I had survived that, more grateful that this was now over.

The judge turned to Mr. Steele.

My attorney stood and said, "We would like Gabrielle Wilson Flores to give her statement."

I touched his arm, but he ignored me. What was this?

Mr. Steele stood, then pushed open the little wooden gate for Gabrielle to come to the side where we sat.

Now my heart pounded like that was my punishment. I'd been prepared for Regan. I knew what she was going to say — or so I thought. I'd had no time to prepare for this.

Gabrielle smiled, though I turned my eyes from her once again. It wasn't until she stood at the podium that I checked out the chic knit pantsuit she wore. St. John's for sure.

Like Regan, she began by thanking the judge. Then she said, "I am so grateful to be standing up and speaking for my sister. There's not much more for me to add to what Regan Givens has already said." Her voice trembled. "But what I can add is that as a sister who just found out that Keisha

Wilson and I were related, there have been few times in my life when I was happier. From the moment I met her, I've loved this young woman. I love her innocence, her enthusiasm for life — and I love the way she loves my daughter, her niece." She paused. "And now I know why." Those words made her have to take another breath. "If we'd had more time" — she shook her head — "I doubt any of this would have happened. We didn't have enough time to discover each other or for me to help her with the hurt she'd had in her life. She was raised by a mom who loved her, but there was so much she missed. I wish I'd understood how to help her get over the loss of her mom, how to help her get over the loss of her baby, which we knew nothing about until the investigators for this case brought that information to us.

"I would give anything to go back so that Keisha would know she wasn't alone. But even though she lived in our home, she didn't know that. And so, Your Honor, I'm asking you for leniency so she can come home . . . to love. So that she can come home to her family, who want to love and nurture her more. A family who will be by her side always."

Again, Gabrielle turned to me. "Our love

is unconditional. It has nothing to do with how you do right and what you do wrong. It's love that lasts forever no matter what."

She faced the judge once again. "So, Your Honor, my father, my husband and I, too, have forgiven Keisha. But we don't want that statement to be only words. We want the opportunity for Keisha to feel our forgiveness with action, and we hope you will give us that chance. Thank you."

By the time Gabrielle turned around, she was crying. From the corner of my eye, I saw Mauricio stand and hug her. And that was when I cried. Because Mr. Steele had told me they were back together, that Mauricio had gone home the same day I'd killed Regan's baby. So even though that had been my plan, I was glad that I'd failed at destroying their marriage, too.

The judge nodded to Mr. Steele, then said, "Does the defendant wish to make a statement?"

Again, Mr. Steele stood. "No, Your Honor."

He said that because that was what I'd told him, but now I touched his arm and stood. "Yes," I said before Mr. Steele or I could change my mind. "There is something I want to say."

His eyes widened, and I understood his

concern. He'd told me anything I was going to say in court had to be prepared and practiced. But what I had to say needed no prep time.

The judge said, "You may speak from where you're standing."

I said, "Thank you," to the judge, and then I did what I'd been avoiding. I turned to the first row behind me. I turned to all of their faces, their eyes all glassy with tears — for me. And I said, "I'm sorry."

Then I sat. Then I wept.

Except for the cries, the courtroom was silent for a few moments before the judge began.

"Keisha Wilson, would you please stand?"

Mr. Steele stood with me.

"You have been charged with and pleaded guilty to assault and voluntary manslaughter in the death of a fetus. This is a charge that the state of California takes seriously. You caused the death of an unborn child, a person to this state."

The judge could have stopped right there because her words would play in my mind forever — a lifetime sentence of shame.

She continued, "I know the credit card fraud was a separate charge that was dropped and is no longer part of this case, but I want you to understand this — that was money that could be replaced. The life of that fetus cannot be."

*Babies don't die.*

The judge said, "However, the statements that were given today, including yours, prove to me that not only is there hope, but rehabilitation and reconciliation is more than possible. Therefore, I am sentencing you to three years, which will be served in one of the women's detention facilities in the state. You will get credit for time served." She paused and almost smiled. "I wish you God's speed, young lady."

She hit her gavel, everyone stood, and Mr. Steele hugged me.

"You got the minimum sentence," he said with joy in his voice. "With time served and good behavior, you may not be there for very long. I'm going to work that out."

This time, I did more than blink; I nodded.

Then he whispered, "I've arranged for you to say good-bye to your father and sister."

But right away, I shook my head.

His eyes, which had seemed so happy a moment ago, dimmed. "Keisha . . ."

"No." I shook my head, then followed the sheriff as quickly as I could.

Behind me, I heard their shouts. "I love you, Keisha."

They all shouted together, so their voices blended. And I still heard them when I stepped from the courtroom. Even as I walked to the room where I'd get to talk to Mr. Steele again, their voices rang in my ears.

But what was different was that by the time I was in that room alone, I still heard them — now their voices were in my heart. A place where I'd never heard anyone before.

Even with that, though, I had no expectations of Gabrielle or Elijah. Yes, I'd heard her, and I knew her words belonged to my father as well. Still, that was what she said now. And what I'd learned in my life was that I never knew what tomorrow would bring.

But as I waited for Mr. Steele, I smiled. Because I didn't know about tomorrow, but I was really grateful for today.

# ABOUT THE AUTHOR

**Victoria Christopher Murray** is the author of more than twenty novels including: *The Ex Files, Lady Jasmine, The Deal, the Dance, and the Devil,* and *Stand Your Ground* which was named a *Library Journal* Best Book of the Year. Winner of the African American Literary Award for Fiction and Author of the Year (Female), Murray is also a two-time NAACP Image Award Nominee for Outstanding Fiction. She splits her time between Los Angeles and Washington, DC. Visit her website at VictoriaChristopher Murray.com.